WITCHMARKED

WITCHMARKED

WORLD'S FIRST WIZARD™ SERIES BOOK 01

AARON D. SCHNEIDER
MICHAEL ANDERLE

LMBPN

DISRUPTIVE IMAGINATION

Copyright © 2020 LMBPN Publishing
Cover copyright © LMBPN Publishing
A Michael Anderle Production

LMBPN Publishing supports the right to free expression and the value of copyright. The purpose of copyright is to encourage writers and artists to produce the creative works that enrich our culture.

The distribution of this book without permission is a theft of the author's intellectual property. If you would like permission to use material from the book (other than for review purposes), please contact support@lmbpn.com. Thank you for your support of the author's rights.

LMBPN Publishing
PMB 196, 2540 South Maryland Pkwy
Las Vegas, NV 89109

First US edition, September 2020
ebook ISBN: 978-1-64971-190-8
Paperback ISBN: 978-1-64971-191-5

THE WITCHMARKED TEAM

Thanks to our Beta Team:

Nicole Emens, Kelly O'Donnell, Jim Caplan, John Ashmore,
Larry Omans, Rachel Beckford, Allen Collins, Billie Leigh Kelar

Thanks to our JIT Team:

Dave Hicks
Deb Mader
Rachel Beckford
Kerry Mortimer
Diane L. Smith
Chrisa Changala
Jeff Goode
Paul Westman

If I've missed anyone, please let me know!

Editor
SkyHunter Editing Team

It lit me up like a torch on a pitch-black night
Like an ember in the needles of a dried-up pine

Lit Me Up, Brand New

"Woe to the rash mortal who seeks to know that of which he should
remain ignorant, and to undertake that which surpasseth his power!"

Vathek, William Beckford

Magic

Sandra's seen a leprechaun,
Eddie touched a troll,
Laurie danced with witches once,
Charlie found some goblin's gold.
Donald heard a mermaid sing,
Susy spied an elf,
But all the magic I have known
I've had to make myself.

Where the Sidewalk Ends, Shel Silverstein

This book is dedicated to my mother. You were the first one who made me believe in magic. Thank you, Momma.

— Aaron

To Family, Friends and
Those Who Love
To Read.
May We All Enjoy Grace
To Live The Life We Are
Called.

— Michael

PROLOGUE: NULL VICTORIA (JULY 1936)

Afghani Overrun

Captain Cassio Magrid cursed as he read the telegraphed text. Being as he was a proper Italian officer of the glorious 9th Regiment, when he swore, it was akin to improvisational art: a blistering stream of obscenities with gravitas, metaphor, and nuance. The majesty of the profane declaration was wasted on his attendants, administrative staff, and junior officers. They were sitting at what passed for the officer's mess in the worm-holed mountains, and many gawked with food still in their mouths. Before they could recover, he started barking orders in a thunderous voice.

"Withdrawal protocol!" he bellowed at his junior officers as he rose from the table. "Tell the sergeants to get their tunnels wired or collapse them."

The junior officers responded with reasonable aplomb, but Magrid still chased them out of his presence with a pointed salvo of curses. The captain knew that he was not an exceptional tactician, and strategy was often beyond him, but by the Virgin Mother, he knew how to motivate men.

To that end, he rounded on the bloodless corporal who had delivered the message.

"Don't stand there like a landed fish," he growled, shoving the crumpled piece of paper into the boy's front pocket. "Get back down there and send a telegram to the major. 'We are withdrawing to Bamyan, and if he has any sense, he will pull the rest of the cohort and follow suit.'"

The messenger stared for a second, mouth still hanging open, then spun and fled toward the communication center as another onslaught rumbled in the captain's chest.

"The rest of you, get this mess sorted and my camp struck," he shouted over his shoulder as he marched in the direction the corporal had run. He forced himself to keep a measured pace, knowing it wouldn't do to have any of his men see him act frantic. Angry was fine—after all, angry men got things done—but a frantic man was one step away from panic, and that man was no use to anyone.

Magrid was very close to frantic, even if pride and training were keeping him together for the moment. His honor guard fell into step behind him, but their presence offered little comfort.

With the godforsaken Afghanis routed, he had minutes, maybe less, before those pasty devils of the German Army were pouring over and through the tunnels honeycombing the mountainside. Amir Amanullah's forces, the rabble their allies called an army, had been the bulwark between his forces and the far more numerous enemy. Without that bulwark, the northern brutes could sweep him and his men away in a single assault.

Magrid didn't think of himself as a coward, but he did not relish the idea of such an inglorious defeat. The second he'd read those two words, he'd known he was not going to throw his career or his men away in a futile defensive action. These cursed mountains had already taken their toll on his forces, with absolutely nothing to show for it. If he'd wanted to spend his time in a meat grinder, he would have stayed on the trench-striped wastes of Crna Bend or Monastir.

A percussive thump resounded from the tunnels.

The air was choked with dust and sulfurous smoke.

Another bark of profanity, less skillful than those before, spewed out of Magrid's mouth, along with foul-tasting grit. The dust settled across the passage, turning the crimson uniforms of the Italian soldiers to a musty shade of rust. Blinking like owls at dawn, the men in his guard turned to their captain.

He spun on his heel and headed for the freight tunnels.

The explosions could only mean one thing: the enemy was already advancing through the tunnels. One of the rigged tunnels, probably the one Alpha *principi* was responsible for, had blown, sealing it shut, but that was one of six main tunnels that fed into their position. Magrid's mind raced, trying to come to grips with the reality that the German soldiers had covered half a mountain in such short order.

"Doesn't matter," he snarled, shaking his head savagely as he accelerated to a jog. He was thankful to hear the boots of his honor guard behind him.

He had to get to the freight tunnels, where the rails could carry him out of the blasted mountain to Jubal. From the fortified town, he could assess what had become of his command.

Another boom shook the dust from the overhead lights strung throughout the tunnel, and the captain fought to keep from flinching. His pace quickened as he tried to remember which passage was the quickest way to the freight lines. He choked back a scream of frustration as he passed a sign for the secondary armory chamber up ahead, realizing he'd taken a left instead of a right. He would have cursed the mute soldiers huffing behind him, but he was heaving air in and out in great blowing rushes.

Swiping sweat from his eyes, he took the next left and nearly sprinted down the winding tunnel. His heart was hammering in his chest, and not just with the effort. Screams had begun to echo through the tunnels, punctuated by the reverberating cracks of rifle and pistol fire.

He needed to reach that rail.

Like an answer to prayer, the tunnel unfolded into a cavern filled with crates stacked upon sagging pallets. Clusters of lights dangled from poles jutting ceilingward between the maze of wooden boxes, their glare casting sharp shadows across the floor but failing to reach the vault above.

A firm hand took Magrid by the shoulder as he made to forge his way between the crates.

"Please, Captain," said the steady voice of Sergeant Major Pavoni, the head of the honor guard. "Let us secure the area."

Magrid's face twisted with the competing fears of an ambush and the enemy that was smashing his forces to bits behind them. A wild, almost joyful scream sounded from the tunnel they had just emerged from, then there was a crunching *thump* of a detonation, followed by a billowing cloud of dust.

"No time!" Magrid snapped, pulling himself free of Pavoni's grip with a jerk.

The captain led his honor guard through the stacks, crying out as he spotted the rail carts between an alley in the hastily stacked assortment of supplies. Not waiting to see who followed, he squeezed down the alley, forced to turn sideways to scrape past.

"Nearly there," he wheezed, failing to convince himself that he was encouraging his guards.

He slid free of the claustrophobic passage of stacked wood and gave a whoop of victory that fell apart in his mouth as he looked down the line of squatting carts.

The locomotive had been reduced to a mangled collection of gears and metal shards, and its jagged surface glistened with something dark and viscous. Before Magrid's numb stare, the pile of gears shifted and collapsed in upon itself with an acidic hiss. The air stank of burnt ammonia.

"Treachery!" Pavoni snarled as the rest of the guard unslung their rifles and raised them to their shoulders. "Sabotage."

Magrid continued to gape, unwilling to believe that for the first time in his not-undistinguished military career, he was about to face a battle he could not avoid and could not win. This wasn't what he'd bargained for when he'd taken the assignment to Afghanistan.

"Enemy sighted!" one of the guards barked, and the honor guard turned as one.

The first row to rush in from the opposite side of the cavern was scythed down by a disciplined salvo of rifle fire. Men so dusty their uniforms were almost unrecognizable crumpled to the floor as heavy rounds punched through flesh and bone, many dead before the fatal shot's shell casing struck the stone.

More piled in after the doomed frontrunners, toppling and lurching over their dead comrades. The second volley, more rushed and leveled at the erratically moving targets, only felled half of the men, the wayward shots biting into crates or sparking off the walls.

The honor guards were chambering a third round of fire when Pavoni's voice echoed through the cavern like a mortar blast.

"Cease fire!" he howled, his voice almost pained.

Over a half-dozen Italian soldiers lay dead or dying, while more terrified faces pressed into alleys between the boxes. Like a bewildered herd, the men at the front were driven forward. They stepped on the fallen, whose cries were soon drowned out by the sobs and fearful curses of an entire platoon, some thirty men.

"What's going on?" Pavoni snarled, glaring at the advancing faces of the men, not daring to spare a look at Magrid.

"Something's in the tunnels!" a man shrieked as more men began to jostle forward. "We have to get out!"

Some*thing*? Not someone? The oddity of the statement drew Magrid's mind, kicking and screaming, from his hasty escape plan to the men in the chamber.

"How far have the Germans advanced?" the captain demanded, forcing himself to use his battlefield voice. These sorry cowards were his best chance of getting out of here, and he was determined to get them sorted quickly.

"The *tudro* aren't in the tunnels, sir," said one of the forward men, passing a trembling hand over his terror-pale face. "It was something else."

Again, "some*thing*." The vague menace of the word infuriated Magrid.

"Say something sensible," he snarled as he drew his pistol. "Or never speak again."

Even staring down the barrel of the sidearm, the men advanced another few steps.

"I-I don't know what it is," the forward soldier stammered before taking a fear-swollen gulp as he genuflected. "But it came up through the tunnels. It was huge, dark, and fast, and blessed Maria, it stank."

Stank? Magrid held the pistol steady but dared a glance at the noxious pile of scrap metal that had been a locomotive.

"Cowards!" Magrid spat, sweeping the pistol at the lot of them. "You ran for your lives from some phantom instead of fighting like men! Cowards!"

Then the question Captain Cassio Magrid had been fearing all his life was asked by a sharp voice in the midst of the throng.

"What were you doing, sir?"

Magrid was spared having to answer that damning question when a scream rose from the rear of the formation.

Men turned and saw their death coming. Some made ready to fight, others fell to the floor and wept, and some just stood there in shock. Captain Magrid was one of the latter, despite what he had been told about how his end would come. It was huge, it was dark, it was fast, and when the dark, gnawing tide swept over him and bore him down to a messy end, his last thought was a rather repetitive realization: it *did* stink.

A TEST

Milo knew serving in a penal regiment would be dangerous, but he thought he'd at least make it to the frontlines before looking death in the eye.

"Take him behind the latrines," Jules hissed as his angry, muddy eyes bored into Milo's pale stare. "I want him sucking his last breath face-down in filth."

Milo would have spat in Jules' face if they hadn't already wound the gag so tightly that his jaw ached. Instead, he settled for straining forward and kicking out as Jules' cronies began to drag him away. Tall as he was, Milo's kicks still fell woefully short of their intended targets.

It was early morning, and the rest of the 7th Penal Regiment of the Polish Colonial Forces, the duly named "Mud-Snakes," were busy prepping for redeployment. As such, no one noticed Milo and his rough-handed escorts as they dragged him across the camp. With one man for each arm and one to keep the gag bound tight at the base of his skull, they skirted the various companies that were hard at work.

Supplies were heaped on flat-backed automobiles, draped in canvas, and then lashed down tight, so they resembled nothing so much as ancient, lumpy beasts of burden. Quartermasters shuffled about, counting and cursing as they sought to dredge order from the chaos, while officers gave sharp, nonsensical orders to men who'd learned better than to pay them much attention. The last ten weeks had not beaten any of the criminal nature out of the motley collection of men in the regiment, but it *had* taught them that the disgraced officers placed over them were disgraced for a reason.

As the regimental proverb said, "Princes may turn into frogs, but generals don't turn into mud-snakes."

More than once, Milo took his life into his hands, straining at his captors to try to get the attention of the men he passed by mouth or motion, but it only earned him sharp blows to the ribs. No one saw him because no one wanted to see him. The sort of business done in the shadows of a penal regiment was something no sane soul wanted to contemplate for long. Even when they reached Milo's company, everyone seemed to be looking everywhere but at him.

Which was why, not ten paces from the latrines, Milo nearly choked out a laugh through his gag as someone shouted his name through the bustling camp.

"Volkohne! Milo Volkohne!"

The three holding him froze, and Milo felt something cold and sharp pressed against the side of his neck.

"So much as cough," the man holding his gag whispered, "and I'll split you like an eel."

"Milo Volkohne!" came the call again.

Milo didn't dare move, but he squinted across a row of tents to spy a very large man in an officer's greatcoat. The seeker's clothing was stark black instead of muddy gray, marking him as a member of one of the Federated branches of the Imperial German Army and not one of the colonial branches. Milo couldn't spot the rank on the coat's shoulder, but it didn't matter.

A Federated officer or Blackcoat of any rank had more authority than a general of the colonial forces.

"It's a Blackcoat," the man on his right hissed.

"Shut up," the gag-handler hissed, the steel blade nicking Milo's cheek before drifting away.

"Milo Volkohne! Report at once!"

"If he spots us…" the man on Milo's left wheezed, his grip slackening.

As surreptitiously as he could, Milo started to shift his weight.

"Don't you dare!" the gag-handler snarled in Milo's ear as he hauled back on the gag hard.

Through the filthy rag, Milo grinned as he drove his head back into the man's nose.

Twisting sharply, he tore his left arm free, and just managed to snag the gag-handler's knife hand by the wrist. The man on his right arm yanked, and Milo was hauled sideways as he let his weight drop. The straining knife skimmed just above Milo's hair to sink deep into the meat of the left-hand man's chest. He'd been so busy reaching for Milo's shoulder that he hadn't been paying close enough attention.

The knifed man screamed as Milo and the man still gripping his right arm tumbled into the mud, thrashing and punching. Milo hoped that would get the Blackcoat's attention, but with the ruckus of mobilization, he wasn't going to leave it to chance. He ripped the gag from his mouth and bellowed at the top of his lungs.

"Volkohne! Volkohne! Volk—"

The man he was grappling threw his considerable weight onto Milo and both pitched into the mud, Milo on the bottom. Earthen slop filled his mouth and he felt the bigger man pressing down, both hands ramming Milo's face into the smothering muck while weighty haunches settled on his back. Milo kicked and flailed but even when he managed to twist his head to the side, he was so deep there was still no air, only mud.

He felt his strength failing him as his lungs burned, and the only thing he could think of was how much he wished that wretched name wasn't the last thing he'd spoken. An unshakable mark of the Bellus Orphanarium, he hated that his last breath had been spent uttering it. Volkohne: folk-less in bastardized German. Dear God, how he hated that name.

Somewhere far away, Milo heard the bark of pistol fire, one shot after another.

Are we under attack?

Milo knew he was dying, his lungs throbbing as they prepared to suck in a desperate mouthful of mud. Something inside his chest kicked, a spasm of surrender, and then he was being hauled upward. Muck came out in a gagging spray, and he fought to breathe between wracking coughs that expelled more mud.

"Get up," a deep voice told him, and had he not been occupied with cleaning his airways, Milo might have complied.

As it was, a huge hand gripped the front of his uniform and dragged him to his unsteady feet. Something soft and dry was pressed into his hands, and by reflex, Milo cleared the filth from his watering eyes.

Two men were dying at his feet, whimpering about the darkening bloodstains swallowing the breasts of their uniforms. A few strides away, face down, lay a third man, the back of his coat sporting two ragged holes. Still retching up mud, Milo turned and saw the huge Blackcoat officer looking down at him with a flat expression.

"Th-thank you, sir," he choked out, fighting to straighten up. He thought he should salute, but feared doing so might have him getting sick all over the man.

"Come," the giant growled in a thick accent as he turned on his heel. "We are already late."

Though he'd only been in the building once in his life, Milo recognized the converted compound as soon as they approached.

This was the building where he'd sworn he'd lost his mind.

The 7th had been encamped in a gutted public park a few city blocks to the south of the town square, in which the Central Command of the Coalition Army was sprawled into every available building. This particular building was just across the street from the town hall, where the top brass of Central Command spent their time pretending to be very busy.

Moving down said street, Milo had spotted smartly dressed officers moving about with the swift, sure movements of men who had somewhere to be. Most were in the drab colonial colors, though peppered here and there was the striking black of Federated personnel. A few called to each other as they toted their satchels and bags full of official documents and all the bureaucratic trappings of men ready to send other men to die in their thousands. Men like Milo, men with no choice, and even worse, no hope.

He stared, mouth open, as two young colonial officers threw salutes as they passed, calling to the huge Blackcoat leading him.

"Victory through brotherhood," they belted out, which was the "new" rallying cry of the Coalition.

The Blackcoat ignored them, but Milo, feeling momentarily insulated in the presence of his intimidating escort, gave them pitying looks.

Who were they fooling?

Milo didn't know which was a bigger joke, brotherhood or victory.

The colonials from the likes of Poland, Ukraine, Latvia, and many other lands once under the wing of the Russian Empire had flocked to the Germans and the Austro-Hungarians out of desperation, nothing else. Outside the hearing of their new masters, Milo had listened to their true opinions, and even his seasoned ears had been burning by the things they'd whispered about the Blackcoats.

And victory?

That was a dream that had died sixteen years ago in 1918 when Petrograd burned, and the war promised to grind on. Only madmen and politicians still talked about victory.

The Blackcoat barely paused as the soldiers stationed there hurried to pull the double doors open. Realizing his bitter musings had put him out of sync with his erstwhile savior, Milo rushed to catch up.

The building might have been a large boardinghouse or perhaps a hotel before the war, but now it was just one of the many buildings hosting one branch or another of the Central European Coalition Army here in Zabrze, Poland. The lobby had been converted to a typing pool, where men and women in crisp gray uniforms punched keys in front of a wide staircase that led to a second level full of interview rooms. Milo couldn't keep himself from counting over to the one he'd been sent to three weeks ago: Room 7, just before the corner.

A longboard was lashed between the rails lining the second-floor gallery, bearing a sign in German that read, *Offices for the Non-Conventional Application of Tactics (Nicht Konventionelle Anwendung der Taktik).* Milo suppressed a shudder, just as he had on that first day. No one knew what Nicht-KAT really did, and in such fertile soil, rumors, huge and thorny, flourished.

"Captain Lokkemand," called a young woman who rose out of the typing pool with a handful of documents. She might have been the prettiest creature Milo had seen in some time, which wasn't saying much, but the severe bangs cut into her dark hair made her look serious to the point of caricature. The stern set to her jaw didn't help things as she rushed toward the towering Blackcoat.

"Not now," he rumbled, and he swept past her like an urchin on the street hawking yesterday's news rags.

She caught Milo watching her for a reaction as he followed the captain toward the stairs, and her eyes narrowed at him for an instant. Something sharp and acidic curled at the back of her throat, but then her eyes darted over her shoulder, and her mouth snapped shut. Without further complaint or even a glance at Milo, she turned smartly and made for her desk.

Milo couldn't shake the feeling that her glance at the second level was directed at Room 7, and the realization set his teeth on edge.

How could she know? Who else knew?

Not for the first time, Milo Volkohne began to wonder if it wouldn't have been better to die in the mud.

Milo had been in Room 7 for nearly an hour, which struck him as ironic considering the first thing Lokkemand had said to him was, "We are already late."

It didn't surprise Milo, even though it was tiresome.

The truth was that more than the business of being a soldier —no, a conscript, the sergeants had been clear about that—his short time in the Penal Regiment had taught him to wait. Wait and stand in line. Wait inside, wait outside, stand in line in full battle gear, stand in line stark naked. He wasn't sure he was any better at waiting, but he was now keenly aware of how long he'd been waiting at any given time. He told himself it was a way to ensure he knew how long between meals, but a more honest and spiteful voice acknowledged it was his way of defying his masters. Deep down he wanted a record, an account of all the ways his life was being wasted.

Keeping time also helped him ignore the small, shadowy figure lurking at the corner of the room. Milo was glad that so far the little...*thing* hadn't turned around, since that would have made the last fifty-six minutes impossible to stomach.

As it was, when the doorknob of the interview room gave a rattle, Milo made sure to add the time to his tally before bracing himself for what would come next. Out of the corner of his eye, Milo noted the figure shuffle from one foot to another, but thankfully, that was all, even as the door swung open.

Thankful for something else to direct his attention to, Milo watched quizzically as a small trolley, complete with white cover and a silver domed dish, rolled into the room. Within the space of a breath, the delicious smell of seasoned meat filled the room. Milo's stomach gave a lustful gurgle despite the knots it had been tied in. Of all the things he'd expected to enter this room, a delivery of food was not one of them.

Pushing the trolley was a slight man, slow and stooped, who shuffled in without any introduction. He rolled the trolley past the salivating Milo and up to the rough table before stepping around to brace himself against the table as he let go of the cart. The man seemed unsteady on his feet, his movements those of a person very old or very ill. That seemed strange, considering that while thin, he seemed hale enough.

He took the seat across the table, his back to the figure in the corner, and settled in with a sigh that seemed both grateful and apologetic. He looked at Milo for the first time through round spectacles that sat on a square, bearded face.

For a moment, neither man said anything; both just stared at each other.

"Is he still in here?" the man asked in Russian, his dialect impeccable Moscovian.

Milo balked for a second, unsure of how to respond.

"They haven't beat all the *Russki* out of you, have they?" he asked, looking askance across the table.

Milo shook his head.

"*Nyet,*" Milo answered in his admittedly stilted Russian, fighting the urge to cross his arms. "I still speak it."

The man's lips raised at the corners, but something about the expression was not a smile despite the similarity.

"We can speak *Deutch* if you prefer?" the man offered, fluidly switching to German.

Milo's eyes narrowed, sensing a test, but the slight sway of the figure in the corner was a relentless drag on his focus.

"Whatever you want," he muttered quickly in German, trying to keep his eyes from sliding off the man sitting in front of him and toward the corner again.

Again the not-smile tented the corners of the man's cheeks, and a glimmer of something sharp shone behind his spectacles.

"Whatever you want, *sir*," he said a little too crisply for Milo to ignore.

"What?"

"You've broken rank three times, Conscript Volkohne," the man explained, his mild tone belying the growing intensity behind his eyes. "I was just reminding you since you seemed to have forgotten."

Milo's stomach sank as he suddenly realized the small, bookish man who moved like an invalid was dressed in a uniform of matte black with an *Oberst*'s shoulder board, complete with three gold pips marching up its black and white coils.

This man wasn't just a Blackcoat but a full colonel in the German Federated Army.

The thing in the corner was no longer the only frightening presence in the room.

"M-my apologies, C-colonel," Milo stammered, rising woodenly to snap a shaky salute. "Won't happen again, sir."

The colonel looked Milo up and down, his eyes lingering on the exposed tattoos on Milo's arms and neck before nodding slowly.

"No," he mused, his voice icy. "No, I don't suppose it will."

The implied threat hung in the air, but the colonel was talking again before Milo could begin to think of how he should respond.

"At ease," he instructed and waved his hand gracefully at the chair across from him. "Please sit."

Milo sank down, wincing as the chair creaked in protest.

"You still need to answer the question, Volkohne," he stated, eyes dark and inscrutable behind the glinting glass lenses. "Is he still in here?"

Milo couldn't keep his eyes from sliding over to the corner again. The figure had turned its head just enough that a small dirty face could be seen in profile. The eyes were mercifully hidden beneath a ragged fringe of hair, but knowing what lay beneath made Milo's stomach twitch and curl.

"Sir, I..." Milo's mouth went dry as he fought to force words around the bile in his throat. "I'm not sure."

The colonel held up one finger for silence.

"Conscript Volkohne," he began, his voice intense yet indubitably sincere, "the only answer that can save you in here is the truth, whatever that may be. Starting things off with a lie between us will only make matters...more complicated."

Milo nodded even as his eyes shifted toward the corner once more, and he forcefully repressed a start. The thing had not only turned all the way around but had taken two steps forward. It stood only a few feet from the colonel, head still bowed.

Was it smiling?

"Sir, I..."

Everything in Milo told him to lie, to defy the trap yawning before him. They had asked their questions before, and he had seen the looks the interviewer had given him three weeks ago. This was the final, irreversible step into the pit, the last nail in his coffin.

He could escape the grave a little longer if he would just lie, deny, and denounce.

It would hardly be the first time he'd lied.

The thing's soiled face tipped up incrementally, just enough that Milo could see its bloodied teeth spread in a wicked grin.

Milo swallowed and made up his mind.

"Yes, sir," he declared, meeting the colonel's gaze as levelly as he could. "He's still in here."

The colonel nodded and sank back against the chair neither had noticed he was on the edge of. Another sigh passed his lips, and this one had the sweet music of relief in it. Milo's heart skipped in his chest.

"I'm glad you are finally being honest," the colonel said, his voice carrying no reproach. "Very good."

He'd passed. What he wasn't sure, but he'd passed, and that was something.

Milo let out his own sigh and nearly choked when his gaze turned back to the thing behind the colonel.

It was glaring at Milo with periwinkle eyes that didn't belong in such a young face. They had seen too much, borne witness too often, and looked on horrors too many times. They were Milo's eyes, and as they bored into him, he felt the rest of the world unraveling into fractals of light and color where darkness yawned between the threads.

"Tell it to leave, Conscript Volkohne," the colonel's voice instructed from somewhere outside the thing's gaze. "Tell it to leave your presence."

Unwilling to release him, his eyes in the mock-child's face pinned him in place as it raised small grubby hands to grip its ratty black hair by the fistful.

"Can you see it?" Milo hissed, his throat tightening it.

"I see the darkness it is composed of, just a dark blur, but that doesn't matter," the colonel explained, his voice patient but unyielding as stone. "Tell it, no, *command* it, to leave."

Milo looked on in horror as the homunculus pulled its hair, tearing itself in half with a soft, wet rip. Behind the ragged edges that flapped and shuddered was a patch of darkness as tangible and tangled as a nest of webs.

"What is happening?" Milo whined, his chest suddenly too tight to hold his hammering heart. "What did you do to me?"

"Command it to leave, Milo." The colonel's words were sharper but more distant, javelins hurled from a distance shrinking toward oblivion's horizon. "On your life, boy, tell it to leave!"

The colony of un-light shuddered once, and a flickering image with too many eyes and too many legs skittered out. The unblinking gelatinous gaze studied him hungrily before it advanced, each limb reaching out to him. Milo wanted to run, to hide, to scream in terror, but he was frozen in terror.

Then something, some deep power, maybe inside or beside where a soul might lie, awoke.

"*BEGONE!*" the power cried, and with a shock like ice water, Milo heard the command in his own trembling voice.

The nightmare twisted back on itself, its body rupturing with the violence of the movement.

"I said, *BEGONE!*"

The horror came apart into numberless fragments, each fleeing member frantically crawling away and disappearing into the voids between the lines of light and color. The emptied sack of woven shadows gave a wheeze like a deflating bladder, and a breath, cold and rancid, slapped Milo's face.

He coughed, his nostrils and tongue revolted by the assault, but by the time he'd finished, it was all gone.

He was sitting in Room 7 in the Offices for the Branch of Unconventional Tactics, and the colonel watching him with a true smile spread across his weary face. No one else was there.

"What just happened?" Milo gasped. He swallowed hard at the colonel's strange expression, "I mean, what just happened, *sir*?"

The colonel straightened in his seat, and in his deliberate manner, reached out and laid a square-fingered hand on the covered tray on the trolley. The dome rose with tantalizing slowness, revealing a steaming pile of pierogi, their sides glistening with butter.

"You, Conscript Volkohne," he said, the slightest tremor plucking at his voice to catch Milo's attention, "have just performed magic. Now, would you like something to eat?"

2

A CHOICE

Despite everything that had just taken place in Room 7, Milo's enthusiasm for the food on the tray was undiminished.

The colonel, who had introduced himself as Colonel Heinrich Jorge after handing over the plate, was happy to explain.

"You've just completed a bit of ritual magic. Banishing a minor shade to be precise," he said as Milo sank his teeth into the first pierogi within reach. "As I understand it, it is mostly a matter of will and minor magical ability. Still, you've shown more magic than any human ever, and I've been told the experience is quite...taxing. I guessed you'd be quite hungry."

Milo was too busy with his food to note the somber shadow that flickered across the colonel's face. For his part, the man recovered quickly, his satisfied smile refusing to remain hidden.

The dumplings, stuffed with ground pork, onion, and goat cheese, had the masterful flavor only hunger could impart to hearty food. Milo could not remember when he had eaten anything so delicious, and for the first three, he didn't have attention to spare for anything else, including all this talk of magic. Before Jules had finally decided to put an end to the "Volkohne problem," he and his goons had made a game of intimidating the mess staff to ensure Milo always got the leavings. They knew he couldn't steal anything better because doing so meant a bullet in the head for a penal conscript. Magic or not, he hadn't eaten well in weeks.

The first trio having vanished, Milo came up for air and took a dumpling in each hand before looking at the colonel.

The colonel waited, his smile unmoving even as his eyes remained watchful.

For a moment, Milo didn't know what to say, and he might have started gorging again if he hadn't suddenly remembered the past ten minutes with painful, nauseous clarity. The food in his stomach became a lead weight, and he slid the two pierogi back onto the plate with numb, trembling hands.

His eyes darted around the room as he remembered the skittering horror that had disappeared between the lights. His fingers raked through his dark hair, nails scraping his scalp before they entwined with what hair they could grip.

"Magic," he breathed, his eyes sliding in and out of focus. "You did say magic, sir?"

The colonel nodded, his expression guarded behind a wooden smile.

"Yes." He nodded, his scrutiny unblinking. "Magic. An alchemic branch of necromancy if I understand it correctly."

Alchemic? For Milo, the word conjured thoughts of long-nosed and long-fingered men surrounded by beakers simmering over flames and great tomes full of spidery scrawled formulae. Combined with the grisly title of necromancy, he felt something twist violently in his stomach. He opened his mouth to demand a justification or even an explanation, but then he remembered that awful day three weeks ago in Room 7.

The odd, trivial tasks: lighting a candle, pouring the water into a bowl, drinking it, and snuffing out the candle with his fingers. Milo had just assumed it was a sobriety check or screening. The abuse of liquor and other substances was hilariously commonplace among the colonial forces and the penal regiments particularly, so it had seemed sensible.

When the child with his eyes had appeared, he'd told himself there was something in the water he'd drunk, something to thwart the drunks and addicts. He'd told himself it was just an adverse reaction to that mysterious medication. Fearing being thought a degenerate, he'd said nothing, though he'd noted that the proctor for the test had noticed his furtive, anxious glances.

"The test," he muttered, dreading how thick his throat felt and how his stomach trembled threateningly. "It was some kind of spell?"

Jorge nodded, his eyes boring into Milo.

"A ritual," he clarified as he leaned forward and slid a hand beneath the white curtain of the trolley cover. "Which I am led to believe is different from a spell in some ways."

Ritual. Sorcery. Witchcraft. Hellfire. Damnation.

The words danced a merry jig around Milo's smoldering conceptions.

His stomach rebelled as the colonel produced a metal pail from the trolley. Milo forfeited the pierogi, along with whatever thin gruel had clung to the inside of his stomach. Head bowed, he felt somehow disconnected to the wretched thing he was, being sick in a bucket with mud still clinging to his ears, throat, and hair. How had so much gone wrong so quickly?

"This isn't possible," Milo muttered into the bucket. "How could I do magic without knowing it?"

Colonel Jorge chuckled, having settled back into his chair, hands resting on the table.

"It is a fair question," he acknowledged with a tilt of his head to regard Milo with owlish scrutiny. "But not the one I had expected."

"What might that be, *sir*?"

The officer's calm replies and knowing stare were beginning to irk Milo, and he was distraught enough to let his military etiquette lapse. The colonel blinked away the breach, too busy watching to take note.

"Most would deny the existence of magic," Jorge said absently. "It is my experience that even being very religious or superstitious doesn't keep a person from questioning whether magic—real magic—exists."

Milo paused at that, allowing himself to wonder, but then he remembered the child ripping himself in half and the patch of midnight that had been left behind. Somehow, dismissing magic seemed incredibly futile at this point. Either the colonel was toying with a madness in Milo he had been unaware of until now, or something supernaturally sinister had just taken place. Either way, he felt like the world was closing in on him.

"So, you tricked me into doing witchcraft?" Milo pressed as he put the odiferous bucket down between his feet. He'd thought to set it to the side, but saying those words made him think it would be wise to keep the pail at hand.

"I suppose that is one way to look at it," Jorge affirmed with a nod.

"How?" Milo wheezed, choking back more bile.

Colonel Jorge crossed his arms, seeming uncomfortable for the first time.

"There is a simple but unsatisfying answer, which is, 'I don't know.'"

Milo stared, wondering if the hollowness he felt was better or worse than what had provoked the vomiting.

"What?"

Jorge shrugged and shook his head, a strangely vulnerable and humanizing pair of gestures.

"I'm afraid we are in the woods on this one," he said. "The fact is that of all those we've attempted the experiment with—I think the total is nearly one hundred and thirty-eight thousand last tally— you are the first viable case."

Milo supposed he should have been pleased that he was special, but Jorge's sheepish expression pricked at his hardship-honed instincts. For the first time, he realized the colonel was holding something back. Milo knew that most must have been fine because his fellow conscripts who'd also been tested did not report anything like what Milo had experienced. The camp had been abuzz for a week over what the odd test was about, with all sorts of theories regarding testing medications, new chemical weapons, or things that were even more frighteningly esoteric. When no one got sick or grew new body parts, the chatter had moved on. Milo had written the whole unsettling business off as nerves.

Now, though, Milo felt his head spin but forced himself to focus.

"To be honest," the colonel began in the way all lies do, "I am amazed that we found a successful candidate so quickly."

"Always had the Devil's own luck." Milo snorted and then grimaced at the implication. Some of the boys at the Dresden *Krieg-Waisenhaus*, an orphanage for the war's cast-offs, had told him his blue-black hair and silver-blue eyes were signs that he was a witchling. Milo, between beatings both given and received, had told them that was hogspit, but now he wondered.

Your momma was a witch, Volkohne.

Shut up!

Your momma danced naked with the Devil, and out you came.

"I understand the Russians hold some very...colorful ideas about the supernatural," Jorge said before the silence could lengthen, perhaps reading Milo's forlorn expression. "To be fair, it is not just Russians, but many people, and as this damned war has dragged on, more and more people are looking for something to believe in, even if it frightens them. I suppose that is how I was drawn into all this."

The confessional tone, more than words, punctured Milo's suffocating malaise, and he looked at Jorge. The colonel's gaze was distant, racing down dark, uncomfortable corridors before he felt Milo's eyes on him. He came back to the present with a self-deprecating nod. Milo didn't like it, but the look they exchanged was a familiar acknowledgment: men recognizing they were on the same sinking ship. The last time he'd known this moment was with Roland, getting their first tattoos together.

Milo spat into the pail full of sick, then slouched back in his chair.

"So, what's next, sir?" Milo grunted when his old, pugnacious tone crept into his voice. "You've turned me into a witch, and now what? You going to teach me to put a curse on the French? Or maybe the Italians or the English? Is that it, *sir*?"

The air grew a little cooler as the colonel straightened, but his intonation remained as steady as ever.

"I think you've missed something, Conscript Volkohne," he replied mildly. "As I've already explained, I know very little about magic and understand the workings of what I know even less than that. If you are to be of use to anybody, you'll need to be trained by someone who knows magic."

"Another witch?" Milo asked, feeling dread fascination despite himself.

"I prefer 'magus' or 'wizard,' truth be told." Jorge sniffed, then leaned forward slowly before tenderly plucking up a pierogi. "'Witch' carries such...baggage, especially among certain circles."

"Another wizard, then?"

Jorge shook his head as he swallowed.

"There are no other human wizards, Milo. You are the first scientifically recorded case of a human successfully engaging in a magical exercise and not going insane."

"Successfully engaging" dug at Milo, but he pushed that to the side in pursuit of what seemed like a far larger and more ominous enigma.

"Then who is going to teach me, sir?" he asked, his mouth going dry as half-formed suggestions and insinuations began to bubble toward the surface.

"In official reports to the General Staff, I cite them as non-conforming assets. So far, no one has asked to what these assets do not conform."

Jorge frowned, considering his words then gave a surrendering shrug.

"As far as you and I are concerned, we'd call them monsters. I am sending you into the dark to learn from monsters."

After Jorge's pronouncement about monsters, Jorge had recommended they leave the room before the smell became intolerable. Milo might have been embarrassed had he not been in a state of utter turmoil. In truth, even with the bucket right between his feet, he hadn't noticed the stink.

Walking with a measured gait that was so slow it was almost painful, the colonel led him out of Room 7 and across the railed gallery to a pair of French doors that opened to a second-story patio.

This side of the building faced away from the command plaza and out toward the park, which had been turned into a muster field. Milo stood watching tiny figures scuttling about in the distance, looking for all the world like ants going about their futile tasks just before the boot descended.

"Have we reached the denial stage of the process?" Jorge asked as he settled into a dusty chair, not seeming to care how it powdered his uniform. "I always find that stage the most tedious, but I suppose it is only natural."

Milo turned from watching the soldiers and crossed his arms as he considered Jorge.

"You are talking about the unsuccessful, sir? The insane?"

Jorge frowned before replying stiffly, "I was referring to anyone who accepts the new *magical* reality."

"I'm all ears, sir," Milo said, leaning forward a little.

He knew he was taking liberties left and right, and he knew that quietly, patiently, Jorge was acknowledging and dismissing each one, but he couldn't bring himself to care. It seemed only fair, considering Jorge had blithely strolled in to turn his world upside down.

Ten minutes a wizard and already putting on airs. Careful, Milo.

"Well, I suppose it won't hurt to say I have had to endure the strained transitions of those who came to grips with this new reality," Jorge answered sagely, stroking his beard thoughtfully. "After I recovered from my shock, it became a matter of who and when in regard to letting others *in*. But you still haven't answered the question."

Milo frowned at the realization that this secret horror was not so secret, then mentally berated himself for the childish reaction.

"I suppose," he began, trying to pick through the long-toothed and cantankerous thoughts racing around in his head, "that I'm not up for denying it. I mean, I suppose I could rationalize it was all drugs and conditioning and such, but that sort of thinking is at least as uncomfortable as what we're talking about."

"Fair point," Jorge commented as he fished out a cigarette case. The cigarette had barely begun to move in Milo's direction before he snatched it. They spared a minute to get the tobacco lit and savor the first few drags. Jorge drew over a small table with an ashtray, while Milo flicked the gray leavings over the balcony.

"As you surmised earlier, we've had a few others react to the process," the colonel explained, his eyes sliding toward the occupied park. "The first was an administrative aid working out of a typing pool in Luxembourg. A good woman by all accounts, widowed with two children, a boy, and a girl. You see, once I had a method of testing, I was perhaps overzealous, and, well, honestly, things were just sloppy. That was nearly two years ago. I had been given clearance to pursue this fully, so I was dividing my time between this and other Nicht-KAT duties."

Milo drew in another lungful of smoke and sent it out in a single rippling ring. The colonel was stalling.

"What happened to the good woman?"

"She died." Jorge sighed into a cloud of smoke.

Milo waited, and to his surprise, the colonel succumbed.

"Seems her encounter apparition was an amalgam of her children. Unlike you and others, she acknowledged what she had subconsciously conjured. We wrote down the details, and we were pleased to see the apparition was bound to where it had been summoned. She seemed a little shaken but stable enough that we escorted her home with plans to have her try to interact with the apparition the next day. Once home, she locked the doors, shuttered the windows, and promptly killed and dissected her children and the young lady who lived with them and watched the children, an orphaned cousin, I think. She said she was looking for the stitches when we came to collect her the next morning, before turning the knife on herself."

Milo had subconsciously begun drawing deeper on his cigarette until it bit his finger. He dropped it with a quiet curse. The glowing stub smoldered at his feet, forgotten before it landed on the stone tiles.

"We've learned since then," Jorge said flatly, then more solemnly, "*I've* learned."

"How many others?" Milo asked, his mouth tasting more acrid and bitter than even the tobacco could manage.

"Five more, all dead within a week," Jorge said, stubbing out his cigarette in the ashtray. "Making you lucky number seven."

Milo didn't bother to turn his head to spit over the rail.

Jorge tensed a little, the first signs of a temper. Despite a lifetime of belligerence, Milo couldn't hide the thrill of fear that ran through him. Wizard or not, he was a colonial penal conscript speaking to a federated officer. One word and the colonel could have him shot, and no one would bat an eye. Some might even thank the officer for it.

Colonel Jorge spoke slowly, his voice perfectly, frighteningly even.

"This is all very disruptive and even terrifying, I understand, but I think we need to make it clear that there are only two options here."

Gripping the arms of his seat, he rose unsteadily to his feet. There was the slightest sway for an instant, as though his own two feet were untrustworthy, and some of the dust from the chair tumbled off his uniform. He righted himself and somehow looked Milo squarely in the eye despite the older man being several inches shorter.

"Your choices are darkness or dissection," he said simply. "You either cooperate with my investigations and meet with the monsters in the dark, or I comply with a directive from the General Staff to have you sent back to Berlin for exhaustive and ultimately fatal testing."

Milo's eyes widened, and his crossed arms gripped his coat to hide the shaking in his hands. Visions of men in white coats with black gloves and long, long needles filled his mind.

"Y-you would defy an order from the General Staff?" Milo pushed the words out on an unsteady tongue.

"General Staff doesn't need to know about our successful trial just yet," Jorge said, another smile creeping under his mustache. "By the time the information has time to trickle back to them, you and an attaché will be thousands of kilometers away, and in contested territory, no less."

Milo frowned and looked at the park.

"But the Mud-Snakes are heading west to reinforce the garrison at Metz."

"You're not a Mud-Snake anymore, Milo."

Milo swallowed, and for the first time in a very long time, a genuine smile spread over his face.

"All right," he breathed, thinking that such a monumental decision should have been made with a poetic flourish. "There's one thing I need to do first."

3

A BONUS

Milo felt a kind of nervous energy crackling through him as he stood waiting in the depot down the street from the Nicht-KAT offices. Somewhere between agreeing to be Jorge's operative and coming back down to the typing pool, he'd shed the horror and disconnection that had threatened to swallow him.

He was a witch, a magus, a wizard, or whatever other name could be conjured up. That was something he would have to get used to. It also meant there was a new mystery and a new world. A tingling, almost painful yearning to learn and explore danced along his nerves.

For the first time in his life, there was more.

Since his earliest memories back at the *Waisenhaus*, he'd found the world to be dreadfully disappointing. The world was an ugly, flat, miserable place, filled almost exclusively by small, shallow, and ultimately petty people. His education had taught him that the universe hated life, and his experience among callous and cruel people reminded him of that daily. Even in the days when he ran with Roland in their little gang of rebels and would-be gangsters, he couldn't shake that for all their bluster, they were just more cogs finding their own grinding path in the brutal and blind machine that was existence.

This disaffection, as far as Milo could tell, was not born out of some innate superiority. After all, he felt his own cowardice and lust and stupidity keenest of all, but that did not change that he saw the world for what it was: a prison too solid, too inescapable. Roland, the brother and mentor he'd longed for, had fostered hope for something else, a borrowed dream. When that dream had come crashing down and Milo had found himself with either the prison laborers' or penal regiment as his only option, it had seemed that the crushing reality had won. Milo was biding time, fighting for a life he fell out of love with more each day. There had been nothing else but to survive without hope or reason. Nothing to live for. Nothing more.

But now there was more.

Terror, danger, and quite possibly madness, but oh, so much more.

That realization galvanized him, awakening him for the first time in a very long time until he was practically bouncing on the balls of his feet. However dark, there was wonder and mystery in the world once more, and what was better, he, humanity's first wizard, could seek it out and experience it.

Colonel Jorge had instructed him to report downstairs to the captain for further instruction and to be outfitted as part of an investigative team. The captain had been waiting at the bottom of the stairs, as dour as ever, and wasting no time in ordering Volkohne to report to the woman with the severe bangs. Once there, she'd asked him for his uniform measurements, which he could not remember quickly enough to avoid more sour glares. Scowling beneath her burdensome shelf of hair, she tugged a completed requisition out of her typewriter and practically threw it at Milo, who realized that in spite of everything, he was smiling broadly.

Form in hand, he returned to Lokkemand, who headed out of

the building without comment, Milo scrambling after him. Two blocks down the street toward the park, a small supply depot had been set up in the shell of a mortar-scoured building. A squat, canvas-back truck that had not been there when they'd passed the structure earlier sat idling in front of the building, its tailgate hanging down in what seemed naïve expectation.

Within the depot, a Blackcoat quartermaster and a colonial soldier stood at the head of a room crammed with rows of crates and boxes, a rough-topped table between them. The quartermaster was berating the colonial in a profane and impressive mix of German, Russian, and Polish. The colonial took the verbal lashing, which seemed to center around appropriate clearance and paperwork, with much grinding of his bared yellow teeth, and he seemed ready to respond in something quite contrary to the supposed spirit of unity. He stopped when he noticed Lokkemand standing there. He sized up the captain at a glance, and seeing the balance was not in his favor, turned to leave. Milo, still basking in the glow of his recent revelation, didn't notice the sharp, low look that came into the man's eyes as he spotted the new magician on his way out.

Lokkemand grunted an instruction for Milo to hand the form to the glowering quartermaster, a stout man with an impressive if lopsided mustache who took the paper with a huff. He scanned the missive, then raised an eyebrow and looked from Lokkemand to Milo and back before he set off among the rows of crates, muttering blasphemies and curses in several languages.

Outside they heard the truck rumble to life and then set off with a congested blat.

"Get sorted and then wait here," Lokkemand had instructed. "I'll send your bodyguard to collect you shortly."

"Bodyguard?" Milo asked, emerging from the happy haze for the first time since leaving Jorge's presence too late.

Lokkemand was gone.

So it was that Milo stood in the depot, mind aching and

whirling with wonder, yet never happier. He was so lost in thought, he was nearly bowled over when the quartermaster returned and tossed a canvas bag into his chest. Fumbling like a drunken juggler, Milo just managed to keep the bag from hitting the floor, and then, realizing the bag was undone, he made another quick scramble to keep its contents inside.

"Try it all on, just to make sure," the office grumbled in Polish. "I'll get the rest sorted."

Milo peeked inside the bag and saw a folded uniform, along with a bundled greatcoat. Everything was matte black. Milo would have argued that there was some mistake, but when he raised his head, the quartermaster had disappeared among the rows of crates again.

"This day isn't shaping up so bad after all," he mumbled to himself as he fished out the greatcoat and let it unfurl in his outstretched hands.

The Federated armies had adopted the black uniform to distinguish themselves from the colonial forces a decade ago, which was plenty of time to imprint a powerful image in people's psyche: a tall, grim officer clothed like the Grim Reaper striding the hellish battlefield, unafraid and implacable. Milo knew, intellectually at least, that the reality was far from this prosaic creation, but it had its appeal.

With childlike haste, he put down his bag and slid into the coat.

It fit well across the shoulders and was long enough, but he was keenly aware his taut, wiry frame did not fill it out, especially through the arms and chest. All the same, it felt good. Powerful, even.

He looked into the bag and thought maybe the uniform would help make up some of the difference in the size. The thin, threadbare rags given the penal conscripts were often described as "whatever the moths couldn't stomach," and were mismatched to boot. Pants too short and a shirt so wide he had to fold it in on itself had been par for the course for him for months.

He shucked off the greatcoat, but he was careful to bundle it up and place it reverently back into the bag. He imagined he'd get dirty soon enough, but for the moment, he'd keep it pristine if he could.

Milo began to draw out his new regalia, grinning as he gathered the pieces in his arms: starched trousers and shirts, even a crisp undershirt that was so clean it must have been unused. At the bottom of the bag, he spied the glint of a new belt and new boots. Milo had never known a proper Christmas morning; such luxuries were rare for children with intact families these days, much less a foreign orphan, but what he felt wasn't far from what such lucky darlings experienced.

He let the garments slide back into the bag and looked at the uniform with a giddiness he would have been embarrassed to express. He began to untuck his shirt, eager to be rid of the sweat-soured memento, when he remembered what lay in the interior pocket. It was something he could no more cast off than his own skin.

In the small receptacle that rested over his tattooed chest was a folded tarot card, scorched along one side and frayed on the other edges. Its back was a series of strange, silvery constellations on a pitch-black sky. The face of the card, or should he say faces, were better known to him than every scar that marked his frame, but he could not bring himself to look at it.

There had been few happy moments in his young life, and he was determined to not sully this one with aching visions and melancholy.

Palming the card, Milo began to yank his clothes off to try his new uniform. His months as a conscript had expunged any shyness about being naked long ago. The first time he had been forced to stand bare and shivering with those who would be his platoon for inspection and delousing, he'd come to accept it as one more necessity of his grueling existence. Now naked from the waist up and with his trousers unbuttoned, he didn't have the wherewithal to be thankful that no modesty impinged on his eagerness.

The quartermaster didn't quite see it that way, though.

"What the Devil are you doing?" the man barked as he emerged from the stacks again, dumping an assortment of sundries onto his table.

Suddenly and keenly aware of his exposure, Milo grabbed at his pants before they fell below his knees and tugged upward.

"Y-you said to try these on," Milo stammered, gesturing with his free hand to the new clothes.

A stream of profanity curdled the air, and the quartermaster jabbed a finger toward a narrow door set in the wall left of the entrance.

"Use the room for such things," he snarled, mustache quivering.

Blushing from forehead to the tops of his shoulders, Milo scooped everything up and darted toward the door. It swung open on squealing hinges, and though there was no electric light inside, a long, smeared window let in blurry sunlight. The pale illumination of the morning shone on a room that was little bigger than a closet. A washbasin stood opposite the window, sharing the wall with rust-spotted milk can that must have served as a chamber pot. He could smell a strong odor, sort of industrial soap and ammonia.

"And don't come out until you're in a respectable state. Blasted colonial savages!"

Milo closed the door behind him, blunting another salvo of polyglot abuse.

As quickly as he could, Milo finished undressing and began putting on his uniform. As he did so, he heard the rumble of a diesel engine that sidled up next to the depot. Idle curiosity had Milo peering through the begrimed window, but he only had a vague impression of a truck through the streaked glass as he buttoned his shirt. As voices filtered from outside, he supposed that it was just some men to pick up last-minute supplies. Maybe the lambasted soldier had gone and gotten the right piece of paper.

Milo had just fitted his cap on his head, noting its pips were pentacles instead of crenelated circles, and was slipping into his greatcoat. Outside the room, there was a bellow and a heavy crash loud enough that he jumped as the coat settled over his shoulders.

Typically Milo would have been too careful to rush into the situation, but the oddness of his day combined with the empowerment of his new uniform kept him from thinking clearly. Drawing himself up straight, he threw the door open and swept into the room.

"Don't make me ask where he is again..." a chillingly familiar voice was saying as all eyes in the room turned on Milo.

The quartermaster's table was upended, its contents strewn across the floor, and the quartermaster was currently being roughly handled by three men in the greasy, mud-colored uniforms of penal conscripts. The quartermaster's profane tirade had been forestalled by the trench knife one conscript held in front of the man's face.

Three more conscripts whirled, pick handles in their hard hands. Milo's stomach sank when he saw the man at the center of the bludgeon-wielding trio.

"Should've spent more time wipin' *Fritzy—*" Jules began to chuckle, but the laugh died as recognition flashed in his piggish eyes. "Well, well, well."

"Told you I seen 'im," called a voice from the door, and Milo recognized the verbally berated soldier from earlier.

"Shut up, Kasper," Jules spat, his eyes roving up and down Milo's new uniform as his lips curled. "How did a little crow like you fetch a Federal commission, eh? What song did you have to sing to get that costume, Volkohne?"

"I didn't sing on anyone," Milo spat, the old refrain of him being a treacherous informant sparking his anger to burn through the fear. "I never have and never will. I leave that sort of stuff to you."

"If I'd known you knew something that valuable," the petty thug continued as though Milo hadn't spoken, "I might've taken my time in carrying out Roland's wishes. Who knows, you might've lasted all the way to Metz if you sang that pretty for me."

The mention of Milo's one-time criminal mentor found its way deep into old wounds, but at the moment, he had to focus on more immediate threats. He felt as much as saw the two men flanking Jules edge forward, cutting off his hope of escape.

"I always knew you were stupid, Jules, but I never thought you were crazy," Milo snapped, relying on his well-practiced skill at sounding tough when he was terrified. "You really think you're going to kill two Blackcoats a stone's throw from a command post and get away with it?"

Jules shrugged, his expression nonchalant even as his eyes shone with hateful triumph.

"Regiment's moving out," he said with a jerk of his head. "By the time they find you two, we'll have fallen in, and if they even have a sniff of who did it, we'll be on our way to Metz. One paper-pusher and one songbird don't seem worth stalling a whole reinforcing regiment to me."

One of Jules's goons rushed forward, thinking to pounce while Milo was distracted.

Milo gave him a broken nose for his trouble and had almost managed to pry the pick handle from his grip when his companion charged in low. Entangled as he was, Milo could only try to twist away from the chopping strike to the back of his leg. The heavy greatcoat took some of the bite from the blow, but in his distraction, he lost his grip on the pick handle. He flailed after it, but gripping it in both hands, the bloody-nosed thug checked Milo hard across the chest.

Milo hit the wall behind him and staggered from his head rebounding off the plaster. He shook the shock off just in time to watch the compatriot slam a heavy swing into his belly. The air rushed out of him, and he gasped like a landed fish as he dropped to his knees. Something in his mind rallied and roared for him to keep fighting, and he almost managed to retake his feet when the one with the broken nose kicked him squarely in the chest.

Milo was thrown back against the wall again, his head and chest aching abominably as everything took on a dreamy, translucent quality.

"Get him up," he heard Jules command. "Can't get that pretty coat dirty."

They hauled him to his feet and then pinned him to the wall by his shoulders.

"Not sure if they've finished the paperwork," Jules mused as he tucked the cudgel under his arm and bent to scoop up a bayonet blade on the floor. "But do you think they'll at least bury you in that pretty black coat?"

Milo spat at Jules, tasting blood.

The men holding him in place laughed as Milo strained sluggishly, fighting for breath and his thoughts to start moving freely again. He was supposed to be a wizard, so why now of all times couldn't he manage some sort of magic? Milo refused to give Jules the satisfaction, but he felt something like bone-deep regret stealing over him.

So close. So close to having and being something more.

"It's not the latrines." Jules grinned as he stepped forward to flash the long steel blade in front of Milo's watering eyes. "But once I gut you, I suppose you will die smelling your own filth."

The point was brought level with his belly, and Milo willed

himself to meet Jules's leering gaze. He didn't want to die, but if he was going to, it wouldn't be as a coward.

"Don't worry," Milo hissed as he broke into a snarling smile. "Your breath is close enough to the real thing. I guess you really are what you eat."

Jules' nostrils flared and the muscles bunched along his arm.

There was a gristly crunch and a surprised squeal as Kasper toppled away from the doorway.

Ambling—waddling, really—into the depot was a brawny figure who made the sturdy quartermaster look svelte by comparison.

"Pardon me, didn't see you there," he muttered softly in a lilting accent, then looked around the room with a shocked expression. "Good gracious me, what's going on here?"

The man was dressed in a uniform of the old Prussian style, complete with brass buttons on the faded blue fabric, all of which strained to contain his massive torso. His chest was like twin slabs of granite balanced over an iron cauldron of a stomach, as round as it was hard. His bandy limbs strained the fabric of his coat and trousers, and with every move the hulking creature made, Milo was amazed the ground didn't shake.

"You seem to be lost," Jules growled, brandishing the bayonet. "Can you find your own way, or do I need to help you find it?"

The interloper squinted at Jules, his eyes so deep-set they looked like old jade glittering at the bottom of a well. He rolled his jaw to one side and then the other with an audible crack, bristling mustache and sideburns twitching.

"I'm here for that one," he said, pointing one blunt finger at Milo, his genial tone falling to a dangerous rumble deep in his cavernous chest. "Hand him over in reasonable shape, and I'll be on my way."

Jules looked at Milo, eyes narrowed as he used his unenviable intellect to sort out the growing complications in his plan. Kasper whimpered on the floor, gripping a leg that seemed to be pointing at an uncomfortable angle.

"Or else what?"

The newcomer shook his head and clucked his tongue forlornly.

"No or else for you, young man," he replied, one scarred eyebrow cocking upward with a warning look. "Don't be foolish."

Milo couldn't see so much as a knife on the man's belt, much less a pistol, so his confidence was somewhere between comical and unsettling. Milo hoped for his own sake that the latter won as Jules took an aching handful of seconds to reply.

"I suppose they'll hang me for three easy as two," Jules chuckled, and the dark laugh was taken up by his cronies.

The bulky man let out a weary, almost sad sigh, then surged forward with a speed that was terrifying to witness and seemed impossible for his ponderous frame. He smashed into Jules, though whether with his fist, shoulder, or wide stomach, it was too fast to tell. The only thing that was certain was that Jules, a brawny fellow by most standards, went flying through the air. He collided with the man holding the knife on the quartermaster, and both of them tumbled into the foremost stack of crates in a lumpy, grunting heap.

Then things became disorderly.

Milo used the distraction to put a knee in one of his captors' groins and swept the winded man's leg with a stomping kick to the shin. The unfortunate thug fell back heavily, and Milo used his newly freed hand to jam a thumb into the other one's eye. The man screamed and instinctively twisted away, letting Milo come away from the wall. No longer pinned down, he gave the reeling, half-blinded man a hard shove that sent him staggering right into the path of the advancing form of the big interloper.

The man, who he had only now put together as his bodyguard, grabbed Milo's would-be captor by the arm and gave a short, sharp twist. There was a wet snap, and the man's arm bent at a wholly unnatural joint. The man gave a thin, shrill scream and the arm hung useless, the pick handle tumbling free. The bodyguard scooped the bludgeon up, and with a nod, tossed it to Milo.

"Be a good boy and clean up after yourself," he instructed the man staggering to his feet, one hand cradling the damaged goods between his thighs.

Without waiting to see the outcome, the big man advanced on the two brutes grappling with the quartermaster.

Milo hefted the pick handle, savoring the solid weight as he stepped toward the stricken wretch. With one look at his compatriot on the floor, the man took a wild swing at Milo that was easily deflected, then executed a limping vault over Kasper's crawling form as they both made for the door.

Milo almost went after him, eager to let the man taste the hardwood stick, but he heard an angry bellow that drew his attention back across the room. Jules was on his feet, one side of his face sporting an ugly purple mass. The bayonet was still in his hand, and with murder in his eyes, he advanced on Milo's bodyguard, who was hoisting a thug in each hand as though they were naughty puppies.

Gripping the handle in both hands, Milo bounded toward Jules. Hoping to catch him off-guard, Milo made a wild swing at the man's head, but something alerted him at the last second. Swaying like a snake away from the blow, he wrong-footed Milo and lunged in, bayonet plunging for the guts. Milo checked his advance and scrambled back to avoid being spitted.

"I'm going to carve off your face and stitch it onto a handkerchief," Jules frothed, lashing and probing with the long-bladed knife. "Then when I send it to Roland, he can blow his nose in your pretty face whenever he wants."

Milo batted away a swipe with the cudgel, but the strike was a feint, and he lurched back. Jules leapt forward, and the blade missed Milo's nose by less than an inch.

"Maybe not." Jules huffed, flicking the blade around to tease Milo. "Maybe I'll have your face sewn onto trousers instead. What do you say, little bird? Front or back?"

In a desperate gambit, Milo swept a blow low, knowing Jules could avoid it easily. When he did, Milo pulled the swing upward, connecting with the thug's chin as he leapt to the attack. Jules's head snapped back, and he rocked back on his heels. Reversing the swing, Milo brought the cudgel crashing back down, and the teetering brute collapsed to the floor in a boneless heap.

Panting with shock as much as exertion, Milo looked around and saw the fight was over.

The quartermaster was nursing a wrenched wrist, rolling it back and forth, while Milo's bodyguard stood watching his charge with an appraising eye. At his feet were the two who'd been grappling with the quartermaster, along with their knife-wielding friend. All three were so still, it took Milo a moment of staring to realize they were still breathing.

A look over his shoulder told him the man with the broken arm had joined his bruised compatriot and Kasper in flight.

Milo's hands began to shake, and he gripped the club to calm himself.

"Not bad." The big man sidled over to Milo, making a bit of a show as he stepped over Jules. "Footwork's atrocious, but that pulled strike wasn't anything to complain about."

Up close, Milo realized that though the man matched or outweighed a titan like Captain Lokkemand, he was shorter than Milo by half a head.

"Simon Ambrose," he intoned, wiping a hand on the hem of his jacket and then extending the huge paw. "At your service, sir."

Milo gawked at being called "sir" so long that Ambrose began to withdraw his hand. Shaking his head to clear the aftershock,

Milo awkwardly thrust a hand out, which the big man took in a crushing grip.

"Milo Volkohne," he muttered numbly.

"Oh, I know." Ambrose chuckled, his green eyes twinkling. "Now we best get you sorted with the quartermaster. Coat looks good on you, by the way."

4

AN OPERATION

"Afghanistan?" Milo shouted over the chugging diesel engine. "Where's that?"

In the orphanage, his schooling had been basic, to put it mildly. Milo was keenly aware of that, but since he was headed there with Ambrose and Lokkemand's team, he couldn't let embarrassment stand in the way of gathering intelligence.

"Somewhere between the Devil's backside and Hell's chamber pot," his bodyguard growled without opening his eyes. The boulder of a man had parked himself next to Milo, folded his hands over his belly, and shuttered his eyes as though set for a long nap. Apparently, he woke up to offer useless geographic insights.

Lokkemand, who seemed to experience only the unique emotion of perpetual annoyance, rolled his eyes and set about unfurling a map on his lap. It took a minute longer since the truck bed rocked as they crossed a cavernous pothole.

"Afghanistan is a Mohammedan kingdom on the other side of Persia," he explained, his words sharp and irritated even through the rumbling of the vehicle they rode in. "Their emir rejected overtures by both the Kaiser and the Ottomans some time ago, and since then, we've been obliged to waste troops fighting the heathen and their British allies in their miserable caves."

"Caves?" Milo asked as he watched Lokkemand's finger trace a quick circle around the nation in question.

"Nearly half the wretched place is jagged heaps of rock," Ambrose said, allowing one eye to slide open enough to squint in Milo's direction. "And if that weren't enough, those rocks have holes in them. One giant worms' nest."

"You've been there?" Milo asked.

Ambrose's eye snapped shut, and he made the sound of a snore in answer.

"We aren't going there for a holiday," Lokkemand observed dryly, ignoring the bodyguard's antics. "We are going there so you can make contact with a nonconforming asset."

"One of the monsters?" Milo asked, unable to keep the eager tremble out of his voice.

"Nonconforming. Asset." Lokkemand said, each word punctuated as hard as a punch. "That is what it is."

"But Colonel Jorge…" Milo began but stopped when he saw the baleful look in the captain's eyes.

"Colonel Jorge is a senior officer and a mentor," Lokkemand explained, his words so precise and sharp they might have been used as surgical implements. "But during this operation, you will answer to me. Due to your unique…station, many liberties have been afforded you, but you need to understand that this is my mission."

To facilitate the point, the strapping officer reached over and tapped the topmost pentacle on Milo's cap sharply. Milo smothered the instinctive response of throwing a fist into the bigger man's throat.

"You may be the star of this little production, Volkohne," he said grimly. "But for now you are on my stage, and it is your job to make sure I'm happy with the performance. Understood?"

Milo glared at him but nodded.

"I'm sorry," Lokkemand said, raising a hand to his ear. "I couldn't hear you."

Milo ground his teeth together and sucked in a breath. It seemed some aspects of military life didn't change even for burgeoning wizards.

"Yes, sir!" he barked over the engine, and Ambrose gave a convincing snuffle as though he'd just been awoken.

"We'der'yet?" he grumbled, blinking and pawing at his face as he sat up.

"And this," Lokkemand said with a curl of his lip toward Ambrose, "is also part of your job. Make certain this deserting scum keeps to his duties and nothing else. If he steps out of line, either you deal with it or I will, with the understanding you won't be getting a new pet anytime soon. Keep your guard dog on a short leash."

"Bow-wow," Ambrose remarked coolly, meeting Lokkemand's glare with defiant indifference.

The captain held the look long enough that Milo felt certain something might catch fire if it passed through the tension crackling between the two men.

To Milo's surprise, it was Lokkemand who broke away from the exchange first, turning back to Milo positively bristling.

"Once you make contact with the nonconforming asset, you will engage in whatever instruction is offered. Colonel Jorge has invested a great deal in securing cooperation from the asset, and as such, you will make every effort to excel. Not just your life and freedom, but the solvency of the Nicht-KAT is at stake."

"Yes, sir," Milo replied, wary of the furious gleam in the captain's eye. "I understand."

"Your personal reservations and preferences mean nothing," Lokkemand continued. "The asset is to be appeased, and you are to learn everything you can. Keep records and be thorough since you will be expected to pass any and all information back to me."

Milo frowned, feeling as though this was turning into a

school assignment rather than a face-first plunge into the world of the supernatural. Lokkemand possessed a knack for sucking the joy out of everything he touched, which perhaps explained his perpetual perturbance.

"We've come to understand that these assets do not value things as a more rational mind would," Lokkemand warned, settling back against his seat. "As such, there is always that one who will decide this arrangement is not to their liking, and you may find your well-being at risk. If such does occur, it is your duty to return to our base of operations at Bamyan, or barring that, ensure the records you've kept are returned."

"He'd hate to go to all this trouble for nothing," Ambrose chuckled.

"Do you understand the parameters of the operation?" Lokkemand asked, pointedly ignoring the bodyguard.

Milo swallowed, trying to remember every instruction given to him in the last few minutes. It seemed to him that there were large gaps left in regard to procedures, but he supposed this operation was strongly results-based. Milo had to learn magic, and despite Lokkemand's rigid manner, he understood that it didn't matter much how it was achieved.

Was this what it took to learn from the dark?

"Yes, sir," Milo answered, unable to shake the disquieting feeling settling over his shoulders.

Milo looked out the train's window as they chugged along the coast of the Caspian Sea, nearly a week out from that first debriefing as they left Zabrze in a small convoy of trucks.

Since the day that had ended in them boarding the first of many trains, Lokkemand had been scarce, busying himself with the entourage of communication officers and technicians and administrative assistants who made up the rest of the team.

When he did appear like some looming, black-wrapped specter, it was to instruct Milo on the next leg of their travels. Every time he spoke, it seemed he had refined his repertoire of instructions to use fewer words to communicate the necessary information.

Given his feelings toward the captain, he appreciated the officer's practiced communication skills.

Still, Lokkemand could learn a thing or two about terseness from his underlings. The other members of the team met Milo's presence with stony silence, so he quickly learned that talking to them was an exercise in futility. Whatever gossip or storytelling they were engaged with immediately came to a stop when Milo appeared and would resume as soon as he began to depart. Questions were answered with simple nods, headshakes, or not at all. Once one of them had pointed him in the direction of the water closet on the train, but that aberration was never repeated.

As a result, Milo had no choice but to amuse himself with Simon Ambrose in what was proving to be a rather uneven series of exchanges. Despite the incredible explosion of physical prowess displayed when they first met, Ambrose was one of the most slothful creatures Milo had ever met. Peculiar for a bodyguard, he spent a good deal of time sleeping or at least pretending to sleep, and the fact that Milo still couldn't tell the difference was troubling.

Eyes closed and hands folded over his belly, Ambrose whiled away hours and hours, politely declining whenever Milo asked if they could engage in some distraction such as cards, dice, or even a smoke. If Milo did catch Ambrose while he was humoring the world with consciousness, the man would listen to Milo's grievances with a sympathetic ear. He offered consoling noises and platitudes but he never joined in, violating the time-honored tradition of soldiers whining about their situations.

Milo slipped deeper into melancholy, until finally on that train skirting the inland sea, his reserve broke.

"Why did Lokkemand call you a deserter?"

Ambrose had been timing his snores with the rhythm of the train, but the grinding exhalations stopped as Milo finished the question. One eye slid open, pitching a bushy eyebrow upward.

Milo stared at him, refusing to hide from the pressure of the big man's cyclopean gaze. He wasn't sure, but he could have sworn he felt a thickening of the air, almost a pressure emanating from his bodyguard. In a way he didn't quite understand, Milo pushed back against the pressure, feeling a strange etheric ripple in response.

Ambrose's other eye popped open, and he regarded Milo for a second longer before closing his eyes again and baring his teeth in a dangerous smile.

"Well, will wonders never cease." Ambrose grunted, straightening in his seat. "I think we're going to get somewhere with you, Volkohne."

Whether it was nerves or isolation making him raw, Milo couldn't hide his habitual wince at the surname he despised.

"What's that about?" Ambrose asked, then covered his mouth. "It's not my breath, is it? Damned if my gustation doesn't get uppity from time to time, and that gives me fierce halitosis."

"No, not that," Milo said quickly, though he couldn't now escape the realization that Ambrose often smelled like pickled meat. "It's just I don't much like that last name."

Ambrose's brows gathered into a single furry knot.

"Care to illuminate me on that one?"

"Well," Milo began but stopped and gave Ambrose a sly look. "How about you answer my question first, and then we'll see if I'm up to sharing, eh?"

Ambrose met Milo's eye and a passing feeling of that same pressure began to congeal between them, but then the bodyguard gave a low chuckle and shook his head in surrender.

"You win." He grunted again, then reached inside his tortured coat and drew out a small leather wallet and a pipe. "But I think I'll need a smoke for this conversation."

Milo watched forlornly as the big man packed his pipe. Ambrose noticed the look and offered him the wallet, which had both tobacco and rolling papers. A pair of match strikes later, the cabin was full of aromatic smoke.

"Never had anything like this," Milo noted after a lazy exhale, savoring the sweet, velvety flavor of the smoke.

"English Cavendish with coconut and rum," Ambrose grunted as he took a long draw on his pipe, something old and sad swimming behind his eyes. "Traded an entire lorry of munitions for this pouch."

He tipped his head back and blew a titanic ring, then smiled through the trailing tendrils.

"Absolutely worth it."

Milo took another drag and cleared his throat.

"Deserter?" he prompted.

Ambrose shook his head.

"I believe the words our good captain used were 'deserting scum,'" the big man corrected, then tapped the stem of his pipe on his lip thoughtfully. "Though I suppose if I had to choose between the two, I'd take your version."

Milo threw a wry look to his bodyguard, prompting a nod of admission.

"I'm stalling, yes," Ambrose confessed. "I'm not sure how much needs to be shared at the moment. Sensitive subject and all, you understand?"

"Not hardly." Milo sighed, massaging a spot between his eyes with his thumb. "And we aren't getting any closer to me understanding at this rate."

Ambrose switched the pipe from one side of his mouth to the other and let out paired contrails through his nostrils.

"Captain Lokkemand, along with the entire Federated Army of the German Empire, is operating under false pretenses," he explained. "I can only be a deserter if I swore service to the empire or was conscripted as a citizen of the empire. As neither

AARON D. SCHNEIDER & MICHAEL ANDERLE

is true, I'm merely an expatriate caught up in a case of mistaken identity."

Milo frowned, and his eyes wandered to the archaic Prussian uniform.

"So, is this some sort of political statement?" he asked, gesturing to the faded blue fabric and dingy brass buttons. "A protest against the unification of your country?"

Ambrose looked down at his uniform as if considering it for the first time.

"Not my country." He shrugged. "Prussians, Bavarians, Saxons, and every last gutter-tongued Hun can call themselves whatever they want. I just put the thing on a few years ago and haven't seen fit to replace it."

Milo tried to process the comments, all given in impeccable German.

"Wait, so you aren't German?"

"Never said I was," Ambrose replied flatly.

"So, what are you?" Milo asked, sitting back as he cast a speculative gaze toward the big man. "And how did you get this assignment if you aren't even a soldier?"

"What I am is your bodyguard, and your best hope of surviving that worm-nest we're about to crawl through," Ambrose said coolly, pointing his pipe at Milo. "I'd think that after that dustup at the depot, you'd understand how I got the job."

A ripple of muscles that could not have been coincidence moved across Ambrose's frame, and Milo vividly recalled the sickening sound of a man's arm snapping like wet kindling.

"I'm not one of you dandy soldiers, but I'm the best God-cursed warrior this side of the Apocalypse," he stated, his voice low and heavy. "I killed men good and bad in more wars than you have fingers and toes before your mother even met your father. I'm here to keep you safe, and the way I'll do that is by killing everything and anything seeking to do you harm."

This wasn't the first or the hundredth time Milo had heard a boast like that from bravos and tough guys, but this was the first time he believed every word of it. Some intuition, maybe magical, told Milo that Simon Ambrose was the type of man who didn't need to lie.

Milo let a slow, impressed curse slide out with the smoke as he basked in the afterglow of Ambrose's declaration. After a moment's reflection, he shook his head and popped the train window to toss out the stub of his cigarette.

"Not doubting your obvious credentials," Milo said, one hand raised in warding placation, "but that only answers part of the question. I want to know why someone in your unique situation would take this position?"

Ambrose nodded and reached over to tap his pipe out through the open window before Milo drew it shut.

"That Colonel Jorge saved me a good deal of headache and then promised me something," he said as he stowed his pipe. "I'm going to see you through this to make sure he keeps that promise."

Milo sat back and began to wonder if there would be a time in the near future when a question he asked would not lead to a dozen more.

"My turn," the bodyguard declared, capitalizing on the momentary silence. "That is, assuming you are satisfied and prepared to move on?"

Milo wasn't, but he nodded anyway.

"So," the big man began, sinking back and folding his hands across the belly, "why don't you like the name Volkohne?"

Milo sucked his teeth and considered taking a page from the other man's book and pretending to be sleepy, but since this was the first real conversation he'd had in some time, he decided he could endure a little longer.

"'Volkohne' is the name given to every child taken in by the *Krieg-Waisenhausr* without a family name," Milo said, trying his best to keep his voice steady and monotonous. "Even among orphans, having a name like that sets you apart, and when it comes to kids, it's never a good idea to be set apart."

Ambrose pursed his lips, his mustache flaring as he studied Milo.

"So, some snot-nosed urchins made fun of your name." He shrugged. "You're not a child anymore."

"But it's not my name!" Milo snapped, the words rushing up like bile, hot and bitter. "That's the name they stuck me with, like branding livestock. And that's just what I was to them—some stupid animal fostered for slaughtering. Do you know what happens when you age out of the *Waisenhaus?*"

Ambrose shook his head.

"To repay the *generosity* of the Kaiser, you are *obliged* to either join a colonial regiment or serve a term of service as an indentured worker in the mines or factories. Death in the trenches or being mangled by machines and mishap."

"But you don't have to join a penal regiment," Ambrose observed, an infuriating twinkle in his eyes. "And let's not forget the getup you're wearing now."

Milo looked down at his black coat and strangled the biting reply he felt rising in the back of his throat. Ambrose wasn't wrong about any of it, but the self-satisfied look on his face was irritating in the extreme.

Silence stretched between them as the train rolled southward and the sun began to sink.

"So, what am I supposed to call you?" Ambrose asked at last. "I can't help noting they gave you that getup without any insignia of rank except those devil traps on your cap."

"You could call me Milo," he offered. "That is my name, after all."

"No," Ambrose muttered with a shake of his head. "I knew a Milo, and that boy was a whiny wretch."

Milo shrugged, feeling tired and hollow.

"I'm thinking...Magus," Ambrose said with a final nod. "Milo Magus, or probably just Magus."

Milo allowed himself a small smile. It was better than most of the names he'd been called.

"Not sure I can live up to the name," Milo said, turning toward the window. "But thanks, I suppose."

Ambrose gave him a lopsided grin as he yawned, and his eyes settled back to their customary position.

"You'll grow into it," he muttered drowsily. "Like that new coat, I suppose."

Milo absently plucked at the coat, feeling the vacuous space within, wanting to believe the big man was right. Simon Ambrose didn't seem the type who had to lie.

5

A STAIR

The last leg of the journey seemed determined to remind Milo that though he was Magus to Ambrose, he was still a soldier, and that meant marching.

The rail line had taken them to a ferry across the Caspian, where they had joined a larger contingent of Federated troops, the venerable 33rd East Prussian Fusiliers. Captain Lokkemand seemed to be at ease as their attaché perched among the seasoned regiment like a vermin-eating bird on a behemoth, separate but still sheltered. Lokkemand was hosted by a fellow officer every night for some time, returning the next day bleary-eyed but less irritable. For Milo and his burly shadow, nothing much changed. They were instructed to keep to themselves lest they, as novices in shadowy operations, let something slip over a game of cards and some schnapps.

Despite this moratorium on contact, Ambrose did manage to acquire a bottle of *Ansatzkorn*, a potent beverage the big man described as being "a dirtier German version of vodka." They'd only intended to sample it the night they made the crossing, but as it turned out, Milo had to be carried by Ambrose like a child in the aftermath of the empty bottle clutched in Milo's fist.

After the crossing, the team and the regiment boarded another train that took them to a city called Merv. The ancient city, Lokkemand explained, marked the edge of secure territory, and that from here on out, the 33rd would be acting as a combat escort as they moved up and along the Murgap River. The river, which began deep in Afghanistan, was supposedly under German control, but there were no regular gunboat patrols, and attacks from British-friendly locals were not unheard of. The 33rd elected to disembark at the bend where the river rounded the edge of the Band-i Turkistans, a craggy range of low mountains that Ambrose promised were only a shadow of the things to come.

From there, it had been marching across the barely passable, barely habitable lands that were lashed by unrelenting winds as they made for Bamyan. Despite having a vague notion that this part of the world was sun-scorched, Milo found he was thankful for the sturdy greatcoat as they trudged along. In his old colonial rags, he would have been scoured raw and shivering, but as it stood, he only had to deal with perpetual fatigue and the monotony of trudging onward.

As the days stretched on, Milo began to wonder if anyone lived in the desolate place, but Ambrose and conversations he gleaned from eavesdropping assured him that there was more to this place than met his unfamiliar eye. Milo remained suspicious of any human life besides their own until in the distance, he spied what looked like a child tending a flock of rangy goats.

Milo had watched the little shepherd scamper up a scruffy hillock, half-heartedly corralling the beasts in his haste. As more of the herd scattered, Milo wondered at the child's poor tending until he caught a clear glimpse of the youth, who cast sharp looks over his shoulder at their company.

It was only then that Milo noted a squad of men had detached themselves from the marching order and were heading toward the shepherd and his flock. Rifles in hand, they loped across the rough terrain like dark-pelted wolves from some parable.

"Seems like a lot of work for a little goat," Milo observed, squinting at a small kid skipping spryly across a boulder. "I'd be more worried about getting lost among all these god-forsaken hills and valleys."

Ambrose paused, shielded his eyes from the pale glare of the sun, and tracked the progress of the pursuers.

"They're not going to catch him," he said at last, catching up with a quick scuttle. "And it's not the meat they want but the boy."

Milo jerked his head around so quickly his labor-stiffened neck gave a pop.

"What do you mean?" he asked, pitching his voice low.

All the terrible things one heard about orphanages were not true of most such institutions, but the Dresden *Krieg-Waisenhaus* was not most institutions. As such, Milo was never shocked but always on guard against the depredations of wicked men.

"Not that," Ambrose muttered as though reading Milo's thoughts, though he seemed to take no joy in the dismissal.

"Then what?" Milo pressed.

Ambrose cast a look around the hills flanking the column and then assessed the column itself.

"The officers in the 33rd are not fools," he answered in his low rumble. "That boy's going to scamper off to whatever village or band is lurking around these parts. From there, any man with a gun or a rock and a love of British coin is going to descend on us like flies on a corpse."

Milo felt an itch between his shoulder blades and forced himself not to do his own fearful scan of the hills.

"We'll be ready, then?" Milo asked, throwing a surreptitious glance at the men in the column around them. "If they know it's coming."

Ambrose shook his head, his voice still barely above a conspiratorial whisper.

"We're stretched out across a few kilometers at least, and tightening things up is going to slow us down. You'll see more sentries, maybe a few more recon patrols, but any bandit-turned-mercenary is going to know how to hide in these hills."

Milo didn't bother to suppress a shudder as the itch became an icy claw racing up his spine.

"So, we're going to be ambushed?"

Ambrose nodded.

"Several times, unless we're incredibly lucky or unlucky," he said, chewing his lip. "They're opportunists, little better than scavengers, so they aren't going to be doing anything more than taking a few shots before skittering off to do it again."

"What are they going to do?" Milo asked, nodding at where the senior officers rode in growling Land Rovers commandeered from the British.

"Do?" the big man asked, seeming shocked by the question. "I know you're young, Magus, but I thought you were trained as a soldier."

Milo blushed, hating himself for it, then shrugged in an attempt to seem unflappable.

"The training of a penal regiment is hardly exhaustive." He laughed, a tart, biting sound the wind snatched away. "March, fight, and die in that order, over and over. Didn't take things like tactical appraisals into consideration."

The bodyguard gave a concessionary nod as he nodded toward the setting sun.

"Maybe tonight, maybe tomorrow night, but once things get dark, we'll see the fighting and dying part, mark my words."

Milo sighed.

"At least that might spare us some of the marching."

The first attack came on the second night after the shepherd escaped.

Milo had just managed to convince himself that the attack wasn't coming, despite Ambrose standing guard for the second night in a row. Their position was more defensible than the trench of a valley they'd been in the night before, being a broad, level patch in front of a craggy hillock. The 33rd had placed two concentric rings of sentry posts around the camp, and the rattling hum of generators powering massive searchlights seemed a comforting din.

Unfortunately, the lights only served as excellent initial targets.

The first went out with a snap, and it was a full two seconds before the crack of the rifle was heard—a long shot by a good marksman.

The rest of the camp hadn't woken to the danger, and Milo was still blinking when Ambrose hauled him out of the tent.

"What?" Milo slurred, his feet scrabbling on the hard ground as he was half-dragged, half-carried. "Wh-where are we going!?!"

Lokkemand had them bunk down in the center of the camp, which seemed a simple if cold calculation to put as many of the 33rd between them and the enemy as he could.

Another light winked out, followed by another rifle crack, and the rest of the camp began to stir. Men shouted in German and tent flaps fluttered as the remaining lights raked the surrounding hills. A siren's blaring wail sounded and was soon echoing off the surrounding hills in strange, unsettling tones.

"Move it," Ambrose snarled, tossing Milo out in front of him.

Ambrose had a rifle in his hands. It looked like the *Gewehr* 98s some of the older Federated Regiments carried, but it somehow seemed a little thicker, almost blocky. A bandolier festooned with five-round clips hung across his huge chest.

"Where are we going?" Milo shouted as a handful of soldiers raced past them.

"That way," the big man barked and stabbed a thick finger at the crown of the craggy hill.

Milo fumbled to get his pistol from his belt, realizing his rifle had been left in the tent. He'd been outfitted with the Luger P08 back in Poland, but Ambrose had *acquired* a rifle for him during their march since his training had been exclusively with rifles in the Mud-Snakes. Now staggering in the dark toward a looming face of rock, it seemed Ambrose's gift would be wasted.

The sporadic pops of smaller, more excitable arms and marksman sounded along both flanks of the camp.

"We're surrounded!" Milo called back to Ambrose, whose crushing presence kept driving him forward for fear of being flattened.

"Shut up and move, boy!" the bodyguard bellowed in a voice that made Milo's bones feel like water. He somehow quickened his pace.

Like a lion at bay, the 33rd roared to life, and the Prussians sent rippling volleys across the undulating hillocks around the camp. Slipping bladelike through the gaps in the cacophony of wailing sirens and gunfire, men could be heard dying on those hills. Only two searchlights remained and they swept over the jagged terrain, picking out a crumpled form here and there. The 33rd gave a cheer at the sight, only for more sporadic fire to draw their eyes and rifle barrels to another lump of earth.

"Sounds like we are winning," Milo panted as they reached the foot of a rough hill that was nearly a cliff.

"Sounds like you and the Prussians are all fools," Ambrose growled and stabbed his finger forward. "Those miserable idiots in the hills are a distraction."

Milo wanted to question how he was going to get up the rough wall of stone, but when he looked at it in the moonlight, he saw rough shelves of stone jutting out in a zigzagging pattern up the face of the cliff. Drawing a breath, he started up the stone staircase, throwing one last look over his shoulder.

More of the 33rd was pouring out to the left and right of the camp in lethal, disciplined order. Under the streaking, searching lights, he saw the Afghan raiders attempting to flee, some having abandoned their rifles in haste. Everyone he saw illuminated in the stark light of the searchlights toppled in seconds like stringless marionettes as the 33rd's rifles bayed for more.

Milo, torn between cheering and hollering at Ambrose in rebuke, found his mouth hanging open as his eyes were drawn to the front of the camp. A second after he saw the rushing, gleaming shapes, he heard the thunder of their hooves.

A contingent of horsemen mounted on spry-footed steeds was pouring into the camp, angry red sparks flickering in their hands.

Leaping the low tents or trampling them underfoot, they made for the center of the camp. The men of the 33rd, intent on their chastising of the flanking ambushers, were slow to realize the true attack. Officers bellowed, but the sounds that filled the valley were the shrill screams of riders and horses, triumphant as they plunged like arrows into the heart of the camp.

"Keep climbing!" Ambrose shouted to Milo, who sluggishly obeyed. "And keep your eyes open when you get to the top."

His limbs felt like lead as he saw sullen sparks fly from the riders' hands. The tiny flames nestled amongst command tents and stockpiles of munitions and fuel before bursting into flames. The incendiaries lit the entire plain, stretching the shadows of the wheeling, shrieking horsemen across the camp like huge specters of death. Swords, lances, and pistols flashed in their hands as they set about striking and hewing at men or machines that lay within reach.

Milo felt his arms begin to burn while below him, the gutted camp smoldered.

The 33rd had turned about-face and was pouring into the camp, their faces grim and hard in the light of their decimated caches and tents. Some opened fire, smiting horse and rider, while others had affixed bayonets and charged in for a more visceral retribution.

Milo had just mounted the crown of the hill when he saw the lunging, wailing riders begin to flee. They'd lost nearly a quarter of their number, but the devastation they had wrought on the material resources of the 33rd was substantial.

"Well, those boys earned their coin," Ambrose growled as he joined Milo at the top of the hill. "Perhaps a touch too eager to bask in their handiwork, but I can't say that I blame them."

Milo looked down, a mix of horrified awe and guilty gratitude inside him. One rider whose horse had kindled in the leaping flames took a smattering of shots to the chest and he fell, dragging the burning animal down with him. Together they smashed down on Milo's tent, and in seconds, their death throes had set the whole thing ablaze.

His mouth tasted of ash as the acrid smell of burning canvas and oil washed over the hill in a foul wind.

"How did you know?" Milo asked, his eyes still watching the last of his tent crumble into cinders.

Ambrose spat and turned away from the sight.

"It's a bold but sensible plan if you've got a doughty company of foot soldiers like the 33rd," the big man explained as he moved farther back on the moon-painted top of the hill. "Especially if you've got the proper information and assurances that you'll be handsomely rewarded by both sides. Would seem worth the risk."

Milo dragged his eyes from camp as the last of the riders sped into the hills, plumes of dust glowing red in the light of the fires. Down below, squads of soldiers were performing as fire brigades, with middling success thus far.

"Information?" Milo rolled the word, as though it felt strange on his ashen tongue. "I thought these were a bunch of bandits, not trained soldiers? And what do you mean by both sides?"

Milo turned around and saw that his bodyguard was ambling over the boulder-strewn hilltop, looking for all the world like an animate hulk of stone in the silvery light. He went over to one of his lumpy brethren and seemed about to have a serious conversation.

"Hey!" Milo shouted, striding after the big man. He felt the pistol in his hand, its rounds shamefully unspent as the camp burned below. "Did you hear me?"

"Shhhh, keep your voice down, Magus," Ambrose hissed as he turned, scowling. "The raiders should be gone, but we don't want to attract any attention in the dark, now do we?"

Then he turned back to the rock and addressed it in a low, indignant tone.

"Not from any proper folk."

A surge of anger and confusion gripped Milo, and without much thought, he laid a hand on the big man's shoulder to haul him around. Milo realized too late that he may as well have tried to get the hill to turn.

"Stop your hissy-fitting," Ambrose chided, still glaring at the rock. "And put that pistol away before you hurt yourself."

In a fit of temper, Milo nearly pressed the barrel of the Luger to the big man's thick skull to show his displeasure and get some attention, but he wisely thought better of it. Cursing incoherently, he secured the weapon with a shove and a snarl.

"What the hell is going on?" he snapped.

"Our rendezvous is late," Ambrose muttered, turning from the rock and squinting across the hilltop. "Unless Lokkemand got it wrong, and I wouldn't put it past the *jaeger* snob."

Milo's head spun, and he turned back to see the slowly shrinking glow of the camp. Pieces began to click into place with stomach-turning alacrity, and Milo turned back to Ambrose, who still seemed preoccupied with the local geological deposits.

"You mean, this was some sort of setup?" Milo asked, numbness creeping up in the wake of the realization. "Lokkemand planned this."

Absently, the bodyguard nodded.

"A bit flashy for my taste, but it removes any reasonable doubt that we both died in the fires of the raid," he stated matter-of-factly. "Enough scorched corpses down there that any attempts at identification by General Staff's bloodhounds should be satisfied or at least frustrated to the point of surrender."

This last thought seemed to appeal to him, and a low chuckle passed his lips.

"Men—soldiers—died down there," Milo said. He wished he sounded more horrified, but the insulating dissociation already had him. "Now you are telling me they died for me?"

The lack of feeling, the cold shell that had been his armor for years, was almost as painful as accepting the burden and promised no relief or closure. He wanted to rail, to scream, even to weep for the men, but instead, he stared mutely at Ambrose, his question hanging in the air.

"Wasn't it some Prussian who said soldiers' lives are the currency officers must spend to purchase victory?" Ambrose asked with a shrug of his huge shoulders. "Seems like something the boys from the 33rd would appreciate. Good soldiers from what I could tell."

"Dead soldiers," Milo muttered, his shoulders sagging.

"Not so many," Ambrose said. "And besides, ours but to do and die, right?"

Milo looked at his bodyguard with a mix of confusion and irritation, the only things he could feel at the moment.

"What?"

Ambrose, for the first time, looked abashed, his cheeks plainly colored, even in the moonlight.

"It's from a poem." He grunted and shook his head. "Never mind."

Milo was about to say something caustic about poetry or perhaps ask what they were supposed to do now that they'd faked their deaths. He never got the chance since two shadows detached from the boulder Ambrose had been staring at. Milo's voice deserted him as the long, stooped shapes with gleaming pale eyes lunged forward, too-long limbs outstretched.

One alighted on Ambrose's broad back, and the big man gave a pantherish twist that saw both him and the living shadow rolling across the ground. The other landed on Milo and bore him to the ground, where cold, sharp fingers cut into his arms.

Instinct kicked in, and Milo's feet and fists lashed out against rubbery flesh that took the abuse without effect. Milo had an impression of many teeth snapping in front of his face, then breath like an offal pit in summer lapped against his face.

"Hold still, meat!" a voice rasped next to his ear. "Hold still, or I'll tear out your throat."

Too terrified to reason, Milo redoubled his efforts, managing to twist one hand free and grope for the pistol at his belt.

The fanged shadow hissed words in a tongue old and wicked before changing its grip to take Milo by the head. A dull thrill shot through Milo when he got both hands free to try for his pistol, but the thought was dashed out of his head when the shadow beat it against the stony ground.

The first impact sent stars spinning through his vision, and the second left him limp, with the world tumbling around him.

He vaguely recognized he was being dragged, and he raised his battered head to see where they were going. A cleft that had not been in the boulder before yawned wide as the shadow dragged him toward the waiting dark. Between the thin legs of his abductor, Milo could just make out a set of stairs glinting bone-white in the moonlight, plunging from the heart of the boulder into the darkness of the earth.

6

AN INTRODUCTION

Milo's passage down the stairs and through the dark was not pleasant.

The being gripping him by his shoulders and dragging him did not seem to much care that the stone steps were rough-edged and unyielding against Milo's back, buttocks, and legs. It also didn't seem to care that the entire trip was made in a darkness so complete that even when Milo's senses began to come back to him, he realized he could not see his own feet as they thumped down the steps. Sometimes he thought he could glimpse the faintest shine of the thing's eyes above him, or maybe that was its teeth, but then another steep spike of pain lanced up his lower body.

Just when he feared the abuse was going to lead to permanent damage to his ability to walk and considered another futile struggle, their descent leveled out. Milo felt the texture of the floor change beneath him to a soft, fibrous mat. With careless strength, the shadow rolled him onto his stomach. The fingers that had been biting into his shoulders disappeared and Milo hit the ground with a soft thud. The floor beneath him tickled at his nose and lips, almost hairlike strands sliding across his face.

"Get up," the voice of the shadow directed. It was a step or two ahead of him. "I'm not carrying you all the way to court."

Milo's fingers took hold of the dense, tangled stuff beneath him and used it for leverage to get to a kneeling position. Everything was still black as pitch, and Milo, his body aching from a thousand short, sharp bounces down the steps, was in no hurry to comply.

"I need a light to see by," he muttered, reaching toward his pocket for his matches.

The air stirred in front of him, and the rotten, icy breath washed his cheek.

"Meat," it breathed, so close he could hear the air whistling between its fangs. "Draw that pistol, and I'll see you carrying it on the inside of your flesh, understand?"

Milo nodded stiffly, sinking both hands into his pockets to hide their shaking more than to search for matches.

He took a steadying breath, drew out the matches, and made to strike one, but the dark and the closeness of the creature worked against him. Twice he tried to strike a match, and twice it broke, snapping off below the head without so much as a spark.

"Hurry up."

The command sounded different, almost distracted, and Milo began to wonder what the thing could be waiting for. Its fellow shadow, the one who had attacked Ambrose, maybe? As if in answer, a snarling sound echoed from somewhere above them on the stairs. Milo felt a chill run through him as he heard that ancient, evil language used again. Then a distinctly human voice rumbled something he couldn't make out.

"Don't move," his shadow said with more than a hint of a snarl in his voice.

Too late to stop, Milo's third match caught, and there was a flare of light in the tunnel.

Milo had only a fleeting glimpse of a stretched figure darting past him. It had the graceless quickness of a pouncing spider and was wrapped in something like oily black skin.

He told himself it was the speed of the things passing that had knocked the match from his nerveless fingers, where it quickly smothered with a whiff of acrid smoke in the woolly gray material that covered the floor. Beneath his self-delusion though, Milo knew the truth. It was one thing to be told that there were beings dwelling in the dark and believe in their existence, and a whole other matter to experience them. He had felt, smelled, heard, and now seen, not just a play of shadows, but this entity who was other. No clever beast, no deviant human, this inhuman, alien creature was real, and Milo's mind swam with the recognition.

"You wanted more, remember," he reminded himself breathlessly as he fumbled for another match. "You were the damned fool who wanted more."

Behind him were more wicked whispers in the strange tongue, much closer this time, and then a voice that was almost as sweet as sunshine in that dark, low place.

"None of that now," Ambrose growled, his voice more annoyed than angry. "It was your fool idea to have it go down this way. If you wanted to play that game, you should have made sure everyone knew the rules."

"It was supposed to be alone," another shadow voice hissed, this one tighter and shriller but no less unsettling, "and we had as much cause for secrecy as you."

"The risk is as great for our tribe as it is for your petty kingdom," Milo's shadow snarled as the voices moved closer. "What we are doing is without precedent in the history of our kind or any of the other *shayati*. There are many who would punish us for such blasphemous congress with meat like that one."

"'That one's' name is Magus," Ambrose rumbled. Milo was fairly certain they were on the level patch just a few steps behind him. "Now, move it before I take another hand."

How was Ambrose, who seemed to be herding the two creatures, able to see in the dark? Milo saw no torch.

He had retrieved another match, but the sound of that unholy dialect made him shudder, and he paused before breaking it. He only had a few left.

"You are fortunate her maiming is not permanent, or this alliance would have ended before it began," Milo's shadow warned, so close he might have been able to twist back and touch it. "She is the get of our Bashlek."

"And I'm the son of a shepherdess," Ambrose replied flatly. "You all right, Magus?"

Milo shuffled about, still on his knees with the match and matchbox still in hand.

"I'm fine," he lied, turning his head this way and that in a vain attempt to discern something other than utter blackness. "I see you are better at making friends than I am."

Ambrose chuckled, and Milo heard the soft tread of his boots before a broad mitt slid under his arm and gently raised him to his feet. Milo was happy to find that despite everything, his legs still worked, though he was grateful Ambrose didn't let go until he'd found his footing on the cushioned floor.

"Well, now that me and my charge are reunited, I suppose we can commence with introductions," the bodyguard said in a genuinely jovial tone. "How about you two go first since we're guests?"

"Um," Milo interrupted, turning toward his best estimation of Ambrose's position. "I can't see a thing, and I've only got about four more matches left. Do we really intend to have this entire conversation in the dark?"

"I'm sorry, you're right," Ambrose said, and Milo heard his feet shuffle softly as he turned. "Perhaps our hosts can arrange to fix the situation. Seems only polite."

The two creatures spoke to each other in their language, which sounded more sinister in a huddled whisper, especially since Milo realized they'd noiselessly slid past where he stood in the tunnel. The conversation lasted long enough that Ambrose gave a huff of irritation, shortly after which he heard some strange sounds.

There was a sound like rotten cloth tearing, then the rattle and clink of glass against glass. A second later, there was scratching like a dull knife rasping over bone. This was followed a heartbeat later by the distinctly unpleasant sound of snorting and hawking, then someone spat into something with a wet splat.

"Here," Milo's shadow said, and Ambrose could be heard stepping forward to take something.

Milo ached to ask his bodyguard how he was managing all this in the stygian tunnel, but interrogating his only ally in front of two monsters seemed ill-advised.

"What good will this do him?" Ambrose asked in a bristly tone.

"If he is what he claims he is, it should be a simple matter to catalyze the essence," the other shadow replied curtly. "It is very fresh."

"He came here to learn magic, sweetie," Ambrose drawled. "You have to teach him how."

Both creatures made a disgusted sound and then lapsed into a thickening silence.

"*Put the vessel in its hands,*" Milo's shadow instructed, and Milo found himself gripping something hard and smooth except for a fine layer of grit across part of its surface.

Milo thought it didn't feel like any container he'd handled before, but the texture of the surface was familiar, although he couldn't place it. It seemed rounded and had two rough handles. As he held it, he heard small granules shifting within, and in a strange way, he detected a faint vibration or resonance coming from within. When he pressed his palms against the surface, he realized he was sensing the subtle movement, though it wasn't through his fingers or palms. He knew it was there, as real as the dust beneath his digits, but it wasn't physical.

A tremor of excitement and delicious terror raced through him, and he fought to keep from visibly shaking.

"Try to relax and do what they say," Ambrose whispered. "And don't drop it."

"Call to the essence," the she-shadow said. "Whisper the command 'Light,' then breathe over it."

It seemed a strange, almost comical, instruction, but the thrumming presence between his hands beckoned him to try.

"Light," Milo said as confidently as he could, then he blew between his hands as though coaxing tinder to life.

Like embers stirred by bellows, a soft viridian light spilled from three apertures in the vessel. The illumination filled the stony tunnel, for that was what they were in, and Milo nearly grinned like a babe after uttering its first word to doting parents.

The smile was snatched away as he realized the openings through which the light poured were the cavities of a goat skull's vacant eyes and nose sockets. The handles were the horns of the beast

Willing himself to not drop the luminous skull, he looked up and saw his instructors. As he stared at the two nightmares given form, he wondered if perhaps he had been better off in the dark.

Milo's first teachers were stooped, gaunt creatures, bent nearly double, so their knobby spines stood out along their backs, while their gangly arms hung to the floor. Their skin seemed like oil, dark but possessing a glimmering opalescent quality that made them seem like slimy creatures of the deep. Their outthrust heads on bowed necks were too elongated, narrow, and sharp to be anything but vaguely humanoid. Their eyes gleamed over a squashed snout of a nose and a nest of fangs.

Milo, gaping in revulsion, looked from one to the other, noting that the larger of the two held one arm curled against a sunken chest, the wrist a ragged stump. His stomach turned when he saw the severed appendage in her other clawed hand.

The smaller of the two, the one who must have been Milo's abductor, stood a little in front of the wounded one, shielding her from the light.

When their glinting black eyes faced the light, they squinted in distaste, but when they looked at Milo, there was an intensity, almost a hunger, that made him uneasy. It was hard not to stare at their hooked fangs and remember that they had called him meat more than once.

"What are you?" Milo murmured, keeping the skull lamp steady in his hands.

"We are *ghuls*," Milo's captor said as it inched forward, eyes locked on Milo's face. "And you are the first humans to have seen our kind and lived for centuries, if human you are."

A defiant spark blossomed in Milo's heart at the implication, and he stoked it until it rendered enough heat to drive back the grip fear had on the organ.

"Why would I be anything but?" he demanded, and the light surged in sympathy that made the *ghuls* recoil.

"We don't know," the wounded female snarled, her eyes narrowed to suspicious slits. "But no human has ever worked magic in the memory of our people or any of the *shayati* we have heard tell of. I would not have believed it to be true if I hadn't seen it."

"You travel with one who looks human but is not, so it is not so strange to think there is some deception here," Milo's ghul said defensively, one gnarled finger leveled at Ambrose.

Some part of Milo felt sure this was a trick, a distraction to draw his attention elsewhere so they could attack or flee, but a sinking sense of dread and curiosity drew his eyes to his bodyguard.

Ambrose was glaring at the ghuls with an intensity that the monsters must have felt, and he refused to meet Milo's eyes.

"I'm half-human," he said by way of explanation. "On my mother's side. I wasn't joking when I said she was a shepherdess."

The ghuls hissed and shrank against the wall of the cavern as one.

"Jurhumidon!"

"Son of Gamorrah!"

Befuddled by the strength of their reaction, Milo's gaze darted between Ambrose and the recoiling ghuls.

"Simon, please help me out here?" Milo said, unable to keep the note of pleading from his voice. "What's going on?"

"We cannot take you to our Bashlek, not now!"

"Ambrose?"

"Treachery! Did you think we would let you deliver this assassin to the heart of our tribe?"

"You can kill us now, Fallen One. We are ready to d—"

"*SILENCE!*"

The bellow came from Ambrose, but it was more than mere sound. Milo recognized it as being akin to the pressure he'd felt on the train when he'd met the big man's stare. This was far more potent, a palpable battering force that drove Milo to one knee and sent the ghuls to huddling on the ground.

Milo felt a heat that did not touch his skin but his soul radiating from Ambrose, and despite the terror that filled him, he turned and beheld his bodyguard.

Ambrose stood in the tunnel the same as he would anywhere else, his jacket straining around his lumpy form, but he was more. Not just taller and broader, though the tunnel seemed to strain to contain him, he was suffused with an alien light that seemed to smother Milo's pitiful skull lamp. He was a black sun bleeding enervating red light, a corona of crackling wrath surrounding his hands and head.

Eyes that had become bloody stars turned to regard Milo, and he saw strange twisting symbols form amidst the dancing flames swaddling Ambrose's hands and face. They were writing, words of living flame.

Milo could read them if he wished.

If he dared.

Across gulfs of infinity, a voice whispered a promise.

Milo's heart seized in his chest and his hands flew to his face, unwilling and unable to bear what he saw. The skull lamp fell to the matted floor, and its light winked out. Mercifully, the world returned to darkness.

It was some time before Milo found the strength to grope for the skull. To his uncomfortable surprise, he saw as the light returned that both his monstrous instructors and his terrible guardian remained. Ambrose was just Ambrose again and the ghuls were no longer cowering, but it was a long, strained moment before anyone said anything.

"So," Milo murmured, slowly meeting the eyes of all in attendance, "I believe we had somewhere to be and someone to meet, right? Perhaps we should just get going."

7

A THRESHOLD

It took a little more cajoling to get the ghuls to comply, and from the onset, Milo could tell it was a ruse. If Ambrose even sniffed, they twitched and cowered.

On they went, down the woolly-floored tunnel, the two ghuls loping in front, just at the edge of the illumination cast by the skull lamp. Milo's legs had begun to stiffen from the bruising treatment they'd received earlier, but he kept up well enough. An arm's length behind him strode Ambrose, quiet and brooding.

The passage wound slowly down into the earth until Milo was certain they had to be several stories deep. The thought of so much earth pressing down around them, not to mention the company he was keeping or their destination, had Milo feeling very small and very vulnerable as he walked through the dark. The tender yet venomous glow of the goat skull in his hands seemed a small comfort as they marched on.

After a time, the ghuls began to whisper to each other so softly that Milo couldn't tell if they were using their blasphemous language or not. He thought about demanding they speak words everyone could understand, but he reminded himself that he was going into someone else's territory—their home, even.

He decided it was probably wiser to be diplomatic.

"Is it much farther?" he called, squinting at the ghuls' dark, iridescent forms.

They were inky puppets moving across a black curtain, distinguishable only by their movements.

"We will come upon the first gate within the hour," the female ghul, the one related to the Bashlek, called back. "Once he learns what walks with us, he will seek to stop us, but I think I can persuade him to let us pass."

"The court after that will be another matter entirely," Milo's ghul warned. "It is already a wonder they were convinced to allow a human, much less a celestial mutt."

"Maybe you shouldn't mention anything about my pedigree," Ambrose called from the rear. "No need to waste our time and yours with arguments with some gatekeeper."

To Milo's startled surprise, the two ghuls stopped dead in their tracks, turning as one to look first at Milo and then beyond at Ambrose, who came up behind his ward's left shoulder. For five long seconds they stared at the big man, then made an awful bubbling sound like blood from a torn throat. Finally, they clacked their fangs together.

It took Milo and Ambrose a moment to realize the awful noise was laughter.

"There is no gatekeeper," the royal ghul remarked as the mirth subsided. "Only the gate. You must remember that among the *shayati*, things do not work as they do among mortal men."

Milo and Ambrose exchanged concerned looks and might have asked more questions, but the ghuls had begun to move again.

"I am not sure if that was meant to be a threat or not," Ambrose whispered, addressing Milo directly for the first time since the revelation at the foot of the underground stairs. "What-ever is up ahead, you need to stay close to me. I don't trust these troglodytes."

At the word "trust," Milo couldn't repress a bitter snort.

Trust was growing scarcer.

"What?" Ambrose asked, sensing something off in Milo's manner. "What's wrong?"

Milo gave the big man an unimpressed deadpan stare.

"Oh come on, just spit it out already," Ambrose growled. "Are you a blushing lady I've been courting? Just tell me what's going on in that magical brain of yours."

Milo ground his teeth together, shuffling the skull to one hand so he could knead between his eyes with a thumb.

"You complaining about trust just strikes me as funny," Milo said in an overly precise manner, his voice icy. "Especially considering that we've been working together for weeks, and you didn't mention that you aren't human."

Ambrose breathed out a long sigh behind Milo and muttered a few exasperated curses.

"Technically, I am human, or at least part of me is," the big man reminded him, keeping close to Milo's shoulder. "If your mother was Russian and your father wasn't but you lived among Russians all your life, wouldn't you just call yourself Russian? It's the same with me. Especially if you know nothing about your father except he isn't Russian."

"I'm not sure it's the same," Milo muttered, but the parallels to his own story robbed some of his indignation. "But keep talking, and maybe I can find my way to seeing things your way. What's your other half, then?"

Ambrose fell silent, and Milo imagined him chewing his lip beneath his mustache as he'd seen him do before.

"All right," Ambrose said softly, his voice low and sullen. "I'll tell you, but you have to remember that I know almost nothing. I'm a byproduct of this world, this darkling reality, not a guide through it."

"Fine," Milo said with a nod. "You don't know much, but you know more than me, and right now, that's enough."

"My mother was a shepherdess near Toul in France," Ambrose said, obviously making an effort to keep his tone level and calm. "My father is Oro'zion'Nrzim, former Keeper of the Tree, He of the Flaming Sword."

Milo threw Ambrose a sidelong look meant to convey his confusion, but the big man was walking with his eyes fixed on the ground.

"Not to be rude," Milo said, drawing Ambrose's attention, "but so far, the only part I understand is that you are half-French. That is ironic considering our current allegiance, but not particularly revealing."

Ambrose chuckled, but it was a shallow, mournful sound.

"My father is an angel," Ambrose said, his voice becoming as hard and flat as ice. "A fallen warrior of Heaven who took my mother on May 22nd, 1813. Same day Wagner was born, if you can believe it. I think Napoleon also won one of his great battles around then too."

Another chuckle, this one even more hollow, passed the big man's lips.

"Busy time in the world, I suppose."

Milo gaped at his bodyguard, his pacing slowing so much the ghuls noticed and hissed for them to keep up.

"So, you are a century-old half-angel," Milo breathed, the words coming out of his mouth feeling strange, almost wrong. "I suppose if there are things like magic and ghuls that live in the bowels of the earth, why couldn't there be angels?"

Ambrose nodded, the two now walking side by side.

"The term used in the Bible and other Christian works is 'Nephilim,'" he offered. "Though I'm not sure if that referred just to the ones in Genesis. You know, a specific breed of half-angels, or all half-angels. The ghuls have their own name for us, and obviously, they know enough to be scared."

Milo looked ahead and saw the ghuls throwing sharp glances over their stooped shoulders. Whether it was fear or hatred or both on their faces was impossible to tell in the gloom, but there was no denying they'd heard what had been said, and they weren't arguing.

"So, there's a lot of you then?"

Ambrose raised his head and cocked an eyebrow.

"You'd figure one would be enough, wouldn't you?" he said with a grimace that couldn't quite bring itself to be a smile. "There are obviously some of us from ancient times, but otherwise, no, there are not many of us. In the century of traveling and warring I've put in, I've heard about half a dozen others like me and only met two face to face. One seemed like the real thing up to the end, and the other could have been, but somehow he seemed so different I wasn't ever sure."

It was Milo's turn to raise an eyebrow.

"In the end, does that mean what I think it means?"

Ambrose looked ahead, pretending to scrutinize the ghuls.

"So, you're the only one left?"

The big man shrugged and gnawed his lip for a moment.

"I suppose I am until the next time some godling decides a mortal is worth going to Hell for." He gave Milo a sidelong look. "We're a rare breed, true enough, but as long as there are pretty women, we'll never go extinct."

Milo gave a nervous laugh, but it was half-hearted, and not just because of the implications of angels and Hell and therefore Heaven and a God to rule it began to weigh on him. He knew many of the boys at the orphanage had been dogmatically orthodox by dint of their dead parents, while others had been violently atheist, again by dint of their dead parents. Milo, with no memory of his parents, had never picked a side. The truth was that given what he'd seen, when the chips were down, both types were the same. Like any outcast cynic, he'd taken to quietly mocking, but now, walking in the dark with ghuls and something like Simon Ambrose, his flippancy seemed more than a little cavalier.

They both fell silent as they trudged along, the ghuls' voices ahead so soft they could barely hear them over their own scuffing footfalls on the turfed tunnel floor.

The weight of Milo's thoughts along with the oppressive darkness might have engulfed him in melancholic black musings, but a curious spark flared as he brooded. He looked at Ambrose, hope suddenly burgeoning inside him.

"So, you've been around for a long time?" he asked tentatively.

"As some would measure it, sure." The bodyguard grunted with a nod. "But the longer you're around, the more you come to understand that what little time you've been around, it never seems like very long."

The curious spark flared and ignited a flood of questions that Milo only barely managed to contain.

"You've seen quite a bit then?" Milo probed as gently as he could.

"Are you about to ask me if I was there at some big event or met some great historical figure?" The big man snorted as he shook his head. "I promise you the answer will probably be no, and if it isn't...well, let's just say you're bound to be disappointed."

Milo drew up short at that, pondering for a second why that thought hadn't occurred to him. After all, it was the most natural thing in the world, but his interest wasn't in anything so mundane.

"I was more thinking about the other things," Milo said, finding himself at a loss for a word to use that didn't sound silly. "You know things that are, uh, magical?"

Ambrose gave a little head-bob of understanding and adjusted his rifle on his shoulder.

"You hoping I'm kind of a field guide to the dark and mysterious world behind the curtain?"

Milo studied him carefully.

"Are you telling me you're not?" he asked, holding his breath with anxious excitement as he waited for the answer.

Ambrose let out a deep sigh that turned into a resigned splutter.

"I'm afraid I'm going to be a disappointment on that score, Magus," he declared. "Jorge put me on this detail because I'm the most dangerous weapon that doesn't require wheels, and I don't spook easy. That's it."

Milo couldn't keep from frowning.

"But you just said you've heard about other Neph, er, Nephilim, and even met some?"

"Sorry, that's it," Ambrose growled, ready to bristle but thinking better of it when he saw Milo's downcast expression. "Sure I've seen strange things, any man on campaign has, but almost all of them could be chalked up to the madness and strangeness that comes with war. I've heard rumors and witnessed what I couldn't explain, and I've met at least two of my kind, but otherwise…"

His voice trailed off, and he shook his head before giving a derisive snort.

"Funny thing is that Jorge had hoped for that too when he brought me on after learning what I was. You and he must be cut from the same cloth because his face looked a lot like that, too."

Milo attempted to reset his face to neutral, but it was harder than he thought. Suddenly having something to care about was a reality he was still adjusting as well.

"Quiet now," the she-ghul called from up ahead. "Silence as we approach the gate, and do not speak unless spoken to."

Ambrose nudged Milo in the arm, and it was all he could do not to lose his grip on the skull lamp.

"See, you're about to be up to your eyes in this magic business," the bodyguard whispered. "You'll be sick of wonders and mysteries soon enough."

Milo wanted to tell him it was unlikely, but he shoved the thoughts aside as his body began to tingle with a heady combination of fear and excitement. His chest tightened as his steps quickened, and a voice in the back of his mind warned that he was rushing to his doom.

Nerves caused Milo to breathe heavily as his viridian light played across the surface of the gate.

When the gate looked up and regarded him, Milo found he couldn't take in air.

It was a wall of bone, or more precisely, it was a wall of bones.

Columns of vertebrae formed curving pillars that reached from floor to ceiling, and between them, a veritable thicket of ribs intertwined into a woven osseous mesh. Situated at seemingly random intervals along the assemblage of spines and ribs jutted skeletal arms, their joints held together by scraps of flesh that glistened black in the lamp's green-hued light. At the center of the gate was a ring of eight bare skulls without their lower jaws. Milo would have assumed the skulls were all from humans, except on closer inspection, he saw that the teeth lining the remaining mandible were long and curved like fangs. The skulls revealed a cavity in the wall that seemed to be little more than a dark pit where the jagged edges of broken bones could just be seen.

Each skull was mounted on a stump of the spine, and every one of those stumps had their skulls pointed directly at Milo.

He tried to tell himself it was just a trick of the light and the nature of their empty staring sockets, but as he crept closer, he realized the gate was intent on him, just him.

The ghul princess stepped forward and performed a vulturous curtsy before raising her voice in her wicked language.

"Do you know what she's saying?" Milo whispered as quietly as he could to Ambrose.

Ambrose gave a quick shake of his head, adjusting his grip on his rifle sling.

"This is all new to me, Magus," he murmured back. "Allies or no, I say be on your guard, no matter what happens."

"Silence," the other ghul growled.

Ambrose bristled, but Milo leaned forward and watched intently.

After she finished her baleful whispers, which Milo now guessed was some sort of ritual, he couldn't suppress a shudder when he heard the bones rattle against each other and then slither this way and that.

The skulls that had been watching Milo turned as one and regarded the ghul in front of them with hollow stares. The troglodyte princess muttered one more declaration, then the skulls began to slide around the cavity until four were lining the top and four the bottom. Above them, skeletal limbs spasmed to life and reached over, gripping each other to form ovoid hoops. The bones inside them whined and hissed as black vapors rose before congealing within the hoops.

There was a titanic rasping breath from within the skull-framed cavity, and Milo felt air drawn across his face toward the awakening gate.

The skulls flexed like scaled horny lips around the yawning mouth of the cavity, while above, the churning pools narrowed to scowl at the ghul before the gate. With a spasm in his mind to make up for the momentarily frozen organ in his chest, Milo realized the entire gate had become the vast simulacrum of a face.

"*IMRAH MARID, DAUGHTER OF BASHLEK MARID, YOU ARE KNOWN TO US*," the gate announced in a deep, cavernous voice. "*FAZIHR JUBAL, SON OF HAMOTH, YOU ARE ALSO KNOWN TO US.*"

The gate then directed its gaze to Milo and Ambrose, turning from one to the other.

"*YOU ARE NOT KNOWN TO US,*" it declared, cold breath

hissing between the fangs of the arrayed skulls. *"HOLD FAST, OR YOU SHALL BE CONSUMED."*

Milo and Ambrose exchanged concerned glances, but neither moved.

More skeletal limbs extended from the gate, some emerging from the layers of ribs and vertebrae. They gripped the walls, floor, and ceiling of the tunnel, and with a sound like a thousand splintered fingers raking stone, the gate dragged itself forward. By reflex, both men tensed, and Milo prepared to run, Ambrose unlimbered his rifle. The dark, liquid eyes fixed both of them with a cautionary glance but did not repeat its warning. It didn't need to.

The ghuls shuffled back to make way for the gate, sliding around Ambrose and Milo.

"If this is some sort of trap," the bodyguard said in a soft, deadly whisper even as he stood perfectly still, "I will make certain you both are sent to Hell screaming."

"Peace, Jurhumidon." Imrah's words were sharp, but her tone was strikingly sincere. "Rousing the gate's anger could kill us all."

Milo didn't kid himself that he could read ghul body language after having learned of their existence only hours ago, but he did notice that both Imrah and Fazihr seemed to be watching everything with rapt, almost anxious attention. Whether that was because they feared the gate or they feared that the gate would kill them remained to be seen.

It crawled forward until Milo could have stuck his hand into the skull-ringed orifice the gate spoke through. This close, the light showed a space lined with spurs of jagged bone stretching beyond the reach of the lamp. The thought of being drawn into that barbed throat to be pierced and torn filled Milo with a horror so potent he almost broke and ran right then.

"BE STILL," the gate instructed, and the mass of bones began to writhe and undulate. Skeletal hands composed of bones so long and thick they couldn't be human reached out of the rattling

SCHNEIDER & MICHAEL ANDERLE

corpus. Fingers as thick as Milo's wrist reached up and dipped into the stygian pools that served as eyes. As slowly and solemnly as at any christening, the gate bent its limbs downward and touched Milo and Ambrose gently upon their scalps.

Milo's entire body shrank as cold the likes of which he'd never known stole over him. Goose flesh covered him, and he felt as though his organs were retracting. A blast of air slipped between his numb lips, coming out a plume of condensing vapor. Desperate, futile shivering wracked his body, and he lost his grip on the horns of the skull lamp.

For the second time that day the light vanished, and for a heartbeat, everything was swallowed by blackness and obliterating cold.

But as suddenly as it had come, the cold left, and a second later, Milo had the horns of the lamp pressed into his hands.

"Thanks," he muttered as the light rekindled, expecting to see Ambrose's grin.

Instead, a skeletal hand retracted back into the gate, disappearing with a series of dull clicks.

"*MORTAL MAN AND CHILD OF THE FALLEN,*" the gate intoned. "*NOW YOU ARE KNOWN TO ME. BASHLEK MARID AWAITS YOU.*"

The huge skeletal arms reached for the cavernous mouth, gripped its edge, and pulled. There were more awful sounds of bones rasping and scraping, then the cavity widened into a portal just tall enough to accommodate Milo and wide enough to allow Ambrose.

Milo looked at Ambrose.

"It says that we are awaited." He had done his level best but failed to sound cheerful.

Ambrose grunted and stepped forward, moving through the shadow of the gate with chin thrust forward and eyes roving.

"Somehow, that doesn't make me feel much better."

Milo tended to agree, but he felt that saying as much in front of Bashlek Marid's daughter might not be the best idea. Swallowing as he tucked the skull lamp under his arm, he followed his bodyguard through the tunnel within a tunnel, trying not to think about the thousand needles of bone mere inches from impaling him from hundreds of different angles. The air in the tunnel smelled of dust and old blood.

After emerging out the other side of the gate unscathed, he stood with Ambrose and waited for the ghuls to emerge.

"The gate wasn't so hard to convince after all," Ambrose noted, his mustache twitching. "Almost like it knew what was coming before she revealed my identity."

"Perhaps Imrah has more authority than she understands," Milo offered with a shrug. He turned to see the glint of the ghuls' eyes coming through the tunnel.

"Maybe," the big man conceded, his face expressing anything but concession on the point. "Or maybe our escorts weren't privy to information their leader has. My point is, careful what you say. Our host might not thank you for being too honest."

Milo nodded his understanding as Imrah and Fazihr emerged from the gate's shadow.

"See?" Ambrose called jauntily. "Not nearly as much trouble as you thought it would be, eh?"

The ghuls exchanged glances, then stared blankly at the bodyguard. Milo wondered how a species could look so sinister just standing silently, but then he looked back as he heard the gate close with a wince-inducing chorus. The magical construction of bone returned to its original shape, the back of the gate looking identical to the front when they first came upon it.

"So, that," Milo said to the ghuls while pointing at the gate. "That's the kind of magic your people will be teaching me?"

The ghuls exchanged looks again, and Fazihr gave a blood-chilling laugh, his head wagging.

"The creation of a bone homunculus of that order is a matter for the masters," Imrah explained, her voice curdled with scornful amusement. "You've lit a spectral lamp so far. Don't get ahead of yourself, meat."

Milo was surprised when he found himself in well-trodden territory with these ghuls. They, and no doubt most of their kind, thought little of Milo and his abilities. He had been underestimated and devalued and was expected to prove himself. The reality of the situation and his familiarity with it awoke an old defiant flame.

"Whatever you've got to teach, I'm here to learn," he declared, crossing his arms. "Just need to give me a chance."

Imrah stared at Milo, her predatory gaze needling him, but he glared back with cool, practiced indifference. Fazihr was the first to crack as a stalemate set in.

"We'll see," he hissed, placing a clawed hand gingerly on Imrah's shoulder. "Right now we are awaited at court, and we're very late."

"Story of my life." Milo sighed and stepped to the side to allow the ghuls to pass. "Please, lead on."

8

A SHOCK

The tunnel changed quickly as they moved away from the gate.

The rough-hewn walls gave way to panels of stone worked meticulously to form bas reliefs. Depicted in the carvings was an unsettling combination of language and art where what were clearly symbols and signs of a language looped and twisted to form pictures of creatures and scenes foreign to Milo's eyes and mind. It was impossible to say what it was about the depictions set into the walls that bothered him, but the more Milo stared at them, the deeper his sense of wrongness became. Eventually, he decided to ignore the subversive artwork.

The ceiling became a vault that Milo appreciated much more than the alien carvings on the wall. The shaped stone arches made the weight of the earth above them not seem so oppressive. Once after passing beneath one, Milo reached upward, just able to brush a finger over a crenelated buttress. Before the gate, the tunnel had been low enough that he had feared standing on his tiptoes lest he scrape his head.

Soon branches in the tunnels, which now resembled a hall more than anything else, began to appear, and they were at the mercy of the two ghuls once more.

Passages branched off and wound every which way, but like hounds to the scent, Imrah and Fazihr led them on without pause. Once or twice as they neared an intersection, Milo caught sight of other ghuls retreating from the light. They ducked back the way they had come, or darted across intersections, often alone but sometimes in groups of two or three.

"Do you all dwell in one structure?" Milo called to the ghuls. "Like a hive or nest."

Imrah cocked her head to one side, looking over her hunched shoulder at Milo.

"Do we look like vermin to you, meat?" she asked, with a grimace that displayed all her teeth. "Do you think we live underground because we are some breed of rodent or insect?"

Milo felt it would be rude to say that sometimes the way they moved and looked around did make him think of a hideous amalgam of rat and spider. Instead, he ducked his head apologetically and answered in a contrite tone, "No, I'm sorry that my words have offended you."

He spoke as calmly and clearly as he could, mindful of the revelation after passing the gate. "There's just so much about your people that I don't understand."

It was hard to win people's respect if they thought you were picking a fight, even when you had a point. In fact, Milo thought, especially when you had a point.

Again Imrah regarded him with an expression he could not read, but when she replied, the long-toothed sneer was gone, and she seemed to be making some effort to soften her tone.

"It is understandable that this all seems strange to you," she rasped before turning back to the winding corridor. "Maybe now that you are here to learn, you will one day understand the great debt the world owes us, and how even as you war over our heads, you stamp upon the homes of a great and mighty people. And no, we do not dwell in a single nest or hive."

Milo had been with her until her declaration about a great and mighty people.

Ghuls were sinister creatures, and that was before one considered their magical abilities, but so far, all he had seen was one bone homunculus and some barren corridors filled with carvings that were probably hundreds if not thousands of years old. Milo guessed the ghuls might have been something great before, but not anymore. He imagined they were like many lingering peoples, clinging to the bones of their ancestors—in this case, literally. The Bashlek Marid's court was probably a ragged assemblage of his dwindling tribe.

They passed through a small round antechamber whose passages led off like spokes in a wheel. Imrah and Fazihr headed doggedly for the fourth spoke from the portal they had entered, and Milo passed beneath a very ornate arch without noticing.

They stepped out onto the landing that led down to a wider plaza, which was filled with the sights and sound of creatures busy about their commerce. From it sprang a great stone causeway leading to a massive, tiered city that glowed like a poisoned gem over a yawning abyss.

"Behold Ifreedahm," Fazihr declared with obvious pride. "Jewel of the Stygian Realm."

That was when Milo realized exactly how wrong he had been.

"Are we under a mountain or something?" Ambrose muttered as they shuffled toward the central citadel. "We have to be under a mountain, right?"

The structure rose like a serrated spike of black tourmaline in the middle of the city, reaching toward the cavernous roof. The azure glow of the vast braziers that kept the city in perpetual cold twilight danced along the jagged edges of the towering structure so that it almost seemed to breathe. The idea of such a vast structure hidden in the depths of the world, much less the city that surrounded it, strained the edges of Milo's understanding. From the moment his foot struck the causeway, he'd felt like a man caught in a drunkard's mad dream.

A dream that teetered toward a nightmare.

Flowing up and down the causeway were rivers of ghuls, often with some form of magically animated corpse acting as a porter or a beast of burden. Here and there Milo saw spectral entities, some bearing the shapes they had worn in life, while others were little more than fractured images or vague clouds of darkness or phosphorescence.

Milo felt a shudder of disgust when he looked at the specters, remembering his first encounter with a shade in Room 7. He knew he'd have to contend with the incorporeal eventually, but for the moment, he decided to study the living denizens of Ifreedahm.

Many of the ghuls were similar in form and appearance to Imrah and Fazihr, but there were variations—what might have been deviant strains of the creatures. Some were shrunken, spindly things that looked like pictures Milo had seen of the monkeys and lesser apes that dwelt in southern jungles. A cart whose wheels were rounded blocks of granite drawn by a team of animated ox bones hosted what looked like a family of the goblin-sized ghuls. The smallest of their number peeked over the edge of the cart, staring at Milo with pale, bulbous eyes.

Another deviation was hulking brutes, built along similar lines as Ambrose but the height of giants. Even stooped with their knuckles dragging the ground, Milo would have had trouble touching the monsters' craggy chins. A pair of the immense horrors stomped by, heads swaying from side to side on their thick necks, and up close, Milo saw they had no eyes. Above their tusk-festooned mouths and snuffling snouts were bony wrinkles where eyes ought to have been.

As they passed, one snorted and swung its barbarous head

around to glare sightlessly in Milo's direction. He wondered what they would do, trapped as they were on the causeway, if the monster took offense at the scent of their party. Milo had a pistol and Ambrose a rifle and a bayonet, but looking at the malformed muscular bulk of the huge ghuls, Milo wasn't sure those would be enough to stop them. As he felt the weight of their tread shake the causeway, he wasn't certain an artillery shell could stop them.

Thankfully, the pair went on their way, and the escorted humans continued into the city. In truth, though they received many questioning glances, Milo was amazed that they were not accosted by any of the traveling ghuls. Given that Imrah and Fazihr had said no human had ever been here, it seemed strange that the denizens were so sanguine about their presence.

When he raised this question as they neared the city, Fazihr had twisted his neck back to answer as he continued to follow Imrah's lead.

"Imrah is known to many," he stated simply. Seeing the humans' furrowed brows, he added, "And it is unwise to hinder the daughter of Bashlek Marid."

They entered the city by passing through a wide arch, where ranks of unliving people and beasts stood in burnished baroque armor as silent, unflinching sentinels.

They came to a harbor of sorts among the tall, narrow buildings that comprised most of the city. In this broad space, a sort of market or bazaar had been built. Stalls and blankets and tents littered the area in sporadic rows, creating twisting avenues and alleys between the various merchants hawking their wares. All of them called out in the ghul tongue in a chorus of viperish rasps that set Milo's teeth on edge. It was just as well that he couldn't understand them because the assortment of objects they hoisted into the air or displayed for inspection seemed only to have being bizarre and grisly in common.

"Dear God," Ambrose whispered. He elbowed Milo before

pointing at a wide red and black domino blanket. "Would you look at that?"

Spools of what might have been glistening entrails or perhaps immense veiny worms sat on red squares, while assortments of small bones with jewel inlays lay on black squares. The ghul proprietor sat cross-legged, smile proudly displaying gem-studded fangs. Just past that, corroded bells and keys on strings of knotted hair jangled in one stall across from a pavilion where smokeless green flames burned and a chorus of whispers could be heard every time someone moved within the shadowy canvas.

"The markets of Ifreedahm offer goods and services to rival any in the world," Fazihr remarked after noticing their gaping. "An absolute necessity when you think about how many ghuls there are, and all the supplies and alchemical reagents they require."

"Naturally," Milo commented as they shuffled past a huge ghul looming over several tables, where skins of varying shapes, sizes, and colors were stretched on racks. All were liberally decorated with more of that bizarre writing that made uncomfortable pictures. Milo wasn't sure which was more disconcerting, the images formed by the script or that some of the skins still bore recognizable features, confirming that they came from humanoids.

Following their ghul guides as close as they dared, Milo and Ambrose passed through the market and into another part of the city. Here buildings lined the broad streets, though all were open-faced so that they resembled roofed stages more than shops. One glance said that these places offered trinkets, materials, and products as strange and macabre as those in the market.

It was here that Milo and Ambrose saw other living humans, or at least some near cousin to their species.

They were on a broad platform under a sharply pitched roof with rows of barbed chains stretched between stony pillars that formed the front of the establishment. Ashen-skinned, bent, and stout rows of them stood in a line with heads drooping so their lank, colorless hair hung over their thick features. A common ghul stood behind them with a whip composed of a spine and red sinew coiled around one hand, while in front of them, one of the smaller simian ghuls cavorted and gestured just inside the chains to other ghuls and stranger creatures who stood pointing and inspecting.

Milo stopped dead in his tracks and called to their escorts, one finger stabbing at the offending shop.

"What is happening there?"

An anger he could not quite put into words coated the back of his throat and burned all the way down his gullet.

Ambrose gave him a confused look but slid to his side in silent support as the ghuls turned and shuffled back to address him.

"We are late," Imrah informed him curtly. "If you wish to peruse the shops, you will have time once you have your audience with—"

"I don't want to *shop*, I want to get answers," Milo snarled. "Is that a slave market?"

Milo had of course heard of such things, degenerate places in savage lands where people were traded like livestock. To see something that resembled such barbarism, only with the purchasers being fanged and gloam-eyed horrors like the ghuls made something rebel inside of him. He couldn't say why this was the bridge too far, not with all the horrible and alien sights they'd seen already, but he found his feet planted in the middle of the broad street, and he would not be moved.

Imrah looked at where Milo was pointing, then glanced at Fazihr, who nodded in a most vulture-like fashion as he stepped forward.

"It is no slave market," Fazihr said, uncurling his claws. "Though what it is will not in truth make you any happier. If it helps, I will tell you that those creatures, the *goyisch*, though they resemble your kind, are little more than animals."

Milo felt a tremor inside him, somehow certain of the answer before he asked it.

"If it isn't a slave market," he said, tasting bile at the back of his throat, "what is it?"

Fazihr looked at Imrah, who nodded.

"It is a meat market," he said, hands splayed apologetically. "Something like the butcher shops you humans frequent."

Milo felt the lead weight in his stomach plummet toward the ground. He wasn't sure if he was about to be sick, storm the abominable place, or attack Fazihr. For a long heartbeat, he stood rooted to the spot as the triptych of choices spun in his head.

You wanted more, his own voice whispered in his head. *No one ever said you'd like it.*

"Magus. *Milo*," Ambrose whispered at his shoulder. "It sours my stomach too, but let's not do anything rash. We just got here, and we both still have a lot to learn, you even more than me. Before we start overturning tables, let's make sure we know which temple we're in."

The full effect of the biblical analogy was wasted on the religiously illiterate Milo, but the big man's calm voice broke the back of his anger. It slunk into a dark corner of his heart to fester, but Milo felt its stranglehold loosen.

"This isn't how I expected things to turn out," he confessed to his bodyguard, not caring that Fazihr could hear. "This is not the kind of place I thought I would…"

Ambrose rested one strong paw on Milo's shoulder and gave an affectionate if painful squeeze.

"I know," he said. "Things rarely turn out the way we hope. But you have one advantage most people don't."

Milo let out a sigh and rolled his eyes.

"I'm a witch," he muttered as they followed Fazihr, who had turned without comment to walk with Imrah again.

"Not much of one yet," Ambrose chuckled. "Besides, that's not what I was talking about."

"Do tell," Milo remarked dryly, exercising all his will not to look back at the downcast creatures, the *goyisch*, one last time.

"At least you were told that you'd be learning from monsters," the big man said with a sweep of his arm at Ifreedahm. "Most folks don't find out how awful their mentors are until it's far too late for it to matter."

Milo's shoulders sagged as he pulled out a desperately needed cigarette and the requisite match. The honest flame of the lucifer seemed a pale, puny thing before the unnatural light that bathed the city.

"Sometimes, Simon," he said, taking a deep drag as he shook out the match, "it feels like my whole life is a study in too little, too late."

It was Ambrose's turn to roll his eyes.

"Young people," he sputtered, shaking his head. "Always so dramatic."

9

AN AUDIENCE

Milo had a sneaking suspicion that their travel through the rest of Ifreedahm had been modified to make certain the two humans didn't see anything that might spark more delays.

With Imrah leading the way, they soon left the wide thoroughfares and slid among the alleys and side streets until they came to a broad stair that descended to a lower level of the city.

"It will be quicker, and there will be fewer chances for interruptions," Fazihr explained as Milo and Ambrose paused at the top of the stairs. "Truly, we should have traveled this way upon first entering the city, but I would have thought you'd appreciate being spared more darkness. I understand it is uncomfortable for your kind."

The steps descended into shadow, and Milo had to admit that as bizarre and awful as the city was, he didn't relish more tunnels with their smothering darkness.

Still, getting to the Bashlek's court quickly was just fine with him. A growing desire to learn what he had to, rather than all he could, had been growing in Milo, and the quicker he got things started, the sooner he could leave.

"Let's just get this over with." He grunted as he shifted the lamp so he had a hand on each horn and its green light shone down the steps into the dark passageway.

"Quickly," Imrah urged from just beyond the light, and Milo followed, feeling as though they were traveling down the moss-floored tunnel again.

He quickly learned the Underpassage of Ifreedahm was far less peaceful than the quiet, steady seclusion of the tunnels that led to the ghul realm. The skull lamp shone on worn walls and floors, their surfaces pitted and scored, and a few times, he spied great, many-fingered cracks on the floor. Occasionally these uneven places nearly turned his feet underneath him, and only Ambrose's steady hand kept him from pitching forward.

In the untouched blackness beyond the lamp's light, the impression of many creatures moving swiftly and quietly nearby could not be ignored. Ghuls seemed naturally cat-footed, but there were so many of them that they could not be completely silent. There were other noises of movement as well, rustlings and flutterings that Milo would not dwell on. At irregular inter-vals, there was an eruption of ghul speech, sometimes soft and insistent, other times sharp and combative, but it always set Milo's teeth on edge. Once he felt something pass within inches of his arm, moving so quickly it was only a dark, spindly blur. He heard the awful torn-jugular sound of ghul laughter echoing behind him, growing fainter with maddening slowness.

His nerves deadened to the terror of the Underpassage as time dragged on, but Milo was becoming more and more aware of his discomfort. Since the interruption of his sleep and the abductive introduction by the ghuls, they had been walking for several hours, and he was tired and sore. After taking no fewer than three twisting turns that led deeper under the city, Milo began to wonder if Imrah really did intend for them to see her father.

He was just about to raise the question when they rounded a bend in the upcoming passage and stood before a baroque door made of worked bronze and set in a wall of the same dark, gemlike stone as the central citadel. In front of the door stood two ogrish ghuls, their blind heads crowned with glowing ridged helms that nearly scraped the ceiling. Their huge hands were encased in scalloped gauntlets, and around their necks hung thick chains from which several glass orbs dangled. In the light of the skull lamp, something noxious and hungry seethed within the glass.

Both guards, nostrils flaring, bowed deeply to Imrah.

"The Bashlek's guest has arrived," she stated in a voice that presumed attention and obedience. "He had word sent that he and his consort were to be taken to the southern antechamber of the court in preparation for their audience."

Both creatures bowed again, then in unison, they slapped their metal-shod hands to the gate and rumbled a single bass note.

The door swung inward with a groan on heavy hinges.

"Consort, eh?" Ambrose chuckled as they moved toward the yawning portal. "You'll have to let me know if that's a promotion or demotion after this is all done."

The interior of the ghul citadel was a strange combination of bleak and alien that left Milo vacillating between shock and near boredom until they reached the antechamber.

They moved through labyrinthine corridors that all seemed very much the same, little more than passages of dark stone smoothed and shaped to inhuman aesthetics. Their odd, slanted design was at first unsettling, but as his mind accepted the foreign geometries, they blurred one into the other. Even the pale-blue witchlight that illuminated the place could be accepted as commonplace.

That lasted until they came to a gallery of bas reliefs full of strange and sometimes animated art or passed a room where an unliving servitor was busying itself with a menial task. Then the reality of where he was came crashing back in, and Milo was torn between disgust and dread fascination.

By the time they arrived at the antechamber, a circular room with several low couches and tables, Milo was thankful for a place to sit and compose himself before meeting the ruler of the city. One of the goblin ghuls was waiting for them when they arrived, and it displayed a maddening combination of excitement and irritation at seeing them. It rubbed its knobby hands together as it eyed Milo and his lamp before pulling a puckered look at Imrah.

"Mysuchastate," it gibbered in a breathless string of sound. "Maimedandsmellingofthesurfacewhatwillyourfatherthink."

Imrah held out her stump of a wrist and examined it as though just remembering what had happened to her hand.

"If he notices, I will be shocked," she replied tartly. "But I have a regenerating salve and all the necessities. Go let him know we are about to be announced, and I'll get things sorted."

The simian ghul gave an irritated little prance as it made its way to a door opposite the one they'd entered.

"Notlikelynotlikelyatall," it sing-songed as it capered. "Andyou'llstillstinkofthesurfacenomatterwhatyoudo."

Imrah's jaws clacked in irritation, and the shrunken ghul gave a shriller rendition of a ghul laugh before tugging the door ajar just enough for it to slip through. In the room beyond, voices echoing in a great hall could be heard.

"This will take a minute," Imrah explained almost apologetically, then paused to look Milo up and down thoughtfully. "Actually, you might want to watch this."

Milo looked at Ambrose, who shrugged, and together, they stepped over to the ghul princess.

"Perhaps you will learn this someday," she said, then, reaching her clawed finger to her collarbone, she dragged a line that split her inky skin and tugged away a loose flap.

Milo and Ambrose swore in shock and horror, drawing Imrah's startled eye. Seeing the faces of the two humans staring at the flap of hide she'd sheared from her body, she gave a derisive snort.

"Be silent and learn," she hissed irritably, then pulled hard on the flap.

Milo heard a familiar rending sound akin to what he'd heard in Room 7 with the shade, but instead of a crawling nest of darkness, there was a gray-skinned body beneath. In truth, the exposed flesh was nearly identical to what he'd already seen, only a different color and less slimy-looking.

With a start, Milo realized the skin of ghuls was some kind of shell, a skin-tight coating, and what he was now seeing was Imrah's naked flesh. The revelation sparked what was left of his underdeveloped decorum, and Milo wondered if he should look away.

When Imrah reached inside her skinsuit, he was glad he hadn't.

There was a clink of glass, then she drew out two vials with wax stoppers, one containing what looked like pale splinters, while the other was a deep bronze color. The vials were small enough they both fit in her hand, but Milo found it hard to believe there was enough room in her snug garment for such items to fit unnoticed. His disbelief was compounded when after looking over what lay in her hand, she palmed the glass containers and fished out another vial full of what looked like ink.

Imrah, her skin suit flapping open, turned to Milo as she shuffled the vials into her other hand.

"Each of these is part of a formula for a regeneration ritual," she stated, holding them up for Milo to get a good look at. "How much and what combinations, you will learn with time. Initially, you will need to follow strict recipes to avoid...accidents. However, once you understand the basic principles, there will be some variations and improvisations available."

Milo, realizing he was being taught magic on the fly, nodded to show he was paying attention and not wondering about ghul conceptions of nudity, and more troublingly, sexuality.

"This is not your mortal chemistry," she said as she gave the vials a shake. "All the reagents in the Underworld will do you no good if they are not commanded to obey, bound by will and intent."

She raised the vials to her mouth, and with one practiced motion, tore all three wax seals free.

"Necromantic alchemy uses the essence left by once-living things to interact with magically-charged ingredients," she explained, passing the open vials beneath her nose with a sniff. "It is art and science, as well as conquest. The finest ingredients can be wasted without essence to fuel their transformation, and even with the essence, an unfocused mind will not be able to control their reactions."

She displayed her teeth in a Ghulish grin.

"For the weak or timid, what should heal could turn to poison in an instant," she explained, then threw back her head and emptied all three vials into her open mouth.

As Milo watched her shudder, he heard her utter a word in the ghul tongue, and he felt...something. Some internal pressure from Imrah thrumming against his mind. For the briefest of seconds, he experienced, not sensations, but impressions of sensations. A thrill, then yearning, and then pain. It was almost dizzying how quickly one bled into the next, and as he wrestled with them, he lost his sense of time and location for a moment.

As such, when he heard Ambrose's voice, he woke as though from a deep sleep, struggling to remember where he was and how long he had been there.

"Well, that's quite the trick and no mistake."

Milo started and saw that Imrah's mutilated arm now boasted a skeletal hand that smoked and hissed. Before he could recover from the shock of the new appendage, before his very eyes, the vapors began to contract and congeal into her ash-colored flesh. In the time it took to utter a profane exclamation, Imrah possessed a complete hand.

As if to show off, she raised that newly formed hand to her mouth and licked her thumb with her black, wormy tongue, then drew the flap of her skinsuit back into place. The new moistened thumb pressed the torn corner into place, and there was a soft cracking like flesh over a fire. When she drew her hand away, her black suit was whole, and within a blink of an eye, it had crawled over her regenerated hand.

"This is what lies within your grasp, Magus," Imrah said as she curled and uncurled her hands in a demonstration.

The door to the Bashlek's court swung open, and the shrunken attendant thrust his head in.

"Youraudienceisbeingannounced," it chirped. "Bestgetoutthere."

Milo had stumbled halfway to the door before claws closed around his arm.

"Take this."

Milo turned around and felt the skull lamp pressed into his hands.

"You might need it," Fazihr said, sharing the least reassuring smile Milo had ever seen.

"Welcome, Magus," Bashlek Marid rasped from his throne. "I trust your introduction to my realm was a tender one."

Despite sitting high upon a throne on an elevated dais, the ghul monarch's gravelly whisper carried down so that it felt as though Milo was within arm's reach of the old predator.

That was exactly what Marid was: a predator.

Years in the Dresden war orphanage had honed Milo's instincts about such things. Even as a young child, those who survived in such environs learned very quickly to distinguish between predator and prey. This understanding grew very quickly to the realization that these roles were fluid for most, with the average individual acting as predator or prey as events unfolded and they were given or denied opportunity. Anyone could fall upon the broken or be fallen upon, but the true predators and true prey never changed, one always hunting and the other always running scared.

One look at the venerable monster—the tilt of his head, the flex of his claws—told Milo everything he needed to know.

"Yes, thank you, uh, sir." Milo fumbled. "On behalf of my commander and the, uh, German Empire, I would like to extend my thanks."

"Your gratitude and that of your people is noted," the Bashlek replied as he leaned back on his throne, smoothing the crimson mantle and stole he wore. "We are glad to be the first to extend a hand of friendship in your kind's first steps onto the path of true civilization."

Voices rustled around the hall, ghuls whispering and scheming in the tiered galleries lining the audience chamber. The braziers hanging in a row from the high vaulted ceiling did not spill their cool light far beyond the center of the room, so Milo could only guess at the expressions of hundreds of eyes watching him. A quick flutter of panic stirred in his stomach to have so many eyes on him, but he squashed it ruthlessly.

There was only one set of eyes he needed to worry about right now, and that set scrutinized him minutely after tossing out a barb tucked into his magnanimity.

Milo nodded, allowing himself half a smile so the Bashlek knew he was in on the game.

"Great Bashlek, I am eager to begin learning," he declared,

pitching his voice so it was clearly heard by everyone present. "Knowing that humans cover the whole of the earth, yet we still have so much to learn fills me with...excitement for the days to come."

Marid inclined his head slightly as he sank deeper into his throne, acknowledging Milo's riposte even as he displayed unconcern.

"Truly, I can only imagine the eagerness you must feel," the wizened ghul said and offered a telltale smile that made Milo very nervous all of a sudden. "In fact, I was told you displayed some of your talents on your road to join us today."

Milo became aware of the skull with its glowing sockets tucked under his arm.

"A trifle, I am sure." Milo shrugged, hoping he sounded modest and not rudely dismissive. "It wouldn't have been possible without some impromptu education by Imrah and Fazihr."

Milo heard more whispers, many of them angrier and more urgent than before. He wondered if perhaps he had said something wrong, and he couldn't help himself; he tried to peer into the shadows beyond the spheres of light. A low, drowning chuckle passed between Marid's emaciated lips, snapping Milo's attention back to the monster he could see.

"I am well pleased that those I sent offered you such assistance," Marid said, leaning forward fractionally on his throne. "Indeed, I would love an opportunity to see your abilities, for my own edification and that of my court."

Milo smelled something funny in the request, but it seemed clear that refusal at this stage would be unwise.

"I am at your disposal," Milo said with a short bow and was glad for a chance to hide a wince. Given what ghuls seemed to do with humanlike creatures, he suddenly wondered to what extent these creatures might take such an offer.

"Excellent," Marid said, though his tone had become deadly

serious. "Taking the lamp in your hands, I would ask you to command it to shine brighter. Strong enough that none here may doubt that you are what you claim, my dear Magus."

Milo drew the lamp in front of him, hands gripping the bases of the horns, feeling the trembling auras there still, though they were a touch thinner and more strained than when he'd first encountered them in the tunnel. All around him, he heard the unsettling sibilance of the court whispering, prognosticating, and simmering with suspicion. Milo was sure how it was to be done, but taking what he'd learned from Imrah moments before and the initial ritual, he guessed it was a matter of will at this point.

"BRIGHT," he said and breathed across the dome of the skull.

The skull's illumination flared for a second but settled back to its original level as though it was too tired to answer to his instruction.

Marid said nothing, only watched through narrowed eyes as the susurrating sea of whispers grew louder.

Command it, he told himself angrily. *Predator or prey, Milo. Which is it going to be?*

The words shot through him, reviving deeply buried memories—hard, ugly things. Milo drew on that anger and repugnance like a flame drawing breath from a bellows.

"BRIGHT!" he demanded, blowing over the skull, then thrusting it up over his head.

Brilliant rays of light, stabbing out in shades of emerald, lanced from the skull's open sockets. Milo could feel the alchemical ingredients within thrumming, a trembling force caught between his hands. Turning in a slow circle for all to see, he watched, gratified, as the now-silent courtiers recoiled from the stabbing light as it played across their hunched forms.

His display done, Milo lowered the skull in front of him, noting that the light shone so bright he could see it slipping through the hairline seams in the skull, a spiderweb of illumination. It was warm in his hands too. Not uncomfortably so, but he nonetheless sensed the change.

Milo looked up at Marid, who was studying him intently; the predator was scheming and assessing. Milo could hardly guess his aims, but the consideration was enough. It seemed whatever happened, Marid could not dismiss him.

While thinking about dismissal, Milo wondered how he could still feel the magic thrumming through the skull, but he found that explainable enough. No sooner did he feel the desire growing in him than the light within began to dim. Soon it was only a faint glow, less than it had been before.

The reality of magic responding intuitively to his desires set off a distant alarm in Milo's mind, but before he could examine it, his attention was drawn back to the throne.

"Exceptional," Bashlek Marid declared, his tone implying both regard and what might have been warmth. "I confess I was doubtful about your leader's message that one of your kind possessed the gift, but I see now my suspicions were unfounded. With such a display, none can doubt—"

"That he should be destroyed!"

The declaration came from the back lowest gallery to Milo's right, and the eyes of man and ghul swung around to search for the speaker.

Emerging from the shadows, a tall, whip-thin ghul strutted into the light, an ivory mantle upon its narrow shoulders, complete with stole. It didn't move with the customary hunched skulk of its kind, instead stepping forth with sure strides, head held high. Upon its pointed brow was a thin band of barbed iron and bone on which an assortment of crystals hung from thin fob-like chains. With each defiant step, the crystals swung and set up a sound like shards of glass falling.

"Welcome, my Lady Ubhalla Dazk," the Bashlek said in a tone that conveyed no hint of welcome. "I am glad to see you have returned to our court at last."

"Not for any love of it, I can assure you," the strident she-ghul replied, continuing to advance with slow, measured steps. "I have come only to do my part to preserve our people from this blasphemous endeavor."

Milo was so focused on the exchange between the monarch and the noble that he hadn't realized Ambrose had moved to his side, which turned out to be just as well. From behind Lady Dazk, a pair of ghuls with clubs made from sigil-marked femurs appeared, and behind them was one of the ogrish ghuls, wielding what looked very much like a very ornate and very filthy meat cleaver.

Milo searched the room, expecting guards, either armed ghuls, or maybe some of the animated dead in their baroque armor, to emerge, but none did. For the moment, it seemed Milo and Ambrose were lethally exposed.

"Blasphemy is a serious charge, my lady," Marid remarked dryly, clearly unimpressed. "But if you hold it to be so, why not test this Magus and his consort? Let us see if the Powers Beneath bear out your charge."

"Don't play games with me, Marid," the she-ghul snarled as she came to a stop a few strides away from where Milo and Ambrose stood. "Swear the Contest of Abjuration here and now before all if you are so confident. It should be a simple matter. Otherwise, the human should be brought to the temple for sanctification by excruciation."

Milo only understood part of what was flying back and forth between the ghuls, but what he did understand had him drawing his pistol. Ambrose already had his rifle to his shoulder.

"One word, Magus," he murmured, his voice icily calm. "One word and I make the front end look like the back end. Topsy-turvy, simple as that."

Milo almost gave the order, content to go down fighting since whatever their rituals, he didn't imagine the ghuls would take kindly to gunplay at court. Still, he wasn't about to be handed over to some monster's priest to be tortured for whatever mad reason the devil had. Thankfully for all involved, Marid spoke before Milo could give his answer.

"A very inhospitable way to conduct court, my lady," he chided, stroking the length of his crimson stole thoughtfully. "But I suppose you have your rights, here most of all. However, before we commence, please let me explain the situation to the poor things since they seem terribly confused. The portly one looks ready to shoot you if you hadn't noticed."

"Topsy-turvy?" Ambrose muttered hopefully from the side of his mouth.

"No tricks, Marid," Lady Dazk warned, then turned sharply and skulked back to her brutish entourage.

Milo, careful to let his pistol hang down at his side, glanced at the Bashlek.

Ambrose didn't move a muscle.

"Some clarity?" Milo asked.

The Bashlek turned from the lady and looked down at Milo before giving a slightly distracted wave of his claws.

"A minor inconvenience." He sighed. "She's drawing on ancient traditions to try to embarrass me. Dispose of the minor annoyances she's about to throw at you, and we can get you settled into your...educational schedule."

Milo looked at the hulking ghul looming across the hall.

Minor annoyances were apparently larger in the Underworld.

10

AN IMPROVISATION

When the violence happened, Milo was almost caught unawares.

The ceremony for the Contest of Abjuration seemed lengthy and convoluted, and it was conducted entirely in the Ghulish tongue. Several successive advances and retreats by the Lady Dazk and her retainers had seen Milo and Ambrose nearly start shooting, convinced this was when the fight began. Each time they'd barely held back, which was just as well because it was soon revealed it was just another part of the ceremony.

"When we finally get this thing started," Ambrose had whispered to Milo, rifle still at his shoulder, "I'll take the big one. Pretty sure that little Luger will just make him angry."

Milo looked at the pistol and agreed with the bodyguard, though given the size of the beast they faced, he wasn't sure the Nephilim's rifle would do much better.

"How can you tell the males from the females?" Milo asked.

Despite the skintight garments every ghul was wearing, Milo had been unable to determine obvious indicators of sex among the creatures. It was an odd thing to be vexed about at the moment, but he had nothing better to do.

"I can't," Ambrose confessed, one side of his face hitching up in a lopsided smile. "But I'm hoping something that big and ugly is male. Otherwise I might have to pity her...uh, it... Damnation, see what questions get you? Him!"

Milo chuckled a little at that. He didn't feel braver or more hopeful, but if he had to face death, he'd be glad to do it beside someone like Simon Ambrose.

The glow of camaraderie vanished the second Lady Dazk, standing clear of her chosen champions, gave a final shriek and stabbed a condemning claw in their direction. With an inhuman bellow, the huge ghul bounded forward, the smaller ghul loping along behind it, femur clubs in its knobby fists.

"Finally!" Ambrose cried, a wild, joyful sound.

His *Gewehr* 98 roared, the sound the very bellow of war in that stony hall.

First blood was theirs as the heavy round punched into the bulging deltoid muscles beside the brute's head, exiting in a gout of blue-black ichor. The beast's roar grew louder, but it did not go down or even miss a step.

Ambrose had already worked the bolt on his rifle, a thoughtlessly fluid motion that chambered another round. He corrected his aim and fired again, sending this one glancing off the creature's skull and then, as smoothly as a well-oiled machine, he sank another shot into the massive chest. The big man was chambering another when Milo realized he too was armed and should probably be shooting.

One of the ghuls was behind the bulk of the charging ogre, but the other was swinging wide, like a wolf encircling prey.

"Brighter!" Milo bellowed to the skull cupped in one hand, and a trio of intense green beams shot forth.

The ghul hissed and recoiled under the light, one hand still holding the club while the other covered its eyes. Its steps stuttered and slowed as it wilted in the lamp's brilliance. It called out to its companions in its sinister language and pointed with its club as it staggered to almost a complete stop, pinned by the stabbing illumination.

Milo knew he wasn't going to get a better shot, so he leveled his Luger.

The cracking pop of the weapon seemed almost effeminate next to the roar of the *Gewehr*, but all three rounds found their mark in the ghul's narrow chest. Thick dark blood bubbled out of its wounds, glistening on its breast, and with a wet gasp, the ghul pitched over.

The thrill of success lasted until Milo saw that the huge ghul had reached Ambrose.

Despite nearly a half-dozen bloody wounds, the monster moved with frightening speed and power, bearing down unerringly on Milo's bodyguard despite its lack of eyes. Its arms swept wide, it leapt forward even as Ambrose dove to the side to escape the fatal embrace. He was still bowled over by the sheer mass of the beast.

Ambrose rolled one direction across the floor and his *Gewehr* clattered in another, the man and his rifle separated by a roaring monster. By the time he sprang to his feet, he'd drawn a knife, a butcher-bladed *Seitengewehr* with a saw-edged spine. Ambrose didn't wait for the larger opponent to come for him but leapt forward, dagger flashing.

For all his bodyguard's ferocity, Milo wasn't sure what a third of a meter of steel could do against something so massive, but he was spared the consideration because in the spectacle, he had forgotten about the other ghul.

He swung his pistol around a fraction of a second too late and only managed to send a round whining off the stone floor as an engraved femur smashed across his shoulder. Milo staggered sideways, reeling from the blow and desperate to keep his grip on his Luger. Spinning, he tried to bring the blinding lamp and his sidearm to bear, but the knobby pommel of the bone cudgel crashed across his jaw.

Milo was thrown back and landed hard on his rump. He tried to raise the pistol, but hard claws seized the weapon and gave a cruel twist. Milo fell back and screamed as his trigger finger gave a gristly pop, then the pistol was out of his hand and skittering across the floor. Throbbing, thought-destroying pain surged from his mangled hand, and more by instinct than artifice, Milo kicked out, planting his foot in the belly of the ghul.

Common ghuls seemed to be viciously fast, unnaturally strong, and grotesquely resilient, but for all that, they were stooped, thin creatures. With his back braced against the unyielding floor, Milo's agony-fueled kick sent his attacker tumbling back and bought him a few precious seconds.

As he forced himself to breathe, Milo knew he couldn't even form a fist to punch with his right hand, and the ripples of pain were making it hard to think. Beneath them, he felt a bone-deep lethargy almost like a sickness threatening to well up and drag him into unconsciousness. Milo raged against the unnatural stupor, feeling a malign will press against his own before he finally shook it off like a clinging parasite.

Gritting his teeth as he drew and expelled hissing breaths, Milo hefted the only thing left to him: the skull lamp. Unsure if he would try to blind his enemy like the last ghul or just smash it into the thing's face, Milo gingerly gripped the horns with both hands.

Milo's gaze swung up, and he saw that the ghul was on its feet again and coming for him. He was doomed. He was a few bludgeoning strikes from that unholy bone smashing his face in.

Then he felt the trembling powers within the skull and remembered another element of Imrah's demonstration.

"There are variations and improvisations available. What should heal could turn to poison in an instant."

Marshaling himself despite the pain of his broken finger, Milo called out to what lay within the skull.

"BURN!" he commanded.

The light vanished for a single heartbeat and the ghul sprang forward, club ready to deal the fatal blow.

With a snarling rush, venomous jade flames rushed out of the outstretched skull. They struck the ghul in the chest and enfolded it like the tentacles of a hungry sea demon. The ghul staggered back, weaponized femur falling from its fingers, and threw its head back to scream. The greedy tentacles of flame enclosed its head and swam down its throat, drowning its shrieking in their crackle. Milo's attacker staggered back one more step before sinking to its knees and pitching onto its side. The witchfire quickly lapped across the body, eagerly devouring it.

Milo turned, skull still clutched in his throbbing grip, as he heard a bullish bellow behind him.

Like an enraged bovine, the huge ghul twisted and bucked, sometimes on all fours, sometimes standing. Gelatinous strands of ichor flew, and for a second, Milo couldn't tell what had possessed the brute. Then with a great crashing heave, the creature threw itself to the floor, and Ambrose flew off the monster's back just in time to avoid being rolled on.

The big man tumbled across the stone floor toward Milo and was on his feet in an instant. His bayonet blade was still in his hand, slick with the dark, stringy blood that also covered his hands and the sleeves of his coat up to the elbows. The strained buttons of the coat had finally failed, and it flapped open to reveal an undershirt smeared with ghul blood. The tectonic slabs of his powerful chest flexed as the coils of muscle banding his wide stomach rippled under the filthy, clinging cotton.

"Where's your pistol?" Ambrose huffed, keeping one eye on the floundering beast that had just realized Ambrose was not on its back.

Milo shrugged, then held up the skull lamp.

"And?" Ambrose asked, cocking an eyebrow as he started to tug off the coat. "What's that going to do?"

Milo smiled hungrily, and the big man gave him a sidelong glance before nodding at the huge ghul that was struggling to its feet.

"Watch and learn," Milo instructed. He stepped toward the ogre ghul, quietly and desperately hoping he wasn't being fatally arrogant.

The vibrations within the skull were even more strained than before, but Milo believed, or at least very badly wanted to, that it would be enough. Besides, the creature was bleeding profusely, and supporting itself on tree-trunk legs, its whole body trembled.

"Surrender or die," Milo called as he stood his ground, the horned lamp held out before him.

The ghul growled something deep in its chest, punching down with one huge fist to shiver the floor in front of it. As chips of stone flew out, Milo suddenly felt far less confident. One blow like that could take his head clean off or ram his sternum into his spine. The skull suddenly felt heavy and yet was so small, a lead weight that he'd been foolish enough to jump into deep waters with. Now he was in over his head.

Command! Milo screamed inside his head. *Will it so, or you will be dead!*

He saw the immense muscles bunching across the ghul's legs, back, and shoulders and knew this was it. Digging deep into every pain, injustice, and fear that had shaped him, Milo gripped the skull tight, snarling through the pain from his broken finger. Teeth bared, he gathered breath along with his will as the brute launched its charge.

"BURN!" Milo howled, and to his relief, the skull replied.

Once again, jets of verdant flame shot forth, climbing the huge creature. Pits began to gape across its massive frame as the flames gnawed down to the bone. It was horrible to see, but even more awful because it was getting closer to him. Although it was bleeding from a dozen wounds and swaddled in ravaging flames, the ogre came on, its arms raised, huge fingers curled into claws

Realizing too late that his magic hadn't stopped the creature, Milo barely had enough time to scramble back before flaming paws got hold of him. Talons scored the stone where Milo had stood, but the beast would not be deterred, even as it sank to one knee. One side of its eyeless face had kindled, the flesh running like wax or curling in on itself, but on it came, snarling and bellowing as its blood smoked and sizzled.

Milo tried to reorder his thoughts, fighting to command the skull, but the reagents within were spent, nothing more than a few stray fragments rattling around within.

The beast lunged again. Milo evaded the swipe by falling backward, but the dying brute loomed over him. The skull had fallen from his failing grip to split open with a crack on the stone floor. The ghul reared back for the final stroke.

The *Gewehr* spoke in its bellicose voice, once, twice, thrice, each bringing a fresh jet of sizzling blood.

The beast's furious expression went slack and its arm fell as its jaw hung loose, then it toppled forward. With a crablike skitter, Milo barely managed to avoid being trapped under the burning giant as it collapsed. The beast lay still as the flames continued to feast.

The Contest of Abjuration was over.

"You might be a proper witch after all," Ambrose called over the charring corpse, tucking his rifle under his arm like a safari hunter after the big kill. "But maybe we ought to leave the killing to the professionals, eh?"

Milo snorted and jerked his thumb toward the corpse and the ashes of his two ghuls.

"Unless we're going by weight," he replied with an outthrust chin. "I think I've got you beat two to one."

Ambrose put a hand on his hip and opened his mouth to argue, then gave an equine splutter.

"Fine, fine," he said, stepping clear of the burning corpse to stand at Milo's side. "First round goes to you, Magus, but remember that I'm just a consort now. I'm working from a handicap."

"Excuses, excuses." Milo chuckled.

"Well," Bashlek Marid burbled as he spread his claws expansively, "who can doubt you now, good Magus?"

There was a rustling reply from the gathered court that sounded more like surrender than acceptance, but Milo would take it all the same. He just wanted to sit down and get his finger tended to. It was swollen to twice its size, and the throbbing was miserably distracting.

"You really don't expect me to believe you have had no instruction in our ways?"

Milo squeezed his eyes together tightly, then forced them open wide, trying to keep his focus.

"I," he began, then paused to steady himself, hollow weariness weighing down his body. "Uh, that is, I have had no instruction apart from what your daughter Imrah gave me."

The chorus of evil whispers that sprang up was nearly deafening, and combined with the pounding that raced from his hand to his head, Milo wobbled. Ambrose's strong hand slid under Milo's arm to prop him up.

"Steady," the bodyguard murmured.

Marid noticed but said nothing. He was still reclining on his throne, stroking his crimson stole thoughtfully as though it were a favorite pet. He seemed to be in no hurry.

Milo wondered if he was supposed to say something, maybe offer further explanation or a self-deprecating remark. He knew he couldn't explain further because his success had only been a matter of Fazihr's and Imrah's limited instruction and some intuitive leaps. He supposed he could just go with self-deprecation, but the pulsing ache in his hand seemed to have spread to his whole body like a fever, and his thoughts were turning soft and sluggish. He was afraid that in a few seconds, the only thing keeping him upright would be Ambrose's grip on his arm.

As surreptitiously as he could, Milo looked around the room and spied Imrah standing at the edge of the gallery nearest the throne. He expected her to be glaring at him while waiting for a response, or maybe even trying to subtly prompt him, but she wasn't even looking at him. Her eyes were turned upward, fixed on her father. Milo was still struggling with how ghuls emoted, but as he watched, her expression tightening into something hard and angry.

What was she mad about?

Milo found out a second later when the Bashlek stirred from his thoughts, the room still filled with whispers.

"Very well," Marid said, sighing though there was a gleam in his eyes Milo didn't like. "It seems clear to me what needs to happen."

"It does?" Milo asked, his voice sounding loose and drunken to his ears. Dear God, he needed to lie down.

"Of course." Marid beamed and his gaze swung toward his daughter, who glared back in open defiance. "My daughter has shown an aptitude for instruction. It only seems right that you should begin your tutelage under her instruction."

A series of sharp sounds in Ghulish that Milo needed no interpretation for came from Imrah's spot on the gallery.

"Simply overwhelmed with excitement, I'm sure," the Bashlek said with a forced chuckle to his court, who obliged with Ghulish laughs that sounded even viler when forced.

"I'm h…uh, honored, your majuzty." Milo slurred as his eyes grew heavier and he leaned harder on Ambrose's hand. "But I don-don't want to be any tr'uhble."

The big man's fingers tightened, probably more than they needed to, but Milo was past caring. He'd never been this tired in his entire life, and the thought of falling asleep in a room of man-eating monsters didn't seem such a bad prospect as long as they didn't wake him up as they devoured him.

"No trouble at all, Magus," Marid cooed, sounding quite pleased with himself. "I'm afraid you are under a lethargy vex from that ensorcelled club. Have no fear, we'll see you put right. You can begin your tutelage tomorrow after you've recovered. I'm sure my daughter is eager to begin your instr...u...c…"

Milo plunged into a welcoming darkness, a place where nothing hurt and the monsters lurking in the dark were content to prowl silently. It wasn't precisely peaceful because somewhere deep in his slumbering mind, he knew the monsters both outside and inside his head were still there, but for the moment, they were content to let him be.

Right now, Milo would take that gladly.

11

A LESSON

"We need to get some things straight," Imrah said. "Think of it as the cultural part of your instruction."

Milo crossed his arms and nodded slowly. His sleep had been unnaturally deep from the lethargy vex, not to mention the busy day he'd had before. When he'd woken, so weary just lifting his eyelids was a work of herculean strength, Ambrose had ladled curatives down his throat. They were putrid-tasting concoctions, but unfortunately, he had been too feeble to vomit them back up. Even with those, he still felt worn out and hungover, but his new teacher had been insistent, so he'd gone to attend her upon a wide platform of crenelated stone at the rear of the citadel. Below the granite-toothed rim of the platform was a black pool like a miniature underground lake that nestled against the citadel's wall and was surrounded by smaller manors on all sides.

Milo had a brief impulse to throw himself into the pool to escape his throbbing head and Imrah's grating voice, but he decided against it. He was too slow, and he was confident that if he tried it, Ambrose would drag him back to start the whole business over.

"I did not want this honor my father has bestowed upon me,"

Imrah practically snarled as she paced in front of a series of stone tables. "This is clearly a punishment, or maybe some sort of gambit of his, but you don't have to worry about that. All you have to worry about are the rules."

"If they're so important, why don't you tell me what they are?" Milo muttered, not particularly caring if she heard.

"What was that?" she snapped, rounding on him.

Milo repeated himself as clear as day, too out of sorts to worry about sparing her feelings.

Imrah stood, shaking with rage, claws flexing as her thin lips peeled back from her fangs. Milo thought she might pounce on him like he thought he recalled her and Fazihr doing yesterday, which now seemed very far in the past. Thinking about it hurt his head, so he settled for staring mildly at her.

She drew in a long, snorting breath and let it out slowly, whistling through her teeth. Slowly she held up her alchemically repaired hand and raised a single sharp digit.

"Rule one," she began, her voice strained but level. "When we are on this platform, I am your lord and master. As far as you are concerned, I am god within this stony rim. What I say must be obeyed without fail, or you might kill us both."

Milo had heard instructive introductions like that before. In truth, the one by Training Sergeant Dubiki had been far more compelling and intimidating. Hardly taking a breath, he'd bellowed out a well-rehearsed speech about making soldiers out of scum, complete with enough profanity and vivid imagery that even those who didn't speak Polish got the picture.

Milo didn't mention that, but something on his face must have irked Imrah because when her second digit rose, her hand trembled.

"Rule two," she intoned in a chilly voice a step above a whisper. "You are neither to perform nor research this magic without my express permission. As I've said, this is extremely sensitive and dangerous work, and careless action or even careless thought could result in disaster."

On this point, Milo did take notice.

He remembered the skull lamp responding to his thought to dim without a command and how uneasy that had made him feel. Magic was a frightening enough prospect, but such an intuitive response meant controlling it would be precarious.

Milo decided that perhaps Imrah's introductory speech was more valuable than he'd given her credit for.

"Rule three," she said, her tone flatter. "Don't trust anyone. Not in this house, not in this city, not in the Underworld. There are conspiracies and vendettas and secrets whose roots grew before your kind discovered fire. You have no friends here, and assuming you do will put you at risk, and therefore me."

Milo restrained the urge to point out the internal flaw in her logic, but smarminess aside, this seemed another fair point. If the audience with Bashlek Marid had proved anything, it was that those in Ifreedahm were not happy to see Milo and were willing to do terrible things in response.

"Do you understand?" Imrah asked, three talons still raised in front of her.

Milo nodded.

Imrah's eyes narrowed suspiciously. "Prove it," she hissed.

Milo heaved a sigh and straightened like a soldier bearing up under a tedious parade examination.

"Rule one, you're in charge. Rule two, don't do anything magical without your say-so. Rule three, trust no one."

It was Imrah's turn to nod.

"Good," she rasped, then turned toward the tables, her arms stretched out in a sweeping gesture.

"What do you see there?" she asked, her back to him.

The tables were covered with all manner of containers: bottles, chests, jugs, jars, sacks, pouches, and boxes. All were spread across the table in what seemed to be no particular order, and from the few he could see through and distinguish their contents, it seemed a wholly macabre collection. A number of misshapen eyes floated in yellowish brine, while hanks of hair threatened to spill out of an open-topped sack. Others were less recognizable but no less unnerving. A blood-red concoction that seemed to be swirling of its own volition frothed in a jar, while one crate sported a collection of fist-sized segmented body parts Milo could not begin to identify.

"I'm praying it's not breakfast," he quipped, looking away a second too late as one of the hanks of hair twitched and fidgeted at the top of the sack.

"That will depend entirely on your performance today," she warned, flashing him another toothy grin. "If you don't want to make do with the scalps of the murdered and pickled frog's eyes, you best pay attention."

Ambrose, who was standing at the edge of the platform fastidiously cleaning his *Gewehr*, raised his head and gave a commending nod.

"Now that's a lady who understands motivation," the big man called.

Imrah's eyes narrowed at Milo's bodyguard.

"And you best not distract him," she warned icily. "Food only comes when I say the lesson is finished."

Ambrose nodded gravely and snapped off a jaunty salute.

"This is power," Imrah said, turning back to the tables and her lesson. "These are the secrets of the cosmos wrapped in chaos, frozen by death, and waiting for the worthy to seize them. I can give you the tools to claim them, but only you will be able to determine if you have the will to wield them. Among our people, it is a birthright, a badge that we are the great Djinn's children, but for you, a man born of mere flesh, it will be a path of pain and despair."

She reached toward a small chest and flipped the latch open with one flick of her claw. Within, bones were piled on top of each other like a child's haphazard collection of pebbles, delicate and beautiful. She snatched up a tiny ribcage fit for a young swallow or starlet.

"So tell me, Magus," Imrah whispered as she crushed the ribcage in her palm, grinding until she held out a hand full of dust, "are you ready?"

Milo was spared having to answer the thankfully rhetorical question. The truth was that he wasn't sure he was ready, but he saw no path other than forward.

Imrah spent most of that first day going over the principles of alchemical necromancy, or what might just be called necromancy by the uninitiated. Necromancy in its truest sense, she explained, was communication with shades of the deceased, which she explained were not the souls of the dead or anything so theological.

"Just as a footprint fills with water," Imrah had explained after whispering over the crumbled ribcage and set the fragments to form a cloud a few centimeters over her hand, "so living things create cavities for mystical energies to pool."

With another whispered command, the cloud spun out into a dancing ribbon of bone particles, looping and coiling in on itself like an eel.

"When the life is gone, those energies remain, trapped in what they touched but most potently in the corpse. Sometimes those energies hold echoes or ripples of what once was, some of them strong enough to use for shape and voice. They aren't a true part of the dead. Only the foolish, the desperate, or the very greatest spend their time on such unreliable sources of information."

"The greatest at manipulating essence, the true virtuosos, can feel the imprint of the dead more clearly and precisely, and so can force the essence to a truer shape. Such experts can question these shades and receive truths the living might have forgotten before their deaths."

Milo's head snapped to her from the ribbon of bone dust. "Masters?"

Imrah nodded with a strange, hungry light in her eyes.

"So, what happens to the true part, the soul?"

Imrah shrugged as though the question was insignificant.

From there, she'd gone on to explain that most of ghul magic involved taking the energy provided by the dead, the essence, and using it to fuel magical reactions. That was where alchemy came into play.

She diverged slightly to explain the difference between ghul and human concepts of alchemy and chemistry.

"These reactions require ingredients that have little to do with their physical properties, but instead are connected to the magical energies that have infused them."

She noted that for whatever reason, most magic seemed to be tied to life, whether directly or indirectly, with a few exceptions. As such, a piece of quartz dug from the earth had limited applications. That same quartz made into a pendant for a youth's lover was infinitely more potent and valuable.

"Even more so if that pendant was bathed in her tears when he abandoned her for another." The she-ghul grinned, seeming to take pleasure in the thought. "Why, if the quartz was splashed with the blood of the gift-giver after she discovered his infidelity, you could name your price in the markets of Ifreedahm."

She went on to explain that deciphering the nature of the ingredients he worked with was going to be the first step. She illustrated by taking two small bones from a crate and wrapping them in strands of hair, one strand from a pouch, the other from a small chest. Holding them up in front Milo, they looked almost indistinguishable, bare bone wrapped in wiry hair.

She placed one in his hands and asked him to tell her what he felt.

"The bone is light and the hair is wiry—" he began, but she cut him off with a sharp shake of her head.

"No, no," she interjected, her tone as sharp as her teeth. "Those are physical properties, crude information pumped to your brain by imprecise organs. Tell me what you sense beyond that."

Milo swallowed, confused. He expected nothing but more crude data as he closed his hand around the hair-wrapped bone. Pushing aside the information of his eyes and gripping hand, he tried to see if there was something, anything else. For a second there was nothing, only the distraction of the physical, but just for an instant, he felt a tremble, almost a flash of something...unpleasantly warm and rough against his soul. Was it anger?

Feeling more than foolish, he confessed what he'd experienced and waited for a reprimand. Instead he was treated to a Ghulish smile.

"Good," Imrah replied and swapped the bones out. "And this?"

That one was harder, and it took him longer to push his mind past the physical. Finally, like an icy river current touching the edge of his soul, he felt fear that would drag him into raving paranoia if he let it.

"Fear," Mil said with a shiver, ridding himself of the offending bone. "Very strong fear."

"Very good," she said, then walked a few steps away and placed both bones on the ground.

"Watch," she instructed and whistled, drawing the writhing bone-powder ribbon to her.

She breathed a command in Ghulish, and as swiftly as a well-trained falcon, the ribbon dove down on the hair-wrapped bones. Particles of bone coated both. He watched as the bone he'd named as feeling angry turned into a cloud of smoke where cinders danced. The other bone frosted over, and a second later, ice crystals bloomed outward, daggers arcing several inches from the bone in all directions.

"Knowing the nature of the ingredients is paramount," Imrah said, nodding thoughtfully at her handiwork. "Even great members of our kind have fallen prey to arrogance and imprudence when they did not check ingredients that were mislabeled or tampered with. Knowing to verify is as important as knowing what each does."

Milo nodded, trying to ignore that there seemed to be a face in the cinders that was watching him.

"Got it: safety first."

Imrah laughed, and Milo found that her laughter was paradoxically the best and worst of all the ghul laughs he'd heard. It didn't have the thick, viscous quality of most ghuls', and if he didn't think too hard about it, it could almost have passed for human. That similarity, knowing she was most certainly not his kind, left him torn and uncomfortable.

If she noticed, she didn't think it worth expressing, and the lesson continued. The rest of the day was spent having him handle various ingredients and seeing if he could sense their "composition," which was always a potent emotional reaction. He often couldn't tell, and if he stood there too long, Imrah would pluck the ingredient out of his hand without explanation and replace it with something else. Before they ended for the day, he'd held the contents of nearly every container, from burnt slivers of wood and dented spoons to the brined eyes and several varieties of shriveled organs.

Milo realized more than ever that this sort of work was not for the squeamish or the faint of heart. More than once, the "resonance" he experienced left him trembling and sapped of both physical and emotional strength. He was ready for a meal and more rest.

After Imrah relieved him of what seemed to be a petrified horse hoof or a very peculiar rock he could get no read on, she dismissed him for the day. Milo was glad to leave, but the distress that so many of the ingredients had eluded him refused to let him leave just yet.

"Am I doing something wrong?" he asked as Imrah began sealing containers.

She turned back, her expression inscrutable.

"What I mean is," Milo continued when she offered no immediate response, "is there something I could be doing differently? You know, so I could feel all of them?"

Imrah looked over her shoulder at the ingredients and then back at Milo, her brows knitting over her unsettling eyes.

"Can you teach an eye to see a color or an ear to hear a sound?"

Milo pondered the question for a moment before answering.

"In a way, yes. You can help someone to look for specific things or pay attention to certain sounds."

Imrah shook her head.

"That is teaching them to understand what they are hearing or seeing. To differentiate between the stimuli that are already present."

Milo wanted to argue, mostly because the implication was far from encouraging if she was saying what he thought she was. In the back of his mind, he wondered if there had been more in the artifacts than he had detected, and his anxiety about his calculations grew.

"So, I'm never going to be able to use those ingredients, then?" he asked, frustration making his voice sharp.

He knew it was petulant to be angry at her for his inability, but the sense of being robbed persisted. After everything he'd gone through, it felt like doors were closing to him before he knew they were there.

She gave what struck Milo as a very delicate response. "Not necessarily. Just because your sensitivity is lacking, it doesn't render the ingredients inert. It will just make them harder to control and certain formulas more difficult."

"Great," Milo spat, hating himself for how childish he sounded. "Already starting off at a disadvantage, and now this?"

Imrah stared at him for a second, then took a step forward. Her eyes searched his face, and she slapped him. The bony knuckles along the back of her hand split his lip and had him staggering back a step in shock. Blood and curses flew, and Milo's hands balled into fists as he glared at the ghul.

Arms trembling with anger, he took a step forward, ready to vent—by word or fist, he wasn't sure. Before he could say or do anything else, he was brought up short when Imrah let loose leopard-like snarl and launched into him with cutting words.

"I thought your people sent a man, not a child." She scoffed. "You are the first human in the annals of your fecund species to have both the opportunity and ability to learn *magic*. To stand upon the shoulders of sorcerers and alchemists throughout the ages to pluck a fruit long denied even the greatest among you."

Milo's hands remained knotted, but he couldn't muster the will to keep his anger burning.

"I show you how to bend death and matter to your will, and you whine?" she hissed. "No, Magus, this will not be easy, and you will have limitations. The cosmos does not bow to anyone, not even the ghuls, but with patience and determination, you have it within you to bend it to your will."

Milo's hand uncurled and he swiped the smear of blood from his lip, silent in the face of her rebuke. Imrah turned away and walked back to the table, where she stood for a long heartbeat.

"Don't ever waste my time like that again," she whispered.

"Yes, ma'am," Milo said softly, then, straightening, he added: "Thank you."

Imrah didn't so much as twitch in response, and they stood in silence before she finally spoke in her familiar rasp.

"Go. Fazihr will have arranged for food and reading material for tomorrow."

Milo replied in the affirmative and joined Ambrose at the edge of the platform.

"What was that about?" the bodyguard asked quietly, nodding at Milo's lip and shooting a look toward Imrah. "You picking fights on your first day of school?"

Milo sucked his lip, appreciating the sting and the taste of blood on his tongue.

"Just learning my first lesson," he answered, then gave the big man a sly look. "More importantly, she told us to go find Fazihr and get some food."

Ambrose grinned and adjusted his rifle on his shoulder.

"Now, there's an assignment I'll take to like a fish to water."

———

"Your reading material will be sparse, especially at first," Fazihr, who had turned out to be Imrah's personal retainer, explained. "Most of these texts are not written in anything resembling your modern languages, so I've employed a scrivener to translate the bare bones of the information."

Despite that statement, the leaves of parchment, which were packed with tightly scrawled German translations, were more than sufficient to keep Milo reading the rest of the day. In the orphanage, he'd learned that he enjoyed reading and possessed considerable retention, but he was not a fast reader. As such, despite the pounding in his head, he took the codices offered and dove into them before they'd even received their lunch. The food, which turned out to not be a prepared meal but rather bulk supplies to provide for several meals over several days, was delivered by a pair of shuffling skeleton porters shortly after Fazihr left their quarters.

The apartment they'd been given in the citadel was a small suite of rooms, with a large bedroom for Milo with an attached lavatory, a common room, a second water closet, and a small cell-like room for Ambrose. Milo had cleaned off his lip at his sink and then come out to peruse the first text Fazihr had given him.

"The dead lads brought lunch," Ambrose said, waving a hand at a pile of sacks and waxed leather parcels.

"Huh?" Milo responded, only partially listening.

The codex was compiled from the text *Awakening Moro: An Introduction to the Necromist's Trade* and acted as a primer for understanding the basics of practical necromantic alchemy. The reading was dense, sometimes relying on assumed knowledge Milo simply didn't have, but through contextual clues and by referring back to earlier paragraphs, he was piecing things together.

"Are you much of a chef?" Ambrose asked hopefully as he hefted a few sacks onto his shoulder and leveraged a crate against his hip.

"What?" Milo muttered, looking up from his parchment and blinking. "No, not much."

"Figures." The big man sighed and moved toward the corner of the common room. "I suppose it's up to me then, huh? Some form of soup work for the busy Magus?"

"Uh, yeah," Milo murmured, diving back into his book as he sank onto a low couch in the center of the common room. "I suppose."

Ambrose looked at him and shook his head as he laid his burden on a smooth granite counter in the corner. This part of the room seemed dedicated to meal preparation since there was a small but feisty hearth where a pale green fire crackled on one wall. A small fountain set into the other wall provided perpetual cool water. Around the sources of heat and liquid were stone countertops, above which bronze cookware hung from iron pegs.

As Ambrose brought the rest of the supplies to his "kitchen" and took stock of things, Milo was piecing together the basic differences between various kinds of magic.

Milo had deciphered that ghuls, as opposed to other shayati, were magical beings who created magic that was bound up in physical objects. The text made reference to how fey worked their sorcery spontaneously and the Hiisani used ritual invocations. That information was lost on Milo, but the text then stated how ghul magic—the superior magic, it insisted—was not just in alchemical reactions but in objects created or treated with such reactions. It went on to say that the only ones who came close were the Dwarrow, and its brief thoughts on those creatures and their works were dismissively bitter and scornful.

Milo made a mental note that ghuls didn't mind letting others know how they felt about the Dwarrow and their works.

"Most of this seems edible," Ambrose said mostly to himself. "Rice, beans, some dried meats, though I won't ask what animal it came from."

Milo ignored the bodyguard's dark chuckles as the text laid out the most common categories of ghul magic.

There were elixirs that were ingredients and sources of essence. These were meant to be ingested or injected into the body, and Milo supposed the regenerative draught Imrah had made was an example. It went on to describe fetishes, which were pieces of dead beings, beast or otherwise, "treated" with alchemical ingredients and then used through commands to create magical effects. The skull lamp sprang to mind as he read the description, and despite himself, Milo felt a small surge of pride. Before he'd even known what they were, he'd created his first fetish.

"Some of these bits have me stumped," Ambrose called, his rustling among the crates obnoxious to the engrossed Milo. "And you've got to remember I've been a lot of places and eaten a lot of strange things. Hello, what's this?"

Milo grunted irritably, turning his back so he could not see what Ambrose held—an ovoid shape with a glossy nightshade shell.

"Maybe an egg?" Ambrose muttered as he set it down on the

counter and fished out two more from a small sack. "Had some soup with eggs in it in the Orient when I was fighting for Tsar Nikki in the Aughts. Willing to give it a try?"

"That's just fine," Milo answered peevishly as he set to reading about animates both corporeal and incorporeal.

Corporeal animates were broken down into two categories: the Qareen, which were animated corpses like the skeletal porters, and the Homunculi, which were fabricated from multiple bodies or even inorganic material, like the Gate that had let them pass into the Underworld. The incorporeal animates had their own divisions as well, with the Hatif and Si'lats. Hatif were shades that were incapable of interacting with the physical world, apart from being seen and heard when they wished. Si'lats, on the other hand, were...

The crash of pans and an oath in a language Milo didn't recognize came from across the room, jarring Milo from his reading. With a frustrated growl, he slapped his papers down and sprang from the couch toward the kitchenette.

"Not to be ungrateful," he snarled, "but could you please—"

The words died in his mouth as he saw Ambrose scrambling over crates and sacks, trying to fence with a flying horror with only a small bronze paring knife. The intruder in their kitchen was black and granular, as though its body was made from glistening black sand condensed into a shape that was part scorpion, part bat. Erratic wingbeats sprayed black grit at the bodyguard's face, while a stinging tail jabbed at his chest.

By reflex, Milo groped at his waist. He found his belt and pistol weren't there, having been left lying on the bed after his trip to the lavatory.

Cursing with each breath, he vaulted over the couches and low tables as Ambrose frantically parried stab after stab. Milo snatched the pistol, drew and cocked it fluidly, and spun.

The monster had chased Ambrose into the common room, and with his door hanging open, Milo could draw a bead on it.

"Drop!" Milo shouted, hoping to God that he'd been heard as he started snapping off shots.

Ambrose dove and flattened as much as his lumpy frame would allow as bullet after bullet ripped through the apartment with echoing cracks. The bullets struck home, launching jets of black grit behind the abomination with each strike. Milo's ears were ringing so loudly by the time he reached the end of the magazine that he didn't hear the customary twang. He managed a useless pull of the trigger before he noted the open mechanism on top.

The flapping fiend turned its malformed face toward Milo, mouth opening to reveal gnashing mandibles. Its tail, arching beneath its punctured form, it launched toward Milo as he spun to grab his belt and the extra magazine that hung from it.

Seeing the speed of the demonic creature and the lack of effect of all eight shots, Milo knew in his heart he was doomed, but he threw himself on the bed and rolled as he snatched at the belt. The bat-thing zipped by overhead, its raking stinger missing by centimeters. It swung around and made for a dive bomb as Milo rolled off the bed onto the unforgiving floor.

Milo fought to pry the magazine clear of its sleeve as he saw his death descending upon him.

An intervening sack saved his life. Ambrose deftly scooped the sandy construct into an empty sack. The creature launched into wild spasms and stabbed with mandibles and stinger, but swinging the sack like a sling, Ambrose raced back into the common room. The stinger had just punched through the sack in two places when the bodyguard reached the kitchenette and hurled the monster-laden sack into the fire. Before the fiend could spring free, he snatched a large bronze platter and slapped it over the opening of the hearth. There was a strange hiss like a kettle about to boil over, along with fierce scrabbling against the platter.

With a piercing screech like metal being torn, black grit

sprayed out around the edges of the platter. Milo felt something shift in the space beyond reality, a previously unnoticed pressure dissipating.

Ambrose still held his ground, even as the sound of his flesh cooking on the heated bronze platter filled the room.

"You can let it go," Milo called much louder than he needed to because of his damaged eardrums. "I think I felt the essence leave."

Ambrose didn't need to be told twice.

Hissing and spitting profanity, Ambrose let the smoking platter fall from his seared fingers, and more inert black sand slid across the floor in a small pile. When he held his hands in front of him, they were in far better shape than they had sounded seconds ago. He stumped over to the fountain and gingerly lowered them into it.

Even as a small sigh of relief passed the bodyguard's lips, he twisted around and glared at the entrance to their apartments.

"Best get that peashooter loaded," he called in a pain-roughened voice. "Whoever sent that thing might be coming by to finish the job."

Milo nodded, finished loading his pistol, and went to check that the door was latched and locked.

He made it halfway across the common room when the door burst open and a contingent of ghuls led by Fazihr stormed in. They staggered to a halt when they saw Milo leveling his pistol and Ambrose, hands still dripping, holding a heavy bronze jug ready to throw.

"What is going on?" Fazihr hissed, his eyes darting between the two humans before settling on Milo. "Are you hurt?"

Milo didn't lower the pistol as his eyes took in the troop of ghuls at a glance. All were armed with one esoteric weapon or another, which went from clubs made from femurs to whips made from sinew and vertebra, along with other stranger things. His eyes locked with Fazihr's.

"Someone sent us a little surprise in the food your skeletons delivered," Milo said, his voice hard and flat. "A creature made of black sand that tried to kill us both."

"Stowed away as a couple of black eggs," Ambrose put in, wearing a fierce smile below wild, roving eyes. "Thought you'd sent us a tasty treat, but it turned out to be inedible."

Fazihr's eyes widened at the implication, and after a short hiss in Ghulish, his entourage lowered their weapons.

"My sincerest apologies, Magus," Fazihr said with a low bow his fellow ghuls imitated. "I was told to provide for your needs, including security, and I clearly failed. When we heard the sounds of violence, my guards and I rushed up here, but we were not fast enough. We will arrange for a pair of guards to be present at all times."

Ambrose gave a derisive snort and might have thrown the jug at Fazihr right then if Milo hadn't spoken up.

"Don't bother," Milo said as he lowered his pistol slowly. "We handled things."

A strange look, fear and outrage twisted together, passed over his face. Milo wasn't sure he was reading the ghul correctly, but he was more determined than ever not to trust him.

"I am afraid I must insist," the ghul retainer began in a strained, wheedling tone. "If not for your sake, then for mine. The Bashlek will have me flayed and restitched many times over if any harm comes to you on my watch."

Milo shook his head as he stepped closer to glare down at the stooped creature.

"I'm afraid I must insistently refuse," Milo said coolly, raising an open hand toward the door. "Now, please leave so we can clean this mess up and make some lunch."

A look of undisguised loathing squirmed across the Fazihr's face, but he bowed and put on his best Ghulish smile.

"I understand," he burbled wetly, then hissed another

command that saw his guards file out. "Just remember, we are only just down the hall from here should you need us."

Milo fixed the ghul with a stare, a challenge shining in his pale eyes.

"Oh, don't worry, Fazihr. I'll remember just where you are."

The ghul turned sharply on his heel, and the door latched behind him as he left.

"Interesting," Ambrose mused after setting the bronze jug on the counter behind him.

"What?" Milo frowned, still glaring at the door. "That we've been here less than two days and these creatures have already tried to kill us twice?"

"Well, there's that." Ambrose nodded before looking at Milo with twinkling eyes. "I was more pondering you saying 'we' were going to clean this place up."

Milo turned from contemplating the door to the chaos that had claimed most of the common room: spilled food, upturned crates, scattered cookware, and of course the black sand that seemed to be on everything.

"You've an ear for detail, Ambrose." Milo sighed as he bent down and scooped up a wayward tuber from the floor.

"All part of the job, Magus," Ambrose said with an officious sniff. "All part of the job."

12

A DEVELOPMENT

"For the next time," Imrah said the next day as she handed him a black cane topped with a raptor's skull. Milo didn't know which bird of prey it was, but judging by the size, it would have been an impressive creature.

As soon as Milo's hand closed around the smooth shaft, he felt the energies thrumming within. When Imrah released her hold on the cane, he felt the sudden weight and realized it was not made from lacquered wood, but from polished black rock. It was not as unwieldy as it seemed at first blush, but Milo did expect that if he failed to use magic effectively in the next attack, he could just beat his assailant to a pulp.

"So, you just had a skull cane lying around?" Milo asked, lowering it to give the floor a good tap. It was a little tall for a traditional cane, but he found he liked it more the longer he held it. It had heft physically and magically, and it felt reassuring in his hand.

"It was a gift for my late brother," Imrah said, looking at the staff. "He never had a chance to use it because he tried to depose my father before he was ready. I thought you could put it to use."

Stunned by her bald statement about family matters, Milo felt strange for so jauntily inspecting the item earlier. He told himself ghuls must think differently about such things because Imrah didn't seem any more sour than usual, but he was still eager to change the subject.

"So, this would be classified as a fetish, correct?" Milo asked.

"Are you asking me or trying to show me that you did the reading?" Imrah replied as she led him toward the center of the platform they'd used the day before. The stone tables had been rearranged and the assembly of items on them had been reduced to a few orderly collections of containers.

"More of the last, I guess," Milo admitted. "But I suppose it never hurts to ask."

"If only that were true," Imrah said, and Milo noted the tremor as she laid her hand on the table in front of her.

"Is everything all right?" Milo inquired, shuffling up next to her right-hand side but not looking directly at her.

Imrah frowned, and her lower fangs slid free of her thin lips with the gesture, but then an angry light sprang into her eyes, and she turned to him with a scowl.

"No, it's not," she answered tartly. "My pupil was attacked yesterday by regressive reprobates, and when he was assaulted, rather than using magic to defend himself, he fired a gun like an ignorant human."

What had first seemed like an expression of affectionate anger on his behalf had transformed so quickly into a rebuke that Milo felt his head might start spinning.

"How was I supposed to use magic?" he replied, doing his level best to sound curious and not irritated. "I had nothing to do it with. The only magic I've ever consciously done has been with the skull lamp, and that was spent from that Contest thing."

Milo near cried out when Imrah snatched his arm and raised it in front of his face. One barbed nail plucked at a vein, causing a tiny red jewel to bloom on his skin.

"As long as you have this," she hissed, dabbing the end of her claw in the blood, "you have something to do magic with."

Milo twisted his arm away, but Imrah had already let him go and turned back to the table.

"You wanted me to bleed on the thing?" he asked, incredulity curdling his tone.

"A few drops of blood on the Si'lat would have catalyzed it," Imrah growled impatiently. "A creation as simple as the one that attacked you might have been disapparated like a minor shade or even usurped so we could learn who sent it."

Milo stood, trying to master his anger, but also, as much he hated it, seeing her frustration. Besides any embarrassment Milo had caused her by emptying a clip into a Si'lat, she'd missed out on the chance to discover who was trying to kill Milo.

"I'm sorry," he said, the words coming out limp and hollow, but not angry. "I didn't know or at least didn't think about it that way."

"Of course you didn't!" Imrah snarled, and Milo braced himself for more of her spleen. "How could you? You are the first of your kind, and I didn't teach you that."

Stunned by what sounded like a confession, Milo missed a beat before recovering enough to speak.

"Wait, you aren't mad at me?"

Imrah looked at him and made a disgusted noise.

"Did I say I was?" she asked, scornful of the suggestion.

Milo let out a bemused, spluttering breath.

"I just thought," he began as he crossed his arms, and then stopped as he fought for words. "I mean, you seemed, uh...angry about um...something."

Imrah nodded and reached over to a small chest in the left-hand table.

"I *am* angry," she said, flipping open the chest to draw out a fistful of gray sand. "But not at you. Your ignorance of life among our people is excusable, but mine is not."

"What do you mean?" Milo asked as she let the powder spill into a small stone mortar, beside which lay a bone-handled pestle. Though this was far finer and lighter-colored stuff than the black grit from last night, Milo couldn't pretend he wasn't anxious at the sight.

"I mean, for a long time, too long, Ifreedahm and all the other outlying ghul communities of the Underworld have been embroiled in petty rivalries and wasteful acts of assassination and sabotage. My father set me to this task, and I should have expected this and planned accordingly."

The she-ghul selected a few delicate bones and deposited them in the mortar. She began grinding the brown remains with one hand while with the other, she drew a thin dried plant stem from an open jar.

"So, what can we do now?" Milo asked, feeling a strange sense of responsibility to shake Imrah out of her melancholic self-deprecation. He told himself it was because she needed to stop moping and teach him, but as he stood watching her prepare this new formula, he admitted he was beginning to like her.

"Prepare you," she replied staunchly before holding up the bowl of crushed amalgam in front of him. Milo could feel the barest tingle of magical potential coming from the bowl.

"Spit," Imrah instructed, and after inspecting Milo's reluctant offering, raised the bowl again. "More."

After providing enough saliva to make his mouth feel dry, Milo watched her mix the spittle and ground dust into a grainy paste.

After that, she dabbed a claw in the mixture and turned toward Milo.

"Where is that going?" he asked, leaning back as her hand strayed toward his face.

"On the lids of your eyes," she muttered distractedly as she strained upward. "Now, bend your head down and hold still."

Milo took a deep breath and forced himself to hunch forward and hold very still. Willing himself not to even breathe as it was applied, he waited as she dabbed a thin layer of the gunk across his eyelid. Then, with her cold carrion breath sliding across his face, she intoned something in magically charged Ghulish. A prickling sensation spread across his eyelids and then his eyes, making him wince, but he kept his hands from pawing his face. A second later, the prickling subsided and he couldn't feel anything on his eyes.

"Open your eyes," Imrah said, and when Milo did, a breathless curse of amazement tumbled out of his open mouth.

The world had been reborn in brilliant shades of darkness and twilight.

Ever since coming to Ifreedahm, the smokeless fire of the azure braziers and green hearths had kept the darkness at bay, but only enough so that everything was in perpetual dusk. Milo could see well enough to move around, but everything was cast in stark lines, and the shadows were deep, almost solid barriers. Now, though the colors had not changed, Milo could decipher between the shades of unlight, a nameless palette of blacks and grays so fine and yet so definite that he could decipher everything as clearly as though it were broad daylight, or perhaps even better.

Turning this way and that, he beheld the towering spires of the citadel and then the manors in the city below. It was like he was seeing the capital of the Underworld for the first time.

"Is this how you see the world?" he asked, marveling at the fierce but beautiful architecture of the citadel again.

"More or less," Imrah said, and though he wasn't looking at her, Milo could almost hear the satisfied smile tugging at her mouth. "At least it should keep you from groping for so much ugly light."

Milo nodded and then noticed that the lights did seem a touch harsher. Not painful, just unpleasant to look at.

"Why have the lights at all?" he asked, turning back to his teacher. "And is this permanent?"

Imrah had set the mortar and pestle aside and was busying herself with combining several ingredients on a bronze tray.

"Because ghuls are not the only beings to frequent the city," she answered absently. "Even now, my father is meeting with fey envoys who will see him by those lights, though admittedly, the pix don't need such accommodations."

Her assembly done, she turned back to Milo.

"And no, it is not permanent, but you will learn to make your own soon enough. First, though, we need to go about waking up the rest of you. Don't worry, none of this should be too painful."

By the end of that second lesson, Milo was not sure human and ghul tolerances for pain were comparable, but he was sure that it was worth it.

It was like he'd been sleepwalking through the Underworld since he'd been dragged down those steps, but now for the first time, he was awake. The paste for his eyes—a combination of candle-wick ash, moonflower stalks, spit, and bone meal, he reminded himself—had only been the beginning. There was a salve for his ears that rendered him able to understand any language, even Ghulish, and a wafer that, once dissolved, allowed his speech to be understood by any creature, even the undead and beasts. After that had come a fetish worn as a pendant that when anointed with a drop of his blood and worn around his wrist, let him sense magical energies that were within arm's reach more quickly.

"If there is magic in your food or drink and you didn't put it there, it would be wise to abstain," Imrah had warned.

She showed him the ingredients necessary for all she had done or made for him, having him transcribe the formulas onto parchment and then repeat them to her. She told him that once he began to make these things on his own, he would detect the resonances in them and should be able to supplement them with his own tailored ingredients. Just as some of the ingredients were not responsive to Milo's intuitive probing earlier, he would learn that some responded much more powerfully or precisely than others.

Why that was, Imrah wasn't sure.

"There are theories that it has something to do with a combination of fate and celestial alignments." She shrugged as though the subject didn't interest her. "Others suggest it is personal experiences and the Magus' psychological reactions to them. For example, you seemed quickest to detect those that were charged with the emotions resulting from fear and direct tragedy. The theory would be you've been shaped by tragedy and fear, so that is what responds to you."

"Fear and tragedy," Milo mused, subconsciously letting his hand slide to the folded tarot card in his pocket. "I think that's not too far off."

"In the end, it doesn't matter." Imrah sighed, not seeming to notice Milo had even spoken. "Things are the way they are, and they don't seem likely to change."

Despite being drained mentally and physically by the magic experienced and formulas learned, the last part of the lesson had been Milo's favorite. Imrah had instructed him to take up his new skull-topped cane, and in a process that was uncomfortable at first and intuitive afterward, she had him place his hand on the avian skull and then placed her sharp grip over his. She reached inside the skull and down into the rod of stone it was mounted on, prodding the alchemical agents preserved within with little pulses of her will.

She showed him what could be called on to produce light, what could be coaxed to produce flame, and what would provide the strength and speed to wield the weighty fetish as a weapon.

After that, she had him try, still with her hand over his, to more precisely feel what his will and magical ability were doing. He was clumsy and weak by comparison, but with guidance and coaxing, he managed to quicken each of the alchemical processes.

"In time, you may find new uses, new variations, but for now, these should serve you for facing future assassination attempts. Now, let's try you out."

From there, she had stalked to the center of the circular platform, where a small black circle was inscribed. Crouching, she pricked her tongue between two fangs and spat the blood onto the stone.

"*RISE, MOVE,*" she commanded in magic-compelling tones that hours ago would have just been more Ghulish hissing.

In response, there was a shudder throughout the platform, and four blocks of stone rose from the floor, forming square pillars. Those pillars, nearly twelve feet in height, began to move slowly around the perimeter of the platform. Standing as he was toward the center, it was like being in the midst of a giant machine, like an engine or a watch.

"Are they on tracks or something?" Milo asked, marveling at how they moved so smoothly and without the sounds of grating stone.

"They move because I tell them to," Imrah answered, giving him a disgusted shake of her head. "And now you will too."

The simple exercise was then explained: she would point at a pillar and tell him light, burn, or strike, and it was his task to do so.

"Sounds simple enough," he said and instantly regretted it as a wicked smile spread over Imrah's face.

Within a minute, he was wiping sweat out of his eyes.

Producing light was the easiest, of course, but even that required focus since Imrah was not satisfied unless the light struck the pillar squarely. The pressure of her insistent commands and the moving pillars threatening to slide away before he could bring his faculties to bear was very frustrating, and that frustration was the enemy of focus.

From there, things only became more complicated and dangerous with the burning and the striking.

Despite what he had thought, channeling the necessary essence to ignite flames from the skull was more difficult than it had been during the Contest. Not being fueled by mortal danger was part of it, he was sure, but also the construction of the skull and the ingredients' reactions within the leering cane topper played into it. Tightly channeled twin bolts of flame could be launched from the eye sockets, streaking out with blinding speed and force to strike and score stone. Driven with blunt force, the beak of the skull would open and a torrent of fire would emerge, like those *Flammenwerfers* he'd seen some of the Federated regiments using to clear trenches. The first time he discovered this, he'd missed twice with the flame bolts against his chosen pillar. In his anger, he bore down with his will, then nearly fell over in shock as an inferno emerged from the end of the cane.

"Control," was all Imrah had said before repeating which pillar she wanted to be burned.

Activating the physical enhancements of the fetish was even more terrifying.

First, it was a very different feeling than light or fire, coaxing the essence inward instead of outward, and second, the sensation of it working was very distracting, complicating things further. When he called on the alchemy within the cane to share its power, it rushed in with a burning chill that made his skin feel as though he was suffering a terrible fever across his entire body. It was not the empowering sensation he'd expected, and the first few times, he was so struck by the nauseous, shivering sensation he'd almost fallen over and adopted the fetal position.

For all that, when he finally moved, his body responded with amazing alacrity, and he sprang half a dozen feet in one stride to deliver a blow that powdered a hunk of stone the size of his fist.

Despite the heavy blow, the polished stone shaft didn't show a single sign of distress or damage.

By the time he finished, he was puffing and blowing, but also grinning from ear to ear. This was just scratching the surface of what he had to learn, and it was incredible. True, a firearm could do much the same without nearly as much mental effort, but that wasn't the point. With a little bit of stone, bone, and whatever dwelt inside the skull cane, he'd conjured fire and given himself the ability to move with inhuman quickness and might. He could appear utterly harmless before springing into lethal action in the space of a thought...as long as he kept his focus, of course.

He imagined Colonel Jorge could find something useful for an agent like him to do.

As they walked back to their apartment, Ambrose muttered about his plans for the meal and whined about his dwindling supply of alcohol, but Milo's thoughts were elsewhere.

In his mind's eye, he imagined himself stalking through the dark, misty streets of Paris or London. No longer the ragged, lanky product of a war orphanage and rebellious criminality; he saw himself as an agent provocateur, dangerous and dapper. With utter confidence and a suave wardrobe to match, he would move through enemy territory, sowing chaos and disruption. Skull-topped cane tapping across the pavement in challenge, he'd busy himself befuddling enemy agents and dispatching threats to the German Army. By the time the Federated and Colonial regiments arrived, he'd be waiting to hand them the keys to victory before setting off on another daring adventure.

He'd return to Berlin every now and again, donning his crisp black greatcoat to meet with Colonel Jorge and receive secret medals for his discreet service to the Empire. After tucking such medals into his hidden sanctum, he would prowl the fine parties and balls of the great and good of the conquering Empire. He would drink and dance and gallivant with the best of them before duty and danger called once more.

He'd plant a farewell kiss on his latest darling's lips before slipping into the night with a dashing flourish and a mystic flash from his eyes.

Milo the Magus, Humanity's First Wizard, Mystical Agent of the German Empire, the man who would bring victory and eventually the end to the Great War. He would be celebrated, loved, and...

Ambrose's heavy arm slammed into Milo, knocking him out of his reverie and flat against the wall of the corridor.

He winced, and a curse slipped from Milo's lips as his head knocked against the stone, but Ambrose's arm held him fast.

"What's going on?" Milo hissed, raising a hand to rub the back of his smarting head.

Ambrose turned toward him, a finger on his lips.

"Company," the bodyguard mouthed, and twitched his shoulder.

Just ahead was the branch of passages that led to their apartment, and urgent voices could be heard. The words were in Ghulish, which Milo realized with a smile he now understood. Raising a finger to his own lips, he craned his neck to listen.

"I don't care if you've a missive signed by Azazel himself," he heard one voice replying with unmasked belligerence. "The orders are that only those chosen by the Bashlek may see the Magus, and that is a shortlist you aren't on."

That must have been one of the guards Fazihr had posted. The ghul retainer had respected their wish for no guards in the apartments, but one was stationed in the corridor right outside their door.

"You fool," the second voice said in a lofty tone Milo took a dislike to instantly. "This isn't an idle request to gawk at the humans. This is a call to appear before the Nether Council immediately."

The first voice gave a vicious laugh.

"Last I checked, the Nether Council advises the Bashlek, not the other way around. You want to guess which one I'm more worried about?"

The second voice snarled in frustration, its tone growing more frantic.

"Do you understand who came to court today, cretin?"

Milo could imagine the shrug in the intervening silence. It was followed by a disgusted sound in the back of the throat of the haughty voice. Ambrose began to lean over to peek around the corner, but Milo grabbed his shoulder. When the big man turned to him, bemused, Milo again pressed a finger to his lips and then tapped his ear.

"A troupe of the meddling fey," the second voice hissed. "For all their long-nosing about, the pix are good for something, and that is news. They shared a tidbit that requires the Nether Council to question the human."

"Question, is it?" The guard snorted. "First an appearance, now questions. If we send the Magus down, do you think he'll make it before the questions become an interrogation, or will you just skip the whole business and make it an execution?"

Milo found himself liking this guard despite himself. He could appreciate the ghul's sarcasm, even if it was delivered in a tongue as vile as Ghulish.

"If an army of humans is marching over our heads mere days after a human arrives in Ifreedahm, don't you think the council should ask questions?"

The silence that followed was wrenchingly potent.

"A human army?" the ghul guard burbled less certainly. "When? How many?"

"Am I going to see the Magus?"

There was a low hiss, then the clack of teeth snapping irritably.

"The Magus is still in training with Lady Imrah," the guard said quickly, as though the words were hot on his tongue.

"Fine," the second ghul said with obvious strain. "Do you know when it will return?"

Not sure what he was doing but determined to figure things out, he slid free of Ambrose's arm and bid the man follow him.

"It has just arrived," he declared sharply as he rounded the corner. "Now, tell me what you fine gentleghuls want with a humble man such as me."

He finished with a flourishing bow, one hand extended and clutching his skull cane.

Both ghuls gaped at him as though he were a demon summoned by their conversation. Milo wondered if they'd have been less surprised if he *was* a fiend. Shock and what looked suspiciously like hunger shone in their wide eyes.

"Laying it on a bit thick," Ambrose grumbled under his breath. He stepped forward to address the unblinking stares of the ghuls.

"All right, fellas," Ambrose called, giving his hands a clap before rubbing them together. "What's your business here?"

"The Magus must attend the Nether Council," the guard ghul answered, his claws picking nervously across the knobs of his vertebrae whip. "They've some questions to ask."

"Do they now?" Milo asked and fixed the ghul with a steady glare as he moved to stand shoulder to shoulder with his bodyguard.

The ghul gulped and looked away.

"Indubitably," the second ghul replied, straightening his bone-white mantle on his narrow shoulders. "There have been developments that require immediate consideration."

Milo looked at Ambrose, who wore a wary scowl.

"You're a popular fellow, it seems," the big man muttered.

"It does seem that way." Milo shrugged, wishing he felt like the dapper operative he'd imagined only moments ago. "Fine, take us to the Nether Council."

The mantled ghul nodded and swept past them to lead them down the citadel's winding corridors.

"Hope you know what you're doing," Ambrose murmured at Milo's shoulder.

"They were talking about a human army being near Ifreedahm," Milo whispered. "Do you suppose there are some of ours?"

"Haven't a clue."

"Well, this is how we find out, isn't it?"

Ambrose's frown remained fixed, and he shook his head.

"I suppose, but I don't like it," he grumbled, adjusting the rifle on his shoulder. "The only thing more useless than one bureaucrat is a council full of 'em. And that's before you get anyone's nethers involved."

13

AN INTERRUPTION

Seeing fey for the first time would have been memorable enough, but seeing them in the gloomy halls of the ghul citadel was a moment Milo would never forget.

They shone like jewels filled with beautiful light, their very skin giving off a soft illumination that defied the twilight of the audience chamber. They wore heavy gray cloaks and gloves that hid most of their bodies, no doubt a consideration to the ghuls, who winced whenever they looked at the lovely creatures. Beneath their hoods, they shone. Even more striking than their height and features, providing an uncanny combination of feral vitality with inescapable courtliness, was the variety displayed between the three. Each was different from the others, yet some aesthetic marked them as one species.

One's skin was the color of grass shoots, and from neck to temple, delicate vines curled and swayed in an internal wind. Another, tall and regal beyond human proportions, bore a perpetual smirk and had skin of polished bronze as his ruby eyes took in the world with a fiery stare. The last, the shortest of the company at eye level with Milo, was a creature of moonlight and lilac who seemed perpetually uninterested yet keenly aware.

All three magnificent creatures, living gods as Milo saw them, stood in a court of monsters who seemed to be working themselves into a frenzy.

"Let's see what the meat has to say for itself," his newly awakened ears caught as the white-mantled go-fer led him across the floor.

"Did they really think they would get away with this?" another voice hissed from somewhere in the gathering beneath the galleries. "The arrogance!"

"Now we'll touch the bottom of this swamp," a ghul behind Milo croaked in a deep voice. "The council will wring the truth from them, just you watch."

"I hope it refuses to speak and the council must...encourage it."

"To think it took the fey to bring us this news."

"Let's hope they make an example of him."

"Filthy humans!"

Milo felt the muscles in his neck coil like springs, and soon, his hands were aching as he gripped his new cane. A potent mixture of anger, fear, and unease roiled in his chest, and Milo soon found his wonder at the fey eclipsed by the reality of the ghuls around him. He could practically feel the pulsing, suspicious energy of Ambrose at his side.

"This isn't good," the bodyguard muttered. "We might've come with news, but we might have to stay for a trial."

Milo grunted in agreement, then, seeing past the trio of fey for the first time, he nodded so Ambrose could see.

"And that jury doesn't seem likely to give us a fair one."

Beyond the fey, a group of nine ghuls sat in high back chairs that were practically thrones, wearing ivory mantles and stoles, before the empty throne of the Bashlek. With gimlet eyes, the Nether Council watched Milo draw closer. It was impossible to escape the feeling that they were ready to pounce. Milo knew next to nothing about ghul development from womb to tomb, if the wicked things were born or died in the first place, but something about each member of the Nether Council struck him as a very old kind of evil. Not decrepit or frail, but old in the sense that ancient trees will become twisted against the wind, growing gnarled and hard.

"Stand here and wait to be addressed by the Nether Council," the go-fer instructed as they came level with the fey envoys.

Milo planted his feet and then let the cane tap the stone in front of him as his hands sat upon the skull. He hoped he struck the audience as confident, even untouchable, as their vitriolic whispers slithered around him.

Nonchalantly, he glanced at the fey and saw that all three of them were looking at him. He nodded at them and then listened in dismay as the verdant one with the vines giggled softly, the sound as soft and pure as wind through the trees. Feeling his cheeks burn, he fought to keep his face expressionless as she whispered behind her hand up to the bronze colossus. The towering fey's smirk broke into a broad smile, and a laugh like thunder rumbled out of his chest. It was a chuckle of such power and grandeur that Milo wanted to join in even though he knew he was the butt of the joke.

For a moment, the whispers quieted to a low susurration, the ghuls in the dark glaring with envious, glinting eyes.

"That's enough," came a soft whisper from the smallest fey, her face turning toward the Council before Milo could get a good look at her.

The huge fey shrugged, and his face returned to its knowing smirk. The emerald fey flared her eyebrows teasingly at Milo and gave him a wink before joining her two companions in facing the council. The whispers began to encroach again.

Now that he was no longer under the fey's direct scrutiny, Milo felt like a weight had been lifted off his chest. He could breathe deeper, and as he did, he was thankful for the tall cane he leaned on.

"Making friends everywhere we go," Ambrose muttered, eyeing the fey with open suspicion. "Just everywhere."

"The Nether Council is called to order once more," croaked a ghul whose wide mouth and thick, wattled throat made him seem like someone had bred a ghul with a toad.

The whispers subsided again, and the toad-ghul nodded toward another ghul who looked remarkably like the one who had sent her cronies to die in the Contest of Abjuration.

"Thank you, Lord Speaker," said Lady Dazk. "We are also thankful for the patience of our honored guests."

With one hand sweeping toward the fey, she dipped her head in a shallow bow. They nodded in silent acknowledgment.

"Now to business," she said, turning to Milo with a triumphant smile that displayed her jagged teeth. "It seems you have a good deal of explaining to do, Magus."

The title came with a sneer that made Milo wonder if it was kosher to challenge a member of the Nether Council to a Contest of Abjuration. The thought had Milo smiling coldly into the leering face of the ghul aristocrat.

Just a thinner, uglier Jules, Milo told himself. Upon consideration, he thought, *Well, not that much uglier.*

"Do you think to defy this council with your silence?" she asked in her shrill voice as the whispers began to climb in volume. "Is human arrogance so great that even now, with your treachery exposed, you think this august council beneath you?"

The whispers began to buzz angrily once more.

"Lady Dazk," Milo said as steadily as he could manage, "if I knew what treachery I'd supposedly committed, I might know what to say. I don't know if the ghuls have magical ways of reading minds, but I haven't been taught them yet, so it would be helpful if someone started explaining things."

The only thing louder than the eruption of Ghulish growls was the verdant fey's laughter. Milo felt good about himself then and made to wink at the giggling fey, but Ambrose surreptitiously bumped Milo's elbow and nodded at Lady Dazk as he cleared his throat.

The ghul's claws dug into the arms of her chair as she quivered with rage. The ornaments hanging from her circlet audibly jangled.

"You cover your sins with levity," she said in a low, vicious whisper that sliced through the whispers and stilled their owners. "You would bring annihilation to our doorstep, even as we embraced you like one of our own! We've come to expect very little from your kind, Magus, but even for your duplicitous ilk, this is treachery most foul. Was the world above not enough for you?"

"Again, Lady Dazk," Milo pressed with forced patience, "if you could tell me what you think I've done, maybe I could give an answer to the council."

He looked at the other council members pleadingly.

"Will someone please tell me what wrong I've supposedly done?"

Milo had gotten a clear picture of the accusation from what he'd overheard outside their apartments and Dazk's ravings, but he'd be damned if he'd start justifying and denying before anyone had leveled an accusation.

Lady Dazk made to continue her tirade, but another ghul spoke up, ignoring the needle-tipped glares received from Dazk and several other council members.

"These envoys bring word that on their way through the mountains, they spotted human airships," the ghul said, her voice as thin and brittle as ancient papyrus. "It is the belief of many on this council that they are here as part of a forward force by a human army to secure the mountain because of intelligence you have passed to them."

"Knew it was a mountain," Ambrose muttered to himself before Dazk drowned him out with her sharp cry.

"They will not stop there, Lady Hrawn. They will invade our

city!" the excitable council ghul cried, turning to look first at the right gallery and then the left. "They seek to pluck the heart out of the ghul people and the Underworld with one decisive strike, a strike that would not be possible without the magus' treachery!"

Whispers rose again like angry vipers hissing, and Milo wondered how long he had before they fell upon him in a rending mob. His eyes wandered to Marid's empty throne, and his heart froze as he realized Dazk had followed his gaze. She turned back to him, teeth glistening in a huge, murderous grin.

"The Bashlek is away on business," she declared with mock solemnity. "It falls to the Nether Council to see to the defense of Ifreedahm in his absence."

The smugness in her voice might have driven Milo to spit and curse, but the loaded galleries seemed ready to explode at any second. He had no intention of tempting that hair-trigger.

"Lady Hrawn," Milo nearly shouted to be heard over the angry noise enfolding him, "I assume the airships that you are talking about are zeppelins, which are indeed used by the armies of the nation I serve, though they are not the only ones."

Though odds are nine to ten it was the Germans, Milo thought to himself. He remembered the many times the skies over Dresden had seemed clogged with the trundling airborne behemoths.

"See, he does not deny it!" Dazk crowed even as Milo's voice swam against the tidal surge of frothing ghuls.

"I am sure the Nether Council is aware there is a war, what my people call 'the Great War,' being waged on the surface, and the land above is no exception. Since I have not contacted anyone since being invited by the Bashlek, I imagine the zeppelins are reconnoitering enemy positions."

"Our position is what he is talking about, no doubt," Dazk persisted, her words flecked with venom.

"Ifreedahm is deep underground," Milo snapped, his temper flaring as he turned to her. "What good would it do to bring large and expensive machines like zeppelins to scout out an area that you need to explore from the dirt down and not from the sky?"

Dazk let out a disgusted hacking sound.

"Again, such arrogance," she hissed. "You think that just because we dwell underground, we know nothing of how humanity wages war, crawling across the surface like a ravening swarm? No doubt, they are plotting the routes for your forces to envelop the entire countryside. We may not wage war as wastefully as your kind, but we understand strategy well enough to know an invasion when we see it!"

Milo had to admit that it was possible, but in his estimation, it was extremely unlikely.

First, not only was the Empire largely ignorant of the nation underground, but one of its secretive elements had gone to serious effort to ally with the ghuls. It seemed unlikely that such subterfuge and brokering would be wasted if the army blundered in with an invading force. It seemed far more plausible that they would try to extract as much information and sorcery from the ghuls as they could before attacking them.

Second, and perhaps far more importantly, was that the German Empire, even with the windfall of fresh men and materials from Eastern Europe, was stretched thin. Germany had been on the brink of surrender just before the Red Rebellions shattered the Russian Empire. So many desperate countries, preferring German autocracy to the mad bloodbath of the conflicting Russian claims, had been the infusion needed to forestall defeat. Yet, even with those reinforcements, even a lowly conscript like Milo had known that victory or even an armistice was a distant, foolish hope. With such an insecure position, why would the Empire make an enemy of those who, up to this point, had been a relative non-factor?

No, Milo decided with a shake of his head. This had to be something to do with the conventional war being fought above.

"Do you have anything more to say, Magus?" Lady Hrawn asked, sounding tired or perhaps very bored.

Milo realized that as he'd been weighing things in his mind, the Nether Council had sat stewing in the roiling whispers of the galleries. If the looks among the Council had been hungry before, they were ravenous now.

"My word might not mean much to you," he began, provoking the first affirmative response from the ghuls in the gallery, "but I'll tell you the truth as far as I know it, with my promise that it *is* the truth."

The audience hall seethed, then seemed to hold its breath as Lady Hrawn nodded.

"I was sent here to learn the ways of magic from your people," Milo said, feeling much smaller in the sudden, smothering stillness. "It cost my bosses a lot of money and the lives of many good men to get me here. The men I work for aren't nice people, or even probably as good as the men who died so I could come here in secret, but they're not wasteful or stupid."

At least, Milo thought, *not most of them.*

"They're at war right now with a lot of enemies, and those are just other humans," he continued. "Why go to all the expense in blood and resources just to find another enemy to fight? They've already got enough of those. They aren't going to go around looking for fresh fights, especially not with a people they know almost nothing about."

The whispers had begun to creep back in, but either delusion or hope convinced him they weren't as hostile as before.

"So whatever those zeppelins are for, I don't think it's to wage war on you and your people. When you're fighting a war like they are, you don't spend what you can't spare to make new enemies. You spend it to make new friends."

Lady Hrawn, the amphibian-faced speaker, and a few other members of the council nodded and exchanged meaningful looks. The crashing wave of whispers descended again, but in the little snippets he caught, there seemed to be as many who were leaning his way as those calling for him to be drawn and quartered.

The speaker, at a slight inclination of Lady Hrawn's head, shifted ponderously forward and raised his deep amphibian voice.

"The council will take these points into consideration and compose a proper initiative to propose to the Bashlek," he intoned, then swung his heavy gaze to those in front of him. "Our thanks and appreciation to Contessa Rihyani and the magus for their willingness to testify before the Nether Council—"

A piercing shriek rang from Lady Dazk's seat, and when Milo swung toward it, he saw that it was empty. She was advancing toward Milo, gesticulating wildly as she ranted.

"You bring the enemy to our gates, and still you stand and smile at us! You talk about friendship and good lives lost while you plot our destruction! Does your swollen pride have no limits?"

"Get behind me," Ambrose rumbled, thrusting himself in front of Milo. The rifle was still slung over his shoulder, but the body-guard radiated a primal willingness for violence. While tall for a ghul, Dazk wasn't eye to eye with the big man, and one of his beefy arms probably weighed more than her.

Milo knew her physical prowess was not the threat. With her denouncing screams, he felt the temperature in the room change again.

"Ah, the mighty magus cowers behind his slave when faced with the truth," she screamed. "See the heart of those who would be your conquerors, Ifreedahm! See and know that if we strike now, strike first and strike hard, we can break their spirits and safeguard our homes."

A few of the other council members made to speak, some in dismay, some in support, but it didn't matter. Lady Dazk's indignant rage was carrying the day, infectious and empowering.

"And if we are to strike," she snarled, coming to within arm's length of Ambrose as ghuls great and small from the gallery began to slink forward, "I know just where to start."

Milo's eyes searched the audience chamber, and he saw only a mob of monsters creeping toward him. His hand tightened on the cane, feeling the energy thrumming within it in time with his pounding heart. He searched the crowd for a thin spot, a place where, with a torrent of flame, they might be able to break through.

It would be a futile move since he and Ambrose were still in the belly of the beast, but he wasn't going to become someone's meat without knocking a few teeth out first.

The magic quickened within the skull, witchfire gleaming in the empty eyes of the dead raptor.

His eyes still roving, he spied the fey, islands of light and beauty amidst horrors. The colossus still wore his smirk, while the green one looked bored with the entire proceeding. The smaller one, the one who shone silver and shades of violet, was looking at him, her dark-golden-pupiled eyes smiling.

Seeing he returned her gaze, she inclined her head to Milo across the sea of gnashing teeth and hateful stares and gave him a wink.

Surprised to say the least, Milo's witchfire guttered and then was blown out completely as the main entrance to the audience chamber burst open with a tremendous boom.

All froze as, resplendent upon a palanquin born by four ogre-sized ghuls, Bashlek Marid was borne into the chamber, followed by ranks of the baroquely armored Qareen. The animated corpses moved in perfect unison, bearing spears whose points dripped icy fog. Without a word, the battalion of corpses formed up behind the Bashlek in an unliving wall that stretched across the chamber and stood three deep.

Atop his lofty conveyance, the Bashlek looked across the room, thoughtfully stroking the crimson length of his stole. His wily and wicked gaze roved over the entire assembly before, with a heavy sigh, he addressed the chamber.

"My, my this does seem rather serious," he remarked, let his gaze play across any who would meet his eye. "Was I gone so long that you deemed it fitting to assemble a celebration to welcome me back? Oh, you shouldn't have, really."

Everyone stared at him, silent and stunned, though both Ambrose and Milo had expressions of such intense relief on their faces that they seemed ready to faint.

Marid's eyes wandered over to the fey, and his gnarled hands thumped together in a sound too ugly to be clap.

"You brought entertainment. How grand!" Marid cooed, smiling broadly as all but the silvery fey stiffened. "I must learn who is responsible for this grand affair and reward them handsomely for it. So tell me, who do I have to thank?"

The chamber remained miraculously silent, not a single whisper to be heard.

"Come now, humility only gets you so far."

"Bashlek Marid," Lady Dazk began, trying to muster the fiery vitriol she'd had moments before, "the Nether Council was called—"

"The entire Nether Council is here?" Marid asked with grotesquely exaggerated excitement. "My dear Lady Dazk, you've truly outdone yourself. I'll have to arrange something very...special to repay you for such a gracious return to my city."

Milo didn't bother to hide his smile as he watched the firebrand she-ghul return to her seat in a miserable, skulking cringe. Turning back to see the wickedly gleaming eyes of the ghul monarch, Milo could almost find it in himself to feel bad for the wretched aristocrat.

Almost.

"Well, as merry a meeting as this is, I'm afraid I must bid it disband," Marid declared with a lazy sweep of his claws. "Your

Bashlek understands and appreciates your adulation, but I'm afraid more pressing matters require my attention."

Before the host of ghuls could skitter into the darkness, their proverbial tails between their legs, Marid pointed a claw at the fey and then Milo.

"If both sets of my esteemed guests would attend me, I believe there are a few things we must discuss."

14

AN ADJUSTMENT

After the excitement of the audience chamber, the private gardens of Bashlek Marid might have seemed tame to the point of dull if not for the alien flora that was tended there.

Luminescent fungal blooms the size of small trees sprouted from clusters of stone or clung in cultured patterns across freestanding walls. Flitting among them here and there were tiny creatures that resembled airborne squids or octopi. Their moist skin was nearly translucent, and Milo spied the hair-thin filaments of their internal structure glittering in ever-shifting shades as they sprang from one growth to another, sometimes snaking in floating motes with their outstretched tendrils.

Across the floor of the chamber, Milo was treading across the same woolly base that had covered the floor of the tunnel. His eyes now enhanced, it resembled coarse gray hair.

They followed the Bashlek to one corner of the garden, past a central mushroom as tall as any tree Milo had seen, to a place where the hairy carpet did not reach. In this bald patch, stone stools were arranged haphazardly around a little pool in whose center was a pile of stones. Shimmering and shifting shades of yellow, orange, crimson, and magenta glowed in the spring that rippled up within the pile of stones to spill down into the pool.

The Bashlek took the seat in the far corner of the garden wall, emitting a groan of relief as he settled against the mossy buds that coated the two walls.

"Please." He sighed, gesturing to the stools. "Have a seat, and have no fear. We need only be ourselves here."

To illustrate the point, the Bashlek leaned to one side and released a tremendous fart. The air filled with the smell of rotting flesh and something that might have been an abrasive chemical cleaner. Milo fought not to gag as his eyes watered. He glanced at the fey, who unfairly seemed immune to the stench or the grotesque display. Ambrose swore in a few different languages and stepped back a step.

"Go on and have a seat, Magus," Ambrose grunted, eying the malodorous monarch warily. "I'm just going to enjoy the scenery, such as it is."

The stools were low and sized for ghuls, a fact Milo was convinced was not lost on the ghul monarch as he squatted to perch uncomfortably. Looking to the side, he saw the moonlit fey who must have been Contessa Rihyani slide gracefully onto the seat. A strange impression, a ripple almost across his sense of the unseen, flitted by. Milo noticed he was staring, and she was staring back.

Milo coughed and cleared his throat, which made it more noticeable when he turned away. To his great discomfort, he found that Marid was also staring at him, his shriveled lips having slid up just enough to show his tangle of fangs.

"You've turned out to be a lot more work than I bargained for," the ghul said after a lengthy foot-shuffling pause. "More helpful than you know, but even so, it seems that every time I turn around, someone is trying to kill you."

Ambrose gave a not-so-subtle sniff that was as good as his "making friends" jibe.

Milo opened his mouth to apologize, then shut it. A lifetime of monsters, whatever their species, warned him that an apology was not in order.

"I was just thinking you should rename the audience chamber 'the arena,'" Milo quipped, doing his best to seem at ease despite the precarious seating. "At least that way, guests have some idea of what they are getting into. You know, good sportsmanship."

The Bashlek chuckled and conceded the point with a nod as the contessa offered a brief smile.

"You handled the situation better than most," Rihyani said in a soft yet powerful voice. It was the kind of voice that didn't need to be raised to get attention.

"I'm not sure we were in the same room then, Contessa," Milo replied, battering down a sheepish grin. "I'm pretty sure I was seconds away from Lady Dazk picking out bits of me from between her teeth."

Marid snorted a laugh at that, but the contessa just gave another cryptic smile as she tilted her head back.

"Perhaps," she said, eying him with a gaze that was both aloof and flensing. "But you provided solid reasons, if not evidence, for your innocence. The Nether Council's more moderate members will be shaken by the Bashlek's display of power, and the more conservative members will have your words to swing them over to their side."

Milo's eyes wandered to the Bashlek, who'd closed his eyes as he nestled in the blooms like a dog enjoying a roll in the grass. Even so, he nodded slightly at Rihyani's assessment.

"Radicals like Dazk aren't going anywhere," she continued. "But they've played their hand, twice now if I hear correctly, and failed both times. They'll have to consider other methods to challenge the Bashlek and get rid of you. Subtler ones, and if Dazk is any evidence, it is something they are ill-equipped to do."

Milo wondered if sending a Si'lat after him in the food

AARON D. SCHNEIDER & MICHAEL ANDERLE

delivery counted as subtle, but before he could say anything, Bashlek Marid cleared his throat as his eyelids rose to half-mast.

"Yet for all that, there is still the matter of your army snooping around my mountain," the old ghul said, his gaze sliding to Milo. "Which is why your tutelage will have to be adjusted. Now, just a moment. This is the good part."

"But I just started!" Milo blurted and instantly regretted it. He sounded petulant even to his ears. "I, uh, mean, my mission is to learn magic, and so I just can't, you know, *stop*."

Marid brushed the protest aside with a flick of two claws, eyes sliding closed again.

"No one said you'd stop," he muttered distractedly, nestling a little deeper into the fungal fronds so that nearly half his face was concealed. A shiver ran through his wiry form, and there was a subtle spicy scent in the air. A light dusting of pink and white particles fell from the fungus-encrusted wall to land stark against the Bashlek's inky skin suit.

There was an awkward silence, and Milo, confused to the point of embarrassment, looked at the contessa, who was looking away discreetly. The silence continued, and Milo looked at the other fey, who just looked bored. He finally glanced at Ambrose, who shrugged helplessly.

Another shiver ran through the Bashlek's form and he straightened, opening bright, almost burning eyes. Milo fought the urge to recoil; he knew the eyes of an addict when he saw them.

Subconsciously, he glanced at the fungal patterns on the wall.

"Ohhh…ahhh, yesss, that's better," the ghul purred in a way that made Milo feel dirty as it brushed his ear. "I swear, it gets better every time."

"Nazahr, please," Contessa Rihyani murmured, the words as soft and unhurried as ever, but Milo felt the subtle tonal shift. Was she embarrassed by the Bashlek?

For his part, the Bashlek stared at both of them, mortal and fey, for a few seconds, blinking slowly. Then he looked at Rihyani, who still had her face turned away.

"Oh, fine. I suppose you are right," the ghul monarch groused, drumming his finger on his knee rapidly. "Business needs to be handled."

He suddenly looked around, seeming confused, and then with a stricken look, he turned to the contessa.

"What were we talking about?"

Milo would have laughed if this ghul hadn't saved him from a mob of his enraged fellows less than an hour earlier and remained his best hope of holding those monsters at bay. The latter fact made this scene downright terrifying.

"The adjustments to the magus' education," Rihyani replied in a long-suffering voice. "You were laying out your plans for how he could assist you and still maintain his studies."

Marid nodded, claws drumming on his knees even faster.

"Yes, yes," he hissed, running a tongue over his teeth and then grimacing. "I remember now. Yes, I had it all figured out before I sent you in to deliver the news about the airships. Yes, yes, yesss."

The Bashlek began to rock, his fevered gaze turning to the luminous fountain. The wrinkled folds of his eyelids rose farther then Milo would have thought possible, his face becoming a google-eyed mask fixed on the transition of colors.

"Care to share, your M—" Milo never got to finish his sentence.

"Contessa Rihyani will take you and an entourage of my daughter's," Marid declared in a distant voice to match his increasingly remote gaze. "Your education will continue on the road to your people's camp, then they will establish a base of operations to continue the tutelage as you confer with your superiors. The situation requires your presence to secure our interests, and by extension, your mission. As per my arrangement with your superior, his intervention needs to be at specific times to be effective."

Milo absorbed the eruption of instruction with a scowl.

It very much seemed there was a good deal to Jorge's interaction with the monster that the colonel had not told Milo. Milo had almost assumed that was the case, but having the brunt of his ignorance bear down on him like this was a distinctly unpleasant experience.

"I suppose," he began, trying to keep his head above the surface of this pool in which he was scared to find the bottom. "It couldn't hurt to reestablish contact with Nicht-KAT. That is, as long as Contessa Rihyani is okay with it. I mean, after all, she just got here. If she has other business to attend to, I wouldn't want to make the lady feel rushed."

Milo looked at Rihyani and saw her smiling. An ugly snort and an uglier chuckle rose from Bashlek Marid.

"The lady's business was coming here to escort you," the ghul said. "Do you really think those clumsy flying machines could wander through my domains without me knowing?"

Milo met Marid's hot stare, refusing to be cowed by the mad intensity he saw there.

"It seems you know a good deal more about everyone's business than I do, Your Majesty," Milo replied flatly. "When you're done playing your games, let me know."

The tension thickened, and the air seemed to seethe around the Bashlek.

"Do you find my treatment of you less than hospitable, Magus?"

"I think you've been using me to bait your political rivals since the second I got here," Milo said, his voice sinking lower and growing harder. "And you don't much seem to care what kind of danger that puts Ambrose or me in."

Marid sniffed, somehow managing to show more of his teeth.

"It started before you came, actually," Marid replied with practiced nonchalance. "From the second the rumors spread that I was going to bring a human to Ifreedahm to learn magic. I've been using your arrival like a lightning rod to gather all the dissidents under one burning roof."

"All right, glad to be of service," Milo growled in his chest. "Now, how about you keep your political schemes to yourself from here on out?"

"I have a better idea." Marid leaned forward, giving Milo the coldest, nastiest grin he had ever seen. "You take what scraps you are given, little magus, and I'll make sure all of ghuldom keeps forgetting you're nothing but talking food."

Marid maintained the locked gaze, his upper lip twitching a wormy dance that showed his fangs with every spasm. Milo shifted in his seat, unsure if he wanted to be ready to spring up and run or beat the old monster to the pounce.

Before he could decide, Marid slumped back and laughed uproariously.

"Oh, Magus, you are nothing if not interesting," he croaked between wracking fits of guffawing. "Imrah tells me you have the mind of a scholar, hungry and lusting for knowledge, but I see you also have the heart of a fighter. Now I know why she likes you so much."

Milo just stared at him, too wary of the mercurial king to acknowledge how shocked he was to hear that Imrah felt anything but loathing toward him.

"Let me open your eyes a little more, my young scrapper," Marid said, the laughter dying as his voice turned to ice.

Marid snapped his fingers.

Swirling and roiling around the ghul like a spectral storm, Milo saw an entire squadron of incorporeal animates. Some, revealed as they were swimming through the air, were little more than living cobwebs woven into ghostly visages—the Hatif, who were the unseen, unfelt eyes and ears of their master. Others, denser but still without true substance, were knit from shadows and spite and seemed ready to manifest as that black sand. With a word—probably just a thought—Bashlek Marid could summon a dozen Si'lat to descend on any who displeased on him. Circling like sharks scenting blood, the malevolent shades eyed Milo with hollow, hungering eyes.

"Just remember how small you are, Magus." Marid whispered the warning. "Before you start picking fights you can't win."

"Oh, I could've throttled the little monster," Milo snarled as he paced in the common room. "Every step of the way, he's been dangling and using us!"

Ambrose grunted his acknowledgment from the kitchen, where he watched over a boiling pot of rice. Milo had insisted he was too angry to eat, but the big man had insisted they have something after the excitement of the day.

"And now, after only three days—three days!—he's sending us off," Milo continued. "How am I supposed to learn anything if I am being shoved right back into the fighting? Marid's welching on his agreement with Jorge now that he's done with me."

"Even if that might cost him his daughter?" Ambrose called, still stirring the simmering pot. "He did say he was sending her with us."

Milo paused in his pacing to consider the point but shook his head.

"I think it's pretty clear there is no love lost between those two." He shrugged as he returned to stalking back and forth across the common room. "Besides, a creature like Marid wouldn't care about things like that. Monsters like him never do."

Milo lapsed into brooding and nearly jumped when a sharp

hiss filled the room. He whirled to see rice being drained. Ambrose looked up, his face reddening in the cloud of steam.

"You seem to think you know quite a bit about the Bashlek," Ambrose noted as he hefted the pot onto the stone countertop and began adding spices, minced vegetables, and diced meat.

"Because Marid is like every other petty despot." Milo huffed and threw himself down on a couch, which gave a loud creak of protest. "Call them Bashleks or Headmasters or Officers or Gang Bosses or Monsignors, they're all the same—self-serving predators who have clawed their way to the top of their local garbage heap."

The flood of memories that came with the description dragged Milo's hands to his head, and he kneaded at his temples. His fingers worked vigorously, as though they might squeeze away the invasive recollections.

"Well, *there's* a bit of baggage that screams for unpacking." Ambrose chuckled grimly as he scraped what they both hoped were minced leeks into the steaming pot of rice. "So, you want to talk about your problems with authority figures in general or simply hop into exploring your issues with priests?"

Milo looked out from under his hand to fix Ambrose with a scowl.

"Is that slop you call food ready yet?"

Ambrose raised his chin and looked down his crooked nose at Milo.

"I thought you weren't hungry, O mighty Magus," he replied archly as he continued folding in ingredients.

"I'm just hoping you'll have something to shove into your mouth soon." Milo grunted as he spied the two codices he'd received thus far. He scooped up both and deposited them in his lap.

"It needs to stand for a few minutes," Ambrose said, leaving the food to cool on the countertop as he ambled over to the couch across from Milo. "Which is just enough time for you to explain how someone who seems passably intelligent is being so very stupid."

Milo looked up from thumbing through *Awakening Moro*, brows knitting together.

"What are you talking about?"

"I'm saying," Ambrose grunted as he settled onto the couch that gave a sympathetic groan, "if you're smart enough to know all about how types like Marid work, why are you trying to pick a fight with him? What makes you think that is a good idea?"

"He picked the fight with me." Milo snorted and let the codex flop on the couch. "Sneering about the contessa and rubbing our noses in how this was all part of his plan and he was using us like pawns."

Ambrose shook his head as he folded his hands over his belly.

"That's not picking a fight," he said with a nod. "That's bragging, which is what you should have expected from a—what did you call him?—'petty despot.'"

Milo's jaw tightened, and his teeth ground together as he forced words between them.

"He was being an ass."

Ambrose shrugged.

"So?"

"So?" Milo echoed incredulously. "So we just let him think he can keep pulling our strings, keep using us?"

Ambrose tapped his feet thoughtfully, rocking slightly this way and that.

"You think that getting in a staring contest and beating your chest will stop all that?"

Milo forced a long breath through his nostrils and slowly unclenched his jaw.

"It will at least show him I'm on to his game, and I'm not playing."

Ambrose groaned and raised a hand to mop his face and tug his sideburns in frustration.

"No wonder you were a penal conscript!"

"What's that supposed to mean?" Milo bristled, fixing the big man with a withering glare.

"It means stop doing this," Ambrose explained, letting go of his sideburn and gestured at Milo with a flap of his hand. "This childish posturing and growling, like a cub trying to prove he's not scared."

"I'm *not* scared," Milo snapped back, flicking the other codex off his lap with one hand.

"Then I take back everything I said about you being smart." Ambrose gave a shake of his head. "We're past the edge of the map here, Magus, and you're being schooled in witchcraft by monsters! If you aren't at least a little bit scared, you are stupid, and being that stupid will get you killed. Probably me too, thank you very much."

Ambrose's words punched through the anger that was swelling inside him, leaving him deflated but unwilling to release his grip. He threw himself back against the couch and raised a fist to grind against his forehead.

"What do you want me to do?" Milo fumed. "Cower and fawn over that parasite?"

A smile twitched beneath Ambrose's mustache.

"I'm not sure you are capable of fawning over anything," he said, failing to stifle his grin. "But if you could try to be a touch less confrontational, maybe learn to growl less and listen more, we both might last a bit longer."

Milo let off his forehead to look levelly at Ambrose.

"I've heard you growl plenty."

Ambrose chuckled and then slapped both hands on his knees.

"That's my job," he said before heaving himself to his feet and turning back to the kitchenette. "And the fact is that for what my job is, it works. But your job isn't being the ruggedly handsome guardian of some upstart, pretty boy wizard. Your job is to be that upstart wizard, and that means you've got to try being more sagely and less of a street tough."

Ambrose retrieved two bowls and filled them with the rice mixture, then snatched up two spoons.

"You really think I'm pretty?" Milo asked in his most delicate voice.

"Without a doubt," the big man said with a wink as he handed one bowl and spoon to Milo. "Just don't tell your teacher. Don't want the poor girl getting jealous."

Milo dug around the clumps of rice to find the seasoned meat, shaking his head as he remembered the Bashlek's words.

"I think that more than anything proves how mad Marid is." He snorted, not wanting Ambrose to see how much he enjoyed the savory smell of the food. "Imrah wouldn't put me out if I was on fire."

"I might think about it," a voice called from the entrance to the apartment. "And isn't that a human proverb? 'It's the thought that counts.'"

Milo nearly gagged on his first bite as he spun on the couch to see a naked woman standing in the doorway.

She was short and shapely, fuller-figured than might have been fashionable, but she would have been quite pleasant to look at had her appearance not been so sudden and she not so nude. After a single uncertain second, she closed the door behind her and strode into the room as Ambrose watched suspiciously. Milo was caught between choking and gawking.

"Who are you?" Milo wheezed, then fought to clear his throat.

Dark eyes turned toward Milo, framed by black, straight hair cut along a severe line. Even through his watering eyes, Milo couldn't help noting something familiar glittering in her gaze. Something which, until very recently, he'd taken for barely suppressed loathing.

"Imrah?" Milo croaked.

The woman nodded, then frowned at Milo's bemused expression.

"What is wrong with you?" she snapped, glaring at his stunned expression and then turning to Ambrose. "What is wrong with him?"

"You do look a little different, ma'am," Ambrose offered. "He might be having a hard time adjusting."

She who was apparently Imrah gave an exasperated sigh and turned back to Milo, whose wandering eyes snapped back up to her face. His eyes looked ready to pop out of his head, and if they didn't, his cheeks were burning hot enough to cook them inside his head.

"How in Styx am I supposed to accompany you?" she demanded. "Humans are notoriously oblivious, but I'm fairly certain they will notice if a ghul is with you."

"I, uh, I guess, um, that makes sense," Milo muttered. "So will you, uh, be traveling with us, um, like that?"

Imrah raised a hand, and both men thought she was about to slap him until she reached over with her other hand to give the meat of her forearm a squeeze.

"If you'd done your reading, you would know this kind of skin-shawl requires considerable time and resources to prepare. Once it's put on, removing it will destroy it. So yes, *Magus*, I will be traveling in this meat suit, though Iblis only knows how I'll manage."

"If I may, ma'am," Ambrose interjected as he cleared his throat with a cough. "I think what the Magus meant was, do you plan to put on clothes before we rejoin the world above? A naked woman might not raise as many eyebrows as a ghul, but it would draw more attention than we'd want."

Imrah looked down at herself and then shot a glance to Milo, whose valiant efforts at discretion seemed doomed to failure.

"As if this clinging flesh weren't enough," Imrah fumed,

twisting on her heel and stomping over to the couch where Ambrose's ruined jacket lay.

With a good deal of fumbling that Milo told himself not to watch but somehow wasn't able to look away from, Imrah managed to enfold herself in the big man's coat, which looked like a blue tent draped around her small shoulders.

"Happy?" She huffed.

"Not to speak for the Magus," Ambrose said, giving his ward a wink, "but I'd say we're about halfway there."

15

A WARNING

The next day, their party came together at the arched entrance to Ifreedahm: three fey, two humans, and two ghuls wearing convincing skin-shawls. To the relief of Milo, both ghuls had managed to acquire adequate if eclectic clothing. They insisted their garments were common dress for the area, but Milo was fairly certain the strange collection of drab essentials with brightly colored head coverings and fringed shawls were what-ever was close at hand.

Without fanfare and hardly a word shared between them, they'd crossed the causeway and were soon being led through the tunnels by the two disguised ghuls. The plan was for Imrah and Fazihr to lead them out to the foot of the mountain, which Milo had heard in passing was called Shah Fuladi by the human popu-lation. Fazihr, in the guise of a small man with dusky skin and a mop of curly dark hair that fell nearly to his shoulders, stated that there was an outpost of ghul sentries near the access to the surface who should have a report of any activity involving human ground forces. Assuming they had the all-clear from the sentries, they would proceed to the surface, where the fey, who were far more accustomed to traveling above ground and knew the area somewhat, would bring them along a forgotten road to Bamyan, where the German forces were supposed to be stationed.

Everything after that point would be up to Milo and Ambrose to sort out.

Every step they took in the tunnels leading away from Ifreedahm, Milo felt like his feet were getting heavier. He kept remembering his last glimpse of the venomous jewel that was the capital of ghuldom and wondered if he would ever see it again. He told himself it wasn't that he'd forgotten how the city's denizens had tried to kill him on multiple occasions, but that while he was there, magic was everywhere, and it was somehow easier to believe that he could become a wizard. If magic and wonder, even the most terrible kinds, were water, he felt like he was leaving the only oasis to head back into the desert, and he couldn't say for certain that he would ever return.

Milo tried to remind himself that his teacher was going with him and his pack was stuffed with tomes of magical lore, some translated but many still in the eye-searing Ghulish script. Imrah had promised to teach him how to make a fetish that would let him read any untranslated language so that he could read Ghul-ish. Then according to her, he would have the framework to become "a passable necromist." Coming from his sour tutor, he supposed he should have taken that as a sign to be hopeful, but despite his best efforts, he couldn't shake his melancholy at returning to the drab, dusty, and no doubt deadly world above— the world at war.

Absorbed in such grim navel-gazing, Milo didn't notice the faint silvery light suffusing the air around him until Contessa Rihyani was walking right beside him.

"Magus," she said softly, her eyes locked ahead where her two companions walked.

"Contessa," Milo replied, stifling his shock. "What can I do for you?"

The fey gave him a sidelong glance, complete with a small smile.

"How very genteel of you," she said. "I'd heard that the age of manners and chivalry was gone among mankind, but I am glad to see that isn't true."

Milo studied the elfin creature, certain she was mocking him but not wanting to be rude on the off-chance she wasn't.

"If my manners don't offend you, you might be the first," Milo said with a wry chuckle. "It seems that being abrasive is a singular talent of mine."

"I'll second that," Ambrose called from his place at the rear of the party.

Lady Rihyani laughed, a sound that made Milo's heart ache.

"You don't give yourself enough credit," the contessa said, adjusting her muffling robes as they walked. "The fact is that things have been stacked against you since the Magpie sent you on your way. Unfortunately, much has been shaped by forces far outside your knowledge and control."

Milo wasn't going to argue with that, but the mention of birds struck him as an odd interjection.

"Did you say 'magpie?'"

Lady Rihyani nodded, and few silver strands fell free. She tucked them back behind the tapered ears within her hood.

"Yes, forgive me." She sighed, a gentle sound that Milo felt he could have bathed in. "For a long time, Colonel Jorge and I communicated using codenames and ciphers, each trying to measure the intentions and abilities of the other. I sometimes revert to old habits."

Milo looked at her, unable and unwilling to hide the surprise on his expression.

"How do you know Colonel Jorge?"

Rihyani smiled, and her voice dropped to a conspiratorial whisper.

"I was the agent sent to contact him when he first began his explorations into our world. It was my job to assess him to resurrect the tradition of the Merry Fellows and reconnect our world and the world of men."

Milo eyed the contessa warily. What had first seemed like merely a wandering aristocrat had turned out to be in cooperation with the Bashlek, and she was now telling him she'd been part of the cloak and dagger games when Jorge was in military intelligence. Milo was not adept at games of subterfuge and covert operations, but he felt the conclusion to be drawn was clear.

Contessa Rihyani was not someone to trifle with, and though she seemed friendly enough, he would be a fool to let his guard down around her.

Fighting his natural urge to throw up a rough front, Milo only nodded, and in his most sincerely inquisitive tone, asked her, "What is the tradition of the Merry Fellows?"

"It was once an informal but well-respected collaboration between certain humans and what we fey call the Folk, what you might call supernatural beings."

"What the ghuls call 'shayati,'" Milo offered.

"Precisely," the contessa agreed, giving him a smile. He was embarrassed by how giddy it made him feel.

"When one of the Folk finds an exceptional human," the fey continued, "they determine if that human can be trusted with knowledge of our existence. If they can, a bargain will be struck for their mutual benefit. Rare even in the days before such dark times as these, it is a credit to your commanding officer that he was chosen, though I'm not so certain he feels the privilege outweighs the burden at this point."

Fazihr's human voice called from up ahead, almost blasphemous in its volume, "We will be nearing the gate soon. After that, it will not be long to the sentry post, and then the surface."

"That's a lot quicker than I expected," Milo mused with a frown. "It seems like it's only been an hour or so if that."

"Ghul tunnels are enchanted to speed travel," Rihyani replied with a shrug as if it were not particularly surprising. "Why else would they be carpeted in mort-scalp?"

"Mort-scalp?" Milo breathed, feeling his mouth go dryer with each cushioned step.

Ambrose muttered a string of profanity that involved multiple saints performing rude and anatomically unfeasible acts.

"Every time I think ghuls can't get worse," the bodyguard growled at the end of his irreverent tirade.

"My apologies," Rihyani said, turning to look ahead once more. "I assumed your instructor had explained that."

"That must be part of day three's lesson." Milo sighed, trying not to wince with every step he took across the hairy floor.

For a time, they lapsed into silence. When it seemed that the contessa was about to slide forward again to rejoin her own kind, a sudden thought struck Milo.

"Why the ghuls?" he asked and realized with a cringe the question had been loud enough to echo up and down the tunnel.

"What do you mean?" Rihyani asked, though one look at her face told Milo she knew exactly what he meant.

"What I mean is," Milo began, carefully modulating the tone and volume of his voice, "there are obviously other Folk. I've read about different kinds in one of the books Imrah gave me. My question is, why send me to the ghuls first?"

Rihyani's expression became fixed, a mask that betrayed nothing as she stared ahead in thought. When her golden pupils finally returned to him, he felt a quickening in his heart that was neither fear nor excitement, but something in between.

"There were many reasons, some practical to the nature of the task and some to the reality of the world."

The answer informed him of nothing, and again Milo had to stow his inclination to become belligerent.

"I am not sure I understand," he said apologetically before pressing in. "It might help if you could be more specific."

Again the mask and again the penetrating look.

"One factor is how ghuls exercise their magical nature," she said, her words chosen with surgical precision. "Ghul magic is of a kind most closely related to common human concepts of science. Ingredients, formulas—those sorts of things. We who were willing to consider the possibility of a human capable of magic felt that their methods might be the best for you to learn."

"But that's not the only reason," Milo said, his certainty driving the question out of the statement.

"That wasn't the only reason," Rihyani agreed, and without seeming to quicken her pace, she slid back in line with her fellow fey.

They passed the gate, the massive bone creature letting them pass without comment, and made their way up a gradually sloping corridor. Then more silent trudging, until a quarter of an hour from the gate, something in the environment altered.

Milo noticed it first as a change in the fey in front of him.

The fey did not walk through the world, they strode in the way he thought kings and princes of bygone years might have. Yet not long after passing the gate, Milo saw their stride became a stalk, every ounce of their grace and poise becoming predatory. Even the bronze colossus, whose head seemed about to scrape the ceiling of the tunnel, moved with the coiling gait of a massive feline.

Milo wasn't the only one to notice it.

"Something's up," Ambrose whispered at his shoulder, and a backward glance told Milo the big man was holding his *Gewehr* in both hands across his body.

"What is it?" Milo murmured, one hand reaching for the pistol at his hip. He felt the tremor of magic in the hand gripping the skull cane.

"Not sure," Ambrose answered with a sniff and a twitch of his mustache. "But our fairy friends seem concerned, and there's a smell on the air that I don't like."

Taking his own sampling of the air, Milo noted that there was something decidedly caustic. It was nothing so distinct as a smell, more of an irritant or a tickle in his nostrils and at the back of his throat. A few minutes later, the smell had grown to a chemical stench on the air, like someone had set cleaning products on fire.

If you could burn ammonia, Milo thought, *it would smell like this.*

A prickle of terror rolled up Milo's spine and he turned back toward Ambrose, not caring that he could practically feel the blood draining from his face.

"Could this be some kind of chemical attack?" he whispered, fear sharpening his voice.

Of all the horrors of the war he'd been braced for, the threat of horrors concocted by some sadist in a lab coat had always struck him as one of the most sinister. Bullets, bombs, and shells to rip, blast, and obliterate were more honest and acceptable. A caustic fog that ate your lungs out of your chest or a noxious mist that shriveled your eyes on its way to your brain...

Milo's chest tightened and his jaw popped as he waited for the celestial soldier's assessment. The thought that he'd rather end up in a ghul's belly than choke to death in some hole occurred to him. At least he might gag the monster that ate him.

"A gas attack in tunnels like these only works if you don't plan on taking the tunnels," the bodyguard said after an evaluation. "Not enough ventilation to clear them out, and depending on what poison you're putting down the chute, it could stay toxic for a good while. I'd say it's unlikely."

Milo let out the breath he'd been holding, telling himself the air he was about to replace it with simply stank and was not going to condemn him to an agonizing death.

Up ahead, the fey had come to a halt. Hearing sharp, hushed voices, he shuffled forward, Ambrose at his shoulder.

"Regardless, the mort-scalp is gone, and that's going to slow everything down," Fazihr was explaining as he darted rodentlike glances up the tunnel. "Perhaps we should return to Ifreedahm and see—"

"No," Imrah interjected, making her retainer cringe. "The Bashlek has given us a task, and we will see it done, even if it will take a little longer."

Fazihr wrung his hands, staring at them as though cursing the blunt digits that hid his claws.

"Loyalty is an admirable trait," he said, clearing of his throat. "But of no use if it gets us all killed."

"So, you know what did this?" Contessa Rihyani asked, looking from Fazihr to Imrah and back.

"Well, no," the ghul retainer confessed, wilting under the glare of his mistress. "But the mort-scalp is fashioned to be extremely resilient. It is the corpus that provides the essence, so it needs to be robust, especially in stretches like these that must be ready to communicate a potential invasion. It would take a concerted effort to scour or uproot so much of it."

"Requiring substantial forces then," Rihyani said, following his logic. "We could be heading into a large contingent of soldiers."

"Precisely," Fazihr agreed, turning a pleading eye to Imrah. "Think of the damage it would do to Ifreedahm, to your father, if the Bashlek's daughter was taken hostage by meatsacks."

Ambrose gave a dry cough, and all turned around to stare at the two humans.

Milo stared back mutely until Ambrose surreptitiously dug an elbow into his back.

"I—"

The elbow dug again.

"We don't think it is a chemical attack."

The stares continued.

The elbow dug again.

"So...so, I don't think this has anything to do with the

Germans' forces," Milo continued, feeling squeezed between the stares of the inhuman party and Ambrose's questing elbow. "So, uh, we should press on unless we have a good reason not to."

"Our reason," Fazihr snarled, "is that we have no idea what lies ahead. We could be walking into a trap or something worse. The point is, we don't know."

"But we do know that zeppelins are flying around this mountain," Milo said, his voice unflinching but dispassionate. "Which means there is a better than good chance that there will be major movement in this area. If you get me—ugh, us, us!—to Bamyan, we can make sure a lot more of those *meatsacks* don't start marching all over this mountain."

Fazihr bared his teeth, but a furtive look at Imrah stilled further protests.

"Fine," the retainer spat. "Then may I advise the humans to go first? It's a straight march to the sentry post from here."

Milo looked at Ambrose, who nodded.

"We'll scout ahead then." Milo sighed. "I mean, at this point, we're practically experts at tunnels, right?"

Creeping down the scoured stretch of tunnel was at once tedious and stressful in a manner that Milo imagined was akin to what men in the trenches felt.

Every moment seemed to threaten them with a messy end, but as the moments stretched into minutes that stretched into hours, the sharp edges of the threat grew dull. Instead of a piercing trauma that awakened the body with adrenaline and sharpened every sense, there was the grating rasp of another advance, another step, another breath toward a death that wasn't in any hurry to arrive. After three hours of the grinding experience, Milo found himself fantasizing about what would end his life. Would it be a bullet ripping from far up the tunnel? A mine or some other booby trap to rip him apart or jelly his guts? Maybe a tunnel rat commando springing from a black alcove to plunge a knife into his chest?

The longer he dwelt on how his life would end, the longer and more fanciful his morbid daydreams became. Soon he was layering levels of plot and symbolism, like a ninepence rag's attempt at a modern morality tale.

Thus distracted, it was no surprise that he nearly planted his foot in a splatter of viscous goo four hours into the unaugmented trek to the surface. The only thing stopping him was Ambrose's strong hand gripping his shoulder.

"Hold on," the bodyguard murmured, drawing Milo back a step and then hunkering down to frown at the glistening smear. "Perhaps a little of your light."

"LIGHT," Milo obliged, and beams of green light shone from the sockets of his cane.

The floor, as reported by the ghuls, had been stripped of the mort-scalp, leaving only bare stone whose surface was scoured clean. Milo was no spelunker, but even the dust or damp you might have expected was absent. This gelatinous splotch was the first interruption they'd seen in that sterile length of the tunnel.

"Anything about this or something like it in those books?" Ambrose asked, flicking out a penknife from a pocket. The tiny blade was humorously small in his shovel-sized mitts. "Because this doesn't look like anything I've ever seen."

Milo sank to his haunches, keeping the light fixed on the goo as Ambrose hooked his blade in the largest lump of the translucent sludge. The burnt ammonia smell was enough to sting the eyes, and Milo found himself blinking rapidly and rocking back.

"Some new gel fuel?" Milo suggested as he shook his head to clear the noxious fumes clinging to it. "Something for flamethrowers, maybe? That could be what cleared out the mort-scalp."

Ambrose made a face as he raised the wobbling hunk,

watching with dread fascination as it liquified and dripped on the floor.

"Maybe," he murmured, then made a face as though he could taste the vile blob. "But that means they used fire to scour the mort-scalp, but that seems unlikely on two scores. First, it would have filled the tunnels with smoke and eaten up the air inside. Any commander ordering his men down to scour tunnels like that would soon have the troops staggering out, smoke-blind and gagging, assuming the poor fools came out at all."

Milo nodded in understanding but was unwilling to let the theory go.

"And the other score?"

"The other bit is that it's a big and risky expenditure of men and material," Ambrose explained, fumbling with his free hand for a match. "To scour so much tunnel with fire would mean teams of men taking shifts to make sure the weapons and men didn't overheat, along with men bringing them water and fuel regularly. The only reason to do that is if you know the ghuls use it to work their magic, but that means not only knowing about the ghuls but their magic too, something no one is supposed to know about."

"Supposed to." Milo grunted as though offended by the two words appearing next to each other.

"Fair point," Ambrose conceded, holding up his liberated match. "Which is why we light this little blob and see what happens. If it burns quick, you might be right. If not, we're back to being clueless. Science, pure and simple."

Milo didn't know if the big man's grasp on the scientific method was up to scratch, but he had nothing better to suggest. He nodded in agreement, though he rose to shuffle backward as he did.

"Fair enough," he said, wondering just how big a mistake it would be to light up their position by setting off the fuel, if that was what it was. He comforted himself that given the sight-salve he'd applied first thing this morning, the pitch-dark of the tunnel had no secrets from him, even without beams stabbing out from the skull. It was nothing but a stretch of tunnel curving gently up and to the left as far as he could see. Nowhere for an enemy to hide unless they could pass through the stone walls, which, when he thought about his new reality, was not as comforting as he might have hoped.

"Fire in the hole," Ambrose muttered as he struck the match, sending up a flare-orange flame.

The match advanced toward the blob, and for a second, Milo thought the jellied mass's quivering was shivering away from the flame. The blob gave a small keening squeal as it jumped. It didn't fall or wobble free, but leapt, gathering itself together in the bat of an eye and catapulting free of the penknife, arching as it strained for the floor.

Ambrose was so surprised he dropped the match. It landed on the initial smear, which lit with a *whoosh* of sulfurous flame. The same piercing cry, almost a shriek, rose from the burning splotch, even as fingers of flame slime kindled the fleeing blob.

Milo and Ambrose watched in horrified amazement as the filaments of fire caught up with the retreating lump, then both men covered their ears as an even more terrible sound stabbed through the air. Screaming and burning, the blob continued its lurching, squirming retreat as it fled, and even as they tried to plug their ears, Milo and Ambrose made to follow.

"Doesn't seem like fuel to me," Ambrose shouted as they trotted after it. "Leastwise, I hope not."

Milo was too busy jogging, trying to cover his ears with one arm while the other kept the witchlight trained on the fleeing cohort before he realized how silly he was being. The tortured goo was providing more than enough light.

"What do you think it is?" Milo called. They moved to keep it in sight as it followed the tunnel up and around.

"Very uncomfortable at the moment, I'd say," Ambrose called, laughing.

Milo shook his head and jogged on.

A minute longer, the blob started coming apart, even as it kept trying to escape, bigger and bigger pieces peeling off to curl and twist into puffs of ash. Its keening was now just a high, pitiable whine.

"Where is it going?" Ambrose wondered.

"It better get there fast," Milo grunted. "It's not going to last much longer."

Milo thought that was just as well because despite his fitness, he was struggling to catch his breath as they jogged along. The air seemed thicker, the chemical stench heavier, and something at the back of his throat tasted like metal.

"Maybe we should put it out," Ambrose said, pulling ahead and tugging a long rag from his back as he ran. "Need to have something to show the creepies."

The creature, if such a thing was possible, being so flammable made Milo doubtful, but before he could voice his thoughts, he saw something in the tunnel up ahead that turned his words into a cry of horror.

Ambrose's eyes swung upwards and both men stood, rooted to the tunnel floor.

Seething forward like an undulating tide, Milo saw more of the gelatinous gunk surging down the tunnel toward them. In the vision granted him by the sight-salve, writhing layers of darkness filled the black frame of the tunnel, but as it neared the burning blob, Milo's eyes saw it in the light of the tortured flames. It was gray and glistening, flecked with discolorations across its surfaces and darker shapes writhed in its murky folds. For all its liquid movement, there was a will to the advance, the leading tongue of the tide surging forward to lap up the burning blob.

The tunnel was so heavy with the scorched stench that Milo wondered if he could choke to death on stink.

There was a merciful hiss of flame extinguishing, as the blob was smothered by the mother jelly, but then, with more fury and contempt than anything so amorphous had a right to be, it turned upon Milo and Ambrose.

Rearing back, a pseudopod of slime arched and then flicked a tentacle, hurling gobbets at Ambrose. The big man freed himself from fear's paralyzing grip and dove out of the way, but one blob splashed across the back of his trouser leg. There was a hiss, and Ambrose gave a snarl of pain as white wisps of vapor rose from the congealing slime.

Ambrose swore and kicked as he ran back toward Milo, flecks of goo flying free, along with bits of his trousers and the flesh beneath.

"Run!" the bodyguard shouted, his booming voice battering Milo back to himself. They ran side by side through the tunnel.

One terrified glance over his shoulder told him the huge, squirming horror was closing on them, and Milo knew there was no way they could outrun it. He felt the heavy cane in his hand, and for an instant, thought of throwing it aside but then the magic hummed against his soul as though begging him to remember.

If the smaller blob had burned...

Milo slowed and then spun around, forcing himself to remember the exercises he'd done with Imrah and the pillars. Only this time, he wanted the torrent of flames instead of bolts.

"BUR—" he began, piling a blunt wedge of essence through the skull, but then he saw an avalanche of slime about to descend and his focus crumbled. Time seemed to slow as he watched the arching wave rushing down on him. Through the quavering layers of muddy flesh, he saw the black shapes, limbs twisting and bodies writhing.

That's about to be me, Milo realized numbly, just before a vice-like grip clamped over his shoulder and hauled him backward.

His feet leaving the tunnel floor, Milo flew several feet down the tunnel before skidding to a skin-peeling stop on his back. Looking between his outward splayed legs he saw the living tide slam down on Ambrose. Milo tried to scream, but he was winded, and his efforts to climb to his feet were drunkenly clumsy.

In mockery of Milo's wheezing protests, the wrathful Mother Jelly lifted Ambrose in its smothering grip, twisting hard to the left and then to the right and smashing the big man against the walls of the tunnel. With each impact, there was a wet slap to accompany the bone-crunching thump, treating Ambrose like a slipper in a mutt's jaws.

Milo was on his unsteady feet, cane thrust out before him like he wanted the skull to bear witness.

Will! he screamed internally. *Bend it to your will!*

"BURN!"

With a maniacal cackle, the skull's jagged beak split to unleash a torrent of witchfire.

The emerald flames worked their terrible power instantly, and the slime burst into flames. It recoiled with shocking speed, letting Ambrose's limp body drop to the floor as it slithered backward. Like burning filth sucked down a drain, the mother jelly retreated up the tunnel, vanishing in less time than it had taken for it to appear. Tendrils of caustic white vapor rose from the walls, and a thin sheen of slime smoldered before shriveling into nothing.

"Simon," Milo gasped, limping forward in the wake of the horror's retreat. "Ambrose!"

The big man didn't respond or move as Milo forced his way through the gagging stink to kneel beside him.

Gently as he could with shaking hands, Milo rolled his body-guard and friend over, only to fight back a sob as he beheld a face with features chewed down to the bone.

16

A PROMISE

Simon Ambrose lay on the ground in front of Milo, motionless, unbreathing, dead.

His limp body was pitted and gnawed, ragged holes dotting his flesh where the caustic grip of the gelatinous horror had found greater purchase. Even below the surface, his bones were splintered, forcing his body into odd, unnerving angles on the floor. His clothes were in tatters, hardly enough to cover the expanse of raw meat that glistened in the dark.

The face, though, was the greatest blow to Milo. It rent his heart, yet he was unable to look away. The soft tissue and facial hair were gone except for a few knots that only highlighted the damage. The revealed bone was scarred by the vitriolic touch as well, moldering and pocked by discolored rings. It was a vision of nightmares, but it was all that was left of the only man who might ever have been a true friend to Milo.

"Idiot," Milo said half-heartedly, wishing he could muster the will for more. "Why did you do that?"

Through the hard, bitter years of his short life, Milo had become proficient at hardening his heart, first in the Waisenhaus in avoiding deprivation and abuse, then in Roland's gang to achieve status and therefore protection, and finally as a penal conscript, just to stay alive and sane. Experience had educated him extensively on the virtues of emotional distance, objectification, and hate. He'd understood early on that tears meant nothing when no one was there to dry them, so such weakening sympathies were throttled inside him.

Or so he thought.

A string of the curses and imprecations of the dead bodyguard dripped from Milo's lips.

"Damned fool," he snarled, hoping anger could bludgeon the grief out. "Stupid, swollen, shuffling…"

His throat ached, and his vision began to blur.

"You-you fat moron," he began again, forcing the words around the lump in his throat. "Now I'm alone with the monsters. Now…now…"

Something wet and burning slid from his eyes to roll down his cheeks.

"Idiot," Milo bleated, batting his face before grinding the heel of his palm into his treacherous eyes. "Stupid, stupid, stupid!"

He told himself he needed to stop blubbering over an empty pile of broken meat. He told himself he needed to report back to the others, who were even now creeping slowly up the tunnel. He even told himself the monstrous thing might return, but none of it seemed to matter.

You promised not to care anymore! his heart wailed at him between the quiet sobs. *You promised to never feel this. Never again.*

The tears fell, and Milo could not move until they had. He cursed himself, Ambrose, the ghuls, the German Empire, humanity, and God, but it didn't matter.

He knelt in the dark and cried for a fallen friend.

Then light came to the dark.

Burning, glaring, and hot.

Milo, confused and revived by fresh terror, scrambled back, covering his eyes. Jerking to his feet, he pressed down the panic at the sudden heat and light and tried to get his bearings. Through his swimming senses, he realized the blinding light was coming from Ambrose's body, a living radiance that drove Milo back with its intensity.

It was red, but not the terrible crimson light that had crowned the guard in the tunnels days before. This was different—cleaner and brighter, yet no less terrifying than that previous alien glare.

Milo's back was against the sour-smelling tunnel wall, and despite the stink, he turned his face away and hid it against the stone. The light pulsed and Milo felt the heat of it cut through him. He screamed.

Then the light left, passing beyond the gulfs between spheres, and Milo was in the dark tunnel once more.

Shivering and swearing, he turned back toward Ambrose's body and beheld a new horror.

The corpse was sitting up, mangled face turned toward Milo, red stars glowing from its hollow sockets.

"ויאמר יהוה לא־ידון רוחי באדם לעולם בשגם הוא בשר" came the declaration from a ruined throat.

In Milo's mind the words thundered, carried by the magic of the elixir Imrah had taught him to fashion to reveal all tongues to him.

And the Lord hath not spoken of a man in everlasting flesh!

Then the dead man rose and moved toward Milo, ruined hands outstretched.

Instinct took over, and Milo, gripping the heavy cane in both hands, swung out with a crushing blow.

One ravaged hand caught the shaft of the cane and stopped it dead. The shock of the sudden stop jolted Milo's arms, and he staggered forward and lost his grip on the cane.

Off-balance, he stumbled into the corpse, rebounding off one sloped shoulder before sliding awkwardly to the ground. His former bodyguard and friend loomed over him, and Milo was certain the end had come. The hands descended toward him slowly, and as he watched them, Milo had time to curse himself.

This is what you get for caring, you damn fool.

The fingers closed around the front of his jacket, and Milo could feel the living heat coursing through them. That was strange. He would have laughed—his last thoughts were concerned with the temperature of an animated body before it murdered him. He'd heard that people's lives were supposed to flash before their eyes, but since no such thing happened, Milo assumed his wretched life was simply not worth the trouble to remember.

As the hands, still possessed of that terrible strength their former owner had in life, dragged him upward like a rag doll, Milo remembered the tarot card in his pocket. Suddenly desperate to see it one last time, he snaked his arm around to rummage in his breast pocket.

His fingers had just brushed its worn surface when the grip on his jacket tightened, trapping his hand inside his coat.

Hope is for the disappointed fool, Milo chided himself with what he was certain was his last thought.

Whatever gripped him easily bore his weight as it reached for his throat.

Milo thought about fighting, part of his mind telling him not to surrender, but black despair and powerlessness had sapped his strength. He would stare into the hellish glimmering sockets that had once belonged to his only friend and let the end come. In a perverse way, the cold certainty of it was a comfort, or at least an anesthetic.

The fingers slid under his jaw.

Then along the jawline to his ears.

Then across his cheek, gliding to his nose, where forefinger and thumb traced the shape of it before moving to brush across his eyes and brow.

The grip holding him upright was as hard as steel, but the fingers mapping the contours of his face were as gentle as any human hand that had ever touched him. Milo, whether in fear or surrender, had let his eyes slide out of focus as he waited for death, but in the face of such odd behavior, he looked at Ambrose's ruined face in confusion.

Raw, bloody lips twisted into something like a smile over pitted pink-smeared teeth.

Milo gawked, but not at the horror of such a smile. Seconds before, there had been nothing to smile with.

He stared for a few seconds longer as flesh filled the mutilated visage. It was like watching some gory flower bloom. Fractured bones set, sinews reattached, and after almost a minute, skin began to appear in bald pink patches.

"Ambrose," Milo said tentatively. "Ambrose, can you hear me?"

The big man's head bobbed, though he cocked his head to the side as though he struggled to hear. Milo could see why: even as they repaired themselves, Milo could see that where the man's ears had been were ragged pits in the sides of his head. That he could hear anything was a miracle.

And the miracle wasn't done.

The man was regenerating before his eyes, and not just his face. Looking down, Milo saw bones lurching back into alignment and the body straightening. Beneath his tattered clothes, the wounds in his flesh filled with fresh meat before sheathing themselves in bright new skin.

Inch by inch, Ambrose was being made whole.

Less than three minutes from when he'd laid hands upon Milo, Ambrose was restored. His iron grip transformed into a crushing hug.

"Ho-ho, it's good to see you, boy!" he chortled as he squeezed Milo until he saw spots. "I knew you could do it! Knew down to my boots and back!"

Milo frantically slapped his free hand on the big man's back as the other hand, trapped between their bodies, gave a wet pop.

Ambrose grunted and released his grip, and the two separated.

Milo heaved in a deep breath and shook his head to try to dispel the bleary fireworks going off behind his eyes.

"Must've gotten a little carried away," the bodyguard muttered sheepishly, then reached out again. "Didn't hurt your arm, did I?"

Milo's hand was still in his breast pocket, and with a start, he drew it out.

The tarot card somehow caught on his retreating fingertips and sprang from his coat of its own accord. Milo lurched after it, but Ambrose's reflexes were quicker. Sausage-thick fingers snagged the card on its fluttering path and held it up before his freshly regrown eyes. They had been one of the last things to regrow, and Milo could not say he was sad to be free of the red glow that had come from the sockets.

"Damn you, Ambrose," Milo snarled, an old fear driving away the warmth of the moment. "That's mine, give it to me!"

Ambrose looked up at Milo, hurt and confusion plainly written across his broad features.

"Sure enough, Magus," he said softly, holding up the folded card for Milo to snatch. "I was only keeping it from touching the filthy floor."

Milo swore and shoved the card back inside his coat, unable to meet the big man's searching gaze.

"So, when were you going to tell me you were immortal?" Milo asked as he straightened his coat, the question coming out sharper than he'd intended.

Ambrose took a step back, looked around the dark tunnel, then shrugged.

"Not sure immortal is the right word for it," he said, letting his arms fall to his sides as he realized there wasn't enough of his pants left for pockets. "I'm fairly certain I die every time."

"Every time?" Milo asked as he stepped around the big man to retrieve his cane.

He still couldn't meet Ambrose's wounded stare.

"I don't make a habit of it," he said, shrugging again. "But life is dangerous, especially in the environments I seem to find myself in. By my count, it's happened four times, including this incident of course."

"Of course," Milo remarked drily as he examined his cane.

It seemed undamaged by its time on the tunnel floor, for which he was thankful as he straightened and looked up the tunnel the way the horror had gone.

"So you knew," Milo said, forcing himself to look at Ambrose. "You knew when you threw me back and stood in the way of that...thing. You knew you'd come back."

Ambrose's face scrunched, the expression odd without his mustache. Stubble and a few longer scraggles of hair dotted his face, but it seemed the healing powers the demi-human possessed did not include complete facial hair reconstruction.

"Well, I'm not sure I even thought about that," Ambrose said slowly, chewing things over as he spoke. "But I suppose on some level I might have known. Why?"

It means I wasn't worth dying for, not really.

Anger, hot and bitter, shot through Milo's mind like bile, but he choked it back. He hated himself for the realization as much as he hated himself for thinking it. The thought felt petty and low, but he couldn't shake its hold on him even as he forced a small, disingenuous smile onto his face.

"I'm a wizard, or at least one in training, right?" he replied with a hollow chuckle. "It's my business to be curious about supernatural occurrences."

"I suppose so." Ambrose nodded, though a quick glance confirmed that he wasn't convinced. "But you can stop with all that 'in training' business if you ask me. Driving off that monster qualifies you for professional wizard chops in my utterly amateur opinion."

Down the tunnel they heard a commotion, the clear, perfect voices of the fey mingling with rougher human tones. The rest of the party was coming toward them, and from the sound of their feet and the words exchanged, they were coming quickly because of the sounds of the past several minutes.

The thought of retelling everything sucked the life from Milo, and his shoulders slumped just before a big mitt slapped down on them.

"Please, Magus," Ambrose whispered hoarsely, stealing a quick glance down the tunnel. "Please don't tell them about me dying and coming back."

"Why?" was all Milo could manage as he stared into his bodyguard's pleading face.

"Loads of reasons," Ambrose said. "But most of all, because I am asking you."

Milo scowled, while down the length of the tunnel, he thought he saw the glimmer of the fey's glowing skin reflecting off the stone walls.

"Fine," he hissed. "But you're going to explain yourself when we get to Bamyan."

"Sure, sure." Ambrose nodded vigorously as he stepped back and tried to rearrange his tatters to something a little more modest.

Both saw that the fey and disguised ghuls were indeed jogging toward them.

"And while we're at it," Ambrose whispered, a second before the others were in earshot, "you can tell me why that card's got you all in a tizzy."

17

A LIE

After explaining the events in the tunnel *sans* Ambrose's death and revivification more than three times, neither the fey nor the ghuls had much of anything useful to say.

"I have never heard of such a thing," Imrah said, sounding almost offended at having to make the confession. The situation was the same for the fey, and as though determined to be even less helpful, Fazihr used the opportunity to express his previously dismissed opinion.

"I told you this was foolish," he spat, crossing his arms and throwing an eye toward Imrah, who only sniffed.

"Last I checked," Ambrose rumbled, "you weren't the one that almost got eaten, so don't go getting your snout out of sorts on my account."

Fazihr opened his mouth to object, but seeing nothing but unsympathetic gazes around him, he wisely decided to close it with a dull clack of teeth. He turned toward the surfaceward tunnel and kept a fretful watch, rocking from foot to foot.

"The question is, what should be done now?" The contessa looked Ambrose over speculatively. "Not to be insensitive to your modesty Mr. Ambrose, but we're remarkably lucky that the only damage done was to your clothing. Things could have been much worse."

"Not to argue, but it wasn't just my clothes," Ambrose explained, his eyes cutting almost imperceptibly to Milo before he continued. "That nasty jelly also ate my rifle, my knife, and my pack, which included my best tobacco tin."

The fey stared, their expressions inscrutable, while Imrah looked at the bodyguard as though he was being obtuse.

"I'm sure there will be opportunities for you to outfit yourself appropriately once we get to the human camp," the she-ghul said archly. "But there is still the matter of what to do next, and despite what just happened, I remain determined that we should push forward."

"I think what Ambrose is saying," Milo cut in with a nod to the big man, "is that first of all, he is unarmed, second, that this thing can break down metal as well as flesh, and finally that when we do reach the German camp, we need to have a good explanation for why he is in such a state."

Imrah narrowed her eyes at Milo, then slid her glance to the nodding Ambrose and back.

"Very well," she said slowly, as though sensing something amiss. "The Jurhumidon can stay close to the contessa's retainers for protection, and we can say he was the victim of a trap left by enemy forces, an incendiary of some kind. You did say your people were scouting the area to reach the enemy armies beyond."

Milo looked at Ambrose, who gave the slightest shrug.

"That will do, I suppose," Milo said. "Though we better hope it is not a long trek from the exit to Bamyan."

"In that, our luck holds out," Rihyani said with a smile at Ambrose. "As I understand it, our exit from the mountains will bring us out very near Shahr-e Zuhak, an old ruin that is not much more than ten miles from Bamyan. I am glad to see your boots survived, though, because it is rough ground."

Ambrose wiggled his toes in a gnawed patch of the boot's toe.

"They'll serve well enough, I suppose," the bodyguard said, then blushed at Rihyani's beatific smile. "Which means we should get on our way, eh?"

"Suppose so," Milo said, turning back toward the tunnel, gripping the cane so hard his knuckles popped.

"This is insane," Fazihr whined. "For all we know, that thing is waiting for us to stumble into it again, only this time, it will be ready."

"We'll be ready too," Milo said, raising the skull and compelling just enough magic to make the sockets flicker.

"That's far from comforting, *Magus*." The retainer sneered and turned to his mistress. "Imrah, please! I know you are strong-willed, but this is beyond stubborn. We must turn back."

Imrah eyed the disguised ghul with an intensity at odds with her human form, and the force of her glare had Fazihr shrinking back.

"Your cowardice is becoming obnoxious," she growled, the sound no less predatory for her human throat. "If you are so determined to return to Ifreedahm, why don't you scurry back?"

"By myself?" Fazihr gulped, then, seeing the hard gaze of his mistress, looked at the fey. Contessa Rihyani and her companions stared back, faces so still they might have been phosphorescent statues.

Impossibly and hilariously, the cringing ghul glanced at the two humans, his blunt teeth grinding as oily sweat sprang out on his brow.

"Sorry, Fazihr," Milo said flatly. "This *Magus* has business in Bamyan."

"Don't look at me, friend. I'm naked," Ambrose shrugged and nodded at Milo. "Besides, I go where he goes."

Seeing there was nothing for it, Fazihr swore bitterly under his breath and turned to the tunnel stretching back toward Ifreedahm.

"I hope—" he began, but Imrah's patience was at its end.

"Start running!" she snarled, fingers curled so the tips began to bulge and distend with her hidden claws. "Run, or I will tear out your eyes so they can watch me eat the rest of your face!"

Like he'd been scalded by a jet of boiling water, Fazihr yelped and tore down the passage in the direction from which they had just come. Only once he'd rounded a curve and the slap of his feet could no longer be heard did Imrah turn stiffly to the rest of the company.

"I'll take point with the magus," Imrah said, her tone brooking no argument. "Now that we know the creature fears fire, we should be able to keep each other safe."

There was a rustle in the oversize jacket she wore, and she drew out a small parchment envelope. She took out a pinch of brick-red powder and snorted it up both nostrils, then drew in a heavy breath. A fiery glow shone from within the hollow of her throat. Curls of black smoke slid out of her nostrils, and as she spoke to Milo, tiny tongues of flame licked from her lips.

"Shall we?"

The tunnel was as bare and noxious as the passage before, resulting in more of the grinding, expectant marching Milo loathed.

For hours, with hardly a word between them, Milo and Imrah marched, peering between the shades of darkness granted them by the sight-salve. Nothing emerged to challenge them, and they didn't see any more signs of the gelatinous monster, though its stench was ever-present throughout the corridor. The only thing noticeable was the utter lack of mort-scalp, and at this point, it just seemed an insult to Milo that the predatory slime had to not only threaten their lives but also complicate their travel plans. As the miles unfolded in their perpetual slog upward, Milo tried to remind himself that as a conscript in a line infantry regiment, he should have expected long marches to be the norm. He quieted the thought by deciding that expecting and accepting were two different things.

Pressing into four hours since they'd moved away from Ambrose and the fey, they came upon a place where the tunnel opened into a wider, taller chamber. A few feet into the chamber, walls of packed stone were visible, connecting at off angles. A single narrow lane passed between two sections. Walkways and platforms festooned the tops of the walls a dozen feet above.

"This is the sentry post," Imrah breathed, throwing up more licks of flame. "Now, where are the sentries?"

There wasn't a sound except the scuff of their feet on stone and the occasional crackle of Imrah's burning breath. The silence was so complete and Milo strained so hard to hear anything that soon he felt he had gone deaf to all but the scrape of his feet.

"That slime creature," Milo whispered, desperate to hear something. "Could it have killed them?"

The sacrilege of the whispered words hung in the still air, but when nothing struck them down, Imrah shook her head and looked around.

"I don't know," she murmured, her human face looking frightened despite her draconic countenance. "I'm not sure I know anything anymore."

Without warning, she headed down the lane, and Milo scrambled after her. Within five steps, they were among a labyrinthine series of twists, turns, and intersecting lanes between the looming stone walls.

"It certainly smells like the thing was here," Milo spat as the stink closed around them with the nearness of the walls. "Like someone started to clean a latrine and decided to burn it instead."

"It is peculiar, isn't it," Imrah said distractedly, pausing at a nexus where several lanes crossed. Without explanation, she took the leftmost lane, which led to another circuitous route between the fetid walls.

"Please tell me this convoluted design is intentional," Milo requested after losing track of how many turns they'd taken for the second time. "Is this a defensive measure to trap intruders?"

"Trap? No," Imrah said, pausing to sniff the air and wrinkle her nose. "It is a defensive measure, though. All these corridors lead into side tunnels to the surface. All except one."

Milo, having made the foolish mistake of trying to smell what the ghul had smelled on the air, bit back a retching cough after a noseful of the putrid air.

"Oh," he wheezed, finally mastering his gag reflex. "Not a trap, but a diversion."

"Yes, of course," Imrah said distractedly.

They emerged from between the walls in a small chamber that narrowed into another tunnel. The chamber felt different to Milo, and with a start, he realized that his enhanced eyes noticed dust on the floor. He could also taste a difference in the air. It was a refreshing relief after the oppressive stink of the creature, even though it only smelled of sunbaked earth.

Sunbaked earth? Milo thought. *Dear God, we must be close to the surface.*

Milo, having been raised in cities, had never been the type to thrill at the thought of the open sky and the wide, wild world, but he felt a sudden desperate yearning for sun and sky. If Imrah hadn't been there with him, he was certain he would have pelted down the tunnel until he felt Sol's kiss on his cheeks.

"Where are they?" Imrah snarled, turning this way and that in obvious confusion. "It couldn't have taken all of them. There should have been half a dozen sentries stationed here!"

"If some escaped, wouldn't we have met them in the tunnels?" Milo asked, forcing himself to hide the giddy and anxious urge to race outside.

"There might be side passages, secret burrows, and tunnels,"

Imrah said, though her tone conveyed that she wasn't convinced. "Perhaps one is hiding somewhere. Maybe they're all hiding. Besides their absence, we have no reason to think they're dead."

The last words came out as a statement, but Imrah still turned to Milo with a pleading question stamped on her face. This was not the ghul princess he knew, and her obvious discomfort at the death of the sentries struck him. It might only have been because she was wearing the veneer of humanity, but despite himself, he felt pity for her.

"When the thing attacked us," Milo began searching for the proper, delicate words, "I think I might have seen...remains inside it."

Milo remembered the dark, tortured shapes twisting within the layers of slime and shivered. He hoped the movements were only the spasms of sinews and tendons coming undone bit by bit. Such extenuating torture was a fate no creature deserved, not even a ghul.

"Oh," Imrah said, seeming ready to crumple into the fetal position. "Well, I suppose that seals it then."

She turned toward the outward-leading tunnel, head hanging on listless shoulders.

"Did you know any of the sentries here?" Milo asked, still shocked by Imrah's downcast features.

"No," she said tightly, not looking up. "But I'd hoped the thing hadn't murdered more of my people."

Milo nodded and stepped up beside her. He felt as though he should put an arm around her, though with the Imrah he knew, he feared doing that would ensure he never got the arm back. Instead, he stood quietly as something scraped and gnawed at the back of his mind until he finally fished it out.

More of my people?

"Come on," Imrah said softly, the flame on her lips having diminished to thin wisps of smoke. "Let's go confirm the way up is clear, and then we'll go get the others."

Milo nodded but said nothing.

The afternoon sun, just beginning its reddening descent, was a welcoming sight, even with the somber silence they'd adopted as they left the sentry post for the final push.

For several long, pulsing heartbeats, he stood basking in the light. The oppression of the long dark was over, and though the heat soon prickled on his pale cheeks, he savored the burning kiss. He felt the sight-salve peel and crumble away from his lids, but he'd made enough to last him for some time before he'd left Ifreedahm. Nothing seemed able to intrude on that singular moment of communion with the world above.

Then Imrah gurgled with disgust in the back of her throat and spat across the sun-warmed stones. Where the spittle landed, a flash of orange flame went up.

"Ugh," she grumbled, squinting under the hands cupping her brow. "The world above is such a wasteland."

Milo held his pose—chest out, eyes closed—but it was no use. The moment was spoiled, so with a heavy sigh, he looked at the land cooking beneath the late summer sun.

The country was rough—primeval almost, with bare rocks jutting up like spines of stone segregated from the lower, flatter tiers far below where tough grasses, rugged shrubs, and stunted trees grew. A scrabbling path, little more than a track worn by goats and hinds, led from the cave mouth to a ridge-line that wound its long, meandering way down to a collection of crumbling stone walls that seemed to perch on a cliffside.

"That must be the ruins," Imrah noted, skulking back into the shadow of the cave. "If the others followed the pace we set, we can go back and lead them here and make for the ruins just after nightfall."

Milo nodded, turning slowly from the light of the sun to the yawning dark within the cave.

"Assuming they weren't eaten by that thing," Milo muttered darkly, more discouraged by the thought of returning to the dark than fearing for their companions.

"Yes, assuming," Imrah acknowledged, her posture wilting in a manner Milo wasn't accustomed to seeing from her. Milo again noted how much talk of the creature seemed to affect her, but before genuine pity or concern could take root, that nagging question reemerged.

More of my people? Milo thought. *She'd said she had no idea what it was, but then how could the sentries not be the creature's first victims?*

None of this was helping him work up the nerve to go back down under the mountain. Quite the opposite, but it roused his mind and senses, and he felt his eyes narrow as he watched Imrah shuffle back into the dark.

There was something more going on that she wouldn't tell him, so he had to stay ready in case that secret ended up trying to kill him. Given what he'd seen of ghul society so far, he was pretty sure it eventually would.

"Let's get this over with," he muttered, fishing in his pocket for the snuff box that contained his sight-salve.

After anointing his eyes with the dark paste, he joined Imrah in the dark to fetch the rest of the group.

They did not make it out of the cave until well after nightfall, though thankfully, there were no further sightings of the gelatinous monster.

They emerged from the darkness of the cave to the striking world of the shadows of a cloud-speckled moon dappling the mountainside. Without preamble, the contessa and her fey companions took the lead and guided them down the path, which turned out to be far more treacherous than Milo had imagined. In places, it narrowed or widened with the terrain, but the adjustments were not always welcome to those who walked it. Too far out on a wide path and you'd risk sliding halfway down the slope, and too close in would see your ankles snapping between hidden seams and clefts in the rock.

Even with his enhanced sight, Milo was certain that he'd have been injured, possibly even crippled, if it hadn't been for the well-traveled fair folk giving them directions as they went. He wasn't the only one.

Just before the goat track met the ridgeline, Imrah had skirted the inside of a boulder rather than the outside. Some treachery in the ground saw the boulder shift inward as the she-ghul passed, and as wiry and agile as she was under her human guise, she wouldn't have been able to jump clear. Luckily for her, the bronze titan had been behind her, and with one hand, he steadied the boulder, sparing Imrah from being pinned to the wall by a few tons of rock.

Imrah had muttered a half-hearted thanks, at which the towering fey laughed, a sound that sang across the heights and down the hills. Milo might have winced at the sound revealing their position to possible enemies in the area, but it sounded like nothing a human voice could produce. It was like something an ancient god or spirit of the mountain might have emitted, and Milo very much doubted that any living man would have gone looking for its source.

The going was easier on the ridgeline, apart from the stomach-churning vertigo one experienced when looking to the right more than two paces. The expanse below might have been beautiful to see in the day time, the sun-painted cliffs plunging downward before blooming into pools of greenery in the valley below, but not moving along them at night. A low, hungry wind groaning along the edge reminded you how close to a fatal plummet you were, and it seemed that all it would take was a sudden storm to sweep you from the ridge to your doom.

When they reached the tumbled-down walls at the edge of Shahr-e Zuhak, the Red City, Milo thought he would feel incredible relief to be finished with such a perilous trek, but that was not the case. Even with his alchemically-enhanced vision, the ruin seemed to be a desolate and haunted place, especially in the feeble moonlight.

Ancient buildings clustered along the cliff face, with so many hollowed out windows and doorways that the whole edifice was like Argus's petrified corpse. The whole forsaken citadel seemed husk-like, and even as they moved down the dusty streets, Milo couldn't help remembering that he now knew strange, horrible things moved in the dark. The realization struck even deeper when he remembered that there were things even the monsters didn't know about.

Fingers closed tight around his cane, and his other hand braced on the butt of his pistol, Milo walked as softly as he could, eyes swiveling this way and that.

So tightly wound were his nerves at the thought of a supernatural horror springing on them that when his ears registered the crack of a rifle shot, he felt relief despite the whine of an angry bullet passing inches from his head.

18

A RETURN

"Move and die," came the warning in German.

After the sound of the rifle's discharge, Milo had never been so happy to hear someone calling to him from the dark. The glowing feeling vanished quickly, however, when he remembered that the fey were in his company. When they'd set out, they'd planned to explain the two disguised ghuls, now one, as local guides hired to help them reach Bamyan after they were separated from the 33rd. Explaining how they had also acquired three glowing beings, one who stood nearly three meters tall, was something else entirely.

He supposed they were lucky the soldiers hadn't shot them on sight.

"We're German," Milo called, raising his hands over his head. "We're German, don't shoot."

He was pleased to see that Imrah and Ambrose were following his lead. He wouldn't have been surprised, but he would have been irritated if one of them was shot.

Milo *was* surprised that when he looked around for the fey, they were nowhere to be seen. For a brief second, his mind revolted against the idea that towering, glowing beings could simply vanish, and he questioned if his memories of the fey were real or just figments of his imagination. He felt a dull pressure in the back of his mind to accept this conclusion, the suggestion so subtle he might not have noticed it if he hadn't spent the last several days experiencing the various wiles of supernaturals. He hadn't been formally introduced to fey magic, but he was fairly certain he was experiencing his first brush with it.

"Get down on your knees," a voice from the dark demanded.

Milo had almost sunk down to one knee when Ambrose whispered to him hoarsely.

"You're a Blackcoat, Magus."

Facing God knew how many hidden guns, Milo didn't much feel like the looming specter of authority, especially not in his current shabby state, but Ambrose had a point. If he wanted to be taken seriously, he'd better act the part.

Milo straightened and very slowly lowered his arms, tucking the cane like a swagger stick under his arm, just like he'd seen Blackcoat bigwigs do.

"Who's in charge here?" Milo bawled, thankful the long coat hid his trembling legs.

"Get down on your knees *now*!" the voice roared back.

"Are you blind or just stupid?" Milo snarled, gesturing first at his coat and then at his cap. "I hope to God and the Kaiser that you know what you're doing, *mein Kamerad*."

The silence stretched, soft wind whistling between the gap-toothed stones.

Milo, holding as still as possible, let his eyes rove the ruin, and as the seconds stretched, he began to pick out the shapes of men hunkered among the stones. Their position, as far as he could tell, was exceptional. They'd located themselves among the ruined buildings and dilapidated wall so that they covered the approach from the rear of the crumbling citadel with intersecting lines of fire at various elevations. With this layering, there seemed no risk of crossfire, and any direct advancement to any of the forward-most positions invited multiple angles of attack.

Milo was willing to bet several valuable body parts these were Federated troops, which was both good and bad. Good in that they were less likely to shoot him but bad in that if they did start shooting, they were unlikely to miss.

"Identify yourself!" demanded a different voice farther back in the defensive formation. It was rougher and thinner, as though worn to fibers from a lifetime of shouting. Milo knew a career non-commissioned officer when he heard one.

Straightening a little more, Milo raised his voice to reach to the back of the formation.

"Milo Volkohne, Nicht-KAT," he called sharply. "Returning with a report for Captain Lokkemand."

Milo thought he heard a murmur among the stones, and it didn't sound friendly. Keeping his spine ramrod-straight, he stared toward where the voice had come from, hoping the answer wasn't a storm of bullets.

"Captain Lokkemand came in attached to the 41st," the gruff voice called back. "Why weren't you with those East Prussian boys when they came in."

Milo knew he was being tested, but the specifics of how to respond gave him pause. They'd all been with the 33rd, who were also East Prussians, but what if after the attack and Milo's disappearance, the captain had moved to another regiment?

"When I was with Lokkemand, he was attached to the 33rd," Milo said, deciding to stick as close to the truth as he could. "If he was reassigned to the 41st, this is the first I'm hearing of it."

More silence, but no bullets. That, to Milo's mind, was winning.

"So, you got sent off on some *gruselig* operation then?" the voice asked, the voice as neutral as its gravelly nature permitted.

"Nothing so clandestine," Milo lied, thankful for years of

practice. "I was taken from the 33rd in a night raid, but I escaped, and I've been making my way back to my commanding officer."

There was the scuff of boots on the dusty stones, and a soft click as a harness or belt buckle struck stone.

"Who are these ragged people with you?"

Milo compelled his lips not to smile. They were through. Unless Milo or one of his companions did something incredibly stupid, they were going to be taken back to camp. Then it was only a matter of time before the grinding wheels of military protocol dragged him to Lokkemand.

"The man in disarray is my personal aide," Milo explained, nodding at Ambrose before gesturing at Imrah. "The woman is a local who offered to be our guide when we escaped. I promised her a reward for helping us get back safely."

The silence stretched again, but it was different somehow, more pensive. Finally, out of the doorway of a nearly intact three-story ruin came a slight man in a dark Federated uniform. He had a pistol in his hand, but it was pointed down as he walked across the cracked but venerable cobbles of Shahr-e Zuhak. Dark eyes glittered in long, lupine features as he stepped into a bright patch of moonlight. He surveyed the ragged remains of the company, then his teeth glittered in the moonlight.

"Your aide's a big one, isn't he?" the sergeant said with a thrust of his chin at Ambrose.

"If you're impressed now," the big man called in a bluff, jolly voice, "wait until you get me out of the cold."

There were chuckles from some of the sentries, and the non-com who held their lives in his leathery hands cracked a smile.

"Wouldn't want to miss that." He nodded. "All right, let's get you sorted."

Sergeant Major Vogt of the Royal Bavarian Infantry Lifeguards Regiment struck Milo as a man who was every bit as formidable as the name of his regiment, despite his small stature and slight build. He moved among his men with the easy confidence Milo imagined an old wolf might have in a pack he'd whelped. Every man deferred to him with ready respect.

Given this, it was no surprise that things moved fairly quickly for Milo and his companions. Ambrose was given the biggest jacket and pair of trousers they had on hand, then two soldiers and a lance corporal escorted them to Bamyan for debriefing. The city the German army had occupied was sixteen or so kilometers north from Zuhak, and the road winding down from the mountains had been kept in good order.

Halfway down in the gray light of the predawn, they'd met more Bavarians from the 9th Royal Artillery who were taking a truck down to Bamyan to get some supplies. To help their countrymen, the men from the 9th invited them to hop into the back, ensuring they moved even more quickly down the mountains. Any attempts at conversation were squelched by the rumble of the engine, but it provided Milo and Ambrose an opportunity to take quick naps as they rumbled along. For her part, Imrah seemed intent on watching everything with an almost feral intensity.

"It's all right," Milo called to the disguised ghul, remembering that they were still playing at her being a guide. "These are the good guys."

Imrah looked at him with incredulity, as though he'd suggested it was quiet or the sky was made of spun sugar.

"No such thing," she hissed, her voice barely audible over the chug of the diesel engine.

"Fair enough," Milo admitted, and leaned closer so as not to be overheard by the others. "What happened to the contessa?"

"They're fey." She shrugged. "Apart from extracting a promise from them, which is nearly impossible, nothing can keep them where they don't want to be."

"That sounds useful," Milo said more admiringly than he intended. "I could think of a lot of uses for that trick."

The hunger to know more stirred somewhere between his mind and his belly, despite the fatigue.

"Maybe," Imrah replied coldly. "But you'd have to learn it from a fey, and you might as well ask the wind to teach you to fly."

Milo gave Imrah a teasing smile and winked at her.

"Why, princess, if I didn't know better, I would say you sounded jealous of the contessa."

Imrah clacked her less than impressive human teeth in Ghulish fury before turning away from him in outrage.

Milo shrugged and settled in to contemplate possible tutelage with the likes of the contessa. Somehow the memory of her seemed sweeter than before, and again Milo felt the enchanting pressure at the back of his mind. Like the soft but heavy current of a slow river, it invited him to go where it led. More magic, apparently woven into his memories of the fey. Milo felt a prickle of danger at the thought, but that only seemed to make learning such magic more enticing. He'd only scratched the surface of necromantic alchemy, and there was still so much to learn, it was dizzying.

With his mind occupied, his body found time to enjoy the rocking vibration of the vehicle, lulling him into a shallow but appreciated slumber.

He awoke to bright, burning sunlight stabbing into the bed of the truck as their ride came to a juddering stop, then with a rough shift of gears, began to back up in a wide sweep. Milo raised a hand to shield his eyes, but the invasion of blinding light was cut off by the shadow of the building their ride was sliding back toward. A large pavilion loomed before him, its old timbers jutting from weathered stone speaking of a structure that had served long before the snarl and puff of modern machines had come to squat beneath it. In a glance, Milo saw that it was serving as a centralized motor pool for the various regiments operating out of Bamyan, but the bustle seemed at odds with the aged structure. It was a venerable shelter, more accustomed to the hawking calls of merchants and the smells of asses and oxen.

After their ride came to a stop and they clambered out, Milo noted he could still smell the sharp, musky scents of beasts. After a few minutes, he understood why as he followed their escorts through the hive-like bustle of the motor pavilion, crossed a dusty street of packed earth, and then walked by an expansive stable.

Unlike the pavilion, the stable was a recent addition to this part of the town, a ramshackle collection of scrap wood and metal that had been assembled rather hastily. Milo at first thought the equines were domestic misplaced by German forces, but as they moved past the yard connected to the stable, every creature he saw was wearing a harness with Imperial and regimental colors, though he didn't recognize the latter.

"You're still using horses?" Milo asked. In Europe, though equines for both combat and logistical support had been fairly common with all belligerents at the outset of the war, they'd been almost completely replaced in the last decade. A combination of technological advances and the fact that arable land was used exclusively for human and not horse fodder meant horses were a sign of war's onset, an anachronism shoved out as the war-machine ground on.

"*Jah.*" The lance corporal, a darkly freckled man named Beck, nodded. "In this country of crags and goat tracks, a pony is about the only thing better than your own two feet."

Milo hadn't thought about it, but it was a fair point. From what little he'd seen of the country, the respectable road leading down from Shahr-e Zuhak was the exception rather than the rule.

"Wasn't always that way, of course," Beck continued as they strode down the street, boots scuffing the packed earth. "The whole command had quite the shock when we moved on from Isonzo. We still get to shoot the occasional Italian, but it's the old four-foots that get most of our boys and their kit where they need to be."

One of the soldiers piped up, a youth who seemed even younger than Milo, his lip speckled with juvenile peach fuzz. Milo couldn't remember his name.

"Not that we have to worry about shooting the Romans anymore," he squeaked. His voice cracked, but he hardly seemed to notice. "Now that they've turned tail. It's all Brits and their colonials now!"

"We'll shoot whoever's there," Beck said, a mild note of reproof in his tone. "Otherwise, we best leave such matters for the Rider."

"White Rider always where he needs to be." The other soldier, a sour-faced man named Hort, muttered the words like an incantation.

"Always," the fuzzy-lipped youth agreed solemnly.

Milo looked at Ambrose, who shrugged, then turned back to see Beck looking at him, his expression between a sheepish grin and a defensive scowl. The look did nothing to help his complexion.

"My apologies, sir," Beck said stiffly. "The Rider, or sometimes the White Rider, is our name for Major General Epp. He was regimental commander for our own Royal Bavarian Lifeguard before he rose to command the entire division here on this branch of the southeastern front."

"Funny thing, him being called Rider," Ambrose mused. "You're infantry grunts, and in all my years, I've never heard a footslogger wanting to take on a cavalryman's title."

Some half-heard but distinctly unfriendly mutters rose from

the two soldiers, but Lance Corporal Beck silenced them with a look.

"In all your aide's years," Beck said while pointedly not looking at Ambrose, "I doubt he's ever seen the likes of the major general, especially on that day that saw us marching right into Bamyan. If that old goose Viermann had been listened to, we would not have taken the opportunity to seize more ground in a week than has been taken in years in this God-forsaken country."

Milo wasn't privy to the intricacies of Federated command structure, much less the details of what had happened on this front, but if he understood correctly, this Epp had disobeyed orders and gotten a promotion out of it. Not only that, but Epp seemed to have won a following with his audacity to boot. Such things made Milo nervous, and he suddenly had a burning desire to report to Lokkemand and get back to his mission.

"Well, you boys are lucky then," Milo said. "Such victories are rare nowadays."

There was a low thrum in the air over their heads, and Milo looked up to see a war zeppelin, those great sky-leviathans, churning through the clear air. Its propellers were throbbing almost lazily as it gained altitude, a king climbing languorously to his lofty throne.

"We're not done yet," Beck said, his eyes flashing as one finger pointed at the zeppelin. "Why do you think those are humming around?"

Milo could guess, but since he was feeling more and more inclined to be rude to the excitable NCO, he just shrugged. He felt Ambrose should have subtly complimented him on being so tactful, but one look at the big man told Milo he was having his own struggles with keeping things civil.

"We're not going to be staying in Bamyan for very long," the lance corporal said, a hard look stealing across his features.

They marched on in a silence Milo appreciated. He couldn't quite put his finger on what it was about the Bavarian Lifeguards that struck a sour note with him, but he felt it all the same. Something nagged at the back of his mind when they spoke, not the words so much as the way they said them. It was also in their eyes, an almost manic shine. As they headed across a broad road, pausing as horse-drawn artillery pieces passed, Milo watched the faces of the men passing them, and he thought he realized what it was.

Fanaticism.

These men moved with an energy and purpose that went beyond the brisk economy of professional soldiers about their work. Every man seemed gripped by frantic energy, at once looking like he might collapse into rapture or explode into rage. Milo felt as though his skin had tightened, and he forced himself to keep looking ahead to keep from looking around in horror.

Once he saw it, Milo was amazed he'd struggled to put his finger on it. It was the same look he'd seen on the faces of the young men who'd been in Roland's gang. Milo knew that because he'd seen it and heard it in that desperate band of young men, men who'd done incredible violence at Roland's word. Some of them, barely more than children, had walked smiling into blades and bullets at a word, right before Milo's eyes. He knew it even more intimately than that, even though it ached like a deep scar to remember.

Milo knew that gleam because he'd seen it in his reflection in those early days. Having drunk from the cup, Milo knew what it meant, and how such things should have been feared. The things he'd been willing to do haunted him almost as much as the things he had done.

The sun was seeping through his clothes, and Milo felt an irritable itch that had more to do with his mind than his body.

Unable to stop himself, Milo stole a glance over his shoulder at the younger soldier as they stepped off the road and made their way across a lot of crushed rock. The glance lasted only a second before Beck gave a grunt and pointed across the lot. They were headed toward a squat brick building surrounded by a barbed fence as tall as the two-story building.

A tug in his chest of something that might have been grief or maybe pity as he thought of the youth behind him. He thought about looking for an opportunity to take the young man aside and get him to come to his senses, but the scheme died barely formed.

Milo remembered what his own reaction had been, and that was someone he had reason to listen to. Milo interfering could only end worse.

The guards at the fence gate asked their perfunctory questions, but Beck saw things sorted out quickly. It seemed the sergeant major had a reputation that opened doors.

At the guard's advice, they headed around the exterior of the building toward the rear. The Nicht-KAT station was in the back under a series of canvas tents so they could carry out their business without interference or eavesdropping from the various officers, enlisted, and civilian support staff that passed through the main command hub.

"Best to keep clear of the Black Kats, eh?" The guard gave a chuckle that vanished as Milo straightened to give him an arch look. To complete the display, Ambrose gave a sub-audible growl in his chest as they strode past the paling guard.

"Black Kats?" Milo muttered as they rounded the corner of the building, pitching his voice so only Ambrose could hear.

"Fits, I suppose." Ambrose shrugged. "Hate to tell you this, Magus, but you haven't exactly been a good luck charm."

"It's not like you..." Milo paused, realizing with a sinking feeling in his stomach that his claim would have been wholly untrue.

The entrance to the tent had two more guards stationed outside it. Without invitation, Beck stepped forward to make their introductions.

"Exactly." Ambrose grunted softly as Beck spoke to the

guards. "Three times in nearly a hundred and twenty years, then inside a month of meeting you, I'm up to four, and not without a few close calls."

Milo spluttered and then watched as one guard stepped inside to get clearance for their entry.

"What's going on?" Imrah hissed as she slid up next to both men. "What is taking so long?"

"When we met with your father, we had to wait to be introduced," Milo said as both men looked over their shoulders at her. "Hardly seems worth getting jumpy about."

"My father," Imrah sniffed, "is the most powerful ghul in the entire Underworld. Your commanding officer is part of an organization named after a creature little better than the vermin it eats."

"KAT doesn't—" Ambrose began before Milo cut him off.

"You're just bent out of shape because of all the humans," he grumbled. "Oh, how the tables have turned."

Imrah choked back a snarl and leaned forward so she was practically whispering in their ears.

"If they had even an inkling of what I am, they'd be piling on logs for the fire," she hissed. "I think I have every right to be nervous."

"Whereas in Ifreedahm, they kept trying to eat us," Ambrose remarked with a dry chuckle. "Right?"

"Hard to argue with," Milo agreed with a nod.

Imrah made to argue but snapped her mouth shut with a click and took a step back to sulk properly. Ambrose turned back to the tent, but Milo watched her for a moment longer. With her chin outthrust and her nose in the air, she was a haughty figure, but he couldn't pretend that with the sun shining on her olive skin, she wasn't rather fetching.

Fetching in her stolen skin, he reminded himself with a shake of his head. *Whatever she looks like now, remember her beauty is literally only skin-deep.*

Milo turned back to watch for the tent guard's return. Ambrose was muttering to himself.

"Probably not very tactful to be needling my instructor like that."

Ambrose gave him a wry grin as the tent entrance flapped open.

"Bah, builds the relationship," the bodyguard said as the guard beckoned them forward.

"Let's hope," Milo said out the side of his mouth as they moved into the tent. "If I get extra homework, you're pitching in."

Inside the tent, several collapsible desks had been arranged into a miniature typing pool where two men and three women in uniform hammered away without looking up. Beyond them, four square tables had been arranged into an even larger square, and a map had been spread out. At the farthest corner of this table, another typewriter sat alongside piled accordion files and a bottle of schnapps. Looming over the table was Captain Lokkemand, his cheeks stubbled with the beginnings of a fiery beard.

He looked up as the tent flap closed behind the trio, motioning impatiently for them to join him at the map table. They acquiesced, moving around the intent typists to stand across the table from the brooding officer. The map showed both Afghanistan and neighboring Pakistan. There were many markers around Bamyan, with a few trailing north and west. They might have been troop dispositions, but it wasn't clear, and the little paper notes under each marker were of no help, having been written in scribbled shorthand.

"Captain?" Milo said tentatively after they had waited for several minutes.

"What are you doing here?" Lokkemand drawled, not looking up from the map he was glowering at. "You were supposed to be in training. You can't possibly be done already?"

"The situation has changed," Milo began carefully. "I was sent here by my instructors."

Lokkemand looked up fleetingly, his eyes cutting sharply across the three of them before returning to the map.

"Don't tell me you failed already," Lokkemand said, heaving a heavy sigh. "It would win my bet with the colonel, but it would create a good deal more work than the bottle of aquavit I am going to get."

"No, sir," Milo said, fighting to keep his tone level after the revelation of the bet. "My studies were progressing exceptionally."

Imrah made a sound in the back of her throat, but Milo ignored her.

"The change occurred when zeppelins began flying over a certain mountain," Milo continued, looking at the map to find the mountain under which Ifreedahm sat. "When our allies saw German zeppelins over it, they became nervous. They insisted I come personally to sort things out."

Lokkemand looked up from the map and met Milo's gaze for the first time since entering the tent. His eyes were haggard, his skin was pale almost to looking gray, and his cheeks were on the verge of gaunt. Apparently life in Afghanistan did not sit well with the formerly handsome and strapping captain.

"What do they want?" he asked stiffly.

"They want reassurances that the arrangements made with them still stand," Milo replied, fighting the urge to cross his arms irritably. "The plans, which I know nothing about, even though they are the entire operation."

"The situation necessitates your ignorance," Lokkemand said flatly, then reached for the schnapps. "Trust me, Volkohne, you're better off not knowing these sorts of things."

After a hearty pull on the bottle, a little color returned to Lokkemand's face, and his eyes sharpened enough for him to realize he didn't recognize one of the members of the assembled company.

"Who is she?" he grunted, eyeing Imrah appraising, Milo found himself not appreciating it.

Imrah looked archly at Milo and nodded.

"This is Imrah Marid, a high-ranking member of the allies' command structure," Milo explained. "She's here to continue my education, as well as to ensure the interests of our allies are seen to."

"Really?" the captain asked, then took another drink before sizing her up once more. He turned back to Milo with a questioning look. "Do they all look so...mundane?"

"It is a disguise, you inebriated slab of meat," Imrah replied scornfully, her fingers curling reflexively. "Now, are things still in place for the arrangements you made with my father or not?"

Lokkemand seemed to be surprised she could talk more than anything else, his eyes darting from the seething Imrah to the bemused Milo and back.

"Father?" he murmured, then his eyes moved toward the map again. "The situation may require that we renegotiate the particulars of the service we're to render."

Milo imagined the look Imrah gave the captain would set a lesser man ablaze.

"What did you say?" she asked, her voice on the brittle edge of dangerous.

To his credit, Lokkemand met the disguised ghul's glare evenly. It probably helped that disguise made her look far less threatening.

"Please look at the map," he said coolly as he picked up a measuring stick that was leaning against the table.

Imrah complied, but the look on her face was all the warning any of them needed. This had better be good.

"This is where the battleline was previously," Lokkemand said, using the ruler as a pointer to indicate a dotted line on the map. The line started in a place called Chaghcharān and ran down a jagged path along the cusp of a mountain range designated B. Turkistan before terminating in a place called Sarpol.

"Our forces have been gridlocked along this line for nearly a decade," the captain continued. "At first we sent only exploratory forces. They met hard resistance, but the coalition of Italian, British, and local forces were too disjointed to launch an effective counterattack. The assumption was this country was going to be a skirmishing buffer between us and the British holdings farther south and east."

Here he indicated Pakistan and the north arm of India.

"But after the victories against the Italians in Isonzo and the subsequent annexation of Greece by the Austro-Hungarians, eyes turned toward pushing the boundaries here," Lokkemand explained as he again pointed to the dotted battle line. "But it was no use, until within the last three months the enemy line seemed to crumble. First the Afghans, then the Italians, and finally the British abandoned their positions."

Lokkemand sighed and stepped back to drain the schnapps.

"Command couldn't understand what was happening, and the intelligence reports they were receiving weren't making any sense. Entire regiments routed overnight, sometimes with both men and materiel going missing. It was assumed it was preparation for a flanking maneuver, or maybe some sort of ploy to attempt to draw committed forces out of position. Orders were to hold position and wait for intelligence to thoroughly assess the situation."

"But they didn't count on the White Rider," Milo said, seeing the story unfold in his mind's eye. "Epp seized the opportunity despite his orders."

"I see you've already heard about the Bavarian," Lokkemand said, massaging his temples. "Yes, Major Franz Ritter von Epp threw his regiment at the open lines like a hungry dog on a bone. If the enemy had been baiting the hook, it would have caught in his greedy throat. As it was, he became a hero."

Ambrose shuffled a little and crossed his arms, a look of consternation on his face.

"You have something to say?" the captain asked sharply.

Ambrose looked at Lokkemand coolly, but then after staring for a second, his gaze softened, and the look he gave the fraying officer was one of pity.

"I've never known general staff or any military command to celebrate anyone who takes to ignoring orders. Why does this Epp get a pass, much less a pat on the back?"

Lokkemand, who looked ready to rally for a fight with Ambrose, wilted and started looking around for something. A chair, one sized to better accommodate his stature, was a few steps away, and he sank into it with a groan before continuing. Perspiration had begun to bead on his brow.

"Because Epp wasn't a nobody to begin with." Lokkemand grunted as he wrenched at his collar. "He's Ritter von Epp because he won the Grand Cross earlier in the war, along with the *Pour le Mérite* for his work in Isonzo. Epp's star was rising some time ago, and the general staff sent him down here to stall his advancement."

Lokkemand finally pulled his uniform collar open, but his face was already flushed in a blotchy pattern.

"Are you all right, Captain?" Milo asked, noting that his commanding officer's face shone with sweat. "Are you sick?"

"I'm fine," Lokkemand wheezed in an unconvincing manner as he slumped against his chair. "Someone get me something to drink."

"Water for the captain!" Ambrose barked, and one of the typists sprang to the task.

"I said something to drink," the officer spat weakly, his arms dropping bonelessly into his lap. "Do I look like a fish?"

"You look unwell," Milo said. "Have you been checked out by a doctor?"

"I said I'm fine," Lokkemand replied icily, his gaze sharpening to fix Milo with a warning look before he lolled his head against the back of his chair. "Now, where is that damned drink?"

"Why would they want Epp's career to stall?" Ambrose asked as the typist arrived with a canteen and an unlabeled brown bottle sealed with a cork.

"It's all I could find," she said apologetically as she laid them on the map table.

"He's drunk everything else," the typist whispered to Milo as she withdrew.

"They want Epp to stall," said Lokkemand before he knocked the canteen aside with a clumsy swing. "Because he's part of a growing number in the ranks who are developing rather radical ideas."

He lunged forward to wrap both hands around the brown bottle as though it were his only security in the midst of a wracking storm.

"Is he seriously about to become even more drunk?" Imrah asked, staring at Lokkemand with shocked, bulging eyes. "While on duty?"

Milo fought back the urge to comment on her father's predilections and settled for shushing her with a wave of his hand

"Radical ideas?" Milo asked, his brow furrowing even as he felt Imrah's gaze boring into his back. "Like what?"

The cork was wrenched free, and he got a potent whiff of something whose smell was between alcohol and gasoline vapors.

"Like this war should be won already," Lokkemand said, grimacing as he put the bottle to his lips. "Like our *great and glorious Empire* would be victorious by now if not for certain *impure* elements holding it back. If only the *honest and true patriots, good Germans*, rose up, we'd have a Reich like none before, a Reich with no end."

Milo felt a chill run up his spine and twist in his gut. As a

Russian born orphan in Dresden, he could hear the silent sirens as keenly as any.

Lokkemand threw his head back and sucked down two mouthfuls of the noxious liquor before coming up for air. The smell of the stuff on his hot, panting breath was not much better than the fumes emerging from the bottle. After the drink, Lokkemand curled in on himself as though bracing under the effects of the liquor.

"They do know that before the Russians fell, the war was almost lost, don't they?" Ambrose asked, sharp incredulity knitting his features. "The fact that the Germans and the Austro-Hungarians are still fighting is some kind of evil miracle."

Lokkemand took a few small sips, wincing after each one, before he answered.

"All these bastards know is that they are tired of fighting but can't stand losing," the captain muttered, his words beginning to slur. "They can't admit defeat, but they know thingz don't look like they're winning. Zo they cry and beat their cheztz for *reform* with one hand and work mizchief with the other."

"If things fail, it's because the status quo held them back." Milo nodded, seeing the low cunning of the position. "If things succeed, they'll claim it is because they defied orders and did what they had to."

The bottle took several more draining hits as Milo pieced things together, and like a stupefying potion, the bitter tension began to leak out of Lokkemand. He settled deeper into his chair, the bottled-clutching hand resting in his lap while the other hung limp in the air.

"Ekzactly." Lokkemand coughed, noxious spittle on his chin. "And who do they keep courting, eh? What branch of zervice zitz just outzide normal command ztructurez, with a reputation for zecretz and conzpiraciez?"

Ambrose and Milo exchanged looks, neither needing to say

the obvious: Non-Conventional Application of Tactics. These radicals were sniffing around Nicht-KAT.

"What does Colonel Jorge say?" Milo asked, feeling the urge to look over his shoulder. "He has to know, and Nicht-KAT is everything to him. He doesn't seem like the type to take this sort of thing lying down."

Lokkemand snorted, then laughed sloppily.

"You really think Nicht-KAT means anything to him?" Lokkemand asked with a giggle as he leaned precariously toward Milo. "Anything compared to *you*?"

Milo lurched back from the drunken captain, only partly to avoid his reeking breath.

"What does that mean?" Milo snapped.

Lokkemand slouched back into his chair, both arms dangling now, the brown bottle in nerveless, sweaty fingers.

"Maybe we should see about getting the captain to his bunk?" Ambrose suggested, gently placing his hand on Milo's shoulder. "He's not feeling well."

Milo shook off the hand, knowing it was only because Ambrose let him as he moved to stand over the captain.

"Damn your eyes, Lokkemand!" Milo snarled loud enough that every typewriter in the tent fell silent. "What does that mean?"

Lokkemand looked up at Milo, his face splitting into a wide, despairing imitation of a grin.

"It means my instructions are to play the whore with these wolves and cooperate in any way I can, as long as it keeps your operation free."

Lokkemand let the bottle drop as one long hand snaked forward with viperish speed to snare Milo by the front of his coat. Before Milo knew what was happening, he was dragged down so the captain's voice hissed directly into his ear.

"He's betting everything, *everything*, on you," Lokkemand gurgled. "Even it means my damned soul!"

Ambrose hauled Milo back as Lokkemand looked on with bright, unfocused eyes, his features stretched into a hideous smile.

"So there it is, Volkohne." He giggled maniacally. "Welcome back to the world of manmade monsters!"

19

AN UNDERSTANDING

"I still don't get it," Milo muttered as he paced the room, boots scuffing the bare floor. "How does any of this make sense?"

They'd been given respectably-sized but utilitarian quarters not far from the main road. The furnishings were spartan or so unfamiliar as to be useless, but none of them was going to complain. It was the largest structure in what amounted to an abandoned neighborhood, functionally sequestering them from the rest of the town and the army. This, combined with a large basement beneath the house, made it the ideal location for Milo's training to continue.

True to form, Ambrose had begun to take stock of what could be done in regards to preparing something to eat. Imrah had scuttled to the basement to make "preparations," leaving Milo with his reading. He couldn't bring himself to fish out the codices just yet.

"Is that rhetorical?" Ambrose called from the other room.

"Yes," Milo shouted back irritably, but then thought better of it. "Well, maybe. Do you have something useful to share?"

Ambrose peeked around the doorway.

"That will depend very much on what is vexing you, my good

wizard," Ambrose replied with a look of serious concern. "What doesn't make any sense?"

"What Lokkemand said, obviously," Milo snapped, pausing in his pacing to give the bodyguard a dirty look. "I understand he's a drunk, but what business is he rambling about, blaming me for Jorge's decision to have him work alongside some rebels in the army?"

"Seems fairly simple," Ambrose said, ducking back into the kitchen, where he raised his voice to be heard. "You're the only wizard ever, so you need time to learn, and Jorge is going to give you that time no matter what it takes."

"How does working with that kind of people buy us time?" Milo demanded.

"Because conspiracies, even unmagical ones, work much harder at isolating enemies and potential enemies than they do friends," Ambrose called back. "Exposing Nicht-KAT exposes them, and Jorge knows that."

Milo supposed it made a kind of sense, but the idea of Lokkemand blaming him for the loss of his soul caught and tore at Milo's psyche on multiple levels.

"You seem to know an awful lot about this cloak and dagger business," Milo growled, knowing he sounded petulant and not caring at the moment. "If you were the witch, things would be going a lot smoother, I bet."

"But I'm not," Ambrose hollered. "Now, stop whining about being the chosen one and do your homework!"

Milo tried and failed to keep the smile off his face as he grudgingly surrendered and snatched up his bag.

He drew out the codices, and the smile faded from his face. Only hours ago, he'd been aching to dive back into his studies, but now the sheaves of parchment felt like lead in his hands. Search as he might within himself, he couldn't find that hungry spark, that longing to know. The longer he stared at the codices, the more he felt a fathomless ennui crawling up his body. It wasn't just that he was distracted by what the captain had said, but he actually didn't want to read them, and the thought of doing so sapped him.

What was wrong with him? What had changed?

After staring at them for a while longer, Milo realized the truth.

Ambrose was not only right that he was whining, but he'd been leading him to a point, intentional or otherwise. Milo realized he was fixated on what Lokkemand had said because for the first time, responsibility was settling over him, and he hated how it felt. Milo hated the idea of Jorge hanging everything on him, even Lokkemand's conscience and stability. He hated thinking that if he didn't learn things quick enough, didn't master magic of some kind in time, everything would come apart. The work and lives of so many hung on Nicht-KAT, and if he acknowledged that, he could take it a trembling step farther and remember why Jorge was betting so much on him; the War. Colonel Jorge had bet on Milo being the one who could end it, which if true, meant every misstep or failure meant the War lasted longer and more people died needlessly.

Like a mountain was settling on his shoulders, Milo sank to the floor, still clutching the codices.

"How am I going to do this?" he gasped, his eyes staring through pages of parchment at a yawning gulf threatening to open before him and swallow him.

"Simple," Ambrose called, still shouting in a jocular tone from the kitchen. "You open to the first page and read. Once you get to the end of that one, turn the page and read the next."

Milo lifted *Awakening Moro*, and the effort felt like lifting a bucket of cement.

"Far as I know," Ambrose chuckled, mostly to himself, "all any of us can do is the next thing, right?"

"The next thing," Milo whispered to himself, staring at the spidery script.

AARON D. SCHNEIDER & MICHAEL ANDERLE

Maybe Ambrose, however unwittingly, was right.

Milo couldn't end the War, couldn't save Nicht-KAT, couldn't even rescue Captain Lokkemand from his conscience. What he could do right now was read. Read and study, then maybe eat whatever Ambrose was concocting before Imrah emerged to lead him through another lesson. That was what was in front of him. That was what was next.

Right where he'd crumpled to the floor, Milo settled into a more comfortable position and began reading *Awakening Moro*, not even looking up to see Ambrose peeking from the kitchen to smile at him.

"Wake up."

Milo started with a sharp intake of breath and looked up into darkness. He had a vague impression of someone standing over him, but little else. He felt the stone floor underneath, and his joints gave a small series of crackles as he sat up.

"What's going on?"

He remembered eating with Ambrose and then going back to finish *Awakening Moro*. He'd wrapped up the abridged text, his head swimming with concepts of alchemical combination and necromantic catalyzation as he scooped up the next codex. He must have fallen asleep very early into *Spectral Ruminations: A Guide to Shades and Their Permutations* because he remembered next to nothing about the text.

"Imrah?" he asked and then gave a long yawn. "Is that you?"

"It's time for lessons to resume." The voice confirmed his suspicion. "My preparations are complete, and it is time we begin in earnest."

"Earnest?" Milo yawned again, then scooped up the codices he'd fallen asleep on top of. "What were we doing before this?"

"Testing you," she said simply, then hissed a low syllable.

The room was bathed with light from the miniature eye sockets on Milo's cane.

"I thought testing came after you learned something," Milo muttered as he climbed to his feet. "Not before."

Imrah's face, lit by the witchlight, was positively terrifying.

"Consider it an initial evaluation," she said, grinning wickedly. "Now that I know what you are capable of, I must push you to the brink. That starts with you meeting someone."

"Lucky me." Milo sighed, trying to remember this was the next thing. "Lead on, Professor."

With a growing sense of foreboding, Milo followed Imrah, who carried the lit skull cane to the stairwell down into the basement. Milo's boots thumped on the wooden floorboards, and he found it hard not to wonder what he would meet in the basement. He told himself Ambrose wouldn't let anything too dangerous show up, but Ambrose had already proven less than infallible. As stairs creaked underfoot, Milo allowed some small part of his mind to remember every story of Butzemann and Babay or whatever other fearful figment children could whisper about at night. He tried to dismiss the nagging murmurs, but he'd learned that faeries were real recently, so why not them?

In fact, as he thought about it, he imagined the stories of child-snatching goblins and kobolds that vanished underground could have easily been about ghuls. The thought made him shiver.

His feet landed on the packed earth at the bottom of the stairs, and Milo felt a rush of pressure against his mind and soul. There was magic, potent and tangible, in the basement. As he moved to follow Imrah, the air thickened until it almost felt like wading.

The basement was lit by spectral blue fires in bottles hanging from the cobwebbed floor joists, revealing tables littered with ingredients, along with what might have been drying racks made of bone strung with sinew. In the corner farthest from the stairs, seven bowls, each full of amethyst flame, were arranged in a loose circle around a patch of quivering darkness.

"Where did all this come from?" Milo asked, remembering that the ghul had left Ifreedahm with only a satchel slung over her shoulder.

"All in good time," Imrah answered cryptically.

With a cluck of her tongue, Imrah dismissed the light from the skull and left the cane lying on a table as she moved toward the undulating patch of night in the corner. Milo made to pick it up as he went by, but he heard Imrah calling to him.

"Leave it," she said. "It is safer this way."

Milo's outstretched fingers ached to close around the reassuring weight of the weapon, but he resisted. Muttering curses to himself, he followed Imrah past the tables toward the seething blackness.

"What is that?" Milo called as they passed the drying racks, from which hung what looked suspiciously like human skins.

"That is the lesson after this one," she said softly. "And hopefully not your last."

"Thanks for the vote of confidence," Milo muttered as they drew closer, then stepped into the violet light cast by the bowls.

They stopped an arm's length from the bowls, within whose circle the raw night, devoid of any star, seethed and writhed. This close to it, Milo felt his skin prickle at the chill that suffused the air. Milo had shed his surcoat after eating, his body warmed by a full dinner, and now found himself wishing he hadn't.

"What is it?" Milo asked, his breath misting in front of his face.

"Didn't make it very far into *Spectral Ruminations* then," Imrah said almost as a note to herself. "Your reading habits will need to improve."

Milo looked at her with a frown, in part to remind her she hadn't answered his question, but also because as he stood there, he felt a growing understanding that the darkness was looking back at him. Awareness pushed through the rippling, coiling darkness, and Milo was convinced that whatever its motives were, they were not friendly.

"This is a soul well," Imrah explained. "A misnomer, as you should know from *Awakening* and our previous discussions that souls have nothing to do with the necromist. This is a repository of essence in the form of multiple shades bound around a lynchpin fetish."

Milo turned to the darkness, noting that it rippled like a flame, though there was something intentional about the movements. As he stared, he began to see faces, or at least the impression of faces, form and then dissipate in the blackness.

"It looks dangerous," Milo said, trying not to let the fear he felt reach his voice.

"Oh, it is," Imrah said, her voice almost giddy. "Without proper precautions, this many shades bound together could easily kill us both and then go on to slaughter many more of your people before it finally tore itself apart."

Milo wrenched his eyes from the hypnotic horror of the soul well to view his teacher warily.

"Then why make it?" Milo asked. "It's tied to a fetish, which means you had to make this on purpose. Why?"

"Isn't fire dangerous?" Imrah asked. "And yet, you humans use it for many things. For war, for industry, even to cook your food. Humans use fire, despite its dangers, because it is a source of power they can use. Have you forgotten what shades are made of?"

"Essence," Milo said, the words so automatic he couldn't even feel proud for knowing the answer.

"Good, at least you remember *something*," Imrah said as she produced a long, thin vial from within her garments. "And why is essence so important to the necromist?"

"Because it powers everything they do," Milo said, feeling foolish. "So, you have a large pool of essence here to draw from."

The temperature dropped further, and Milo's skin began to ache from the cold.

"Is it doing that?" Milo said as he rubbed his arms and shivered.

"Yes," Imrah said, her eyes darting to the bowls on the floor. "It is pressing against its containment, trying to find a weakness."

"W-will it f-find one?" Milo asked, teeth chattering. "A w-weakness, I mean."

Imrah's gaze rose from the bowls, and she turned to Milo with another wicked smile.

"We hope not," she said, then raised the vial so Milo could see the grains filling it. "You don't want the soul well loose while you assemble your first Si'lat."

"What?" Milo balked, his mind conjuring the memories of the flapping horror made of black sand that had nearly killed him and Ambrose.

"It is a simple process," Imrah stated, deliberately oblivious to his disbelief. "Using only your will, though later, we'll train with a focus conduit, you draw a shade from the soul well and then compel it to occupy the medium you've chosen."

She rattled the dark granules in the vial with a shake of her outstretched hand. Swallowing heavily and still shivering, Milo reluctantly took the vial.

"There you go," Imrah said indulgently, eyes shining in the amethyst light of the burning bowls. "Now, the hardest part will be drawing the shade out without it dragging too many of the others along with it, which would waste most of the essence at best or breach containment at worst. That is why we are not using a focus conduit yet. It will be harder but safer for you to do it with sheer will."

"Safety first," Milo muttered, looking at the vial and then at the soul well. "H-how do I get the s-shade out?"

"Focus your mind and emotions on the soul well," Imrah instructed. "It will be similar to how you could sense certain ingredients, only the sensation will be more intense. Don't let it overwhelm you, or the shade will try to affix itself to you. Don't worry, it can't because of its containment, but the backlash will sting. Nothing fatal, of course."

"Of c-course." Milo frowned.

"If it helps to visualize by holding out your hand, do so. Just be careful not to stick your hand into the well."

"If I d-do?" Milo asked, his hand shaking in the unnatural chill.

"Well," Imrah said, considering the best way to answer the question, "let's just say you won't be able to make that mistake again, at least not with that hand."

"Naturally." Milo huffed, sending up another gust of crystalizing breath. "This would probably be easier if I had my coat. I'm freezing!"

"It wouldn't help," the she-ghul replied flatly. "The cold you are experiencing is both a physical and a metaphysical phenomenon. You could be bundled in the thickest furs and sweating, but you would still feel as though you were deathly cold."

"S-such a p-pleasant thought." Milo shuddered.

"Quickly now," Imrah snipped. "I'm tired of your whining."

Checking his distance to the soul well, Milo raised one trembling arm and tried to keep his gaze and mind fixed on the roiling darkness. For one aching, straining moment, there was nothing but the perpetual cold, and Milo wondered if Imrah had overestimated his abilities as he sensed nothing. Then, like the sub-audible hum of a live wire, Milo felt the thrumming power of the soul well. At first it was a low, vague thing, easily overlooked; then, like some crazed actor rushing to the foreground, Milo realized it was crashing toward him. Finally, it was on top of him.

It was like plunging his head into a swirling maelstrom of not just physical but emotional sensations. Incredible heat gnawed at his skin, while a desperate longing raked his heart. Sharp, grating pain sawed his bones as a towering rage roiled and blazed in his mind. Every sensation was magnified and writ large on his mind and body, and despite his best efforts, he was dragged into their sucking depths.

"Don't let them drag you down," Imrah hissed in his ear. "Your will is strong enough. Don't let them—"

There was a loud snap, then pain, pure and simple, lanced through Milo's skull. The world vanished in oblivion.

"Get up," Imrah's voice commanded across the gulf of unconsciousness. "Get up and try again."

Milo dismissed the distant demand, yearning for nothing more than vacuous sleep.

"Get up," the voice pressed. "*Get up.*"

Milo was dragged back into wakefulness and instantly regretted it.

His head throbbed with pulses of agony, and when he raised his hands to his face, a gaping wound wove a puckered line across his brow. There was no blood, which was even more unsettling, as though the scabby fissure had erupted from within to gape open with exposed bone.

"Not fatal," Milo groaned, his eyes watering so badly he couldn't see anything but a shimmering blur that made his head pound worse. He decided it would be better to just squeeze his eyes shut for the moment.

"Stop whining and hold still," Imrah said, her voice coming closer.

Hard fingers took hold of his, and Milo couldn't keep a small cry from slipping between his gritted teeth. His face was guided left, then right, and then the fingers released him.

"Don't move and don't resist," Imrah murmured, which did little to ease Milo's anxiety.

Something cold but mercifully numbing was spread across his brow, and Milo felt the pull of magic sliding across his mind. In a process that was harder than he would have imagined, he tried not to resist the pull, slowly allowing it to have its way. As he did so, a different sort of pain, cleaner and easier to bear, suffused his brow. His scalp itched and the skin tingled uncomfortably, but within a minute, the only sensation left was a faint dampness across his forehead. He carefully opened his eyes, feeling a mixture of relief and irritation at the sight of Imrah standing over him, wiping her fingers on a rag.

Slowly, he raised his fingers and ran his fingers gingerly across his newly mended brow.

"Not fatal," Imrah muttered dismissively and held out a hand. "Now, get up and try again."

Milo took her hand and got to his feet.

Imrah pressed the dropped vial into his hand and nodded at the soul well.

Milo hesitated, the vial feeling weighty in his hand. He was neither eager to experience the backlash from the forces containing the shades nor certain he could do anything differently if he tried again.

"Why couldn't we start with the healing stuff?" he asked, stalling for time to catch his breath. "Seems like that would be far more helpful than making a pile of murder dust."

Imrah looked up at him with narrowed eyes.

"Who is the teacher?" she asked, a note of warning in her voice.

Milo took a step toward the soul well, but it was shortened as he turned around.

"I'm just saying, healing others like that seems a far more important thing to learn. We humans already have plenty of ways to kill each other."

Imrah stared at him, her jaw working from side to side before she heaved a sigh.

"First of all," she began, her tone sharp and angry, "I'm not teaching you these things to provide you with weapons, but because they are the building blocks for mastering the art. That you choose to view them as tools for murder is your business."

Milo wasn't sure what other use throwing witchfire could have, but he could tell from Imrah's attitude it was pointless to argue. She would have her say, and it would behoove him not to argue.

"Second," she continued, "regenerative formulae are much more complex and require a subtler application of will. If you get it wrong, either in mixture *or* in application, the results are disastrous. You are using unliving energies to force living tissue to accelerate or even override their natural regenerative processes. If you foul up repairing a small cut, you could end up creating a toxic tumor the size of your fist."

Well, that sounds like a good reason, Milo thought as he imagined his wounded head bowing under a pustulating growth on his forehead.

"Third and finally, healing will be very difficult for you," she stated, pausing just long enough to dare him to speak before continuing, "The ingredients you were exposed to and had a tangible response to had almost nothing to do with curatives and restoratives. They might as well have been inert stones in your fleshy mitts, while all the things that are tied to dominion and fear practically jumped for joy."

Imrah's dark stare bored into Milo's pale eyes.

"You aren't a healer, Milo, not naturally. You might learn in time, but right now, we need to capitalize on your strengths to build your experience and confidence."

"Fear and domination," he snarled. "That's all I'm good for."

Imrah stared back, neither offering comfort nor backing down from her claim, which enraged Milo further. His fingers curled, and he felt a growing urge to leap upon her, to force her to...to...to do what? Tell him what he was doing right then wasn't proving what she'd already observed?

Milo forced out a slow breath and nodded.

He didn't have to like it, but she seemed sincere, and her points were all valid. He was going to have to trust her, just as she had to trust him to protect Ifreedahm. With a pang, he realized he'd forgotten all about the purpose of coming back to the surface in the face of Lokkemand's revealing breakdown.

With that understanding bracing him, Milo turned back to the soul well and fixed his eyes on the undulating shades.

"All right then," he said after a steadying breath. "Let's get to work."

He reached out, determined to not fail this time.

As it turned out, he did fail again, and again, and twice more after that.

Each time, the shades piled on and overwhelmed him. Imrah's wards kicked in, and he was thrown down with some sundering injury. Yet each time, after Imrah's ministrations, he climbed back to his feet, took the dropped vial, and tried again.

On the fifth attempt, remembering the tempo and intensity of the previous assaults, Milo decided to try something different. Instead of bracing under the sensations and emotions, which piled on until he collapsed, he decided to ride them, plunging into each as it came. He writhed in pain, wept in despair, and roared in rage. As he did this, he began to feel he could twist the emotions, leaning into the pain until it hardened into despair, which he stoked until it flared into outrage. He lost his concentration as he allowed anger to spin him in a vortex of senseless anger, but even as he felt himself drowning in the encroaching shades, he smiled.

He had them now; next time, he was going to take one of them, and there was nothing they could do about it.

On the sixth try, practically giddy, he was back on his feet, hand outstretched to the soul well before his wounds were fully healed. He used the lingering pain and discomfort of the mending injury, a nasty gash across his chest, to propel him into the contest of wills. The shades came on. This time he didn't resist them; he didn't even ride the waves they brought. This time he danced with them, giving context and definition to every blind sensation they drove at him from his scarred history. The lonely nights he'd felt his heart shrivel in the orphanage, the ache in his belly on his third night without food, the fury at seeing his dreams dashed by callous and petty people. The shades were only echoes of lives, but those echoes were notes that would not be drowned out. Instead, he composed them to tell his story, manipulating them so their sensations fell in line. Their cries became the chorus that would sing his tune.

So shaped, the shades seemed to dance to his tune, moving about him in accordance with his will. From there, it was a small thing to lead one into a crescendo, free and clear of the others. Like some hungry beast from a fable, he beckoned a groomed shade, one of unquenchable longing, to emerge from the flock to sing its song, then just like the fable, he snatched it.

Milo's mind cleared as he emerged from the energies of the soul well. Before his eyes, a coil of night slid along his outstretched hand to slither across his shoulders and down the opposite arm. The single shade, driven by his unspoken command, wrapped around the vial, and for a moment, Milo seemed to be holding a tube of raw darkness. Then, like water soaking into the earth, the darkness shrank, and he was holding a vial full of black sand.

Milo lifted the tube in front of his face and smiled as he saw grains flutter within. For an instant, he saw a face press against the glass composed of lightless grit.

"I think that does it," Milo said, holding the vial out to Imrah. "What do you say, maestro?"

Imrah, eyes narrowed, took the vial.

"Well, Magus," she murmured, her voice refusing to express the surprise on her face, "I do believe you have done it."

Milo laughed, then twisted his face into an exaggerated scowl.

"You act like you didn't think I could!" Milo cried in mock indignation.

Imrah chuckled, the sound far more appealing in her human guise.

"After the third time you failed, I was honestly beginning to wonder."

20

A SUSPICION

When they finally emerged from the basement, Milo had bound two more shades into vials and worked up an incredible appetite. With little convincing, he'd cajoled Imrah into having them go upstairs and either find something to eat or, he'd chuckled, bully Ambrose until he made something. Though he'd never admit it out loud, Milo was growing quite fond of Ambrose's simple yet adaptable culinary style.

The sun had risen while they'd been below, and slanted beams of light were shining through the shuttered windows.

But that wasn't the first light he noticed in the room.

Countess Rihyani sat cross-legged in the den, the unmasked light of her alabaster skin filling the room with soft brilliance. Her heavy robes lay on the ground next to her. She was wearing a pair of silken gray trousers and a blouse of ivory white, though it was hard to tell if it was just the light radiating from her skin. Her long silver hair was wavy and swept to one side to perfectly compliment her graceful neck.

"Magus," the contessa said, an ethereal smile flickering across her dark lips. "I'm glad to see you."

Milo gaped at her, then realized with a single sniff that something else unexpected greeted him.

On the air was the sharp intrusion of tobacco smoke, and sure enough, a dainty cigarillo, its tip cherry-red and trailing smoke, was in her long fingers. With elegant confidence, she raised it to her lips to take a long drag. Her eyes still locked on his, she drove the smoke out through her nostrils so that, for just an instant, her dark-golden-pupiled eyes seemed like those of a dragon watching him through blue-gray vapors.

Milo cleared his throat, wondering why he felt so warm and out of breath.

"Contessa," he said so quickly it forced him to pause and consider the next thing he was going to say. "I'm, uh, glad to see you too."

Imrah clucked her tongue and gave a sniff.

"Of all the human affectations you could become attached to," Imrah chided the fey over Milo's shoulder. "Really, what do you see in those vile things?"

The tension suddenly crackling through the room was immense.

Rihyani acted as though the question was sincere, turning concerned eyes toward the fuming ghul.

"I'm not sure I can explain it besides saying I enjoy them," Rihyani replied with gentle thoughtfulness. "If it bothers you, I'd be happy to put it out."

"Don't bother," Imrah said quickly. "I won't be around for a while. I'm sure by the time I get back, the smell will be out of the building, as long as my student opens the shutters."

"Where are you going?" Milo asked, tearing his eyes away from Rihyani. "I thought we were going to have breakfast?"

Imrah, who was turning to leave, paused, her shoulders hunching as she turned around. The muscles of her masked face bunched and twitched, and the rest of her seemed to be coiling for a spring.

"I've lost my appetite for human fodder," she said tightly. "And last I knew, masters did not have to explain their comings and goings to apprentices."

"No, they don't," Milo said slowly, confusion stamped on his face. "But it helps their students if they do."

"It seems to me you have all the help you need."

With a final venomous glare at Rihyani and her cigarillo, Imrah turned sharply on her heel and stormed out the front door. A few seconds later, Ambrose came shuffling in, looking bemused and glancing over his shoulder.

"Where's she going?" he asked, hooking a thumb over his shoulder.

Milo threw his hands up with a shrug and turned to Rihyani with a pleading glance.

"I think Lady Marid doesn't like me smoking in the house," the contessa observed mildly, vanishing the tobacco with a flutter of her fingers. "It seems to offend her sensibilities as being an odiously human thing to do."

"I s'pose so," Ambrose said, rocking on his heels a little as he looked around. "Would it offend anyone's sensibilities if I undertook the human ritual of breakfast?"

Rihyani gave Milo a conspiratorial wink before turning a grave face toward the bodyguard.

"Only if you don't make enough to share."

Ambrose threw a hand to his chest in horrified indignity.

"*Mademoiselle!*" he said with a rolling French accent. "I will only excuse such an insult on the grounds that you have not sampled my fine cooking in our brief acquaintance. Simon Dieudonné Ambrose would never let a guest go hungry!"

"What about his ward?" Milo asked pointedly, crossing his arms as his stomach gave an audible rumble.

"You were busy," Ambrose replied, shooing the remark toward the basement steps with one paw. "Doing, uh, witchy things."

"That was not half bad," Rihyani remarked, pushing her bowl away. "And considering I grew up dining in Arcadian gardens, that is saying something."

Ambrose was just finishing his bacon hash, which had been seasoned with the reserves of herbs and salts he always seemed to have. He took the compliment with a bowed head before shoveling in his last bite.

"Wasn't the worst thing I've ever eaten," Milo said, unable to hold back a smile as the big man gave him a wounded look. "But I really don't think the contessa showed up just for breakfast."

Rihyani shook her head.

"No, I'm afraid not," she said, her face becoming more serious. "I've come to see if you have any news of your progress in redirecting the human advance? I hoped I could bring word back to the Bashlek that things are in motion when I return to Ifreedahm tonight."

Milo didn't have anything remotely good to report on that subject but bringing himself to say it proved a challenge.

"Well, we've only been here a day," Milo said, trying to sound nonchalant. "Anything to do with so many men and materiel is going to take time to sort out."

Rihyani gave him a pointedly patient look.

"Then the orders have been issued, and it is only a matter of time?"

"Well," Milo said, his gaze dropping as he searched for the words, "nothing has happened officially yet. We've only been here one day."

"So you said already," Rihyani replied, cocking an eyebrow. "Yet in that one day, you met with your commanding officer, did you not?"

"Yes," Milo said, looking at the fey askance. "How did you know that?"

"You might have noticed at Zuhak that fey are quite adept at not being seen," she replied archly. "You can fill in the rest, but do you mean to tell me that you informed your commanding officer, and he's chosen to do nothing?"

"No, not exactly." Milo squirmed, his mind scrambling. "It was more that it didn't come up."

Rihyani's eyes widened enough that it might have been a humorous sight had the room not just become very uncomfortable. When the fey blinked, it might have been to push her eyes back into their sockets, but Milo thought it rude to ask if such was the case.

"You didn't..." she began and trailed off for a moment before gathering her thoughts once more. "Magus, I'm not sure you understand what is at stake here."

"I think I'll go clean up the kitchen," Ambrose mumbled as he collected the bowls and spoons, then vanished.

"My commanding officer is out of sorts at the moment," Milo said, parsing each word as he said it. "And though there is no love lost between the two of us, it is almost entirely on my behalf that he is in this situation. I don't think you understand what a precarious state he is in."

The contessa listened to every word, even nodding slightly at a few, but when she spoke, her tone was as hard as steel.

"Maybe not, but I don't think *you* understand what is going on," she said. "Humanity has been waging war on itself for the last few decades, and that has placed the entire world in a state of strain. The Folk, while living outside the direct conflict, still experience the tremors of all those marching feet and tanks. In the last five years, many have grown restless as they watch humans claim more resources and push unknowingly against the boundaries of their territory. Factions are forming, Magus, as the forgotten people begin to discuss how to end this human-made apocalypse."

WITCHMARKED

Milo felt a prickle along his spine.

"You mean, end the War?" Milo asked. "How?"

"That's precisely the question," the contessa said. "There are theories galore at this point, but in principle, they align along two camps. One is that the Folk, united under a banner of survival at all costs, wage war on mankind. They know our kind, the magical beings of the world, could never fight humanity directly, but as I'm sure you've realized, there is much we could do to wreak a terrible toll."

Milo imagined it for a second—the varieties of magic he'd witnessed put to subversive use by an embittered enemy. Fey assassins who struck and then vanished without a trace. Ghul necromists who animated graveyards and mortuaries of the dead to attack and terrify cities and towns. Ignorant human armies would blunder and smash, but just one magical being could cripple an entire city.

"Victory would certainly not be assured," Rihyani continued softly and sadly. "But their hope would be to cow the proud nations enough with fear and blood that peace would be reached. It is an ugly and barbarous but direct solution."

Milo's mouth suddenly felt very dry.

"What's the other camp?" Milo asked as he picked up a canteen next to him.

Rihyani looked at him intently for a moment, then with a flutter of her fingers, produced a lit cigarillo.

"The other camp," she began. "The camp that I, Bashlek Marid, and a few others belong to, wants to see us ally with humans to see this war end as quickly as possible. That's why we reached out to the Magpie, your Colonel Jorge."

Milo blinked, pieces he hadn't given more than a passing thought to falling into place.

"Why did you choose him?" Milo asked. "I mean, I don't know the colonel well, though he seems decent for an officer, but

249

choosing him means choosing Germany. Why not the British or the French, or hell, even the Americans?"

The contessa smiled as she breathed out a long ribbon of smoke.

"It doesn't matter now," she said, a sheepish smile drawing up the corners of her mouth. "It was more that he chose us. His investigations brought him close, and we decided he had an open enough mind to be receptive to interacting with us. We made contact, real contact, and from there, our course was set."

"Set with me?" Milo asked, a strange combination of pride and helplessness making him feel light-headed.

"Well, no," Rihyani confessed, taking another drag and letting it out languidly. "You were a happy accident."

Milo frowned and waited for her to explain.

"Our initial thought was to ally with one of the powers that be and provide support and services to tip the war in their favor. We hoped that once this was achieved, their enemies would sue for peace, and the state of the world would settle for some much-needed rest. The Magpie had more, uh, *ambitious* plans."

Milo chuckled at the statement, recalling his brief encounter with the mastermind behind Nicht-KAT. You had only to lock eyes with the man to know he was capable of great and terrible things.

"So, if your whole goal was to help Jorge, and by extension, the German Empire, why is Marid sending me on errands?" Milo asked. "Wouldn't it make sense to keep me at Ifreedahm so I completed my studies quicker and got on to helping turn the tide?"

Rihyani took another toke and sent the smoke curling out of her nostrils before answering.

"Ideally, yes," she said. "But the Bashlek is concerned, with good reason, about such a force stomping around his mountains and caverns. Ifreedahm is one of the largest gatherings of the Folk in the world, and while no official edict has been made,

Marid has made it known his alliance with humans by taking you in. If the army even accidentally stumbles across ghuls and lives are lost, what do you think is going to happen?"

Milo nodded, seeing her point.

"They'll say I betrayed him, and he looks weak," he said. "And from what I've seen, I imagine he won't last long on top with that being the case."

Rihyani let out another plume of smoke, nodding slowly.

"Even worse than that is what it would do to the cause," the contessa added. "Not to seem cold, but Marid, for all his assistance, is not key. What is key is proving that the Folk can work with humans and human fear and ignorance will not win out. In this case, Marid's self-interest runs perfectly alongside the greater movement."

Milo's stomach settled like a lump in his belly, and he felt a drowsiness that reminded him he'd only slept a handful of hours before Imrah had woken him for his lessons. He noticed Rihyani watching him through the haze of smoke. Shaking off the lethargy, he squared his shoulders and met the fey's eyes.

"I guess that tells me what I'm doing," he said, rising from his seat on the floor. "I'll be back as soon as I can with word of what is being done to keep our forces off the mountain."

Rihyani smiled, her teeth flashing white and sharp behind her dark lips.

"I appreciate you taking this so seriously. I'm glad to find we can be allies."

"Is that what we are?" Milo said, holding out a hand to her.

The contessa took his hand, her skin surprisingly cool but still soft and smooth.

"I don't see why not," she said, snapping the nearly spent cigarillo into the ether with a twitch of her fingers.

"If we are allies, there is one thing I'm going to need from you very soon," Milo said softly, staring intently into her eyes.

Enigmatic but clearly intrigued, the fey stared back.

"Oh," she breathed. "What would that be?"

Milo released the hand he'd been holding and raised his own to do a flapping imitation of Rihyani's magical gesture.

"You're going to need to teach me that trick, only I want cigarettes. Students shouldn't be putting on airs."

"I can't remember much from our last conversation," Captain Lokkemand growled as he massaged his temples with one hand and gripped the map table with the other. "But it seems that you've forgotten even more than I have."

Milo took another drink of water from his canteen before responding. The heat in the tent was smothering, and both men had not only shed their surcoats but also had their sleeves rolled up to the elbow and collars undone.

"Captain." Milo swallowed, doing his level best to ignore the sweat dripping down both their noses. "I understand your situation and that of the division, but we are talking about avoiding another front for the war to be fought on. Surely, there has to be some way we can keep them away from the ghuls, or at least direct them around."

Lokkemand frowned at Milo before gesturing at the map.

"I understand you're not really an officer, Volkohne," he said tartly. "But you can read a map, can't you? What's this?"

His fingers stabbed down at a city south and east of Bamyan, its location marked with a star. If Milo was reading the topography of the map correctly, it sat at a lower elevation, and the slope of the land progressively descended from there.

"A city, sir," Milo said with a forced level tone, wiping sweat from his eyes as he squinted at the name beneath the captain's finger. "Kabul."

"Yes, Kabul, the capital of this hellhole," Lokkemand spat, then traced a furious line with his fingers farther south and east, past a border. "And what is this?"

Milo felt the longer this dragged on, the less chance he would have of winning Lokkemand over, but a combination of heat and fatigue was making a difficult conversation even more daunting.

"India, sir."

"And who controls India?"

"The British," Milo said before quickly adding. "But Captain, we are already fighting the British in the west. What I'm talking about is preventing a completely new conflict, one—"

Lokkemand silenced Milo with a dismissive flick of his hand, forcing the magus to grind his teeth as he bit his tongue.

"Yes, yes, you've covered that," the captain snapped. "But what you haven't explained is how you expect me to redirect the flow of this river. You come in here with alarms about an apocalyptic war with monsters, but I have my own world-ending crisis with humans right now."

His finger stabbed down at Bamyan.

"Epp may be a monster in the making, but he isn't stupid. Pushing to Kabul has to succeed and well enough that he can push on to India without too much delay. That means a greater concentration of forces right here, a few short hours from the prize. The ghul king can moan all he wants about soldiers on his mountain, but I've got problems of my own right now."

Lokkemand turned from the map with a growl in his chest, hands bunching into fists.

"Epp and his cronies don't just want intelligence and logistic support and strings pulled and special dispensations. Oh no, that's just because we're good *friends*. They also want me to coordinate an effort to find out what happened to their missing patrols as if this worm-bored backwater couldn't swallow an entire division with barely a whimper. Wouldn't be surprised the drunken Bavarian idiots just got lost and will show up in a few weeks, trailing after the rearguard."

Given that the captain's sweat stank like it had been distilled, it was more than odd that he would be critical of others' alcohol consumption, but that wasn't what piqued Milo's attention.

Missing patrols?

"Missing patrols, sir?" Milo asked, feeling the hairs on his neck pricking up.

Lokkemand squinted at Milo after mopping at his face with a handkerchief.

"Yes," the captain replied. "A few smaller patrols went missing after the general advance was issued. It's not unheard of, especially in this rough terrain and with so many men, but when more were sent out and only half returned, I had Bavarians by the bucket demanding I do something."

Milo supposed it was possible to lose your way in the mountains, but after the revelation in the tunnels, he doubted that was the only thing in play.

"I tried first to just give them search grids to use," Lokkemand said, nodding at the map, where Milo could see overlapping lines penciled in certain areas. "When they pressed it, I reminded them that technically Nicht-KAT wasn't military intelligence, and they went whining to the Rider. Epp came strutting in here and made it clear he wants to be close to full strength before pushing on to Kabul."

"What did he expect you to do?" Milo asked, looking surreptitiously over his shoulder at the collection of typists. Not a crack squad of *jaegers,* that was for sure.

"How should I know?" Lokkemand huffed, grabbing his chair and dragging it closer before plopping down. "Men like Epp make declarations and expect subordinates to figure it out from there. I'm not saying he isn't a capable commander, but when it comes down to it, the man is an ass."

Milo didn't know if telling Lokkemand about the jelly thing in the tunnels would help the situation, but the germ of an idea was beginning to form. With some finagling, he might take something off the beleaguered captain's plate and protect Ifreedahm at the same time.

"So, what if the patrols weren't lost?" Milo asked carefully. "What if they were killed in a treacherous ambush?"

Lokkemand narrowed his eyes at Milo.

"Is that a confession or a question?"

Milo swallowed and tried to keep the nervous flutter in his stomach from affecting his voice.

"A question, sir," he replied crisply. "If the men were all tragically lost, I assume you couldn't just give your word that they were dead. What would have to happen for that to take place?"

Lokkemand leaned forward in his chair, a bead of sweat dripping from his nose onto the map below.

"I suppose," he began gingerly, "I'd need some sort of evidence of their demise. Bodies mostly, along with damaged bits of their kit. Uniforms, broken equipment, and weapons. Even if the enemy took everything serviceable, it would be odd if there wasn't something left."

"Of course," Milo said, nodding to himself. "And you wouldn't necessarily need to have every soul accounted for. Some might have been taken prisoner or something."

Lokkemand swiped his face again with his damp handkerchief, nodding very slowly.

"That's true," he said, watching Milo warily. "Do you have something in mind, Volkohne?"

Milo met the man's pointed gaze and felt his stomach do a little flip-flop. Was he really ready to do this?

"Yes, Captain, I might," Milo said, forcing a smile. "But I'll need two things."

Lokkemand was losing the struggle to keep a hopeful look off his features.

"Yes? What?" the captain said a little too quickly.

"I'll need about a week," Milo said, watching his commanding officer's expression closely. "And how quickly can you get me as many dead bodies as possible?"

21

A COMPLICITY

"Impossible," was Imrah's response when Milo introduced his plan to her. "Mad and impossible."

"But you made yours in a matter of hours," Milo pressed, pointing at her flesh-shrouded figure. "If you teach me how to make skin-suits like that and we had all the materials, we could make half a dozen a day, and with nearly a week, that should be more than enough to cover the majority of bodies."

The ghul princess snarled and began to pace the common room. Milo's eyes were burning out of his skull with fatigue, but he'd avoided his bedroll so he could talk to his teacher as soon as she returned from wherever she'd been sulking. The contessa had left with word for the Bashlek to gather the supplies they would need for his scheme.

"Just teach me how to do it, he says," Imrah muttered to herself as she stalked back and forth. "As if it were that easy. As though he could just pick up what some ghuls never master."

"Oh, come off it!"

The words had surged out of Milo's weary mouth before his brain could stop them.

"What?" Imrah hissed, rounding on him.

Milo knew he was supposed to be working on tact and that you caught more flies with honey, but right then, indignation was the only thing keeping him upright.

"Don't act like you think I can't learn it, or that you don't want to give it a shot. For every challenge you've put in front of me, I've come out on top, from that first fetish in the tunnel to the soul well. I'm not saying it'll be easy, or that we might not be able to pull it off, but I know if it seems so impossible, you want to give it a shot just to stick it to all those leeches in Ifreedahm, not the least your own father."

His little rant finished, Milo leaned against the wall to hide the fact that he was winded. Imrah stared at him for a full pained minute, jaw working. Then she gave a frustrated clack of her teeth.

"Even if this was possible, which is in question no matter your boasting," she said at last, returning to pacing, "We would need many ingredients, most of which are rare enough to be either very hard to come by or very expensive to acquire. Neither of us has the means to acquire the supplies in the time you are talking about."

Milo crossed his arms as he drew a steadying breath, a smile twitching at one corner of his mouth.

"Your father would."

"How would my father know about this?" she asked sharply, eyes narrowing. "And why would he go to such an expense?"

"I'm fairly certain staving off exposure and an all-out war with the world is worth a fortune or two," Milo said, more than a little smug. "And the contessa is on her way to tell him. I'm pretty sure she can convince him."

Imrah sniffed irritably.

"You really think she can huff and puff and blow that house down?" she spat. "But fine, it seems you have me cornered. I'm pretty sure you didn't tell the contessa that my cooperation was in doubt on this plan."

"Well," Milo muttered, breaking eye contact to scuff a boot at the floor, "I might have made the assumption that you would want to help, if for no other reason than because you wanted to show what you could do with even such a poor student."

"You are without a doubt the worst human I've ever taught," she replied with a wry look.

Milo raised his gaze and met her look with a small grin.

"I'm fairly certain I'm the only one you've ever taught."

"That doesn't seem relevant," she muttered dryly.

"I'm learning things from you all the time." Milo chuckled and heaved himself off the wall. "But in all seriousness, thank you, Imrah. None of this would be possible without you."

"I'm still not sure it is possible," Imrah said with a soft snort. "But I suppose we're going to find out."

"All the same," Milo said, taking a step closer to look earnestly down into her eyes, "thank you."

Imrah searched his face for some sign of sarcasm or mockery. When she saw nothing but genuine regard, a strange, forlorn look came into her face. The look passed so quickly Milo wasn't sure it had been there a second later.

"You're welcome, Milo," Imrah said softly, then pressed her lips into a restrained line.

Something in the way she was looking at him made Milo forget that he was looking at a monster in a fetching costume. Her face was softer, her eyes not so hard. He had the mad thought that perhaps, in one wild moment, he might kiss her, and she, just as madly, might kiss him back.

Then a wracking yawn overcame Milo, and she looked away.

"Oh, excuse me," he said as the yawn tapered off. "Well, I guess we'll get started tomorrow whenever the supplies arrive. For now, I need to get some sleep, and I imagine you'd appreciate some too."

"Sleep?" Imrah asked, her expression sharpening. "What do

you mean, sleep? I thought you were committed to this scheme of yours?"

Milo, who was walking away, swung around, a lead weight in his stomach.

"What do you mean?"

Imrah shook her head and gave a disapproving cluck of her tongue.

"We need to get started with the next lesson right away," she said with sadistic eagerness. "You might be certain you'll master the skin-suit, but it is still going to take time."

"But but but," Milo gibbered pitifully as he tried to beat his foggy brain into coming up with a plausible excuse. "Don't we need to wait for the supplies to get here?"

"Oh, I've enough supplies here for you to get started on one," she said, smiling with sickly sweetness. "I mean, you've already been introduced to the basic concepts in *Fashioning the Fetish*, and the process doesn't have to be perfect the first time around. You *have* been reading your copy of *Fashioning the Fetish*, haven't you?"

"Sure." Milo groaned and ran both hands over his face to grind his palms into his burning eyes. "Why wouldn't I have read all those pages when I don't even have enough time to get a decent night's sleep?"

Imrah offered him another shake of her head.

"Poor thing," she cooed in a saccharine voice. "If you are really tired, I have an elixir to help keep you trudging along. You think that might work?"

"Really?" Milo asked, perking up a little. "Well, yeah, I'll give it a try."

"Good," Imrah said sharply, her facade cracking. "Now get to the basement. We've got some skin to stitch."

The elixir was aptly named nightwatch, and to Milo's great relief, it was not nearly as noxious as it might have been. It was deep blue and produced the aftertaste of sweet onions in the back of his throat. Once he'd ingested it, he could feel the essence-infused liquid in his stomach, and with a little nudge from his focused mind, he set it to work.

It was like being filled with pale, cold morning light after a bleak, dark night. It wasn't a manic or hot energy, but there was an impetus to it, a momentum that kept his mind and body pushing forward. Every step was like the last surge before the crash into a well-earned rest. It was discombobulating, but he soon found the loping energy intoxicating.

"This is incredible," Milo chortled as he set about ordering the various ingredients Imrah had instructed him to gather. "How long does this stuff last?"

Milo had experimented with snow and hop when he ran with Roland at Roland's enthusiastic encouragement, but this was unlike anything he'd ever experienced.

"That depends." Imrah grunted as she heaved one of the flapping skins off the rack. "The batch you just took should last you for the next six hours. If you haven't made significant progress in five hours, I'll show you how to prepare another dose, and we'll keep going until we know you can't do it without wasting the supplies."

Milo nodded, taking the statement in stride as he went over to help her manage her awkwardly flexible burden. It was only once they'd brought it over to the table and laid it out that Milo realized she was talking about repeatedly doping him.

"Wait," he said sharply as Imrah began to straighten the uncomfortably familiar shape across the table. "What are the side-effects? I mean, you can't just keep taking nightwatch forever, right?"

Imrah didn't bother to look up as she finished spreading her burden on the table. At first Milo balked at what he took to be flayed human skin, but staring at it, he saw hides of different colors and textures all together to make a human shape. He breathed a sigh of relief at realizing that none of them were human.

Imrah surveyed the hide carefully before turning to scrutinize the materials Milo had gathered on the next table.

"I suppose it would be possible to take it for an extended period of time," she said thoughtfully as she checked a bowl. "Depending on the quality of the batch you make and the level of control in its activation, you could probably go for a week without sleep, maybe two, before you saw any decrease in function."

She scooped up the bowl she'd been scrutinizing.

"You'll need far more dried pupae," she said, holding the bowl out to Milo and nodding at a jar on another table. "Two handfuls."

"Okay," Milo said, calling over his shoulder as he went to get the husks, "but you're saying it won't have any negative effects? What happens once you finally come off the stuff?"

Imrah gave the rest of the ingredients another sweep and then a curt nod before answering.

"Long-term use of any elixir will have side-effects, though nightwatch is mostly cosmetic and behavioral. Nothing serious, and again, that would be with extended use."

Milo tried to block out the dry scrape of the spent pupae on his skin as he carefully drew them out and deposited them in the bowl.

"And as far as when the elixir runs out," the ghul continued, "that will depend on how long you have been using it. If it has only been a few days, then the fatigue will be intense. If you are pushing a week, you'll have minutes, maybe seconds before you collapse. If you've pushed it further than that, well, just don't do that."

Milo gulped at the implications as he came back with his bowl of expended cocoons, offering them to Imrah for inspection. She waved them over to the table.

"Good, now start stuffing the pupae into one of those eels," she said absently as she prowled around the table.

Milo frowned at the long black shapes floating in a murky glass jar.

"I still want to know where you got all this," Milo muttered as he rolled up his sleeves. "It's not like you had time to gather it."

Imrah bared her teeth at him as he removed the glass jar, filling the basement with a rank, fishlike smell.

"If you don't manage to foul this up too terribly, I'll show you," she teased, then frowned as he plunged his hand into the jar. "Mind the teeth!"

Milo swore furiously as he yanked his hand clear of the jar with a wriggling eel fixed on the meat of his thumb.

"These things are alive!" Milo howled as he whipped his hand around, spattering stinking water.

"Obviously," the ghul remarked with wry amusement. "Now quit playing with the vermin. We've got a lot of work to do."

Milo finally managed to pry the needle-toothed jaws from his hand, gripping it behind its blunt head as its black length flopped and dangled. Then, still swearing and cursing the eel to the very progenitor of its kind and the last offspring of its entire species, he began the process of coaxing the ill-tempered fish to eat the pupae. Imrah watched with crinkled eyes as he taunted it into fits of snapping at him that saw cocoons slipping down its gullet. It was a slow, frustrating process, and soon Milo was sweating and so intent on the task he didn't even have time to swear.

He'd made it halfway through the bowl when Imrah finally burst out laughing.

Milo looked up, eel in one hand, bowl of empty pupae in the other, eyes wide.

"What?" the magus asked, his voice sharp and trembling. "What!"

AARON D. SCHNEIDER & MICHAEL ANDERLE

Imrah wiped tears from her eyes.

"I said stuff it, not feed it," she wheezed, barely able to keep herself from devolving into further chortling. "You kill them first. What do you think the ramrod is for?"

To illustrate, she pointed at the bronze cylinder on the table, its baroque filigree twinkling mockingly in the light.

Milo made to argue, but a spluttered curse was all he could manage before turning an accusing eye on the gaping eel.

"I'm going to try to enjoy this," he hissed into the cold eyes. "If nothing else because both of you have been enjoying making a fool of me."

The eel gave no reply except one more defiant snap of its jaws as Milo set down the bowl and picked up a knife from the table.

The ingredients were finally prepared and placed in their appropriate places within the empty skin, which Imrah had described as the easy part. The swollen skin and series of puncture wounds on Milo's thumb begged to differ, but either way, it seemed they were ready to proceed with empowering the fetish.

"The essence to empower the skin will come from this," she said, holding up a small pouch. "It should have all the power you need to complete the process. You'll probably need one for each skin-coat you prepare."

Milo took the pouch, and the second his fingers closed over it, he heard a soft click and rattle within. Certain he wouldn't like the answer, he tugged the top open to peer inside. An assortment of tiny bones was within.

"Birds?" he asked, hating how hopeful he sounded. Somehow, as delicate as bones were, even he struggled to believe that was possible. Animal corpses offered many ingredients and potential alchemical applications, but essence came from one place.

"Of course not." Imrah snorted, then seeing the expression

curdling his features, broke into a frown. "What's wrong? Are you embarrassed that you forgot something so basic, or is it something else?"

Milo stretched the mouth of the pouch wider and scowled at the collection of tiny bones, his skin crawling even as anger rose in his belly. His fingers sifted a few of the bones before settling on a tiny femur, which he raised in front of his face.

"These are bones, Imrah," he murmured, not sure if he wanted to fight or vomit. "The bones of a child, an infant!"

An expression of raw confusion slid across the ghul's human guise, then her expression hardened.

"Yes, so?" she asked, her eyes flat.

"So," Milo snarled, thrusting the bag toward her, "this was someone's son or daughter! It's bad enough that we're going to be handling god-forsaken bodies, but the bones of children are just fuel?"

Imrah's fingers curled and her teeth clacked, but she closed her eyes as she drew in a calming breath. When she opened them, her gaze was steady but softer, and her voice was low and calm.

"I understand that physical remains mean something to humans," she said, each word pronounced with measured slowness. "But if you are going to be a necromist, you will have to accept that they are simply raw materials. Yes, that *was* someone's daughter, but not anymore, just like this skin."

Milo ground his teeth as she spoke. Though he knew it was all in his head, the pouch felt heavier in his palm.

"That girl died years ago, over a decade if I remember correctly. Her mother and father, if they still live, will have moved on with their lives and probably had more children. Nothing we do to those bones will hurt her, but they can help us greatly."

Milo looked at the delicate bones. He tried to tell himself her words made sense in a cool, rational way, but every second he held the pouch, it felt heavier, and his hands felt more soiled.

He imagined a small grave dug into a hillside.

Raw materials!

Milo railed at himself, knowing he was wasting precious time, but he couldn't shake the image of a man and woman leading their other children to that hillside.

Just raw materials!

Despite his internal conflict, the vision progressed as he saw the mother and father kneel beside that small grave, clearing away nature's weedy grip. They taught their other children their sister's name and inched closer to healing a family that had been broken.

Then he thought of their faces when the next time they came and found the little grave plundered.

Milo closed his eyes, and cold, righteous anger stirred in his chest.

"How did she die?" he asked, the question coming out before he could stop himself.

The ghul looked as though she didn't understand the question. After a moment, she seemed to realize he was waiting for the answer, and she made a frustrated sound in the back of her throat.

"Will that really help?" Imrah asked, eyeing him like he was a wounded animal. "Will that make any of this easier?"

Milo swallowed and tightened his fingers around the pouch, wincing at the soft clicks within.

"It might." His voice whistled around the lump in his throat. "It might make all the difference in the world."

The last words came out sharper than he'd expected, but as his misting eyes narrowed at Imrah, he knew certain as stone he meant it. Imrah raked her fingers through her stolen hair as though ready to tear the disguise apart in a fit of temper. Her jaw worked for a moment, eyes blazing.

"It—ugh, fine—*she* died of some illness or another," the ghul said at last. "That's all I know because that was all the merchant told me. The bones of a beloved child pick up a powerful resonance that catches more essence than such a small life would collect."

Milo looked at the bones and couldn't keep himself from wondering what mother would want to know her daughter's bones had been collected by creeping monsters for dark magic.

"How do you know the merchant didn't kill her himself?" Milo asked. "Snatch her up and then kill her to give you the bones?"

Imrah looked at Milo with narrowed eyes.

"I don't know, Milo. How would I be able to tell?" she asked irritably. "Think!"

Milo wanted to snarl that now wasn't the time for a review, but the words died in his mouth. He swallowed the rebuke and nodded his understanding.

"You could sense a difference," Milo said with a defeated sigh. "Such a violent end would affect the essence. *Awakening Moro*, section four."

Imrah raised her hands in front of her and began to clap slowly. If his hands hadn't been full, Milo would have snatched up something to throw at her and might have started with the eel jar.

"So you do read occasionally," the ghul said, her face twisting into a smug sneer. "Now, just to check that I'm telling the truth, why don't you feel those bones out and tell me what you find?"

Milo stared at her, and in silence, he felt the tremble of magical awareness centered around the pouch in his hand. He feared to reach out, not sure if he could bear what was waiting for him. Imrah just stared back, unflinching.

Milo's hand trembled, the bones rattling, and he felt the essence pulsing within the pouch. Throb by throb it was closer, and somewhere in the back of his mind, he wondered if he would get to hear the sobs of the child's mother echoing in his mind.

"Why can't we use a soul well?" he asked. "Draw on shades to power the process?"

"Because shades have too much will of their own," Imrah explained, rolling her eyes. "These aren't skin-coats going on you or me, who can control them. If we put a skin-coat on a corpse, even with instructions to stay put and in the form we give it, it's liable to start changing shape or even crawl away within minutes, certainly within hours."

Milo felt his chest tighten, and his eyes roved around him, searching for escape.

"Milo," Imrah called as though he were a skittish horse, which was how he felt.

"What?" he gasped, unable to focus on her as his mind raced.

"These are the realities of the craft," she said gently. "There are no other sources of essence besides humans, and the only reliable way to get that essence, untainted, is from their remains. If there was another option I would suggest it, but you remember your reading. This has to be done."

With a single heavy breath, Milo shook his head, tied up the pouch, and set it gently on the table.

"No," he said, the word quiet but heavy. Staring at the bag a moment longer, he made a promise to himself that he would find a place to bury what remained of the little girl. He would find somewhere the sun would touch every day. She'd spent enough time in the dark.

Imrah's nostrils flared and her eyes flashed.

"Milo, think about it," she warned. "You are going to throw away a powerful tool just because it makes you uncomfortable. Think of the lives you'll be saving by preventing this war. Aren't those worth a little discomfort?"

The words struck Milo, though not in the way Imrah intended. Moments ago, she'd asked him to recall a section of his reading, and now her words called to mind another passage toward the end of the codex. Part of him trembled even as he snatched up an empty bowl and the knife he'd used to kill that cursed eel.

"I'm willing to endure more than a little discomfort," Milo said after placing the knife and bowl down to snag a few pinches of weapon filings and crematory ash.

"What are you doing?" Imrah asked, her tone approaching a demand.

"*Awakening Moro*, section seventeen," Milo said distractedly as he sprinkled the filings and ash in the bowl. "There's a reference to further details in an unattached appendix, but I think I understand the basics."

Milo spat into the bowl, then drew his focus to a needle point within the container.

"BURN."

A tongue of green flame sprang up from the center of the bowl like an infernal candle.

"You can't be serious," Imrah hissed. "Not only is it forbidden, but it is also incredibly dangerous. Do you even know what you are talking about?"

Milo retrieved the knife and began to pass the blade through the flames, careful to keep his fingers clear. When the bronze blade began to glow along the edges, he held it up for inspection.

"Clearly, I do," Milo said as he watched the burning light pass out of the blade, though he could feel its biting heat. "For once, I did my homework."

Imrah stepped toward him.

"It is forbidden!" she snarled and reached out to grab the knife from him.

Milo stopped her with a baleful look.

"Forbidden for a ghul," he said grimly, stepping over the prepared skin with eyes still locked on his teacher. "But I'm not a ghul."

"Milo, please," Imrah said quickly, watching as the blade drew near his open palm. "Forget rules and traditions; this could kill you, and then what good will it do?"

Milo didn't bother to answer as he drew the blade across his hand. The edge of the blade, searing and keen, parted his flesh in one smooth stroke. A sharp, truncated hiss sounded as blood met the hot blade. Without flinching, Milo clenched his lacerated hand, drawing more blood to the welling wound.

"You're being a fool!" Imrah shrieked, slamming her fist on the table. "For Iblis's sake, you're standing there over what will be a skin-coat you fit on a dead man, you idiot! You probably have more in common with the corpse you'll be using than some whelp who didn't have the strength to see her second year. Where's your outrage for him?"

Blood had begun to drip from Milo's wound, and not wasting a drop, he dribbled it across the skin.

"I've got to draw the line somewhere," he said without looking up, wondering if the heady feeling was conviction or the magic taking hold. "Men, good and bad, die for so many reasons, that's the way of it. Sometimes it's a tragedy, sometimes it's a blessing, and sometimes it's necessary. But a child's death is always a tragedy and never necessary."

He felt it as the blood soaked into the prepared hide. A connection was made, like two wires making contact and the current starting to flow.

"The men we'll be using died in the service of the Empire. We'll just be asking them to serve a little longer. Same can't be said of her."

Imrah looked ready to pounce on him in her fury.

"You're being so arbitrary, so self-righteous it makes me sick!" Imrah shrilled, scattering bowls and jars to shatter on the floor as she picked up the pouch of tiny bones. "What if the world was burning, the whole damned world, and I told you this right here was the only way to save everyone and everything? What then, Magus?"

Milo shook his head and looked at his bloody hand. Blood had been ground into the lines in streaks of crimson, but the wound was dry. The skin-coat had drunk its fill and was now ready.

"If profiting from the death of an innocent is the only way to save the world," he said slowly, gathering his focus to start the reaction, "then I say, let it burn."

22

AN OFFERING

Thankfully using his blood, and therefore his life force, to power the reaction did not prove fatal. Painful, most certainly, but after the first moment of soul-shredding dislocation, Milo was pleased to find he remained alive, and as far as he could tell, whole.

Meanwhile, the prepared hide was going through a rapid cycle of changes.

First, the blood bubbled and hissed like it was boiling off the surface, though Milo felt no noticeable change in temperature from the forming skin-coat. No sooner had the vapors risen a few inches from the coat than they were drawn back down across the surface of the hide, where they hovered like fog. Beneath this layer of mystic vapors, the hide seemed to thin, becoming insubstantial. A few seconds later, the entire hide looked like it was made of glass, and Milo could see the table through the hide.

"Incredible," Imrah whispered, suddenly at Milo's shoulder.

Milo wanted to feel smug, but the rapt look on her face was so intent that he felt a tremble of unease.

"Did something go wrong?" Milo asked, more concerned about her than his oddly behaving project. "Is it damaged?"

Imrah shook her head, not answering, then reaching for the accordion file resting against the leg of the table. She drew out the first collection of sheets held together with a paperclip.

"Here," she said, shoving the papers into Milo's hand.

A photo of a dark and surly-looking fellow with a weak chin was stuck under the paperclip. The papers were the medical records for a soldier in the missing patrols, an unfortunate named Klaus Schuster.

"So, this is supposed to happen?" Milo said, looking up from the paper and nodding at the glassy hide. "It's supposed to look like that?"

Imrah gave an impatient snort, but checked herself, and then bobbed her head in confirmation.

"Yes, that is exactly what it is supposed to look like. In fact, even though I've made dozens of these in my life, I've only had this happen a handful of times. The cloudier it is during this stage, the more imperfect it will be on completion."

Milo gave a grunt and looked at the picture of Klaus again. He felt a slight tug at the back of his mind, where the magic binding the proto skin-coat to his blood sang. Not sure how the process worked, he stared at Klaus and let his mind drag every feature over that thrumming chord at the back of his mind. It was something like sending puzzle pieces down a chute, knowing that they will reach their proper place. As long as he kept feeding the information, it would find its proper place.

Imrah gasped, and Milo was just about to look up when she stopped him.

"Don't stop," she said quickly. "It's working perfectly."

Milo finished with the photograph and then began to read the papers, overlaying numbers and descriptors on the image he'd formed of Klaus from the picture. Height, weight, a slight stoop here, a birthmark there. Within a few minutes of reading, Klaus Schuster was a whole creation in Milo's mind. Somehow, he knew the skin-coat on the table was complying as well.

As the mental image thickened into a three-dimensional creation, the words on the paper swam in front of his eyes, and Milo's head began to spin. He felt that gravity was disproportionately affecting parts of his body, his head and hand were suddenly so much heavier. He was certain he was going to need to lie down very soon.

"Finish it!" Imrah cried at his side, and her shoulder braced him under one arm.

He couldn't remember when his legs had decided to stop working.

"Finish it and break the connection!" Imrah ordered.

Milo struggling to come to grips with soft and slippery thoughts, remembered that chord at the back of his mind. With fumbling awareness, he tugged on that clinging sensation and realized it wasn't just a feeling. It was the anchor of a magical umbilical cord, and it was pumping more of him into his creation. He had to sever it or it would suck him dry, though all this occurred without the requisite fear he should have felt.

His mind was numb and clumsy, but somehow with the last vestiges of his jagged will, he sheared through the magical connection. Like a taut string snapping back into place, his senses snapped back with painful clarity. He was covered in a cold sweat, and he ached in every way possible—and a few impossible ones to boot.

On the table lay what looked for all the world like a deflated Klaus Shuster.

"Well," Imrah said with a grunt since she was still holding him upright, "I suppose for doing forbidden blood magic, that went exceptionally well."

Milo tried to straighten, but his joints sent protesting spasms of pain in rebuke. Instead, he swung his burdensome head around to give the ghul a pained grin.

"And to think you doubted me."

As carefully as she could manage, Imrah lowered him to the floor and propped his back against a table leg. Milo didn't protest, in part because he didn't want to and mostly because he couldn't. He settled onto the floor, a low groan passing from deep in his chest to leave his lips sonorously. His eyes fluttered closed, and he surrendered to fatigue, but then fingers squeezed his jaws open, and that sweet onion taste washed down his parched throat.

The nightwatch's bouncing energy rolled through him, battering his limbs to wakefulness. It wasn't nearly as pleasant as the first dose he'd taken, but by God, it woke him up and dragged him to his feet with fierce intensity. His eyes popped open as though they would burst if he didn't let them loose.

Imrah had already stepped away and busied herself with something in a small cup at the table.

Milo realized with a start that he must have been out longer than he thought because the skin-coat was no longer on the table and the leftover ingredients had been cleared as well. The knife he'd used to open his hand was still there, sitting next to the bowl whose flame had shrunk to little more than the fire to be found on a candle stub.

"So, that was interesting," Milo said a little breathlessly, the nightwatch dancing in his chest.

"Indeed," Imrah remarked, casting a critical eye over the interior of the cup. "I suppose it goes without saying that what you did was incredibly reckless and stupid."

"Maybe." He shrugged. "But it worked. Speaking of which, where is my handiwork?"

His eyes roved around the basement as Imrah turned and held the cup over the shrinking witchfire in the bowl.

"I hung it on the racks, along with the file," she remarked, watching the cup mildly. "If we fold or bundle it up, we're likely to get creases and seams we don't want. They'd fade with time and use, but we might as well avoid it if we can."

"Good, good." Milo nodded over-eagerly. He knew his behavior bordered on manic, but he couldn't stop.

Imrah peered at him, looking weary around the eyes, though her human guise remained as vigorous as ever.

"I suppose your success makes you think you can keep doing things like this?"

"Yes, yes, it does," Milo said as he bounced on the balls of his feet. "Now that I know how the connection drains me over time, I can be prepared. Dump the details into the hide and then break the connection. Simple, simple, simple."

Imrah nodded and sighed.

"Yes, it seems so," she muttered. She lifted the cup from the flame as little gray wisps emerged. "We'll have to be careful it doesn't kill you, but these sorts of skin-coats are relatively simple. Your control is amazing with the blood, but the drain on you physically is a concern. When you begin to learn about protective coatings and replicative adaptations, it will be more dangerous, and I can't imagine you could pull off extra-dimensionals powered by blood alone."

Milo was nodding rapidly, taking in the information and pairing it with fanciful, frantic imaginings. His mind caught on extra-dimensionals.

"What are those?" he asked, then remembering he hadn't said the words out loud, added: "Extra-dimensionals, I mean."

Imrah smiled wickedly through the saturnine vapors.

"How do you think I carried all these things from Ifreedahm?"

Milo balked and stared around the room, his magically stimulated mind tumbling into a freewheeling spin.

"What? Really? All of it? *WHAT?*"

Imrah chuckled and held the cup out to him.

"Drink," she instructed.

His mind still spinning, Milo took the vessel and threw back its scalding contents in one wincing swallow.

"Ugh, that hurt," he said, but his discomfort hardly slowed his train of thought. "Imagine what we could do with that? It would be incredible. It could revolutionize everything, everything! Why, we—"

"Milo," Imrah said firmly.

His mind was working so quickly he could hardly see her.

"No, just wait—"

"Milo!" she snarled

"What?" he shouted back.

"The elixir I just gave you is a restorative," she explained with forced calm. "It is going to counteract the nightwatch I gave you in a few minutes. Unless you want to pass out on this floor, you best get upstairs to something soft!"

After losing a day to sleep, Milo's world accelerated very quickly.

While he'd slept, Lokkemand had arranged for all the corpses they would need to be stored in the empty home next to Milo's "lab." The official explanation was concerns of the dead being infected by a deadly fungus that a specialist needed to examine. The combination of location and the rumor of disease-spreading corpses assured them that Milo could carry out the operation unmolested.

When he had awakened from his alchemically enhanced stupor, Rihyani and her companions had arrived with all the supplies they would require to make skin-coats for the rest of the dead soldiers. Imrah had vanished again, and Milo was in no rush to start the process just yet since the fey brought the supplies in after nightfall. Milo supposed Imrah would arrive soon, and if she didn't, he would start without her after he shared a meal with his bodyguard and the contessa.

The fey companions, whose names Milo still didn't know, had elected to leave as soon as their duty was discharged.

The food, sandwiches made from dense field biscuits, canned

meat, and local goat cheese, weren't bad, but the smell of the moldering corpses next door was ever-present. They'd eaten in silence, forcing down bites, trying to ignore the scent of putre-faction.

Ambrose had managed to find some coffee and was brewing a pot whose smell seemed to drive off the worst of the odor next door. This, combined with the plummeting temperatures of the arid world outside, meant the stink was muffled.

"Any news from the Bashlek?" Milo asked as he brought the contessa her cup on the second-floor veranda. Rihyani decided to smoke one of her cigarillos there in the hopes of not offending Imrah whenever she returned. Milo had at first worried at the stir such a luminous and unearthly creature might cause, even when they were nestled away from most eyes, but she'd insisted she would make certain they were unobserved.

"Thank you," the fey lady said as she took the cup. "There is quite a bit of news from Ifreedahm, not all of it from our friend Marid."

"Do tell," Milo urged as he struck a match to light the hand-rolled cigarette hanging from his lip. Ambrose had also found a way to replenish their tobacco in excess of the commissarial allotments.

Rihyani blew out a plume of smoke, and it turned to silver filigree in the light of the moon before dissipating. She sighed, her eyes distant, then took a sip of the coffee.

"Humans and their marvels," she muttered, then looked at Milo standing at the doorway. "Won't you come stand next to me as we talk? I so rarely get to enjoy tobacco and coffee with anyone."

Milo hadn't brought his coat with him, and even from where he stood, he felt the night prickling his skin with gooseflesh. All the same, he steeled himself, thankful that he had hot coffee, warm smoke, and a fetching creature like the contessa to fight the chill.

"So long as you plan to tell me about that news," he said, puffing on his cigarette as he came to stand beside her. "Among most humans, making comments like yours and providing nothing is called 'being a tease.'"

Her wine-dark eyes studied him for a moment as her head tilted to the side, and one corner of her mouth hitched up in a wry grin.

"Can't two friends just enjoy a moment together? Very soon, you'll be back to your schemes, and I'll make busy running my errands. Can't we just savor the coffee and each other's company?"

In response, Milo took a sip and then a drag on his cigarette to buy time. As he sent a jet of smoke into the night, he realized he wasn't sure what to make of the situation.

"So, we are friends?" Milo said, the words coming out flatter and harder than he'd intended.

Contessa Rihyani paused and frowned over the cup she'd just raised to her lips.

"I'd like to think so," she said, the barest hint of rebuke in her tone. "I've been more forthright with you than most of my own kind, let alone any human I've ever encountered. I supposed I'd hoped that sort of thing would engender trust and camaraderie. Was I wrong?"

"I'm sorry," Milo said quickly, the look in her eyes a warning he was eager to heed. "It's just that, well, you're not only the first fey I've ever been friends with, but also the first woman, or female, I've ever been friends with."

Rihyani laughed, the sound producing that same ache in Milo's chest.

"That's me," she said, tossing her head back to strike a regal pose. "A pioneer all over again."

"I suppose so," Milo said, acutely aware of how blank his mind had gone. "So, uh, the news?"

Rihyani turned to look at him again, and Milo busied himself with enjoying his coffee to avoid the gaze that was making him uncomfortable. She held the stare long enough that Milo was certain he was being rude by avoiding her gaze before letting out a sigh and drawing on her cigarillo again.

"The Bashlek agrees with the plan, obviously," she said as she sent twin jets from her nostrils. "He even recommended some areas that we utilize for depositing the bodies. He says they'll be close enough to the enemy lines to seem reasonable positions for an ambush."

"That's helpful," Milo said, nodding. "We'll just have to make sure that we don't stumble into a real ambush when we go to set things up."

Rihyani tapped some ash off on the rail of the veranda before scattering it with a gust of conjured wind from her fingertip.

"We can scout the locations out ahead of time," she said, looking down into the small courtyard in front of the house.

"Thank you," Milo said woodenly, hating how stiff and distant the conversation seemed. He wished he could say something to put the contessa at ease, to draw her into those familiar tones, but it was no use. With disgust, he thought he might have an easier time talking to Imrah than this radiant creature.

"Fazihr returned to Ifreedahm," Rihyani said once the silence had stretched past the point of discomfort. "But he did not return to the court of the Bashlek."

Milo looked up through his cigarette smoke with a frown

"Where did he go?"

Rihyani took another drink before setting her cup down in front of her.

"To Lady Dazk," she said, her tone making it easy to guess how she felt about the matter. "The rumor is the little worm crawled back to Dazk with all sorts of slander and scandal coming off his poisonous tongue. Tales from the broken House of Marid and the wayward daughter Imrah."

The fey gave a sniff of disgust before drawing and exhaling a dragon's share of pungent smoke.

"It's unlikely a word of it is true, but his treachery could prove an unwelcome complication for Marid. Perhaps it is for the best that all this happened. Now is a most uncertain time for you in Ifreedahm."

Milo let out a long curse along with a plume of smoke.

"Should we tell Imrah?" he asked before flicking the butt into the courtyard below. "Or will she already know?"

Rihyani shrugged.

"In all the time I have known Marid, he's never acted as though Imrah cared that her father was the Bashlek."

She let out a final puff of smoke before vanishing the cigarillo with a flick of her fingers.

"Tell her if you want, but there is something of greater concern for Ifreedahm besides who is Bashlek."

"What now?" Milo groaned after frowning into his empty cup.

Rihyani turned toward him, and he wasn't quick enough to look away. Her gaze pinned him in place, intent that he pay very close attention to her words.

"More ghuls have gone missing," she said, her lips tightening into a grim line. "More outposts near routes where humans have been spotted. There are growing mutters of it being the work of humans, which only stokes fears and produces calls for Marid to do something. He's shut up the city, and precious few are allowed to pass the gates. Still, those who go near the surface tunnels disappear."

Milo swore bitterly and shook his head.

"Almost like someone wants to provoke the two sides to war," Milo growled, cupping the mug in both hands.

"Almost," Rihyani replied with a nod.

Milo chewed his lip before heaving a sigh.

"What are the odds that thing in the tunnels isn't involved?" Milo sighed. "I mean, seriously; disappearing ghul outpost and human patrols, all leaving no evidence, so everyone is poking around and asking more questions. What are the odds a creature like that just shows up now?"

Rihyani gave him a wry smile.

"Most unlikely," she said. "I asked the Bashlek if he'd heard of anything like what you described, and he mentioned very ancient tales of bound demons and forbidden experiments, but he didn't seem to give it much credence. Either way, if it becomes bold enough to attack Ifreedahm, he's been told it doesn't like fire."

"That's something," Milo said. "Thank you."

"You're welcome," Rihyani said and turned back to the court-yard as she gave him a sidelong glance. "If we were friends, I'd tell you I was glad to do it."

"If?" Milo asked.

"If." She nodded.

"If we were friends," Milo said, joining her in gazing across the courtyard, "I'd tell you to be careful, and I looked forward to seeing you in a weeks' time."

"If?" she said softly.

"If."

Imrah did not return from her ramblings, which Ambrose muttered darkly must be finding "ghul-fodder" until early the next morning, but when she did, she was eager to join Milo in making the skin-coats.

Unfortunately, Milo had made adjustments to their resources and division of labor.

They were not appreciated by the ghul princess.

"You did what?" she snarled.

Milo knew she'd heard him, so he didn't waste the effort of repeating himself as he worked at his mortar and pestle. He'd made three coats in the course of the night and was feeling the drain on his soul, something that seemed to translate directly into marked fatigue. To counteract the effects, he was making some nightwatch to keep him upright for the next three.

"We have other options," he said simply as he ground the ingredients with heavy, even twists of the pestle.

"How dare you!" Imrah snarled. "You are the student, I am the master. You don't get to determine which tools I get to use!"

Milo removed the pestle and shook the ingredients into the waiting tincture in a tin cup.

"Actually," he began, keeping as level a tone as he could manage, "this is a Nicht-KAT operation, and therefore, command flows down from Jorge to Lokkemand to me. Lokkemand's given me operational discretion, so I get to decide how this show's going to go, and I say no more kid bones. It's that simple."

Imrah trembled with rage, stabbing a hooked finger at him as spit flew from her lips.

"You wouldn't even know what you were doing if it weren't for me! You ungrateful wretch!"

Milo focused, then threw the nightwatch back in one gulp. He braced for the magical stimulant's effects, which came with their increasingly familiar rolling surge. In the back of his mind, he wondered what habits would need breaking once this was all over, but the thought disappeared as the elixir washed the fatigue out of his limbs and the fog out of his brain.

When he turned his eyes on Imrah's seething figure, his gaze was clear and sharp.

"You can throw your fits all you want, but unless you are quitting the operation altogether, you're going to have to make do," he said firmly, then set about clearing his table to begin working on another skin-coat.

Imrah snarled Ghulish curses that lacked human corollaries and made several abortive attempts at storming away before coming back with a hiss.

"Where are the bones? What did you do with them?"

Milo turned. He would have been nose to nose with her if she was a bit taller.

"They're gone," he growled. "Get over it."

"I'm not using my blood!" she spat. "Where are the bones?"

"Don't use your blood," he shot back. "There's enough resonance in the extra ingredients we have for you to draw essence from them."

"Scraps, and inefficient scraps at that," Imrah replied in a hard, flat voice. "I'm not going to go scrapping like some scavenger. Where are the bones?"

Milo glared at her.

"Where are the bones!"

"Buried," said a voice as hard and blunt as a hammer stroke.

Man and ghul turned to see Ambrose coming down the stairs.

He was dusty, and grimy streaks decorated his face, which was set in a thunderous scowl. One hand clutched the bundled-up bags that had held the infants' bones, while the other rested pointedly on an officer's sword the big man had "appropriated" sometime since they arrived at camp. His boots hit the basement floor and he advanced on Imrah, the bundle raised in front of him.

"There still might be some bone dust in there," he rumbled. "You want a sniff, vulture?"

Imrah recoiled, seeming ready to flee for her life, but Ambrose settled for throwing the bags at her feet.

"There, get a snout full," he said in a low, deadly whisper. "That's the last thing you're going to get out of them."

Imrah's eyes darted to the bag, to Ambrose, then Milo, and back to Ambrose. Her face became a sneering mask even as she cringed and threw an unconvincing shrug at the bodyguard.

"It doesn't matter," she said with forced nonchalance. "I have ways of finding them."

Ambrose took one step, and Imrah flinched back.

"Do that," Ambrose warned icily, "and there won't be enough

of you left to do magic with. Do you understand me? I will end you, then render you down into pieces too small to bother finding."

Milo's stomach tightened and his skin prickled. There was a red radiance in Ambrose's eyes that he hoped the ghul could see. One more foolish word from her might lead to the fatal termination of this argument.

Imrah's gaze fell quicker than even Milo expected, and her shoulders sagged.

"Fine." She shrugged sulkily. "But even scraping every last bit of essence from the spares won't be enough. That isn't an excuse, just a fact."

Before Milo could speak, Ambrose had peeled back one sleeve and stretched his arm out in offering.

"Take whatever you need," he said.

"Ambrose!" Milo exclaimed quickly as he stepped forward. "You don't have to do that."

The guard fixed him with a powerful glare.

"'Have to' has nothing to do with it," he replied pugnaciously. "If this gets things sorted and stops another war, I'm happy to do it."

Imrah eyed the big man through narrowed lids.

"Do you realize what you are offering?" she asked. "Do you really understand the risks?"

Ambrose rounded on her and shook his bared arm.

"Do you understand that you need to shut your mouth and get to work?" he shot back. "We've wasted enough time."

Imrah looked at Milo, who could only nod.

"If anybody knows their mind, it's Simon Ambrose."

"Damn straight!" the big man shouted, ambling over to an unoccupied table to slap his arm down. "Now hurry up before I get bored and use the pigsticker on my belt to get things started."

23

A RUSE

Seven long and grueling days after the fifty corpses had been relocated for Nicht-KAT research, in the near darkness before dawn, fifty uniformed soldiers shuffled out of Bamyan, cutting south and east across a series of broken hills.

Their movements were stiff, their faces slack, and if anyone had bothered to look closely, they would have noticed how vacant their eyes were, refusing to focus on anything. Those deeper in the column's formation had a distinctly mortified appearance, and all manner of questions would have had to be asked.

But soldiers shuffling toward or back from patrol or repositioning were so commonplace that no one seemed to notice. The column of fifty soldiers was summarily ignored even as they followed a tall, rangy Blackcoat, at whose shoulder walked a brute in a borrowed uniform and a native woman as they strode beyond the picket lines.

The last sentries to see them gave them a passing glance, rubbing their eyes blearily. One might have even made a grim joke about the men walking like the living dead, but only a few laughed. They were all tired, and their watch was almost over.

With a long sigh, they watched the forgotten fifty trudge on, rounding a rough hill before they passed from sight and mind.

Two miles from the closest picket line, Milo met the fey.

"We've scouted out these three spots," Rihyani explained, pointing at the map Milo unfolded. "Two shallow valleys and a draw that should provide an open enough space for the bodies to be seen and would serve as a reasonable place for an ambush."

Milo nodded, struggling to concentrate on what she said. The animated corpses shuffling behind them were empowered by bound shades. They'd gone willingly into the prepared bodies, but part of him had to remain focused, or the shades were liable to take their new ride out for a stroll. In the time it had taken him to talk to Rihyani, one of the dead had managed to take three sluggish steps away from the column.

"Good work," he said distractedly as he applied mental pressure. The dead soldier shuffled back into line.

Imrah gave a small sniff and looked up at the fey defiantly.

"Isn't that a little too obvious?"

"People make mistakes," Milo said quickly, wanting to keep them focused on the task at hand. "Especially when they're lost, which is how we're trying to play this."

Two more shades drove their meat vessels to the side and had to be brought to heel with a spike of Milo's will.

Throwing a look over his shoulder, he saw that the other half of the column, those controlled by Imrah, hadn't moved a muscle. Despite how silly and petty it was, he envied her control over the essence-enriched echoes. She clearly had enough control that she could argue with people without letting the Qareen wander. He wanted that kind of control, not just for the power of it, but also because the constant strain of course-correcting the dead soldiers was tiring.

The truth was, he and Ambrose had suffered under the regimen of blood magic. Despite their best efforts with food, rest, and even elixirs, both of them were unnaturally pale, and their eyes were circled in bruise-colored flesh. Milo was looking almost as rawboned as the day the two had met, and Ambrose had clearly lost a few pounds, his round face becoming more angular and blocky. To make matters worse, Milo learned that the "cosmetic effect" Imrah had mentioned from overusing nightwatch was that the circulatory system began to darken beneath the skin. Twisted patches of blue-black veins and capillaries spiderwebbed his body. For the last two days of their work, Milo had avoided his reflection because it was too disheartening.

Both men would need time to recover, but first they needed to see this done. Milo had tried to get Ambrose to stay behind and recover since there was nothing for him to do, but he'd insisted a bodyguard couldn't guard when he wasn't around.

So now they stood, looking more like the uncoated corpses at the center of the formation, eager to get the job done.

"How will the bodies be discovered?" Rihyani asked, making it a point to look directly at Milo instead of the glaring ghul.

"Lokkemand came through for us on that too," Milo said, pushing the fatigue out of his voice. "He's scheduled zeppelin surveillance of the area by midmorning. We need to get this moving so we have everything in place and we're clear of the area before they get there."

"Understood," the contessa said. "We'll stay clear, and no flying while the airships are blundering about."

Milo and Ambrose looked at her with weary, furrowed brows.

"Flying?" the big man asked.

Rihyani smiled and cocked her head to one side.

"Her eyes are blue, her hair is brown, with silver spots upon her wings, and from the moon, she flutters down," she quoted in a sing-song voice, her eyes glinting the steely predawn light.

"Shakespeare?" Ambrose mumbled with an uncertain frown.

"Thomas Hood," Rihyani said, her voice and smile gentle and refreshing despite the correction. "Though from the way both you and the Magus look, I judge Mab hath *not* been with you for some time."

"Fair to say," Ambrose agreed, a grin breaking out beneath his newly grown mustache.

Milo stared at the two of them, unsure if it was fatigue or ignorance that kept him out of the exchange but not liking it either way. He absently wondered if this was what jealousy felt like, but the reflection was broken by Imrah's snarled interjection.

"I thought we had a schedule to keep?" the ghul said sharply, eying them all balefully. "Enough poetry."

"Right," Milo said. straightening and gesturing at the map. "Imrah will take the easternmost location, this draw right here. Ambrose and I will deposit the rest of them along these two valleys. Rihyani and the fey will be in a holding pattern around this north and west hill, which is where we will rendezvous."

He looked at each of them to confirm they understood before he began to refold the map.

"If everything goes according to plan, we'll hold there until we can confirm the zeppelins are inbound. After that, we'll head back to camp. Might even celebrate if Ambrose can rustle us up any booze Lokkemand hasn't drunk."

There were tense chuckles from Ambrose and Rihyani. Imrah's expression remained flat and hard.

"I can't work miracles," Ambrose warned. "But I'll do my best."

"That's all any of us can do," Milo said. "Now, let's move out."

A rock turned under Milo's foot, and he stumbled forward to bark his shin on a jutting lip of stone. He swore when he nearly lost his footing a second time and muttered further profanity under his breath as he rubbed his battered leg.

"This all seemed a lot simpler on the map," Milo growled, then gave a frustrated snort as he felt four of the Qareen lagging behind as they tried to climb the steep sides of the valley behind them. Mumbling vitriolic oaths, he hammered down with a flex of focus, and the shade-powered corpses fell back in line.

"Almost there." Ambrose held out a canteen.

Milo accepted it and took grateful slurps as he looked at the twenty-some corpses coming to a staggering halt a few feet away.

"When I signed up, I never thought this was what I'd be doing." Milo sighed as he handed back the canteen. "But I suppose I didn't expect to last more than a few days in the trenches, so all's well, right?"

Ambrose nodded, took a drink, and wiped his mouth on the back of his arm.

"Very cheerful way of looking at it," he commented and gave Milo a wink. "Though 'signing up' sounds like a rosy way of saying you were conscripted into a penal regiment."

Milo shook his head, climbed to his feet, and opened his surcoat. In the chill early hours the coat had been nice, but after a few hours of clambering and the sun breaking over the horizon, it was uncomfortably warm.

"Except I did sign up," Milo said. "The Leipzig *Werk-Strafrechtlich* I was in, well, they put out the all-call for anyone willing to sign up. I put in my name as soon as my shift was over."

Ambrose gave a long whistle as he capped the canteen.

"You were a Strafie before this?" he said, shock in his tone. "You must have been a naughty young boy to get plopped in there."

Milo nodded.

"The worst." He sighed again and gave a slight groan as he stretched. "Let's keep moving."

They trudged on for a while, the dead scuffing along behind

them, occasionally stumbling but always righting themselves with jerky marionette movements. Before long, they crested a rise and were looking down on the first valley.

"You know," Milo puffed as he wiped his sleeve across his forehead, "you still owe me an explanation of that whole resurrection business."

When Ambrose didn't immediately respond, Milo turned around and saw the big man looking out over the ranks of the dead.

"Something wrong?" Milo asked, taking a step back toward him.

Ambrose frowned, his gaze fixed on the way they'd come.

"Thought I heard something," he muttered and adjusted the carbine on his shoulder. The truncated rifle had been another acquisition, along with the sword on his belt. Milo had offered to ask Lokkemand for goods from the quartermasters, but Ambrose had only laughed and said he preferred to do his own shopping.

"Are you sure you aren't trying to avoid the subject?" Milo pressed.

Ambrose didn't respond. Milo saw the animated soldiers halt and decided to start sending them down into the valley.

"MOVE," he commanded, and the shade-fueled Qareen made to stumble down into the valley.

Milo looked back and saw Ambrose had stopped staring back the way they'd come, though a frown was stamped on his face. He stepped clear so the dead could pass as he gathered his thoughts.

"It's hard to explain," he began. "In some ways, it's a bit like a dream because I know things for certain as soon as I get there."

"There?" Milo asked, sparing a thought to drive a wandering shade back on course.

"There being the place I go when I die," Ambrose said, scratching his cheek. "At least where my, uh…"

"Soul?" Milo offered.

"Yeah, that will work. Soul." Ambrose grunted with relief. "I'm so used to dealing with blunt hard cases that saying the word seemed silly. Forgot I was talking to a witch."

Milo wanted to correct him and say magus, but the big man was already uncharacteristically uncomfortable. More than half the dead had already shuffled past in the time it had taken him to say a few words.

"Anyway," Ambrose continued, "my soul gets to where it always goes, and somehow I know I'm dead. I just know it."

"Like in a dream." Milo nodded encouragingly.

"Exactly! It's always the same place. First time it happened, I was confused because it was just bad luck, you see, me getting killed. It was 1844, late summer in Morocco, and I was a veteran fighting man, but that wasn't any use when a frightened horse—"

A dull *whump* carried faintly on the air, followed by a distant whistle.

Ambrose froze and looked at Milo, his eyes blazing with a savage light.

"I knew I heard something," he roared as he spun and gazed back the way they'd come. "Artillery fire."

Milo fought the instinct to duck as his eyes swept across the truncated horizon created by the mountainous terrain.

"Are they shooting at us?" he asked, hating that he couldn't put a little more iron into his voice. Of all the horrors of the trenches he'd been bracing himself for, artillery was the most horrible. The thought of a sudden, messy, and inglorious end descending from on high took away every last shred of war's glamor for him.

"No," Ambrose said with a snarl, his ears pricking up as another *whump* and keening whine sounded. "They're a good way off...and right where I put Imrah's band."

Milo swore savagely.

"Rihyani said she scouted the areas!"

"Armies move, and you could hide whole regiments in these overgrown gullies," the big man spat. "What's the order?"

For a split second Milo froze, suddenly realizing that everything—the operation, the future of the war, and the future of human relations with the supernatural—rested on him. It was a crippling and awful realization, and it slammed into the magus like a knockout punch. What should they do?

Two rounds of artillery fire, one chasing the other, carried on the air, and Milo uttered his best combination of colorful curses.

"Only thing we can do," he growled, his mouth working before his mind had even recovered. "Go save the cranky bitch!"

By the time they'd closed on the draw where Imrah and her squad were bound, even Ambrose was puffing, while Milo was concerned he was in danger of collapsing. Despite their panting and wheezing, both men noted that the crack of rifles had been added to the artillery fire.

"The more, the merrier," Ambrose snarled as he gripped Milo's hand to drag him over a patch of broken stones. "Good thing it's not just the two of us."

Behind them, the line of dead soldiers formed a meandering trail. Milo had given up trying to keep them together, but they were following in a relatively cohesive direction.

"We're...going to...need... something," Milo wheezed as he doubled over.

The thumps of artillery fire—lighter horse-drawn guns Ambrose had stated some time ago—was now close enough that Milo jumped each time. Through sweat-bleared eyes, he looked down from the hillock and saw bursts of earth where the enemy shells struck. The ground had been so broken and pocked even before the bombardment of the last half-hour, it was hard to tell what they were aiming for besides wanton destruction. Milo thought he spotted dark stains on the rocks that might have been the remains of the corpse soldiers.

Wandering clouds of dust made the scene and its actors all the harder to see.

"I can't see her," Milo hissed between the curses he spat at each *whump*. "Hell, I can't see anything."

Ambrose was squinting at the terrain, mustache twitching.

"We've got the boomers over there," the big man growled, pointing at a ridgeline on the mountain arm that made the top of the draw. "And they're going to be sighting us shortly if they haven't already."

Milo's eyes broke free of the tunneled view of the blasted draw, and he saw the glint of enemy arms and the shapes of men working at low-slung carts. A second later, he saw one of the carts jump and kick up dust as the mortar within belched fire and thunder into the heavens.

He braced himself as the cratering impact hit a few seconds later, this time a few hundred meters closer than all the other strikes.

"That's our cue," Ambrose said, taking Milo by the front of his coat and dragging him down the boulder-strewn slope.

Skidding and scrambling, they managed to fetch up against a nest of rocks at the end of the draw. From where he stood, back against a sun-warmed rock, Milo saw the first of his dead soldiers cresting the hill. In the time it took him to recognize they were following in his footsteps, a shell struck the hill. Swearing in shock, Milo stared at the drifting dust and heard the patter of broken stones and bodies across the hillside.

Before the dust had even settled, more of the dead shuffled forward, boots squelching over the twitching remains of their erstwhile comrades.

Overhead, bullets began to fly with zipping hisses. The cracks of the rifles came half a heartbeat later.

"Flankers to our east," Ambrose reported as he craned his neck to take in the draw. "A ways up, but they'll be advancing, especially if we don't give them any return fire."

Ambrose nodded to the dead who had just started coming down the hill.

"Any chance you can get them to shoot?" he asked as he scooted between sheltering stones. "Doesn't have to be effective. Just smoke and noise."

Milo shook his head.

"If I had a few hours, I might get one to be that coordinated," he grumbled, ducking as a stray bullet skipped across the top of his boulder. "As it is, I'm not even sure how I've kept them with us this far."

Ambrose sucked his teeth and swore.

The first of the dead was nearing their spot, one of those without a skin-coat, its features shriveled and waxy. A fragment of shrapnel or something like it had torn a ragged gash across the thing's cheek, exposing bloodless gums and yellowed teeth. As it stumbled forward, a bullet punched through its shoulder, exiting to kick up the dust on the slope behind it. The shot must have shattered the bone since the arm hung a little lower in the uniform, but the Qareen kept coming, its slow gait undisturbed. Behind it, more of its kind were making their bullet-riddled way down the hill.

"Well, I've got an idea," Milo panted, leaning over to spy out the eastern slope. "It has a good chance to get us killed if it doesn't work, but hey, that's not a problem—for you, at least."

Ambrose gave him a stern look and then heaved a sigh as he unslung his carbine.

"We really need to finish that conversation," he shouted as the enemy's fire intensified.

"We need to survive first." Milo laughed. "Now, get ready to run into the draw on my word."

To the enemy positioned along the ridgeline and the eastern slope, it was a scene of madness.

A mob of German soldiers rushed out of cover, moving with a drunk's rubber-jointed reeling. It wasn't quite a charge since their weapons were still slung across their backs, but they came toward the eastern slope with a reckless energy that couldn't be ignored. The artillery pieces scrambled to adjust their vectors, while the line infantry on the slope halted their advance. There was a stunned few seconds as the line infantry took aim, then salvo after salvo ripped into the German line.

Bones snapped, bodies jerked, and helmets rang with puncturing fire, but still they came.

A curtain of mortar blasts descended on the advancing mob, throwing up a storm of debris. To the horror of the enemy, those Germans thrown down flopped and heaved themselves to their feet, while those peppered by shrapnel did not even slow. Two that had been caught by the blast crawled forward on gory stumps and clawing hands.

Suddenly faced with fearless, immortal soldiers, the enemy's resolve wavered.

Orders were bellowed and conflicting calls made for orderly fire and donning bayonets as the horror-stricken men sent their useless fire downwind. Eventually, someone called for a withdrawal up the slope, and instant consensus seemed to be reached that this was the best course of action. The mangled but undaunted German forces still only halfway up the rough hillside, the enemy infantry scuttled back as the artillery covered their retreat.

In all the madness, no one noted two figures darting from cover to cover in the draw, pausing every so often to search among the dead.

"Imrah!" Milo hissed as he slewed to another nest of jutting rocks. "Imrah!"

The sound of the enemy venting their fearful fury on the dispatched Qareen was moving farther away, but he felt dreadfully exposed as he surveyed the draw.

The dead soldiers lay in patches and clumps, some blasted beyond human resemblance, others looking no worse for wear than they had when they'd set out that morning. It was the sight of these unmolested corpses that filled him with the most dread.

If the shades had lapsed like that, there was a good chance that Imrah was at best unconscious.

"Milo!" came a hoarse bark to his right.

Milo dared a look around his rocky cover and spied Ambrose waving him over from a narrow crease in the earth. Taking a furtive and futile look around, he sprang from cover and raced toward the shallow gully, certain either a bullet or a shell was headed his way.

He threw himself flat, sliding the last few feet into the earthen crevice, to come down next to Ambrose. The big man crouched over a small form, rifling through his pack for bandages.

Imrah lay on the ground, her breath coming in sharp, shallow gasps. Patches of dark ichor blotted her ravaged clothes, and one arm was a mangled mess that flexed and twitched with feeble movements that violently twisted Milo's stomach. On the same side as her wounded limb, the skin-coat had been rent from crown to clavicle, so Milo could see her jagged teeth and wrinkled throat moving with every breath.

"Hang in there," Ambrose said, his voice unnaturally calm as he drew out clean strips of cloth and a length of leather cord. "I've got you. I've got you."

Shuffling around, the big man moved to her dangling arm and nodded at the spot he'd just vacated.

"Over there, Magus," he said, his voice still smooth and even as he set to work. "Just hold her hand and let her know we've got this under control."

Milo shuffled over and took Imrah's limp hand in his. He tried to form words, but his throat knotted up, refusing to work. He wanted to tell her everything was going to be okay, but the lie refused to come.

Imrah's half-human, half-ghul gaze swung over to him, her eyes sliding in and out of focus.

"My...coat. Milo, my...coat..."

"It's okay," the magus said, the words sounding dead and flat even to his ears. "I'll...I'll make you a new one when we get back."

She shook her head, the movement frighteningly boneless.

"No...inside. Inside...my coat."

Feeble as her grip was, Milo felt her drawing his hand toward her wounded side.

"Inside..." she wheezed, and her gaze sharpened for an instant as she croaked, "Kimaris comes!"

The ghul princess collapsed in a senseless heap.

Ambrose swore, and Milo looked over and saw him struggling to fashion a tourniquet with the leather cord as he blotted ichor away with the bandages.

"Damnation," he muttered softly. "Can't tell which part of this mess is her and which part is the skin-coat."

Milo stared at the gory body, trying not to let his mind linger on any one detail too long, but something caught his eye. He spied a curl of seemingly human flesh hanging near the collarbone like the eared dog page of a book. At first, the grotesque sight nearly convinced his stomach it was time to vacate, but then he remembered a vaguely similar sight in the sitting room just outside the Bashlek's court in Ifreedahm.

Inside...my coat.

Gripped by a sudden realization, Milo grabbed the flap of flesh and began to pull.

"What are you doing?" Ambrose cried, his cool demeanor

fracturing under the horrific sight of the flesh peeling back like paper.

As the flap folded over, Milo saw seams across the expanse of ichor-splotched skin. Freeing his hand from Imrah's unconscious grip, he shoved his fingers into the pockets and nearly recoiled in horror as his whole hand slid into a space that could not have been contained in the slim pouch. Forcing himself to remember Imrah's hints about extra-dimensional spaces, he kept groping around until his fingers slid across something made of rounded glass. There were clinks as he gathered everything he could, and when his hand emerged from the enchanted pocket, he held three small vials.

Milo wasn't certain, but he willed himself to believe they contained the ingredients he had seen her use when she regrew her hand before court.

"Get her mouth open," Milo instructed as he yanked the wax seals from each vial.

Ambrose complied, though he nearly lost a finger when she snapped in unconscious reflex.

Hoping he wasn't about to turn his teacher into an alchemical bomb, Milo emptied the ingredients into her mouth. As an afterthought, he sent a small pulse of his magical focus after them as they passed through her gaping teeth.

For a single eternal second, nothing happened, then Imrah's chest ceased to rise as her body went limp, flattening against the ground.

Milo stared numbly as Ambrose shook his head slowly and slid an ichor-stained paw across his forehead.

Then, so suddenly both men lurched backward, Imrah gasped and coughed. A wet hacking sound came from her throat, then she rolled to one side to expel blue-black globules. She tore Ambrose's failed tourniquet off since her arm had begun to steam and mend itself. The skin-coat still hung in tatters of fleshy fringe around her forearm and elbow, but within seconds, the whipcord sinew had returned. Imrah flexed her claws experimentally.

With a snarl, she sat up unassisted and turned her bifurcated gaze on the humans on either side of her. For a moment, only her familiar irritation was present, then her eyes widened with fear.

"You need to get out of here," she rasped, her human voice edging toward gravelly buzz of ghul tones. "Now!"

"We all do," Ambrose said, shoving his remaining bandages back into his pack. "Nice work, by the way, Magus."

"Can you stand?" Milo asked, tentatively putting a hand on her shoulder for support.

"You don't understand!" Imrah wailed, twisting away from his touch. "*You* need to get out of here! Just leave me and go!"

"Not going to happen," Milo said firmly.

From somewhere up by the ridgeline, there was a piercing scream.

"You don't understand," Imrah repeated, looking from one to the other. "Oh, Iblis, please just go! Now, before it's too late!"

"What are you talking about?" Ambrose asked, the first edge of suspicion sharpening his tone. For the first time since they arrived, the air was not being rent by mortars, and even rifle fire was slackening. Ambrose rose from his crouch to survey the enemy positions.

"Milo, please!" Imrah moaned, one human hand and one ghul talon gripping his open surcoat. "You need to run!"

Milo looked down at her and saw a struggle of guilt, fear, and anger writhing behind her mismatched eyes. His stomach sank toward his heels.

"I called to it," she gasped, her gaze beginning to twist slowly toward the ridgeline. "When I first came under attack. I'm sorry."

"What are you talking about?" Milo demanded, yanking her hands off his coat.

"*Mon Dieu!*" Ambrose gasped, and by instinct, Milo heaved to his feet to see what was going on.

Sweeping across the ridgeline and flowing down the rockface toward the eastern slope was a vast undulating tide. Its muddy gray surface glistened as it rolled down over the hillside, rippling layers speckled with discolorations across its filmy membrane. Dark patches at varying depths in its translucent form bore the shapes of men, horses, and things less recognizable. It rolled down from the saturated ridge to lap across the enemy line. Men vanished, screaming beneath grasping, smothering waves.

On the air was a heavy clinging stink of stale sweat and burnt ammonia.

"Come on," Milo shouted, breaking the spell of the horror's appearance as he hauled Imrah to her feet. "We need to run!"

Ambrose shook his head, tearing his gaze away to stare numbly at Milo for a second before giving another whiskery toss of his head and nodding. He slung his rifle back over his shoulder and snatched up his carbine with a seamless economy of movement.

"Imrah, move!" Milo shouted, pulling on her arm, but she wrenched back, nearly knocking him over.

"No, it's too late," she cried, reaching up to dig at the ragged edges of her rent skin coat. "Just stay here."

"What's wrong with you?" he bellowed, pointing up the slope to the slime flood scouring the eastern slope. "We need to get out of here."

"Just stay here and be quiet," she instructed, turning toward the gelatinous horror. With a sickening, wet wrench, she tore the skin-coat off her head so the vacant remains of a woman's face hung like a hood from her shoulders.

"Milo," Ambrose rumbled at his shoulder. "We need to get out of here now."

Milo nodded, his mind freewheeling even as he watched his teacher advancing toward the monster, arms outstretched.

"Okay," Milo murmured, something twisting hard inside his ribs. "You're right."

They turned to run, but their feet refused to comply as nerveless fingers gripped their ankles with dead weight. The dead soldiers at their feet tightened their grip, curling around their legs, even as more rose from the ground to stagger forward, hands outstretched.

"I told you to stay put," Imrah called over her shoulder as she kept advancing toward the eastern slope.

To Milo's and Ambrose's horror, the foul tide turned and rushed down to meet her.

24

A GAMBIT

Milo waited for the living sea of filth to sweep Imrah away, determined to witness her last moments before his own time came.

Yet, just as the cresting wave of caustic jelly was about to swallow the ghul, it halted before her. A glistening wall of murky protoplasm rippled and shone as its previous victims, men and horses, twisted and rolled lazily within its depths.

"Kimaris!" Imrah cried, raising her arms over her head. *"Commander and master of legions, I call you to treat with me!"*

The gelatinous depths heaved and wriggled, and then from the quavering wall of jelly emerged the bile-gnawed faces of the slime's prey. Most were human, some were ghul, and a few were horses, goats, and dogs, all in varied states of digestion. The wall of dripping heads opened their mouths in unison to raise a sodden, quavering chorus.

"BEHOLD! BEHOLD!" they cried in choking, trembling ecstasy. *"THE PRINCE ARRIVES!"*

Imrah stood motionless as the center of the expanse before her grew convex. The forming bubble swelled, then with a wet pop, it collapsed, revealing a figure within.

Tall and slender, with an androgynous aesthetic of elegance, the figure seemed to be composed of the same substance as the sea that birthed it, but shaped and hardened to a glassy smoothness. It might have seemed an impressive sculpture, but floating within its polished form were bits of viscera, meat, and bone. Turning its smooth face to look down on the ghul before it, the figure gave the slightest nod of acknowledgment.

"*BEHOLD THE PRINCE!*" the chorus cried. "*THE PRINCE BEHOLDS YOU!*"

"You have served well," Imrah said, to which the figure raised its chin. "Now I bid you return to the deep and wait for my call once more."

The figure turned its head to one side, then slowly turned and pointed at Milo and Ambrose.

"*THE ENEMY IS UPON THE FIELD!*" the gnawed faces warbled excitedly. "*THE PRINCE RIDES TO WAR!*"

Pseudopods of slime crept forward on either side of Imrah, inching toward the corpses that held the magus and the bodyguard in place.

"Imrah!" Milo shouted in warning.

"Kimaris!" the ghul princess snarled, turning a withering gaze on either side of her before glaring up at the figure. "I am the one who freed you! I am the one who healed you! I am the one you serve!"

The pseudopods retracted, and the figure raised a hand to its chin as though deep in thought.

"*THE PRINCE WILL HEAR THEE!*"

Despite the statement, Milo and Ambrose saw a shiver race through the stinking expanse. Neither could have explained how they knew, but both were certain it was rage.

"This isn't going to end well," Ambrose growled under his breath as he exerted himself, though at the angle he was being held, Milo couldn't see what his bodyguard was doing.

"That's better," Imrah cooed with icy confidence. "Things are going to change now. I've been lax with you, letting you roam free. You will still be fed, but it will be by my hand and whom I choose. Your hunger has already complicated things more than it should have."

The figure straightened from its pensive pose, shoulders squaring indignantly.

"THE PRINCE HAS LAID YOUR ENEMIES LOW," the chorus wailed in outraged testimony. *"EYES AND EARS BEAR WITNESS TO THE SLAIN!"*

"You wiped out an outpost of ghuls!" Imrah cried, a brittle note in her voice. "You were meant to save my people, but now Ifreedahm is bolted shut for fear of you. That was not what I bargained for."

Ambrose gave a straining grunt, and Milo twisted as best he could to see the big man bent nearly double, the dead soldiers nearly burying him under their gripping limbs.

"What are you doing?" Milo whispered.

Ambrose looked up from under a corpse's arm and flashed Milo a strained smile.

"Working on something," he panted.

Before Milo could ask anything further, the chorus sounded again, the unnatural voices rising in clear anger.

"YOU IMPUNE THE PRINCE'S HONOR? YOU WHO STAY THE PRINCE'S HAND UPON THE FIELD?"

The wall loomed over Imrah, a hundred tortured faces glaring down condemningly as the figure crossed its clean limbs.

"Kimaris!" Imrah roared, but one foot slid back reflexively. *"I am your mistress! I—"*

With frightening speed, the figure's hand swept out, slapping the ghul's face with such force that she was thrown off her feet.

"FAITHLESS KNAVE!" the chorus shrieked. *"YOU ARE UNWORTHY OF THE PRINCE! JEALOUS AND PETTY INSECT!"*

Ghulish ichor dribbled from Imrah's lips as she looked up from where she'd fallen. Milo could see the terror in her face, but as their eyes met, incredible sadness stole over her features. She lowered her gaze and shook her head as she climbed to her feet.

Milo's fingers tightened around the cane in one hand, and he began to draw his focus.

"It was always supposed to end like this, wasn't it?" she asked, turning back to the figure looking down its nose at her. "One way or another."

The chorus' cry was strident with triumph.

"YOUR AMBITIONS ARE SMALL! THE PRINCE'S DESTINY COULD NEVER SURRENDER TO YOUR INSIGNIFICANT DEMANDS."

"Your destiny was to waste away in that ruin I found you in!" Imrah spat. Again the hand struck out, and she was upon the ground. Teeth and brackish blood fell from her mouth.

Milo felt the unnatural force begin to flow into his arm.

"SILENCE, WRETCH! THIS IS THE PRINCE'S HOUR! WITH THE WITCHBORN'S DEATH, IT SHALL NEVER END!"

The gelatinous wall surged forward, swallowing the figure as it made for Imrah, who released a handful of twinkling dust that kindled to blue flame midair. At the same time, Ambrose loosed a terrible roar, and corpses flew into the air like rag dolls. Milo twisted free to sweep his cane in a wide arc, pulping fingers and snapping arms.

The living tide that was Kimaris recoiled before Imrah's fiery onslaught but it did not retreat, drawing its leading wave up higher.

Ambrose was free of dead soldiers, sword in hand, hacking and punching with the basket hilt left and right. Milo kicked free of the last corpse clinging to his legs and spun to smash the length of the cane across a soldier groping toward him. With the lingering effects of the alchemical strength coursing through him, Milo's blow sent the corpse flopping to the ground.

Ambrose had hewn a space around them, and without the

direct intervention of Imrah, the remaining corpses milled around aimlessly.

"We need to run!" Ambrose bellowed, turning this way and that, congealed blood covering his blade.

"Imrah!" Milo called, casually blasting a corpse back with witchfire as it lurched forward. "Imrah, come with us!"

From her place on the ground, the ghul's attention alternated between Milo and the towering Kimaris. Her hand was inside her skin-coat, frantically groping for something as the curtain of blue flame began to shrink. The edges of the ocean crept around the waning barrier.

"Hurry!" Milo shouted as he started toward her, reaching out. Ambrose grabbed him by the shoulder and hauled him over the twitching, squirming bodies.

The air began to fill with thrumming.

"Come on, Magus!" the big man growled, outmuscling Milo with ease as the last of the alchemical strength left his limbs.

"Wait!" Milo shouted, fighting his bodyguard's grip ineffectively. "She can still make it!"

"Damn it, Milo," Ambrose snarled as he shook the magus. "She doesn't want to."

Milo shot him an accusing glare, then turned back to see that Imrah had found her feet and whatever she'd been looking for in her skin-coat. An ivory powder horn was in her hand, more of the twinkling dust tumbling from its tip to spread azure fire at her feet.

"I'm sorry, Milo!" she shouted back. "It was too late before I ever met you!"

Her eyes rose above him, and Milo followed her gaze to see a zeppelin churning toward them as it made for the sky over the draw.

"It's over," she called, looking at him one last time. "Goodbye."

With that, she turned toward Kimaris, the crest of his wave nearly thirty feet high.

"Come embrace me, O prince!" Imrah screamed as she raised the horn and upended it over her head.

The air was sucked from Milo's lungs as his teacher burst into blue flames and ran shrieking toward Kimaris' descending bulk. He couldn't even scream as she disappeared in a rush of slime and a cloud of putrid steam.

All he could do was give in to Ambrose's firm grip and start running.

"Don't know which is going to run out first," Ambrose panted as he looked down the slope at Kimaris' converging tide. "Our legs or this hill."

Milo gasped for breath, spat out bile, and forced himself to straighten.

"We need to keep moving," he wheezed and looked down the hillside they'd been climbing for the last ten minutes. The places scorched by his witchfire were covered in the murky slime of the gelatinous horror, so that everything below had a vile sort of icing.

Forcing his concentration into the proper avenue was harder the more exhausted he became, but despite everything, Milo hammered his will through the raptor skull atop his cane. The avian beak swung open, and a torrent of green fury lashed down the hill. The slime retreated before the flames, but only to the edge of its crackling reach. Milo swept left and right, trying to form a wall of fire, but every time he swung to one side, the abomination crept closer on the other side.

With nothing to kindle but bare rocks, Milo knew it was futile, buying them less and less time.

With a gasp, he stumbled back, tasting blood in the back of his throat as he forced air into his lungs.

"I can't keep doing this," he panted, his body burning with frustration and exhaustion.

Ambrose stepped back to watch Kimaris begin climbing again. A string of curses in several languages tumbled out as he turned away sharply, eyes scanning in every direction. Milo had just begun to straighten as the big man pointed at a jagged peak west of the hill they were climbing.

"If you make for that crest," Ambrose said, "maybe you can send up a firebolt like a flare, and the zeppelin will swing by to throw you a line."

Milo looked at the sheer soaring stone, and his legs trembled beneath him. A tight, bitter laugh passed his lips.

"Even if I had the strength," he said, "there's no way we'll make it before that thing catches us."

Ambrose spat downhill and snarled.

"Then I guess I don't need to hold onto these."

From his pack, he drew out two grenades of a type Milo had never seen. They were constructed like a traditional *Stielhand-granate*, or stick grenade, but instead of a canister, there was a trio of ribbed spheres clustered around the top.

"What are those?" Milo asked, eying the wicked-looking devices suspiciously.

Ambrose looked up with a youngster's mischievous grin.

"Tunnel-brushers," he said, stroking the handles affection-ately. "Drop one of these into a dugout, hard tunnel, or even a bunker if you can manage, and it fills it with burning debris that bounces around like hornets from hell."

Milo squatted, knowing in the back of his mind that they had minutes, maybe less, before Kimaris was on top of them.

"One for each of us?" Milo asked, looking the big man levelly.

Ambrose nodded, his smile turning grim.

"Won't take the thing down, I expect, but we might make it regret gobbling us up."

Milo nodded and took one of the grenades.

"Well," he said, feeling the heft of the explosive and trying to imagine pulling the pin and charging face-first into...the end.

"Do you think you'll come back from this one?"

"Don't think so." Ambrose sighed. "But then again, if everything is eaten, not sure I'll come back from that."

The magus shrugged. "I suppose this is as good a way as any to go."

Ambrose chuckled.

"I can think of a few better ones," he said, a wistful look in his eye. "But it'll have to do."

The men stared at each other, knowing that more could be said, but also knowing nothing need be.

"Human lives seem short enough to me as is," a sweet, siren voice called from behind the two men. "Yet it seems men are always looking for an opportunity to end things early."

Both whirled to see Contessa Rihyani sitting daintily on a boulder. Her two companions, the verdant lady and the bronze colossus, lounged on their own jutting stones.

Milo muscled down his surprise and relief and struck an indignant pose with arms crossed.

"Took you long enough," he grumbled.

"I told you we should have just left," the bronze colossus said with a voice like a brass bell.

"I have a soft spot for friends." Rihyani threw a wink at Milo before making a show of looking downhill. "Though if you two would rather take the old Roman way out, I suppose we can't stop you."

"Well, we *could*." The green fey giggled puckishly.

"But we won't," the bronze giant intoned.

Ambrose stole a glance at the creeping advance of Kimaris' reaching pseudopods.

"Is there an exit strategy?" the big man growled. "Or are we going to just keep snarking until we become slime fodder?"

Rihyani sprang off the boulder, as lithe as a cat.

"I do believe you had plans involving a zeppelin."

"What do you think the crew is going to say?" Milo shouted at the top of his lungs as the wind raked across his face and through his hair.

In truth, he was less interested in how the crew of the zeppelin would react and more concerned about not looking down. The sight of his legs dangling hundreds of meters in their air was something he wasn't sure he'd ever get used to.

"Ambrose?" Milo shouted when no reply came. Twisting in Rihyani's grip, he spied his bodyguard held between the contessa's companions, his eyes screwed shut and every muscle quivering.

"Stop squirming," Rihyani chided, her voice barely audible as they soared toward the zeppelin. "You might not be as heavy as Simon, but we don't make a habit of wind-riding with passengers."

Milo might have chuckled because she was on a first-name basis with his bodyguard, but he'd accidentally looked down again, and what he saw was more than disheartening. Besides the sphincter-puckering terror of his altitude, Milo noted the glistening gray river that was snaking along the ground below them.

It seemed Kimaris, now free from whatever hold or guidance Imrah had on it, was determined to come after them.

No, not them, Milo reminded himself. *Me. The witchborn. It wants me.*

He took a steadying breath despite the wind whipping across his face and tried to think.

If Kimaris was determined to get him, fleeing to camp in the zeppelin would make a bad situation worse. If the disappearances of the patrolling squads were evidence, small arms fire was useless, and given the thing's nature, Milo wasn't certain that anything short of fire would harm it. There was a possibility that with enough explosives, most of which produced little flame, along with any and all flamethrowers in the entire division, they might be able to hold Kimaris off. That was if Milo could get everyone organized before they arrived.

Given what he would be trying to prepare them for, he doubted his chance of success.

If they headed back to Command, there was a good chance they would be handing hundreds, even thousands of soldiers over to this fiendish jelly-monster.

Milo swore under his breath and stared across the sky at the zeppelin that was banking for a broadside view of the draw as its surveillance crew frantically took pictures. Desperately, Milo wished it was a bombardier instead of a reconnaissance blimp. With a payload like one of those leviathans carried, they would at least have a chance to punch a few holes in Kimaris, and with an incendiary bomb or two, they might have handled the whole business. The truth was that Kimaris was being reckless, exposing itself above the ground like this, but given the situation, he wondered if it was a calculated risk. Why he was worth taking that risk, Milo didn't know, but he imagined any hope of finding that answer had died with Imrah.

As he stared at the vast blimp, Milo's frustration mounted. So huge, so expensive, so immense, and yet so useless with its vast interior filled with hydrogen bladders…

A wonderfully awful idea began to take root in Milo's mind.

Trying not to twist too much in the contessa's grip, he craned his neck around and spied the sharp peak Ambrose had pointed out when they were on the hilltop.

It was probably insane, but it just might work.

"If you had to," Milo called up to Rihyani, "could you get the crew to safety in short order?"

The fey looked down at him, her silver hair snapping behind her like a banner.

"Why are you asking?" She frowned.

"Could you do it?" Milo pressed, staring up into her golden pupils.

Rihyani looked at the zeppelin, eyes narrowed, and then at Milo.

"Depends," she answered, her caution clear despite her raised voice. "How many men would be on board?"

"A dozen at most," Milo answered, not sure of his answer, which was based on seeing the airman crews moving in a gaggle across the command post.

"If none of them are built like your bodyguard, we could manage it in two trips," she shouted, her face still set in a frown. "What do you have in mind?"

Milo smiled up at her winningly.

"Just some more of that old Roman stuff."

It turned out to be three trips to clear out the zeppelin's crew, which was just as well because it took some time for Milo and Ambrose to get the crew to turn the airship around and sail it toward the peak of Milo's choosing.

He was doubly thankful for the fey as the pilot jabbered on because the potent creatures seemed to possess the knack for enchanting the crew into cooperating. As the moon-eyed crewman lined up in an orderly fashion to be carried away by the wind-riding fey, Milo decided he would insist on learning from the fey next.

Of course, he had to survive the next half-hour, which was far from certain.

"As long as these all stay where they are," Milo said, pointing at the network of controls he couldn't begin to understand, "we should slide right by that mountain top."

"*Jah.*" The pilot nodded. "But you'll need a man to stay and make sure wind currents or something else don't knock you off course."

Milo nodded, then pointed out the open window of the cockpit.

"How close will we pass the peak?"

The pilot's face scrunched around his goggles, and he sucked his teeth as he checked one of the instruments in front of him.

"Within one to two hundred meters," he said, tapping a reading Milo didn't bother to look at.

"Make it half that," Milo said, then repeated the command when the pilot balked.

"That's too close," the pilot protested.

"That's an order," Milo shouted back, tapping the pentagram studs on his cap.

Under the skin of the blimp, amongst swollen sacks of hydrogen bigger than houses, the whistling rush of wind was absent. The only sound was the thrum of the airship's engines, a constant low buzz.

Milo scaled a ladder that connected the crew compartments below with the blimp that kept everything afloat. He emerged onto a gantry walkway that stretched the entire width of the blimp and fit between two hydrogen bladders. A second ladder rose an uncomfortably high distance to the curved top of the blimp's structure, where, if he squinted, Milo could see a hatch.

He tried not to think about how spindly the ladder looked as it stretched upward.

On the platform stood Ambrose, his belly pressed against the railing as he secured one of the tunnel-brusher grenades to the rippling skin of the hydrogen bladder. The other tunnel-brusher was already attached, using layers of powerfully adhesive patches commandeered from the mechanics' stores aboard the ship.

"Crews cleared out," Milo announced as he walked across the gantry, awed by how peaceful it was inside the rigid skin. "Almost done?"

Even the thrum of the engines was almost soothing.

"Just about," Ambrose said softly as he stepped back to review his handiwork. Satisfied, he pulled a roll of thread out of his pack and measured two equal lengths to tie to the rings on the grenades.

"So, some poor fool stands here," Milo said, moving to the middle of the platform between the two grenades, "and pulls the string to get the grenades going."

"Pretty much," Ambrose muttered as he tied off one string and shuffled over to tie off the other.

"And who is that fool going to be?"

"Well," the big man began as he stepped back from the affixed grenade and gave Milo a level look, "I'd be a pretty poor bodyguard if I expected you to be the one to set off the suicide trap."

Milo shook his head.

"You don't have to do that, Ambrose."

The bodyguard scowled.

"After all this, you're going to make it hard on me?" he rumbled, crossing his big arms over his chest. "Milo, someone's got to set this fireball off, and pretty as I am, I'm not the poor bastard who was born with magic up his trousers, so spare me all that rot. It has to be me."

Ambrose turned his back to his ward, pretending to check the lengths of the strings as he muttered, "There's always the chance I somehow come back, and if I don't...well, I suppose it was a long time coming."

Milo sighed and reached into his black coat.

"Simon?"

"What?" the bodyguard asked fiercely, turning on his heel with eyes blazing.

"You don't have to do this," Milo said, shaking a vial filled with black sand. "Because I've got someone else dying to do the job."

Ambrose's eyes widened, and he made several attempts to form a coherent sentence before finally throwing his hands in the air and wagging his head.

"Witches," he growled in disgust as a smile crept below his mustache.

"Come and get us," Milo growled under his breath as he gripped the rail running across the top of the zeppelin.

Despite the reality of losing his grip and subsequently his footing and then sliding off the airship to certain doom, Milo only had eyes for the fang of rock in their path. By his amateur evaluation, they were minutes from passing the summit, and right on schedule, a tongue of murky filth as wide as a football field and three times the length lapped its way up the mountainside.

"Keep coming," Milo muttered. "Almost there."

Despite his fixed gaze, not all of him was present for the unnerving spectacle.

In the back of his mind, he kept the shades animating the Si'lat under tight control, especially the squirrely little thing in charge of the grenades. Besides the one who kept getting curious about grenade rings, Milo had set the other two animate clouds of black sand to watch the controls as the pilot had instructed. Milo wasn't sure if both were required, but it looked like a two-person job to make sure all the instruments and knobs and levers and other such remained just as they were. That and shades were relatively simple things, and Milo's confidence in directing them was suspect.

Still, their presence below meant Ambrose stood next to him, glaring at Kimaris' ascent.

"Where does something like that come from?"

"Hell?" Milo offered. He was half-joking, but the look on Ambrose's face conveyed that such things were no laughing matter.

The guard shook his head and adjusted the straps on his parachute with his free hand.

"Are you sure these things will work from this height?" the big man asked as he eyed the pack suspiciously.

"No," Milo admitted as he ran his thumb along one of his own straps. "But I figure they couldn't hurt."

Ambrose's gaze wandered to the valley floor passing beneath them.

"I think I'd rather blow myself up," he muttered, the words nearly stolen by the whistling wind.

"You and the Si'lat can still switch places," Milo said, jerking a thumb at the hatch. "You better hurry, though."

Ambrose's mustache twitched against the wind as he scowled at Milo.

"You know, you think you are a whole lot funnier than you actually are."

Milo raised a hand to his ear and gave an exaggerated shrug.

"What was that? Couldn't hear you over the sound of trying to save your life."

Ambrose rolled his eyes, and both fell silent as Kimaris reached the peak, wrapping around the horn of rock and straining up into the open air. They were seconds from passing over the monstrosity-laden zenith, and for an instant, Milo feared they weren't going to be close enough. His mind scrambled as he wondered what they would do as the zeppelin barreled by. Looking past the peak he'd been fixated on, Milo learned exactly what would happen when he saw a white-crowned mountain rising barely a few miles from its smaller brother. At this altitude and speed, they would amble past the crucial point and the smash into the taller mountain five minutes later.

Milo nearly said something to Ambrose, but he spied something strange happening just below them.

Kimaris' cloudy bulk began to darken as it gathered itself. The magus remembered the sight of its cresting wave looming higher and higher over Imrah, and then they were over the peak, the gelatinous monstrosity hidden from view.

Then a rope as thick as a truck strained upward. The slime was compacted to give it strength and rigidity, but Milo could still see the tortured forms writhing within the compressed layers. In horrified awe, he watched it strain up over them, then sprout the acid-eaten faces of the grotesque chorus like a rash of pustules.

"THE PRINCE IS NIGH!" they shrieked thinly as the tendril swayed and then descended upon the zeppelin.

Gripping the rail, Milo and Ambrose skittered across the hull of the airship as the tendril slapped down, buckling the forward portion of the blimp several feet inward. The entire airship shuddered and both men lost their footing, boots skidding and scrambling as they held on with both hands. With wide, terrified eyes, they looked up and saw the tendril constricting, wrapping around the airship as it drew more of its bulk up from the peak.

The zeppelin listed hard from the sudden burden, but the protesting engines kept the craft plugging forward. As it moved clear of the peak, Kimaris came with it, a shrinking flag dangling from the airship as it began to spread over the surface.

"Move!" Milo shouted as the metal beneath their feet groaned and rumbled.

Hand over hand, they made for the rear of the ship even as the nose of the zeppelin began to bow forward. A few seconds later, they were fighting not just the wind, but the incline of the vessel as it began to plunge toward the valley floor. It seemed they wouldn't have to worry about the mountain after all, but as more of the slime began to spread across the surface of the blimp and into the compartments below, Milo felt a shift.

Milo drew on the connection with the Si'lat in the vessel's bridge and drove them to apply their efforts to the instruments. He couldn't sense that they were having any success at first, but little by little, the zeppelin leveled out and then began to climb a little. Under his feet, he felt the trembling skin of the blimp, and wondered if its structural integrity, already sorely tested, would hold out.

Only one way to find out, he told himself as he hauled another hand up the rail.

"Incoming!" Ambrose shouted from behind him, and Milo turned around as the stolen carbine opened up. Looking just past his bodyguard, Milo saw not only the advancing waves of hungry mucus pocked with shrieking faces but also the towering manifestation of Kimaris. The glittering mockery of a human form rode the crest of the oncoming wave like the figurehead of a ship, chin up and arms thrust out behind it. Ambrose's shots pattered uselessly into the gray tide, and a round that struck the figure's featureless face only spread a spiderweb of cracks across the hardened surface that quickly vanished as the jelly within swelled to push everything back into place.

Milo swung his eyes to the stern of the airship. They had only a few dozen meters to go, but at this rate, the tide would overtake them before they covered half that distance.

It was time for something drastic

"Fire in the hole!" Milo howled as he swung around and pointed the raptor skull past Ambrose and toward the figure.

"BURN."

Twin comets of emerald fire lanced down the length of the zeppelin, on target to bury themselves in the figure's chest. With unholy quickness, the figure coiled and leapt clear of the tidal slime, which writhed and shriveled where the bolts scorched and burned.

The wave lost cohesion as the flames hissed and emitted contrails of acrid steam. Kimaris sought to smother the agonizing sorcery with its bulk. Milo might have crowed with victory as he and Ambrose continued their retreat, but behind them, he heard the figure land on the blimp with a clang. Glancing behind even as he continued to clamber across the blimp, Milo saw it begin sprinting toward them as the rest of the monster continued its crawling advance.

"It's coming too fast," Ambrose said, slinging the carbine over his shoulder and drawing his sword. "Go now. I'll hold him off!"

In defiance of the trembling surface beneath its feet or the wind whipping across the surface of the blimp, it raced after them like a sprinter fresh from the blocks. Its spry feet dented the metal skin of the blimp, each step like a hammer stroke, raising a terrible clamor as it closed on them.

"Together!" Milo shouted, adjusting his grip to midway down the magical cane. "I'll get him airborne, you spit him!"

Ambrose met Milo's eyes and knew better than to argue.

Milo sent out a rapid series of witchfire bolts in a flurry of mental focus he would have doubted possible before that moment. Most flew wide of the mark and sailed across the sky like fireworks; just as well since there was no slime on the surface of the blimp to keep the burning missiles away from the hydrogen bladders behind the thin metal. The last few bolts streaked toward the racing figure's head, and true to form, it leapt into the air, this time turning the movement into a pounce.

Ambrose was waiting, thrusting upward with the blade as the figure descended. The needle point met the hardened skin, flexing for the barest moment and then plunged through the thing's chest until it sank halfway down the length of the blade. The figure writhed like a bug on a pin, one fist crashing into Ambrose's face, smashing his nose out of alignment and shooting blood through the air.

Despite the ringing blow, the big man kept his grip on the hilt, twisting it hard as he threw his weight against his attacker.

The figure absorbed the shove with a ripple across its form

and snapped back to chop one hand across the blade. When the edge of the descending hand met the spine of the sword, the blade snapped, and Ambrose was thrown off-balance, only to be snared around the throat by a huge crystalline hand.

Ambrose lashed out with the splintered blade and basket hilt, stabbing and punching, but the blows only created cracks that were quickly mended. With inhuman ease, it lifted Ambrose off his feet and shook the big man like a doll.

Behind the looming figure, the encroaching slime swelled to allow the gruesome faces to emerge like dark-crowned boils.

"BEHOLD THE PRINCE!" they cried, keening over the engine and the wind. *"BEHOLD THE MIGHT, THE GLORY, THE—"*

"Behold this!" Milo roared in defiance as he twisted around the rail like a pool shark making a trick shot.

Two lances of emerald flame sprang from the raptor's sockets, passing within inches of Ambrose before burying themselves in the figure's belly.

The avatar of Kimaris lost its grip on Ambrose, and it was all Milo could do to snatch the big man's arm as he began to slide down the edge of the blimp. Ambrose gripped Milo's arm feebly, still stunned, and they hung there as the figure, kindled by Milo's attack, tumbled backward head over heels. By the time it splashed into the seething layers of slime coating the ship, it was blazing in flames of green. The chorus screamed, the disjointed, viscous sound of the drowning damned.

"Nearly there," Milo growled, hammering home the last of his mental fortitude.

Drawing strength from the staff, he hauled Ambrose up to the rail as the big man came to his senses. Bowing their heads against the wind and the screams of Kimaris' maddened choir, they scrambled the last several meters. Behind them, the murky tide roiled and raged, a spout of flame still gnawing at it even as another wave gathered.

Magus and bodyguard reached the rear of the zeppelin as the

tsunami of slime filled with screeching faces launched toward them.

The men looked toward the edge of the zeppelin and back at the oncoming breaker from hell.

"Together!" they shouted in unison and leapt as one.

Kimaris' wave broke just behind them as the men began their skidding departure down the zeppelin's rear and into the open air above the valley. As they tumbled free, cartwheeling in a nauseating spin, Milo let the last Si'lat pull the pins.

There was a rumble half a heartbeat before a massive fist of flame punched up through the very center of the zeppelin, enshrouding it in flame. Less than a second later, secondary detonations from burning shrapnel and gouts of immolating gas set off the other bladders and ripped through the vessel. In the blink of an eye, the airship had become a second sun, blazing over the valley.

In that inferno, the blaze did not just kiss Kimaris, it embraced the horror like a lover, and together they burned and writhed. The chorus ceased, their torment finally snuffed out as they burned with their captor over the valley.

As this singular dawn rapidly approached its noon, two small figures fluttered through the air, their canvas chutes blazing above them. They'd been too close, and the heat had been too intense. They had just enough time to look up and see their desperate gambit play out before they plunged to their deaths on the rocky earth below.

In that moment of embraced inevitability, neither man cried out. Both magus and bodyguard smiled, basking in Kimaris' ruin.

So busy were they in savoring the works of their hands that neither noticed the radiant forms racing toward them, riding fast and free on the wind.

25

A NOVELTY

"Have you heard what they are calling you?" Lokkemand asked, sipping from a canteen, his glass of schnapps untouched.

"I typically don't listen to what people call me," Milo said with a shrug as he finished his own glass. "It's rarely flattering."

Lokkemand nodded and secured the cap on the canteen before dabbing his mouth with a handkerchief. They were alone in the tent, most of the files, maps, and typist materials already packed. The war was moving beyond Bamyan, with Epp leading the offensive toward Kabul.

"It is actually funny," Lokkemand said, reaching inside his coat and drawing out a cigarette tin. "I'd be worried about it being a breach of operational security if it wasn't already making its way into all the dirty jokes and drinking songs."

Flipping the tin open, he held it out to Milo, who took one with a grateful nod.

"All right, I'll bite," the magus said, the cigarette hanging from his lip as he fished out his matchbook. "What are they calling me?"

Lokkemand waited the tantalizing seconds until they'd both lit their cigarettes before answering, "*Der Zauber-Schwartz*," the captain intoned through a haze of smoke. "Though I've already heard a few shortening it to the pet name of *'Zauber.'*"

Milo coughed on a throatful of smoke and took a moment to gather himself.

"What?" he wheezed, watering eyes bright with alarm. "They're calling me the 'Sorcerer in Black,' and you don't think that's cause for concern!"

Lokkemand chuckled, sending out tufts of smoke.

"Well, that's not the only thing they are calling you, just the most flattering. There's *Verbrannt'Hex* and *Feuergeist*. Things only get more imaginative from there."

Milo stared incredulously as the cigarette smoldered in his hand.

"I'm not sure how that is supposed to make me feel better. I thought the fey worked their magic so the men wouldn't remember what they saw."

"Oh, their memories were suitably modified, but don't you see?" Lokkemand snorted. "You're on your way to becoming a legend, a myth amongst the ranks of the fighting men of the German Army. What's the one thing all myths have in common?"

Milo rocked back as he realized the captain's point, savoring a long toke.

"They're not real." He sighed out a stream of hazy blue-gray.

"Exactly." Lokkemand smiled, then picked up the glass of schnapps and held it under his nose. "We couldn't have asked for a better cover if we'd fabricated it on purpose."

Milo nodded, tapping ash into the empty schnapps bottle.

"What about the photos and other recordings? They were on a reconnaissance mission after all, and we didn't search them before escorting them off the zeppelin."

"Duly confiscated by Nicht-KAT," the captain said as he flapped his hand dismissively, cigarette tracing wisps of smoke. "All packaged and on their way back to Berlin."

"To be examined by experts? Studied"? Milo asked with a raised eyebrow. "Presented to the general staff?"

"Wouldn't that be something?" Lokkemand laughed bitterly. "No, I imagine the colonel will peruse them briefly, but he is a busy man, and unless there is something exceptional, he'll mark them to be locked away until some distant, unreachable date."

Milo popped the expended cigarette into the bottle, where it went out with a damp hiss when it met the dregs of the schnapps.

"An enormous sentient jelly monster that killed hundreds isn't exceptional?"

Lokkemand and Milo locked eyes through the haze of tobacco smoke.

"You're special, Milo, no denying it," the captain said, leaning to one side to stub out his cigarette on the gravel floor. "But you've only scratched the surface of this world. Savor the victory, then brace yourself for the next plunge."

Milo crossed his arms, letting the words digest.

"Also, pack warmly." Lokkemand grunted as he leaned forward to deposit the stub. "We're headed north."

"Not following Epp on his glorious conquest of India?" Milo asked. "Isn't that what every true German would kill for?"

Lokkemand glared at Milo.

"Just when I thought I might grow to like you." He sighed and heaved himself to his feet. "Get your affairs sorted. We leave in the morning."

———

Milo had just arranged his bag for the night when there was a knock on the front door.

"Who is it?" he called, his hand straying to the cane resting against the wall.

Ambrose was out disposing of whatever elements of Imrah's laboratory Milo couldn't make use of.

"A friend." It was Rihyani's silvery voice.

Milo rose and went to the door, ignorant of the smile that hovered on his lips.

"In broad daylight?" Milo asked as he drew the door open to see Rihyani peeking out from under her heavy traveling robes. "With so many soldiers roaming around?"

"Many and strange are the visitors of the Sorcerer in Black," the contessa said lightly as Milo moved to allow her inside. "I am only adding to the mystique."

Milo shook his head as he closed the door, and they walked into the den beside the kitchen.

"So, you've heard about that then?" he asked, wishing he could offer her something to eat or somewhere to sit. The only things left in the house were their trunks, packs, and sleeping rolls, all gathered into a heap by Milo.

"Oh, where do you think they got the idea?" The fey chortled softly. "I usually prefer not to be center stage, but I *am* rather proud of that little improvisation. Your commanding officers didn't think it was too on the nose, did they?"

Milo paused for a moment at Rihyani's confession, then shook his head vigorously.

"What? Oh, no, no, they liked it," he said quickly. "Captain Lokkemand loved it. Truth is, he pointed out how building the myth is the best way to keep things from being taken seriously."

"Good, I'm glad." Rihyani smiled, wine-dark eyes glittering.

"Uh, yes, well," Milo floundered, his cheeks flushing and his stomach knotting. "I just wanted to say...um, thank you for saving us...twice...and then with the zeppelin crew, and before that... Well, just, thank you for everything."

The words had come in such a jumbled rush. Milo was winded, and for a moment, he just stared at her.

"You are most welcome," Rihyani said, laughing in the way that made his heart ache. "I only hope the tale of Der *Zauber-Schwartz* and the Lost Patrols grows with each retelling, knowing the tales will never be as fantastic as the truth of what happened that day."

"For sure," Milo muttered lamely and found he was having a hard time raising his eyes above the floor.

For a moment, a silence potent with potential passed between them, then Milo cleared his throat with a grunt and gestured at the piled-up luggage.

"We're moving out in the morning," he said. "Going north, but I'm not sure where."

Rihyani nodded slowly, and then, straightening as though just remembering, reached inside her cloak.

"I heard, which is why I brought these," she said, drawing out a satchel. "Bashlek Marid sends them with his regards, as well as a command to not return to Ifreedahm anytime soon."

Milo took the satchel and found it contained several parchment codices. Combined with what he'd already been given and what they'd found in Imrah's effects, he had months of material to read and practice.

"Why am I banished?' he asked, a frown creasing his brow. "What did I do?"

Rihyani cocked a delicate eyebrow as her dark mouth twisted into a wry grin.

"You mean, besides save his kingdom and bear witness to his daughter being a dangerous traitor and heretic?" The contessa chuckled. "Oh, Milo, it has nothing to do with you and everything to do with ghul politics. You remember what I told you about Fazihr going to Lady Dazk?"

Milo nodded and his mouth hardened into an angry line. The prohibition against Ifreedahm notwithstanding, he would have loved to track the sniveling little rat down.

"Well, just to prove nothing is ever a sure thing," Rihyani began as she straightened her robes, "it seems Fazihr, being Imrah's retainer, was part of finding and liberating that thing. You called it Kimaris, yes? Well, the worm thought sharing that with Lady Dazk would win him favor and provide an opportunity to overthrow Marid. Instead, it saw him delivered rather promptly to the Bashlek's dungeons."

Milo's eyebrows shot up in surprise.

"How did that happen?" he asked, genuinely intrigued.

"It seems that Lady Dazk's primary concern *is* the good of ghulkind," Rihyani said in bewilderment. "Seeing the threat was as dire as it was and knowing that, whatever their differences, Marid would never tolerate wanton destruction, she delivered the bound Fazihr with her personal guard. Since then, she has been a vital asset, working with the Bashlek's agents to track down anyone who knew or even suspected Imrah was consorting with the Guardians."

"Guardians?" Milo said. "Is that what Kimaris was?"

The word seemed too wholesome to describe the nauseating horror, but Milo supposed aesthetics and sanity might be in the eye of the beholder.

"No," Rihyani said, her eyes darting left and right so quickly Milo barely had time to notice. "Kimaris was something older and fouler than we have experience with."

"'We?'" Milo asked, bemused as he watched Rihyani shift her weight to her back foot.

"Milo," she said tentatively, unsure for the first time since he'd met her, "there are aspects of this world, the world of the Folk, that will take time and experience to learn. I've probably shared more with you than I should have. I'm not sure more will be helpful, and it could be dangerous."

Milo bristled, his arms sliding across his chest even as he forced his voice into a level tone he didn't feel.

"That seems to be a popular tune with a lot of people," he said, his eyes locking onto hers. "But considering you've already let a few things slip, wouldn't it be best if you gave me enough information to keep me from coming to the wrong conclusions?"

Rihyani's gaze hardened. Milo wasn't sure if he'd crossed a

line, but he'd planted his flag, and he wouldn't back down now.

"Very well." The contessa sighed, shrugging her cowled shoulders. "You remember when I mentioned factions who want to cooperate covertly with humans and those who want to wage war with humans?"

"Yes," Milo murmured, arms still crossed.

"As you'd expect, it is deeper and darker than that. The anti-humans call themselves the Guardians, and along with stirring up animosity toward your kind, they send what they call Questers out to find secrets and tools or weapons they can use against humanity when they eventually declare their war. Imrah, it seems, was a Quester, and she did in fact find a weapon that could have done even more damage than it had already. Do you know what caused your armies to advance so quickly?"

"The enemy retreated," Milo replied, eyes narrowing. "Some thought it was a trap, but it turned out to be a strategic repositioning."

"The *repositioning* came when Imrah first unleashed Kimaris," Rihyani explained, the words sending a preemptive chill up Milo's spine. "The coalition of enemies arrayed against you, both the native soldiers and those from Europe and India, retreated because they were losing entire companies in a night. The official reports are that your armies used some sort of chemical attack."

Milo shuddered at the fate of so many men, screaming and running through tunnels and across mountainsides, only to be overtaken by the foul tide that would spend days digesting them.

"Dear God," Milo murmured, running a hand over his face. "So Imrah didn't just set loose the monster, but she set in motion the events that nearly saw her people at war with humanity."

Rihyani nodded, taking a step toward the door.

"Yes, though besides the timing, I'm not sure war would have been disagreeable to her sensibilities."

It was before the end, Milo thought, remembering the broken, despairing look in the ghul's eyes as she embraced death.

"Regardless," the contessa continued, seeing Milo was slipping deeper into his thoughts, "such desperate and dangerous schemes seem intertwined with the Guardians' efforts, so among those who seek to work with humans, a faction has emerged that concerns itself with stopping the Guardians and their Questers before they can do too much damage."

"The *we* you mentioned earlier?"

"Yes," Rihyani confirmed, then gave a little bow. "We call ourselves the Shepherds, and while we are few, we are active in ferreting out Questers and keeping the chaos at bay, at least for a day longer."

"Is that why you really came to Ifreedahm?" Milo asked. "Tracking down rumors of Questers?"

"Perhaps," the fey said with a smile. "For now, all you need to know is that I'm very glad you and I have had a chance to work together. I imagine we'll have plenty of opportunities to do so again, assuming you live that long."

Milo gave a derisive snort, followed by a grudging nod.

"Fair enough," he said, eyeing the contessa cautiously. "I suppose it wouldn't be terrible to work with you again."

"You are too kind," she replied as she stepped to the door and laid a gloved hand on the latch. "Just remember something, Milo."

"What's that?"

"The things always go deeper," she said, drawing the door open and letting in a blaze of the red sunset. "There is always another mystery, another riddle, another enigma. The secret to surviving at this game is to know when to dig deeper and when to bury things. It is a secret every necromancer would do well to learn."

"I'll keep that in mind," Milo said, stepping forward.

Their eyes locked for another moment of pregnant silence, then she was out the door and calling over her shoulder.

"Be careful tonight. Don't raise more ghosts than you can put down."

EPILOGUE: SINE SACRIFICIO

The moonlight glinted off the black winds swirling and coiling across the mountainside. Half a dozen spectral currents of glistening darkness slid across the worn earth and chipped boulders, their movements serpentine and exploratory. To the scavengers not immediately frightened by their arrival, the slithering tendrils seemed to be nosing over their feast like huge flying blindworms.

From his position on the opposite hillside, Milo could see the method in the Si'lats' movements, an expanding grid as they searched amongst the scorched and shattered remains. The skeletal hulk of the zeppelin was higher up the face of the mountain, but Milo expected their best chance was to work their way upward amidst the splintered remnants of Kimaris' tortured quarry.

"I'm still not sure this is a good idea," Ambrose grumbled next to him as he puffed on his pipe.

"Let's go with not," Milo said, one corner of his mouth rising in a lopsided grin. A plume of breath rolled from his nostrils, the temperature having dropped drastically since sunset.

"Then why are we doing it?" Ambrose asked before releasing an impatient blast of smoke. "We're headed out first thing."

"You can sleep on the truck ride," Milo muttered distractedly. One of the Si'lats had picked up a bunch of charred bones, but after tossing them about a bit, it went off again.

"That doesn't answer the question," the big man said, kicking a fist-sized rock into a downhill bounce. "And standing out here in an unsecured valley with no support and no one knowing what we are doing is exactly the kind of thing to get two fools captured or killed."

Milo gave his bodyguard a wink.

"You could always head back," he teased. "Leave me to my foolish ways."

Ambrose spat downhill, the spittle staying aloft for a record-worthy amount of time.

"I've said it before, and I'll say it again." The big man sniffed. "You're not nearly as funny as you think you are."

Milo chuckled and turned back to watch his shade-animated agents continue their search. He watched the Si'lats for another handful of heartbeats before he looked back at Ambrose, his eyes narrowed accusingly.

"Hey," he cried sharply. "You never finished explaining your resurrection gimmick."

Ambrose puffed his pipe three times and muttered the word "gimmick" grumpily before heaving a sigh and tapping the bowl out.

"My *gimmick*," he began pointedly as he slid the pipe into his breast pocket, "is anything but. It's a harrowing experience as I cross between the realm of the living and the ghostly realms beyond."

Milo raised a hand to his mouth and gave a choked cry of shock.

"Oh, no," he said with exaggerated tenderness. "Have I hurt your feelings?"

"Anyways," Ambrose replied tartly, then cleared his throat. "Erm, now where was I? Oh, yes, Morocco. So there I was—"

"No," Milo cut in, one hand raised wardingly. "None of that. We only have so long, and I am pretty sure I still owe *you* an explanation."

He tapped the breast pocket of his surcoat, lighting an eager gleam in Ambrose's eyes

"You'll have plenty of time for war stories on the trip up north," Milo said, sliding his hands into his pockets. "Just focus on the real issue. You say you really die, and then you really come back. I want to hear about that."

Ambrose rocked on his heels, and his lips twitched beneath his mustache. His internal dialogue ended with a low grunt as he nodded.

"All right," he breathed, expelling curls of dragon breath into the cold air. "It's like a dream but not. Just like you know things in a dream, just know them for no reason at all, you also can know that you're sleeping or that you're dreaming, or whatever, that's what it's like. I'm dying, bleeding, drowning, or what have you, but then I find I'm standing on my own two legs, whole but different, and by different, you understand that I mean I know I'm dead."

Milo nodded, studying the bodyguard's face as his eyes became distant with recollection.

"It's dark, quiet, and almost peaceful, you see. Certainty comes over you that yeah, this is it. But then one of the titans stirs in the dark next to me, and all the peace vanishes. Just like that, I'm a scared little boy hiding beneath his covers from the monster under his bed."

Ambrose sucked his teeth, his eyes widening at the frightful memory.

"Titans?" Milo asked, trying to imagine what creature in this life or the next could have such an effect on the likes of Simon Ambrose.

"It's just my name for them," Ambrose explained, his words coming out faster and sharper. "I never see them since it's dark, but I can hear them and feel them, and they're, well, enormous. It's like standing at the foot of a mountain and sensing it moving just feet away from you. It seems slow, but that is because it's taking your mind so long to realize something so massive is moving at all. And just like in a dream, I know these things, and I also know they're bound somehow. Restrained, and they're angry. So angry."

Ambrose shoved his hands in his pockets, but Milo could still see them trembling through the fabric of his coat.

"I know all of them hate me and want to hurt me, but one in particular, the only titan I can actually see, is looking for me. I get a quick glimpse of him, as immense and dominating as a mountain against a sky, and red stars in his huge head as he turns to look at me. He calls for me, calls me a name I've never heard in my life, but I know it's mine even as I watch him start wading through the dark toward me."

Ambrose blinked, his glistening eyes unnoticed as he heaved a heavy breath.

"And then," he said thickly, "I feel a hand on my shoulder and a voice, a familiar voice I can never recognize, whispers in my ear, telling me something."

Milo leaned forward in rapt attention, the meandering Si'lat search party forgotten.

"What does the voice say?" he breathed.

"*All that seek shall find,*" Ambrose recited, his voice barely more than a whisper. "*But my spirit shall not always strive with man.*"

Milo stared, bemusement, horror, and wonder, wrestling for control of his features.

"And then I wake up, hurting but alive," Ambrose said. "I recover quickly, but each time, I get the feeling that was the very last time."

Milo let out the breath he was holding.

"That's...something," he said, not able to muster embarrassment for his befuddlement. "And it's that way every time?"

Ambrose nodded solemnly before turning back to the mountainside and wiping his eyes.

"Every time." He sighed.

For a long time, the two of them stared into the night, the Si'lats moving beneath gazes that paid them no heed. Eventually, a chill wind rose, making Milo shiver, and he started as though waking from a dream. He looked at Ambrose, who was still staring vacantly, before chewing his lip as he fetched the tarot card from his pocket.

The grind of Milo's boots on the rocky ground brought Ambrose back to himself, and he looked up to see Milo holding out the folded card.

"Here," he said heavily, giving the card a shake. "You've earned a peek."

Ambrose shook his head.

"No, it's all right. Your secrets are yours, Magus."

"Are you sure?" Milo asked, his arm still extended. "May not ever be another time I'm feeling so generous."

Ambrose nodded and sniffed, running a hand across his mustache.

"I'm sure," he said, squinting at a confluence of black sand. "When you're sharing because you want to and not because of a fast-handed deal, I'll look at the card."

Milo hung there a second longer, card between his outstretched fingers, then drew back and replaced the card in the coat.

"And if that time never comes?" Milo asked, following Ambrose's gaze to the veritable cyclone of Si'lats rushing toward them.

"All things in God's good time, Magus," the big man muttered.

The Si'lats broke upon the hillside like a crashing wave, rippling and swirling around the two men, bits of broken and charred bone held aloft on the gritty gusts. Milo focused his will and held out his hand.

The black-sand tempest swirled across his open palm, depositing a narrow sharp-toothed skull. It was cracked in several places and missing the entire lower jaw and several teeth from the upper, and the whole surface was pitted unevenly.

Milo reached out with his sorcerous awareness, feeling echoes of the life that had once been and trailing his consciousness across the pools of essence left by it.

"Hello, Imrah," he said with a grim smile.

AUTHOR NOTES - AARON SCHNEIDER

SEPTEMBER 25, 2020

Dear Reader,

Thank you.

Thank you for taking the time to read this book and I hope that you feel the time was not wasted. I know that nowadays your options for entertainment and distraction are immense, and I'm humbled and appreciative that you thought what I had to offer was worth your time. If you didn't find it worthwhile then I appreciate you at least giving it a shot.

However, if you did enjoy it I've got good news for you because the next book is going to be right around the corner. Book 02 is coming out shortly. You'll get to ride right along with Milo, Ambrose, and Rihyani as they head to Georgia, the beautiful country not the lovely state, and face new challenges, dangers, and wonders.

I hope you'll keep reading not just to state my fragile feelings, but also because Milo's story has so much further to go. The monstrous and marvelous world of the First Wizard is a deep and wide place I'd love to explore with you, if you'll have me of course.

Now before I leave you for a little while I'd like to say something to all of us facing the weird world of 2020 and all its different shades of madness. With all the tragedies, problems, and terrors some would say that there are more important things to do than read some silly story, much less write one.

Clearly, I think those people are wrong.

For writers like me and readers like you it comes down to one word: escapism.

This word is often treated like a dirty word, a word suggesting dereliction or even cowardice and weakness, of not facing up to the "real world" and trying to hide from it. I'm afraid people touting that sort of nonsense have quite missed the point and not just of novels but of art in general.

We read, we write, we sing, we dance, we paint, we become art all so that we can escape and to escape means to strive to be free. Free to dream, to hope, and to be, and that is the opposite of cowardice and hiding. I would say in a time like 2020 that is exactly the sort of business we need to be about.

So keep escaping dear hearts, and remember that most poignant of conversations between Tolkien and Lewis:

"What sort of men would be most opposed to escape, Jack?"

"Jailers, obviously."

Regards,

Aaron D. Schneider

ACKNOWLEDGMENTS

This book, as with anything worthwhile I've ever done, is the product of not just one man but a combination of fantastic people. First, to my children who had to bear through Daddy locking himself inside his cave to growl and type, thank you for your patience and your love. To my family, who only rarely complained over me finding excuses for missing events to write and generally have been kind enough to put up with my surliness while writing. To Mr. Anderle for being willing to take a chance on me, and being the easiest writing partner I've ever had (How about zeppelins?). To Mrs. Abby, who has, ever since we first crossed paths, been nothing but a dear friend and a staunch ally, honest, brave, and true.

Finally and most importantly, to my wife, who has, without exception, irrevocably changed my life for the better and without whom nothing would ever get done. My love has believed in me when I couldn't and rebuked me when I lost my way. My dueling partner to the death, she is without a doubt the peg o' my heart, and I owe her so very much.

First, THANK YOU for not only reading this story but these *Author Notes* in the back.

Working with Aaron has been a massive pleasure for me. When he and I were introduced, the first thing I noticed was I felt like he was a kindred spirit, a person who would prefer to just help those out in the world and not hurt a soul.

But you don't push him. He is a kind guy, but he has a backbone of rigid steel if pushed. He just doesn't like being in that position.

Now, this is just my opinion. Aaron lives pretty far from me, and we only ever speak over Zoom (video) or the phone.

The second thing I noticed was his writing.

It's beautiful.

He prose takes me away, even in situations I would NOT wish to read about. Somehow, his spirit is entwined within the words he shares. I can't explain how it makes me feel, except to say I this isn't normally a story I would enjoy.

But somehow, here we are.

I hope you join us for books two and three. They are already being wrapped up to present to you as a gift. This wild alternate history where World War I never stopped.

All so we could explain how in a dark time, we reach down into the Earth to uncover a power that perhaps we shouldn't touch.

But extreme times require extreme actions. Milo is our hope, and we trust that he has a heart that has every right to be as black as those reared in the orphanage and streets where he comes from.

But the heart, once uncovered, starts to show its real color: a bright one.

At least, we hope it is since Milo must choose to accomplish great things while wielding energies that might better be used by those who have ethics a bit more...

Malleable.

Join us as we push into book two. The story is just getting started!

Ad Aeternitatem,

Michael Anderle

CONNECT WITH THE AUTHORS

Connect with Bradford Bates

Facebook:
https://www.facebook.com/authoraarondschneider/

Amazon:

https://www.amazon.com/Aaron-D-Schneider/e/B07H8WZ2HT/

Connect with Michael Anderle and sign up for his email list here:

Website: http://lmbpn.com

Email List: http://lmbpn.com/email/

Facebook:
https://www.facebook.com/LMBPNPublishing

OTHER BOOKS BY AARON SCHNEIDER

The Warring Realm Series

War-Born

War-Torn

War-Sworn

World's First Wizard

(with Michael Anderle)

Witchmarked (Book 1)

Sorcery Bound (Coming soon)

Wizard Born (Coming soon)

OTHER LMBPN PUBLISHING BOOKS

To be notified of new releases and special promotions from LMBPN publishing, please join our email list:

http://lmbpn.com/email/